Sergeant Dooley
and the Submarine Raiders

PUBLISHING

Sergeant Dooley AND THE Submarine Raiders

A Tom Dooley Adventure

WAYNE ABRAHAMSON

Sergeant Dooley and the Submarine Raiders: A Tom Dooley Adventure

© 2023 by Wayne Abrahamson

Editors: Earl Tillinghast, Mary Ward Menke
Cover and Design: Emma Elzinga

Indigo River Publishing
3 West Garden Street, Ste. 718
Pensacola, FL 32502
www.indigoriverpublishing.com

Ordering Information:
Quantity Sales: Special discounts are available on quantity purchases by corporations, associations, and others. For details, contact the publisher at the address above.
Orders by US trade bookstores and wholesalers: Please contact the publisher at the address above.

Library of Congress Control Number: 2022911783
ISBN: 978-1-954676-36-7 (paperback)   978-1-954676-37-4 (ebook)

First Edition

With Indigo River Publishing, you can always expect great books, strong voices, and meaningful messages. Most importantly, you'll always find . . . words worth reading.

CONTENTS

CHAPTER 1

AS THE SETTING sun disappeared behind the mountains of the Bataan Peninsula, American supervisors barked orders to Filipino workers transferring cargo from truck beds into nearby warehouses. At the same time, the rattle of four-cylinder Ford engines echoed off the centuries-old stone wharf and across Manila Bay.

"Mack says we're ready," voiced the young officer standing in the doorway of the ship's bridge. "Any sign of our mystery guest, Skipper?"

"Thanks, Kermit, and not yet. He should be along anytime, though. Also, remind Mack about the Number Two Boiler."

Kermit turned his head to look at the four exhaust stacks running the length of the superstructure aft of the bridge, noticing the exhaust from the second stack appeared oilier than the others. "Think the burners will last two months? Till August?"

"The shop supervisor of the Cavite Shipyard said they should, but a prayer never hurts."

"Prayer logged, Skipper," Kermit replied with a quick salute as he turned to join the two men inside the bridge. The greenish light from the compass behind them illuminated their relaxed forms. The skipper, like the men inside the bridge, lit up a Camel and watched the enlisted men smile as Kermit spoke to them. After taking a draw he returned his attention to the man standing next to him. "Looks like our mystery guest is running on island time just like us."

"You ain't kidding," Chief Petty Officer Fowler said as he picked a piece of tobacco from his tongue. "I'm still trying to celebrate my thirty-ninth birthday."

The captain of the torpedo boat destroyer, Lieutenant Rance Hillary, smiled as he exhaled. "Yet you still had no problem beating the hell out of three doughboys at Fort McKinley last weekend. What the hell were you do-ing at an army post anyhow? Chasing some gin-drunk woman while her man is on field maneuvers?"

Fowler answered wryly. "If the colonel is going to take his regiment out for mountain training, why shouldn't I have a chance at a white woman? 'Sides, we're supposed to be on our way to Shanghai. How was I to know we had to wait for a stiff-ass ring-knocker?"

Lieutenant Hillary shook his head. "Boatswain's Mate Chief Petty Of-ficer Ernst Fowler, I know you know that sleeping with an officer's wife is a court-martial offense and warrants brig time if found guilty. I should know."

"You said the magic words," Fowler replied as he exhaled. "If found guilty."

Lieutenant Hillary shook his head. "Anyway, the skipper before me said that you did nothing but pester him about some fantasy island, and since I took command, every time we head one foot north, you harass me about stop-ping at every island that fits the description some drunk Chinese fisherman told you about. You've done your twenty, plus, so put your papers in. Then, you can get your own boat and look for it yourself. And if you do find your Spanish treasure or pirate gold then you can pay me back that twenty you still owe me, and in gold. The last time you paid me back was in paper, and that turned out to be sour dough."

Fowler smiled. "Skipper, if I were to retire now, what would you do with-out me? Anyway, you learned your lesson just like the gunnery officer did. By the way, how is Mister . . .?"

The chief petty officer stopped as something on the wharf distracted him. The ship's captain followed his chief's eyes. On the wharf, under the lamp posts, and among the unloading, stood a naval officer wiping his forehead with the back of his hand. The man wore a dress white uniform along with a khaki musette bag hanging from his shoulder. A Filipino stood behind him holding the handle of a steamer trunk with both hands. A sheathed officer's sword was inserted under the brass-buckled leather straps on the side facing them. The uniformed man saw those on the ship looking down at him. He waved back.

"Told you; just another stiff-ass ring-knocker," Fowler said. "And I'll bet he's only here for sea time, a free trip to Shanghai, and a chance to earn a medal. That chest looks a bit bare. You don't get medals while on flag-ship junkets."

Hillary waved back to the officer while looking at his own ring finger. "Not all Academy graduates are stiff-ass ring-knockers."

"Well," Fowler said as they watched the officer walk to the gangplank, "you only turned out this well because of me. I slipped you that sour dough on purpose."

Hillary replied. "And I almost got my head stove in trying to use them."

"See, wasn't that a good lesson?" Fowler said with a nod, "Now, back to pirate gold."

"Here we go again," Hillary scoffed. "You're about to tell me a tale some toothless waterfront rummy sold you, and you have it for sure this time: an island that looks like a crouching tiger or the breasts of a woman. There are a thousand islands between here and Shanghai."

"Skipper," Fowler replied. "I got square dope this time. I ran into a Chinese sailor who kept repeating an ancient proverb. Something about the sleeping wise ones. Intrigued by the coded message, I did research and found evidence of what I've been told. It matched his proverb, and the island exists on our charts, and it's only two days out of our way. It's called Isla de la Muerte. 'Sides, didn't you study codes at Annapolis?"

"Some, and I also took academy summer cruises which included port visits to Colombia and Pensacola. Places that also have islands named Isla de la Muerte. Seems back in the olden days, seamen had a habit of getting dead bodies off their ships and under an island's sand as quick as possible. My point is there will always be an Isla de la Muerte somewhere."

"Good," Fowler said, "and as captain, your job is to show the American flag, help stranded seamen, rescue typhoon victims, and look out for the welfare of American citizens and property. It's your job to use your discretion."

Hillary responded. "Chief, you're ignoring my point. Anyway, I don't know anything about Spanish treasure, but that rumor of a hijacked shipment of British gold sovereign coins hidden on a secret island has existed since HMS Rangoon disappeared in 1819. A hundred years ago to the year and month. Even if Ching Shih did seize that vessel, I'll bet they spent those sovereigns faster than it took to capture the ship. The idea of buried pirate treasure exists only in the minds of writers and readers."

"Skipper, I know that gold is still there. On Isla de la Muerte; the Island of the Dead."

"If you look at a cloud long enough, you'll always see the image you're looking for."

"No, Skipper. That cache of gold coins still exists, and we can't wait that long," Fowler said. "It could be found anytime now. The Far East is full of lousy characters, and you don't know who else could be searching for it."

"I don't know about any lousy characters north of here," Lieutenant Hillary said, flicking his butt over the railing, "but I know I'm looking at one right now."

Both the men smiled as they looked down at the officer stepping up to the gangway.

Chapter 2

AN ERUPTION OF silvery bubbles exploded from the black depths. The outburst reflected the moonlight while the sound of the bursting froth chased itself into the surrounding night. After a minute of disruption, a submarine pushed the torrent aside as it bobbed to the surface leaving only the sound of water running off the deck to disturb the night air. Suddenly, the squeaking of metal replaced the sound of running water. A silent thin, red grin turned into a wide yawn as somebody inside pushed the hatch open. Five dark-clothed figures escaped the aurora of blood-red light welling up from the hatch and as one of them quickly closed the hatch, the others briefly saw his face and the ragged scar across his cheek. After standing, he spoke slowly while observing their surroundings. "Nice work, Captain Vostok."

The man who spoke went silent as his eyes fell on the nearly invisible horizon. The only light available came from the partial moon, the vivid stars, and the greenish glow of compass lights, which escaped the windows of the two patrol boats protecting the approaches to the crescent-shaped bay.

The man who complimented Captain Vostok spoke again. "Now all we have to do is land my raiders and walk up that cliff face."

The other eyes on the conning tower turned their attention to the cliff a little more than a hundred yards away. At the top, a forest lined the edge, and everybody saw the peaked roofs and upper windows of a *dacha*. Just like the patrol boats, the only signs of life were the occasional slits of weak light escaping from behind drawn curtains.

The man continued speaking while raising one arm. "Let's go over the plan again. Once we unlimber the boats, we will row to those rocks where we will go ashore."

Everybody looked at the bumpy row pointing out from the cliff base.

"We will then run along the base of the cliff to the staircase. According to the information the countess obtained for us, there are four guards and five officers inside the *dacha*, but they've fallen into a routine."

The man dropped his arm as he appraised one of the raiders next to him. While the raider gripped a modern weapon in his hand, the man focused on another weapon inserted into the raider's canvas web belt. "Sergeant Dooley, is that shingle axe worth its weight?"

Sergeant Dooley answered. "Major Utkin, this 1881 Stanley never failed me, my father, or his father . . ."

Major Utkin nodded at the statement before continuing. "What about that Thompson?"

Dooley responded as he looked at the short-barreled submachine gun in his hand. The weapon, now with short strips of canvas dangling from it, was invented as a trench-clearing weapon, however, its production and issue to frontline troops came too late to see combat. "According to its serial number it's one of the first ones off the production line, but I've had the opportunity to break it in. But you know that. Otherwise, I wouldn't be here."

The major nodded again. "Sergeant, you, and your squad, will go up first, and make your way to the barracks. Allow no troops to interfere with our mission."

Dooley, like almost everybody else around him, wore a black wool cap. He also wore his US Army uniform, minus badges, or chevrons. Around his waist, Dooley wore a web belt holstering a .45-caliber pistol along with two magazines, and a sheathed hunting knife. He also wore a musette bag containing two hand grenades, three, thirty-round stick magazines for the Thompson along with an extra drum magazine. Dooley glanced at his hand holding the Thompson and at the trench watch strapped to his wrist. The greenish glow highlighted the black hands, which indicated an hour before midnight. He turned his attention back to the cliff and the metal staircase running diagonally up its face. "No problem, Major," Dooley said as he enjoyed the cool night and relief from oil-tainted air and cabbage farts. He thanked God that nobody smoked on the submarine. It was claustrophobic enough inside that thing without having thick, smoke-filled air to make the closed-in feeling worse. He also shivered slightly. Although it was early June, the Siberian night air reminded Dooley's bones of the winter he fought through only months ago.

"Good," Major Utkin replied as he turned to face another man. "Lieutenant Gorki, you and your men will stay with myself and the countess. We will follow her into the main building. Process everybody else with your knives. Understood?"

The man addressed as Lieutenant Gorki held a magazine-fed, automatic rifle with strips of canvas hanging off it just like Dooley's Thompson. He also wore a pistol belt that holstered a revolver and a sheathed Russian trench fighting knife. Dooley knew what Utkin meant by the word "process" as he had seen the young officer, and his men, sharpen the stiletto-bladed knives nightly since he boarded the submarine. He felt sorry for whoever would be on the receiving end of those vicious blades and enclosed jaw-breaking grips.

Gorki looked at the major's scarred face as he answered. "Process them. *Da*."

Accepting the response, Utkin turned to the smallest figure among their group. "Countess Tolstoy, your task is to let your cousin know we are here to rescue her. Again, are you sure we can trust your informant, and are you sure she will be hiding where you said she'll be?"

The eyes of the men towering over the countess waited for a response. Like most of the men, she wore a black wool watch cap. Although she tried to stuff as much of her blond hair under it as she could, some still leaked out. Her small frame was further diminished by her oversized Russian army blouse and trousers. She reminded Dooley of a Mary Pickford drama where the actress played a tragic character too young to understand her dire circumstances and who only sought some sort of rescue. Like in the drama, the sudden turmoil of the October Coup in 1917, the downfall of the Imperial family, and the subsequent Revolution still eating at the Russian soul betrayed the chaos on her young face. Dooley felt sorry for the countess.

Countess Tolstoy responded. "Again, I would like to thank you for your efforts to rescue my cousin, Major Utkin. And yes, I believe our informant is trustworthy. Before the Revolution, he was a landed gentleman and my family relied on him, and his father and his father before him, to oversee the property during the non-summer months. Now, he is but a lowly manager of a state-owned farm. Yes, his information can be trusted as he would want to return to the way they used to be. There is no reason to mistrust him."

Major Utkin chuckled.

"I said something amusing, Major?" she asked.

"No, you didn't," he responded. "It is nineteen-nineteen now, and everything in Russia is state owned. Even mistrust is a state-owned commodity."

She nodded while continuing. "He was the one who informed me, through the post, that the duchess had been abducted from Shanghai by Reds two months ago and taken to this place for safekeeping, but for what, I do not know. We have all heard the rumors of precious stones cached on the property. A hoard the Reds never had a chance to seize. Perhaps her abduction might have something to do with that."

The countess paused as she looked up at the major. "Do you think her presence will help restore Imperial Russia? Will she be accepted by all Russians?"

"I understand your concerns," replied Utkin, "and yes. She may not have been part of the inner circle, but she was in line to inherit the throne. Her freedom in Shanghai would allow her to gather an audience, which is why the Reds had to get her away from Shanghai. I and my men will rescue your cousin, along with the means necessary to restore the rightful monarchy. I am thankful you allowed me to convince you of this plan. I hate to think of what would have happened if you ended up relying on that trash in Shanghai. Those men call themselves patriots for the Tsar but are simply rabble with rotten teeth, big mouths, and slack backbones who fight for ignorant Chinese warlords. Only to waste their pay in the bars and brothels of an uncivilized city. We will end this mission on our terms and ensure the duchess is retrieved from what you describe as a fairy-tale house."

"This estate was designed many years ago by a Bavarian craftsman," the countess continued. Together, he and my granduncle built a home with internal mysteries. The duchess and I discovered many of them as children, so if the diamonds were hidden there, she will find them."

"Good," Major Utkin replied. "We don't want to alert the soldiers by killing the generator. Its silence would be quite deafening. That said, do you still believe there is no electricity provided for the barracks?"

She answered, "The informant said the only modern fixture is a telephone."

Utkin, who returned his attention to the cliff, responded, "Based on your informant's information, I know the officer in charge, and he truly is a useless dullard. However, even bores know a visible telephone wire leading to the only source of assistance is the first thing an attacker will take care of. So, we can assume that there is a line buried in the ground leaving the exposed line as a decoy. In either case, Sergeant Dooley's men will take care of that wire and remain ready for any opposition. We will be on our way back to Shanghai before survivors can alarm headquarters in Vladivostok."

Utkin paused. "And the patrol boats have no wireless radio? No deck guns?"

She nodded. "He said that the guards take turns on the boats, and all they have are rifles, a pair of old machine weapons, and flare guns."

Countess Tolstoy finished as she turned her eyes up to the American sergeant. Their eyes met and remained on each other for a second.

"Good," Utkin said as he turned his eyes back to the submarine officer. "Captain Vostok, once we launch our boats, station a man there with a Lewis gun and extra magazines."

"*Da*," Captain Vostok replied as he adjusted the bill of his naval officer's peaked cap.

"Excellent," Utkin answered as he bent to the hatch at their feet, cracking it enough to give a quiet order. Dooley again noticed that the dull, red light illuminated the scar on Utkin's cheek.

CHAPTER 3

AS THEY PRACTICED during their transit from Shanghai to the Siberian-Russian coast, the raiders inside the submarine climbed out of the fore and aft deck hatches, attacked the lashings securing the upside-down wooden boats to the deck, and flipped them over before easing them into the water. While the tiller in each boat would be manned by a submariner, Major Utkin, Lieutenant Gorki, and six other men, armed with Fedorov Avtomats, with their twenty-five-round box magazines slung over their backs and pistols and knives hanging from web belts, slid into the boats. Countess Tolstoy followed them into the boat.

Sergeant Dooley, with his squad, slid into their own boat and paddled ashore. While Dooley was armed with his Thompson and his squad carried automatic rifles slung over their backs, one man, Morda, was armed differently. In the bilge, at the man's feet, lay a Lewis machine gun complete with a mounted bipod and an attached ninety-seven round pan magazine. A Russian army musette bag, filled with more pan magazines, lay next to the Lewis gun. As a veteran infantryman Dooley knew it took more than one soldier to operate and carry the Lewis, while keeping it armed and functioning. Despite its length and weight, Dooley noted throughout their training, Morda had no problem handling the machine gun. The only other weapon Morda carried was a wooden-handled entrenching tool. During their transit north, Morda spent his time, when not reading, sharpening its blade and oiling the short handle.

In just a few minutes, the prows of the wooden boats ground into the sand on either side of the rocks. Dropping his paddle, Dooley unslung his Thompson and leaped over the gunwales onto the line of rocks. His squad followed as he raced over the rocks to the base of the cliff. Once there, he ran to the wrought iron staircase noting its disrepair. The moonlight revealed missing sections of balusters poking out of the sand like soldiers standing at attention on a winding palace staircase.

Without missing a stride, Dooley prayed silently as he bounded onto the steps, the barrel of his Thompson leading the way. His men followed. While wearing their old army field uniforms and carrying modern military weapons, they all wore shoes Utkin secured from a sport shop in the British section of Shanghai. Popular with tennis enthusiasts, the athletic shoes were made from canvas and had rubber gum crepe soles. They were a grand replacement for the clunky boots and leg wraps Dooley wore in the army. Dooley listened to the soft padding of feet as his men climbed the metal staircase behind him while feeling the staircase shift under their weight.

It took a minute to reach the top of the rusting staircase. Spread about in front of them was what had once a splendid yard with manicured hedges and trees surrounding a fine home. Now, the hedges grew in disarray and dead leaves, twigs, and branches littered the grounds. Centered on the lawn behind the hedges, was a multi-story ornate summer home built of stone and topped with curved ceramic tiles. The moonlight glistened on the hedges and fairy-tale-like roof. The setting reminded Dooley of the villages he saw in the story books his mother read to him as a child. All that was missing were patches of snow at the base of chimneys and icicles hanging from windowsills. The droning of a hidden generator wafted over the roof of the structure.

"Go down that path, Sergeant Dooley," Countess Tolstoy said, slightly out of breath. She and the others had just arrived. Her extended arm pointed to a path bordering a lengthy hedge. "It will lead you to the corner of the main house where you can access the telephone wire. Follow it to the barracks."

Dooley turned to look at his squad. Like him, they were in their late teens or barely into their twenties, but their faces told him they were ready to fight.

Dooley and his men started down the path. Shortly, they reached the lane, which led through the trees to the barracks housing a company of infantry. Dooley slowed and looked at the man next to him. "Corporal Mashka?"

The young man smiled, revealing sound teeth. "Let's skedaddle."

Skedaddle? That wasn't exactly what the word meant. Dooley stepped out to run past the row of telephone poles guarding the lane. Time for another English lesson.

Corporal Mashka turned to the men behind him and signaled with his arm. They all followed Dooley in a double-time gait down the lane.

As they approached to where the lane pierced the tree line, Dooley watched for any threat ahead as he thought about the man behind him. He also thought back to the last few days aboard that submarine, and his reason for being on the grounds of a dilapidated Russian summer home as a nineteen-year-old ex-soldier.

Major Utkin assigned Mashka to be Dooley's interpreter since Mashka spoke some English, but the corporal was much more. Every night, when the submarine surfaced to recharge their batteries, Mashka was always next to Dooley during their raider drills, from swimming to firearm practice. He took delight practicing with Dooley's Thompson and army-issue pistol, even in disassembling and cleaning the weapons he used. Meanwhile, he used his time with Dooley to improve his English and learn more Brooklyn slang. It was as if the young corporal was trying to be just like Dooley. One last drill, overseen by Utkin, involved close combat. The raiders lunged at each other and parried blows as if they were fit men belonging to a prestigious *ludus* and overseen by a scarred *lanista*. One who stood on the sands of the Colosseum.

While completing their nightly drills, Dooley had taken the time to watch Utkin practice with his 1895-model Nagant revolver and its huge silencer. From his experience, Dooley knew that silencers were a recent invention and did not work with revolvers. Curious as to why this almost one-foot-long, steel tube was able to substantially mute the sound of the Nagant and cancel the muzzle flash, he asked Utkin about it. The Russian officer responded with pride.

"Even though this handgun is of Belgium design, the Tsar's military leaders contracted for its construction, and, by accident, incorporated a gas-seal configuration in the revolver's cylinder allowing for the addition of a silencer. My engineers completed its construction using my designs."

Dooley also thought about one of his favorite authors H.G. Wells where Utkin's combination could have found a place in one of the author's narratives as a futuristic space weapon. Dooley told himself Major Dmitri Utkin is one character that any person should come to fear.

That said, the nightly drills were a welcome diversion from the boredom of the transit, as Dooley had no duties. He spent most of his time watching the submarine's crew operate the vessel, seamen whose stature allowed for easier movement as compared to the bigger, embarked raiders. Watching the seamen, he was amazed at how much had to be done at the same time by so many people to make sure the submarine both surfaced and submerged safely. Having an affinity for fishing Dooley, during their nightly drills, also watched the submarine's cook troll for fish catching mostly tuna and mackerel. Dooley also appreciated the young cook's abilities when it came to preparing excellent tuna steaks.

Bringing his mind back to where the lane cut through the tree line, Dooley saw the forest along the right side. On the left side of the road, occupying an open area and backed by the cliff, was a single-story wooden building with one main entrance on the side facing them. On either side of the double wooden door windows ran the length of the structure. Their panes were shut, and curtains drawn. No lights leaked out. He sniffed at the still night. No harsh Russian tobacco tainted the cool air. Nor did he spot the red glow of a cigarette through the branches.

The building ran diagonally across the open area and, just as he and his squad planned, the men dispersed to their positions. Only Dooley and Morda, with his Lewis machine gun, remained where they stood. This position allowed a view of the front of the barracks. Dooley watched as the big Russian kneeled to set up his Lewis gun and ready his extra magazines. He put his entrenching tool on the ground next to the machine gun. The automatic weapon was developed to be used against humans running across no-man's-land or against canvas-covered, wooden-framed airplanes, but with enough pan magazines, those bullets could chew their way through any obstacle, including thick wooden doors of the barracks. Seeing that the front was covered, Dooley turned and ran to the north end of the barracks.

He followed the edge of the open ground to the corner of the building where the slightly drooping telephone wire connected to the low-pitched roof. Pulling out his shingle axe, he reached up and caught the wire with a v-notch at the bottom of the implement's blade. It fell noiselessly to the ground, and he moved away from the building to complete the circle around the barracks. With a three-hundred-and-sixty-degree arc of fire, everybody settled in to wait for the next event.

Taking his weapon off safety, Dooley lay prone on the damp grass and listened. The night was still, and all that could be heard was the soft hum of the generator muffled by the maze of hedges and lines of trees. Thanks to the moonlight Dooley could see the parade area in front of the barracks and behind it, four long wooden tables where the soldiers could relax when off duty. There was a wooden stand with a line of tin washbasins and water pitchers. Lastly, four small wooden structures occupied the space between the washstand and the trees. A stack of firewood reached halfway up the wall of the one closest to Dooley with a tree stump pinching that stack in place. An axe blade was sunk into the flat surface of the stump. Above the stacked wood he saw a half-moon shape cut into the wall. Having been assigned to latrine duty, he knew what those shacks were for.

As Dooley took in the view with the barrel of his submachine gun pointed at a barracks full of people he did not know, he deliberated his reasons for being on the periphery of the ex-Russian Empire. Though the adventure of the mission thrilled him he hated to think about what he might be forced to do. He also thought about what Utkin had meant by not only rescuing a possible candidate for the imperial throne but also the means necessary to do so. A cache of diamonds? Dooley sighed and focused on the rear double door of the barracks.

CHAPTER 4

AS THEY WATCHED Dooley's squad quietly vanish into the darkness, Utkin turned to the countess and told her to lead the way. She nodded and followed a path bordered by ragged hedges that led toward the estate's main building at the edge of an area once home to a children's playground and a stage for entertainment. Now, everything was in disrepair. The area was covered in weeds, and broken parts of carousel horses reigned over the playground. Half the stage was missing, probably used for firewood.

Crossing the open area, they entered through what was once a grand garden doorway, now closed off with army blankets. At the foot of the door, the blank stare of a pony's head, lying on its side, along with a wide grin revealing a huge set of wooden teeth, greeted them. Countess Tolstoy pushed the blankets aside.

Inside, Major Utkin and the others found themselves in a large room that was now just a shell of its previous opulence. Now dingy and broken, all that remained were remnants of wood paneling and trim, along with patches of plaster and white paint adhering to the rough-cut stones. Leading away from the spacious room were hallways and a winding staircase that led to the second floor where the duchess was housed. All Utkin's men unsheathed their knives, and most of them headed down the darkened hallways. Gorki and one of his men took to the winding staircase with the countess and the major following.

While other blankets covered the windows of the estate, enough celestial light leaked in to welcome their arrival to the second floor. They walked down one of the hallways with the countess in the lead and stopped in front of one room that still had a door. The countess turned to look at Utkin. He nodded as she turned and quietly tapped the door with her knuckles four times in slow succession. After the fourth tap, the countess pushed the door open with her fingers. The door lock and handle once in place were now gone. As with anything else in the house of even the smallest value, the door hardware found a useful home elsewhere.

Behind her, Utkin pushed aside a hanging blanket and looked at the bed and the two people covered with warm-looking bedding. Letting the blanket fall back into place behind him, Utkin stepped to the side of the bed. Standing over one of the sleeping men, he used his thumb to pull back the pistol's hammer, rotating the cylinder. The clicking woke a man with a pudgy face and receding hairline. His eyes opened slowly, and his one long eyebrow furrowed as his eyes struggled to adjust to the dim light leaking into the room. "Dmitri? What are you doing here?"

At the same time, the second form in the bed turned over as well. The young man also looked confused. "Yuri? What is happening? Who is he?"

"Oh, hello, Yuri," Utkin said quietly. "Sorry to wake you, chum."

Still confused, the man addressed as Yuri brought a hand up to rub his eyes. "I thought you were on your way to . . . Wait. Why are you here? I thought you were with Comintern?"

The men in the bed now saw the revolver and the attached silencer. The major brought his arm up and pointed the silencer at Yuri's forehead. "I know you will understand."

The man's eyes widened, and a look of horror took over his face. "Why?"

Utkin answered with the squeeze of his finger. The hollow thud of the shot was followed by a dull crack as the back of Yuri's head exploded against his partner's face. Before the man could scream, Utkin re-aimed and pulled the trigger one more time. The major turned from the bed and saw the countess standing in the doorway holding the blanket out of her way. He saw her shocked look.

"You said that you knew that man," she said with a shaking voice. "Yet you shot him like he was nothing?"

"He always was nothing but a useless Bolshevik. Now, let us call out your cousin," Utkin said as he calmly lowered his pistol.

Shaken by the killing, the countess turned back to the room with the now open door. She stepped in with Utkin behind her. "Olga, it is me."

Both looked into the darkened room. They heard nothing, and all they could see was an unmade bed with a thin mattress, ragged sheet, and an equally shabby army blanket. The only other fixture was an escritoire with a mirror and a wooden chair in front of it. Around the escritoire, on the wood-en-planked floor, were scraps of fancy or frill cloth.

"Olga," Countess Tolstoy said with a bit more emphasis.

After a long second, both Utkin and the countess heard the distant click of a metal latch and the sound of a door being slid back revealing the inside of the built-in wardrobe. In the open frame stood a woman who appeared to be a bit older than the countess's nineteen years and a bit bigger in frame but just as pretty with an innocent face and silky blond hair. The duchess, who seemed to struggle to hold herself straight, wore her hair drawn into a severe bun, a gown that reached to the floor, and an unbuttoned army blouse over the ballroom dress. In each hand, she held leather hatboxes with brass hinges and snap locks. Lastly, she wore what looked like a horse collar around her neck. But as his eyes adjusted, Utkin realized what it really was.

"Zeta!" sighed Olga. "I can't believe it's you!"

The sound of Olga's heels striking the planked flooring thundered in the darkness, and the hard sound gave the major pause to think. *One nice pair of shoes to wear while trying to make an escape.* He then thought about the item wrapped around her neck. He smiled.

Olga, still carrying her load, nuzzled her head into her cousin's neck and responded with a relieved sigh. "Oh, Zeta."

"I am sorry, but . . ." Utkin spoke as he holstered his pistol. The silencer protruded out the bottom of the leather holster almost reaching his knee. "We must leave now."

The two women separated, and the duchess held out the hatboxes.

Utkin grabbed them, and as he did, Gorki stepped up to the door behind him.

"We've processed everyone on the second and third floors," Gorki said, as he turned and pushed aside the blanket hanging in the doorway. He looked at the forms in the bed. "He was always a useless pig, but now he and that whore next to him accounts for everybody."

The three people in the room joined Gorki in the hallway. It was there when they saw the knife in Gorki's right hand. They also saw blood splayed across his face.

"Good work, Lieutenant," Utkin said. "And you are right. He was always useless alive, but now, he just became unbelievably valuable."

Without another word, the four of them stepped down the hallway with Utkin in the lead and Olga and Zeta holding each other's arms. Olga still wore the horse-collar-looking thing around her neck, and Utkin and Gorki could hear the rustle of her clothing. They also heard the thumping of her heels against the wooden floor.

They stopped at the balcony overlooking the large room. The men assigned to the first floor gathered below them. Like Gorki, they all carried bloodied knives in their hands. One of them looked up at Utkin. "One of Reds was awake. He got on the telephone, but I took care of him before he said anything."

A smile came to Utkin's face. "Now it is time to see if our American can earn his five hundred dollars and pass muster."

Gorki replied as he sheathed his knife. "We shall see."

CHAPTER 5

THE MUTED RING of a telephone inside the barracks destroyed the silence of the cold night air outside. It rang only once.

"Shit! There was an underground wire," Dooley cursed as he tightened his grip. At the same time, he saw weak lights fill the cracks and holes in the curtains. The sound of confused voices followed. Dooley aimed down the barrel of his rag-wrapped submachine gun while thinking about the men inside. He prayed silently. *Please Lord, I don't know those men from Adam.*

It finally came. An explosion of machine gun fire ripped the night apart. Though he could not see the carnage directly, Dooley heard the lead from both Morda's Lewis gun and two Fedorov rifles tear into flesh, glass, and wood. He envisioned men, half-dressed and carrying bolt-action rifles, spilling out the front door of the barracks and into withering fire. The burst from the Lewis gun outlasted the short bursts from the Fedorov rifles, but both were accompanied by the screams of men being mowed down. Dooley took his eyes from the rear door of the barracks long enough to look over the peaked roof. The orange-yellowish muzzle flashes interrupted the moonlight.

After what sounded like the death of many men, everything went quiet except for the screams of the wounded who either lay in the grass or made it back inside. Dooley refocused and watched the rear doors which snapped open within two seconds. The feeble lights silhouetted shadows spilling out. Just as Dooley envisioned the distraught men were either half dressed in uniforms or wore long underwear and boots, but all carried bolt-action rifles. Dooley pressed harder on the trigger, lowering the barrel, and the weapon bucked against his shoulder. Rounds tore at the dirt under the mob's feet. As Dooley finished a short burst, the men scrambled over each other trying to get back through the open doorway. The doors, though, were slammed shut leaving two men outside. The men screamed and hammered at the doors with their fists. Their panic, however, was cut short as bullets from Mashka's automatic ripped into them from the side. Both died instantly.

Dooley let go of his Thompson long enough to reach into his musette bag and grab a hand grenade, his second to the last one. He pulled the pin and threw it toward the rear doors. The grenade exploded in a brilliant flash, and fragments lashed at the wooden wall and windowpanes. Seeing someone peeking out the now pane-less window, he grabbed his pistol and fired it six times at the window, emptying the magazine. The man's face disappeared and the lighting inside the barracks went out, followed by a deathly silence.

Dooley reloaded his pistol and grabbed his submachine gun. Surprised the old grenade still worked, he hoped it would convince those inside that any attempt to exit the building would be met with gunfire. They stayed put.

Waiting for Utkin's signal, the seconds vanished one tick at a time, and, after a good number of ticks, the distant shrill of a whistle ripped away the silence. A burst of gunfire from Mashka's position replaced the shrill of the whistle, and Dooley heard the rounds tear into the wood walls of the building. Another burst of automatic gunfire also tore into the barracks. It came from the man positioned between Mashka and Morda. Dooley then heard Morda unload his magazine into it as well. One by one, Dooley's squad emptied the magazines inserted in their weapons as they peeled off to form an organized withdrawal.

Finally, it was Dooley's turn. He stood and, with the Thompson at waist level, pulled his trigger, splaying the side of the barracks with forty-five caliber slugs. Once empty, he detached the drum magazine from the weapon, and placed it into the musette bag. He was about to pull one of the stick magazines from his canvas web belt, but the door of the latrine closest to him slammed open. Dooley looked up in time to see a balding man, wearing long underwear and army boots, bolt from it.

Only three yards away, the man turned and ran straight at Dooley, yanking the axe from the stump as he did. After months of fighting in Russia, instinct controlled Dooley's next move. Dropping his weapon, he pulled his shingle hammer-axe from his belt and raised it above his head while leaning into the assault. The man saw the shingle axe and did the same with his axe. Unfortunately, he didn't see Dooley pull his knife from its sheath. As they collided, Dooley drove it into his gut.

Blood squirted all over Dooley's hand. The man grunted in response, and Dooley saw the shocked look on his face only inches away. At the same time, Dooley brought the hammer end of the shingle axe down on the man's skull. Dooley heard the man's skull crack. He looked into the man's wide eyes. "Damn you!" he cried. "You should've stayed on the crapper!"

Pulling the blade from the Russian's guts, Dooley stood back, letting him collapse on his own. Sheathing his bladed weapons, Dooley cursed the body while wiping his hand on his trousers. He turned to collect his Thompson, which he quickly reloaded with a stick magazine as he ran to join his squad and yelling out, "The rest of you better stay put!"

Dooley rounded the northern end of the barracks and ran to the tree line encircling the summer home. As he did, he saw a dozen bodies strewn about in front of the shredded barracks. Reaching the trees, he saw Mashka kneeling with his Fedorov pointing at the barracks. Dooley ran past him and down the road, passing the rest of his squad who were spaced about ten yards apart and doing the same as Mashka. Once Dooley passed the last man in line, he ran for another ten yards and stopped, kneeled, and raised his weapon pointing it back down the road. The men of his squad repeated the leapfrog retreat. After the last man, Mashka, passed their leader, Dooley stood, but a ragged volley of rifle fire forced him to duck. He heard Mashka grunt as he did. He also heard bullets whistling over his own head. Twirling around with his Thompson held at waist level, he saw figures running down the road. They stopped to work their rifle bolts.

"Dooley!" The corporal grunted behind him.

Hearing Mashka's plea as he struggled to get to his feet, Dooley raised the submachine gun to his shoulder. He peered down the barrel at the men raising their rifles at the same time. They stood twenty yards in front of his muzzle.

"Bastards!" Dooley cursed loudly as he pulled his trigger. "I told you to stay put!"

The submachine gun roared, and the muzzle flash blocked out the line of Russians in front of Dooley. He heard the screams of men over the blast of the weapon. After emptying the stick magazine, he cursed his pursuers again while slinging the weapon over his head. Turning around he reached to pull Mashka to his feet and throw him over his shoulder in a firefighter's carry. At the same time, the others in the squad, still kneeling in their firing positions, allowed Dooley to pass them. The three men waited for any others who might prove to be brave but foolish soldiers. No one followed.

Dooley ran hard, but even though he had been a combat soldier for the last year, it felt as if his lungs were on fire, while sweat streamed down his face. Unable to wipe away the stinging wetness, Dooley ran off the road and onto the path that led to the cliff. Without realizing it, he came around the corner of the hedge and faced Utkin and the others grouped at the cliff face.

"It's Mashka," Dooley exhaled while bending to let the man slip off his shoulder.

Two raiders from Utkin's squad stepped forward to lay Mashka to the ground. Utkin and Gorki leaned over to look at Mashka's face and at the blood saturating the uniform blouse.

The corporal answered Gorki's look by quietly and painfully pointing at his chest.

Utkin stood and said something to the two men. They immediately picked up Mashka and walked him toward the staircase.

Utkin turned to Dooley. "Anybody else in your squad wounded?"

"They're fighting a delaying action."

Just as Dooley finished his words, his squad suddenly appeared, all out of breath. Morda carried up the rear. The big Russian held his Lewis gun firmly in one hand and his unsheathed entrenching tool in the other. By now, the moon had become brighter, and Dooley noticed the sharpened steel of Morda's entrenching tool was dulled by a coat of dark liquid.

While Dooley waited for his men to file down the stairs on the cliff face, he saw the woman they came to rescue. She was a bit bigger than Countess Tolstoy, several years older, and too overdressed for the occasion. He also noticed what looked like a horse collar hanging around her neck. But after a second, he realized what it really was. It was a toilet seat.

Suddenly, a burst of gunfire erupted from behind a nearby hedge, and the woman screamed as everybody heard bullets thud into her back. She fell forward and the toilet seat around her neck flew over her head. Both thudded heavily against the ground. The countess screamed. "Olga, no!"

Everybody else dropped to their knees and Gorki's men emptied their box magazines into the hedge. Once the last shot was fired, two of Gorki's men threw themselves into the hedge.

"I thought we accounted for everybody," Gorki stated. "That slut in Yuri's bed must have thrown off the tally."

"Apparently so," Utkin responded as he kept his attention on the duchess.

The countess, bent over the body of the duchess, sobbed and repeated Olga's name over and over. But the countess stopped when she heard her cousin moan. Like a revenant, Olga pushed herself up from the ground and stood. Falling into the arms of her cousin, everybody was amazed at the woman's survival.

The popping sound of a red flare disrupted their stunned silence. Everybody's eyes followed the rising arch of the flare. It came from one of the patrol boats. The running lights of both patrol boats were now switched on. However, the twinkle of the boat lights was met with a stream of tracer bullets from the Lewis gun on the submarine's conning tower.

The men who entered the hedge reappeared with one of them holding his rifle along with an automatic machine pistol. Dooley remembered seeing the type of pistol before. It was more fitting for an officer to wear while sitting for a portrait as its frail construction reduced its combat effectiveness.

Utkin, still carrying the hatboxes, saw the pistol and turned to his men. "Gorki, collect the toilet seat and take the lead. Morda, stow your entrenching tool and escort the countess. The rest of you follow them. Duchess, you stay with me."

The group turned toward the stair landing at the cliff and followed Gorki after he scooped up the toilet seat and looped it around his neck. Utkin and the duchess followed the rest. Dooley was about a quarter of the way down the staircase when he heard a spine-chilling scream and turned to look over his shoulder just as the duchess and her bulky dress dropped past his eyes. She screamed nonstop while clawing at the air. A second later, her body drove itself into the sand.

The countess screamed unintelligibly, and everybody raced down the steps of the staircase, forgetting about its deteriorated condition. Reaching the beach, they ran to the form. Countess Tolstoy reached out for her cousin, but Morda held her back. Everybody else stood around the duchess, and in the moonlight, they saw she had been impaled by three stair balusters.

"I do not know what happened," Utkin stated. "She was standing right next to me, then suddenly fell over the side. It must have been her shoes."

Utkin stopped to look at his lieutenant. "Gorki, Collect the duchess. Everybody to the boats. Dooley, give us cover."

At sea, the uneven gunfight between the submarine and patrol boats ravaged on.

Morda, carrying his Lewis machine gun crooked under one arm, forcibly escorted the hysterical young woman toward the boats. The others followed. Meanwhile, Dooley raised the barrel of his Thompson and pointed it at the edge of the cliff while keeping an eye on Gorki. The Russian lieutenant adjusted the toilet seat around his neck before stooping to collect the woman's body. Before he did though, he saw Gorki inspect one of the balusters sticking through her torso. Dooley thought he saw Gorki pick something off the end of the three-foot pipe, look at it, and throw it on the sand.

Helluva time to be worried about a piece of gore, Dooley thought.

Gorki seemed to fidget with the back of the duchess's dress for a few seconds before inserting his arms under the body to lift it off the balusters. Once free, he folded the body over his shoulder and turned toward the boat where his men waited for him. Dooley remained as the last man on the beach.

Listening to the firefight between the patrol boats and the submarine behind him, Dooley walked backward while keeping his barrel pointed at the cliff line and his eyes on the sand around him. In doing so, he saw one of the woman's shoes laying several feet from where she landed. For some reason, he side-stepped over to the shoe. It looked like a type of fashionable, but practical, shoe that he had seen in magazines. He didn't remember the heel being that big in the photos, though. He stooped to pick it up and secured it in his musette bag, while looking around to see what else might have fallen off her body. As he did, he saw something sparkle in the sand next to where the shoe landed. Just as he bent over to see what it was, rifle fire from the top of the cliff changed his mind. With bullets punching into the sand around his feet, he emptied his magazine into the cliff top. Morda fired a burst over Dooley's head, and at the cliff, as Dooley ran past him. The other two raiders, with their paddles in hand and the steersman holding onto the tiller, waited for Dooley and Morda. The gunshots from the cliff stopped, Dooley threw his weapon into the boat, and climbed over the gunwale. At the same time, he saw that the other boat was already at the submarine.

Paddling hard, Dooley and his men backed away from the beach and made quick time to the submarine. It seemed to take only a minute before the steersman turned the tiller landing alongside the submarine's hull just aft of the conning tower. Morda dropped his paddle and grabbed at the bowline, throwing the other end to a man on the deck. The man held the line so Dooley, and the others who quickly slung their weapons over their shoulders, could pull themselves up to the deck. As his men squeezed themselves into the deck hatch, Dooley reviewed the results of the gun battle between the submarine and the patrol boats. Both boats were burning, and he heard the screams of the survivors as they jumped into the cold water.

Looking up he saw both Utkin and Vostok standing next to the machine gunner who had ceased firing his weapon but pointed the barrel to the boats rubbing against the hull. The man holding their lines let go and ran to the open the hatchway forward of the conning tower.

Dooley felt the vibration of the submarine's diesel engines and heard the swishing of water at the stern. The Lewis gunner fired into the boats and, as bullets chewed into the bilges of the wooden boats, Dooley stepped over to the hatch and started to slide down the ladder but stopped with his head and shoulders still outside the submarine. The shooting stopped as the submarine picked up speed and glided between the two burning patrol boats.

Dooley felt a warming kiss on both cheeks, while listening to men screaming in the frigid water. He wondered why the gunner did not finish those men off. It would be more humane than letting them drown or freeze to death. Leaving the carnage, he continued down the ladder and thought *maybe working at Pop's wagon repair shop in Brooklyn wouldn't be such a bad idea.*

CHAPTER 6

DOOLEY LANDED ON the deck plates of the crew's aft sleeping compartment. Now, that the raiders no longer needed their night vision, the crew switched off the red lights and turned on the white lights. The brilliance stabbed at Dooley's eyes. Wiping sweat from his eyes, he looked at his surroundings.

While the submarine was one hundred and fifty feet long, the inside was sixteen feet at its widest point, and that was amidships at the control room. Having never been aboard a submarine before this week, Dooley was amazed at how much machinery, brass piping, copper tubing, valves, gauges, and wiring were shoved into such a narrow tube. That didn't even include everything needed to house and feed a crew of thirty-five. This compartment, like all the others, was crammed with only the essentials: a place to sleep and stow personal gear, a toilet closet with barely enough room to close the door once occupied by one man, and an office cubicle stuffed with a desk, wireless radio, typewriter, and book-filled shelf.

Dooley noted the radio turned off and its headset hanging from the mouthpiece. The operator was busy with another mouthpiece, that being the Lewis gun on the conning tower. To one side of the radio was a typewriter and a booklet written by the current American president, Woodrow Wilson. Squeezed between the radio room-slash-office cubical and forward bulkhead was the aft toilet closet. He saw the door ajar, and one raider bent over the sink scrubbing his face. The man's field blouse hung from a hook, and his build pressed against the sweat-soaked undershirt.

Turning to look through the hatch piercing the aft bulkhead, he saw two young men wearing clean coveralls, one lubricating an exposed rocker arm moving up and down with the pistons inside the cylinder. The angled pieces reminded Dooley of the crabs he saw at Coney Island. The other man watched a gauge panel in front of one the engines. Both engineers, small in stature and with close haircuts, reminded Dooley of technicians he saw on the cover of motorcar magazines.

Turning his attention from the engineers, Dooley pulled the sling of his Thompson over his head and stooped through the hatch leading into the crowded control room. A wooden chart table ran the length of the portside of the compartment. Rolled-up charts were stacked like firewood underneath, and a shelf stuffed with books, manuals, and atlases above, a few of which Dooley perused through during their transit north. The man who held the bowlines of the boats stood next to the table in front of an open logbook, with a pencil in his hand. Other men, including the submarine's only other officer, either stood or sat at their stations, watching over the myriad of gauges, valves, and equipment needed to control the submarine. Taking up the center of the packed room was the periscope, in its lowered position and a ladder leading to the conning tower above them. Dooley squeezed around both and stood next to the officer who was about the same age as Gorki. This officer, though, wore dungarees and a naval officer's cap.

All the submariners were waiting for their next order, and Dooley waited just like them. After a few seconds of listening to the marine diesels behind him, he looked up and into the hatch next to his head. Just as he did, Vostok's face filled the open hatch and barked out new orders in Russian.

The submarine officer responded with what sounded like a repeat of the order while looking at the flush-mounted gyrocompass in front of the helmsman. The helmsman responded by turning the large wheel slightly while keeping his eyes on the white-faced dial. The long, black needle settled on one-eight-zero degrees.

We're heading due south, Dooley told himself as he pictured an atlas map of the Sea of Japan in his head. The Siberian coast would soon be behind them leaving the submarine pinched between Japan and the Korean Peninsula. His picturing of the Sea of Japan was disturbed by a metal clanking sound. Dooley turned in time to see the Lewis gun being lowered into the compartment by a length of rope. The man standing next to the ballast tank valves reached out to collect the weapon. Untying it, he cradled in in one arm while opening the door to a locker. At the same time, Utkin, then Vostok, slid down the ladder.

Vostok said something in Russian to the officer before turning to Dooley. Like most of the crew and raiders, the other officer did not speak or understand English. Only Utkin, Vostok, Gorki, Mashka, and Countess Tolstoy understood and spoke at least some English.

"Well, Sergeant," Vostok said with a smile. "I see the legionnaire's fire in your eyes. Are you glad that the Major sought you out in Shanghai?"

Dooley looked at the captain while pulling the watch cap from his head and feeling a diminishing knot as he did. To Dooley, the sixty-year-old officer with his white peaked cap and manicured beard reminded him of Captain Nemo of the *Nautilus*. Dooley wiped the sweat from his forehead with the watch cap. "Nothing wrong with a little adventure, but he still owes me the south half of five hundred bucks, which I assume will be waiting for me in Shanghai."

Dooley paused before speaking again. "What about Mashka?"

Vostok was about to speak again but Utkin interrupted.

"Sergeant, you will get your money, but meanwhile, go wash up, have a cup of wine, and get some sleep. Do not worry about the corporal. He is of sound body, and Lieutenant Gorki is not your simple barrack doctor capable of only doling out expectorants and lancing boils."

Before Dooley could respond, Utkin turned to Vostok. "What is our plan of action?"

Vostok answered quickly. "We will remain on the surface until dawn so our diesels can get us out of this area as fast as possible. At dawn we will submerge and continue south on battery power. We should be out of the Sea of

Japan before noon and, barring any encounters with the Japanese Navy, we will change course and head southwest for Shanghai."

"I agree," Utkin said. "It is assumed that the company guarding the duchess will send out a radiotelegraph message concerning this submarine. It can also be assumed that the Japanese will intercept such a message and will not be happy about an unflagged submarine operating in the Sea of Japan. Even the United States Navy is not allowed to operate a lowly destroyer in these waters without their permission."

Vostok chimed in while looking at both men, "Since we do not have to conduct our raider drills, the transit back to Shanghai will be quicker. Dooley, do as the major says."

Realizing how thirsty he was, Dooley dropped his shoulders while saluting with the muzzle of his Thompson. Lowering the barrel, he stooped to enter the hatch leading into the forward compartments. Careful to not hit his head on a valve again, he straightened up on the other side and looked at his trench watch. It was just past midnight.

Looking forward to cleaning up a bit, he looked to his sides. Next to his left shoulder was the captain's stateroom, now closed off with blue curtains. Dooley listened to the quiet sobbing on the other side. During their transit, it was where the countess stayed, leaving only for the toilet, to get food or tea from the cook, or to enjoy fresh air while watching the nightly drills. She was back in that room again and still alone. Next to his right shoulder was the other stateroom, but this one, with its curtain drawn back, revealed the officers' quarters where Vostok, Utkin, Gorki, and the other submarine officer took turns sleeping. Although tiny, warm blankets softened the austere metal of the stateroom. Just forward of the captain's stateroom was an alcove with padded bench seating wrapped around a table. Able to seat four people, Dooley spent hours occupying the space while drinking wine or coffee and reading. Against the piping-lined bulkhead behind the bench seating was another bookshelf stuffed with books.

Opposite the wardroom, squeezed between the officers' quarters and the forward bulkhead was the forward toilet with its door ajar. Looking around the ladder leading down from the forward deck hatch, he saw Morda rubbing oil into his wet, foppish blond hair while inspecting his teeth. Morda reminded Dooley of American college football stars with women hanging off their shoulders and advertising companies chasing in their footsteps. But this athlete did not look like he needed to bully anybody into doing his homework. While Dooley's eyes paused on him for a second, he thought about the other submarine raiders. Although the submarine crewmen tended to be small in stature, every submarine raider could've been the handsome sons of millionaires making up the elite squad of Harvard's football team or star gladiators belonging to a wealthy Roman's *ludus*.

Dooley stepped around the ladder and stooped through the round hatchway into the crew's mess. To his left was an enclosed pantry. To his right was the galley. Not much larger than the two water closets put together, it was equipped with everything needed to feed a crew of thirty-five men. However, the crew was reduced to make room for the raiders. The only item that stood out in the galley was a framed photo of the Waldorf Astoria Hotel in New York City. Hanging from the seasoning rack, it could not be missed.

Although Dooley walked past the hotel's grand façade occasionally, he was more familiar with the service entrance, which is where he helped his father or brother off-load produce. Some of the kitchen staff were nice folk, but others tended to be snooty. He did, however, have a friend who worked there as a busboy. Jose, barely five-feet tall, told Dooley more than once of conversations he overheard. Being a diminutive Puerto Rican, Jose was amazed at what wealthy patrons would openly say while he picked up after them, especially the half-drunk politicians with their mistresses. Dooley heard a voice come from around the corner. Stepping past the galley and pantry he entered the relative expanse of the crew's mess. On either side of the compartment was a long table with bookshelves, piping and valves running the length of the curved bulkhead behind the bench seating. It was here where the crew ate and relaxed. Tonight, though, it served as both a morgue and a hospital.

On one side Dooley saw a white sheet covering the duchess. Her feet, covered with pink stockings, poked out from under it, but she still only wore that one shoe. Nowhere did he see the toilet seat. Dooley patted his musette bag and was about to lift the flap but was interrupted. To his right he saw bright red blood run down Mashka's torso and pool on the table's surface. The vibrations of the diesels powering the submarine though the sea shook the blood over the edge where it dripped onto the steel deck at Gorki's feet. While Mashka lay unconscious on the table in only blood-soaked undershorts, Gorki and the cook worked to save his life.

The cook, a petite red-haired nineteen year old, said something in Russian as he flipped the pages of the book in his hands. It was a hardcover medical book with images and printed in English. Gorki still wore his field uniform but with his sleeves rolled up to his elbows. Dooley stepped to get a closer look at his teammate. Mashka's eyes were half open, and his mouth was agape. With a vacant, drug-induced stare, his glassy blue eyes seemed to thank Dooley.

Dooley returned the gaze but only for a second. He looked to see what Gorki was doing. Wearing a pair of blood-saturated cloth surgical gloves, Gorki just picked up a pair of bloodied forceps along with retractors from the bloodstained towel spread across Mashka's abdomen. He reached into one of the bullet holes with the retractors to pull the wound open a bit more so that he could insert the forceps.

Dooley, like all soldiers in his regiment, received first aid training before being shipped out, but that instruction was nothing compared to what he experienced in Russia. After his first action, Dooley helped transport the dead and wounded to the field hospital where one surgeon stood out. The surgeon was respected by everybody in the regiment, even while he inspected the off-limits establishments outside of camp.

Unfortunately, that surgeon, who left a New York City practice and volunteered to serve in France before America entered the war, was killed by mortar fire in Russia while tending to a platoon of soldiers out in the field. It was at those times, as he stood at attention while watching a comrade being buried in the dark Russian soil, when Dooley questioned their mission to Russia and the waste of men like the surgeon. War took no favorites as both oafs and prodigies alike were just desserts for the Grim Reaper, he thought as he watched Gorki working to save the young raider's life. It was if Gorki was that surgeon back in New York where fellow doctors gathered to watch him work, and nurses swooned at his wavy black hair and good looks.

Seeing Mashka was in good hands, Dooley reached down to retrieve the shoe, but his throat reminded him of the wine. Patting the utility bag, he bent and stepped through the forward hatch entering the crew's forward quarters, which was also the compartment that housed the main purpose of any submarine: torpedoes. However, there were no torpedoes locked into their deck-mounted carriages under the folding bunks. Because of this mission, the eight, fifteen-foot-long torpedoes that the submarine could carry were removed along with all the equipment needed to house, lift, and move the torpedoes into the four brass-capped tubes. The result was more room for the submarine raiders and reduced crew. Even still, the stature of the embarked submarine raider force, along with their field equipment and the rectangular table Vostok had installed in the compartment, seemed to overwhelm whatever space the removed torpedoes offered up. Especially since all the weapons, gear, and clothing the men carried or wore in the raid were spread about the compartment, including Morda's entrenching tool. Wiped clean, it leaned against a wooden folding chair now occupied by a raider. It was if the entrenching tool was recovering from the mission just like the raiders. Waiting for their turn at either one of the toilets, the men sat half-dressed while enjoying wine and conversation.

They stopped talking as Dooley entered the compartment and turned to flash toothy smiles at him, while lifting their tin cups. After the salute, one of them pointed with his cup at the two metal soup tubs on the table. One was full of fresh water with a couple of pinkish-smeared towels next to it. The other tub contained five open bottles of red wine with several empty pint-sized tin cups around it. Dooley was astonished at how much red wine these men consumed but was even more astonished at the fact that none of them smoked.

The same man reached for a bottle in the tub and filled a cup. Putting the bottle back, he nodded at the cup. The sergeant smiled at the Russians and stepped up to the cup. But first, he laid his Thompson against the chair nearest him and dunked both hands into the tub of water. After rubbing them together several times, he withdrew them and grabbed the cleanest of the two towels. Thinking about the man he stabbed through the gut and the raiders in front of his Thompson, he dropped the towel back on the table and reached for the cup of wine. He took a long, thoughtful swallow.

After a couple winks, and a few more smiles, the men returned to their talking, leaving Dooley to place his gear on his bunk. It was one of the bottom ones, and under Mashka's bunk. Dooley put his cup on Mashka's blanket-covered bunk long enough to lay his Thompson on his own bunk along with his musette bag, axe hammer, and pistol belt. With a sigh of relief, he reached to unbutton and remove his uniform jacket, which he threw over his weapons before picking up his wine. He almost emptied the cup in that second swallow. With his eyes closed he had no idea how thirsty he was.

Dooley noticed the smell of his armpit and looked forward to Shanghai where he could take a proper bath in his hotel's hallway toilet. He also thought about the last two hours. Sighing again, he told himself that all those men had to do was to stay put.

He took a second to look at Mashka's bunk. Like the others, it had a thin mattress and striped pillow, covered with a white sheet and rough wool blanket. Dooley used the cup to smooth out a wrinkle on the blanket, and, as he did, spied the corner of a book under the pillow. Thinking about Mashka's companionship over the week, Dooley reached for the volume. It was thick, like the medical book the cook held for Gorki, but this volume was a chemistry book. Dooley noticed a blank piece of paper sticking out from the top. He put the book down on the blanket and opened it to the marked page. The images were complex, but he could read the text, which had something to do with a chemical called fluorine. Suddenly, Dooley realized the book was in English. Just like the medical book.

A push against his shoulder drew him from the book. Morda, cleaned up and wearing athletic sweater and civilian trousers, stood next to him. His combed blond hair held in place by hair oil highlighted his grin. He held a bottle. "Mashka. Good."

Sighing again, Dooley grabbed his wine cup and held it out. He looked at the men at the table. Their eyes invited him to sit. He nodded and stepped to the table where he put his full cup down and washed his hands again, but more thoroughly this time. Before drying his hands on a fresh towel Morda brought in, Dooley ran his wet fingers through his black hair. He took a second cup of wine and said, "For Countess Tolstoy," and left through the hatchway.

CHAPTER 7

WITH A CUP of wine in each hand, Dooley stepped back into the crew's mess in time to see Gorki wiping his hands on a towel while studying his sutures in the corporal's chest. Dooley also saw that Mashka's eyes were closed, and the cook was sopping up blood from the deck plates with another towel.

The black-haired officer turned and winked at Dooley. "He will be fine, Dooley."

Relieved, Dooley winked in return and stepped behind Gorki, who returned his attention to his patient. Dooley glanced to his right at the still-covered body of the duchess. He saw that the shoe she did wear was now gone.

No sense putting the other shoe back now, Dooley told himself as he entered the officer's quarters. Stopping in front of Vostok's stateroom, Dooley noticed, through the open hatch leading into the control room, that the hatch leading to the aft crew's quarters was closed, shutting out the noise of the diesels. He also noticed the sobbing he heard before had stopped. Behind him though, the curtain for the officer's stateroom was drawn as well, but he heard murmuring in Russian.

Dooley was about to call out her name, but the submarine surged, causing him to spill some wine. After cursing quietly, he spoke, "Countess?"

The murmuring behind him stopped and, after a second, he saw the woman's fingers curl at the edge of the curtain and push it aside. The brass curtain rings scraped across the brass rod as she did. Dooley looked down and into her eyes. Normally, they were large, innocent, and bright blue. Now, they were red, puffy, and melancholy. She still wore the overly large army uniform with the blouse buttoned to the collar. Dooley noted smeared snot on her right sleeve. She had, however, taken the time to remove her watch cap and brush her long blond hair behind the ears. Before tonight, at nineteen, she looked so sweet and angelic. Now, she looked desperate and lost.

Not knowing what else to say, Dooley held up the wine. "I thought you would like tea, but the cook was helping Gorki. Hope wine is satisfactory?"

She lifted the damp cuff and wiped her nose. "The cook's stingy when it comes to his sugar, so drinking tea without sugar is a moot point. Please, come in."

Still holding the curtain back, she stood aside, allowing him to slip into the small stateroom. While Captain Vostok presented a distinguished appearance with his neat uniform and trimmed beard, so did the stateroom. It was like all the attributes of a nobleman's country estate found themselves neatly reassembled inside a children's playhouse. The sparse furnishings were made from varnished red oak and appeared to be custom fitted into the tiny space.

Dooley noted the bookshelf above the bunk and its contents right away. Most of the books, mostly bound in fine leather, were printed in either Russian, French, German, or English. Those written in English covered many different interests from aviation, marine salvage, armored war machines to diving birds and Latin American history. There was even a copy of Woodrow Wilson's book *On Being Human*, just like in the aft compartment. Bottles of wine took up the remaining shelf space. Squeezed against the forward bulkhead was a toiletry cabinet. Installed against the aft bulkhead was a rolltop desk with was a glass-covered wooden shadow box mounted above it. One that could be found in any science classroom, and one that contained desiccated winged insects pinned to a white backing.

"I hope I'm not intruding?" he asked.

"No," Countess Tolstoy said as she squeezed around Dooley and sat on the bunk. She looked at Dooley's face, then at the wine. "Please close the curtain while you are up. I know it will not stop our voices, but it seems more civilized."

Dooley placed the cups on the desk and turned to close the curtain. As he did, he saw her reach for one of the cups. Pulling out the chair and turning it around, he sat. "Mind you, that isn't the same wine you nipped off your father's glass," he told the countess.

Sitting straighter, she retorted. "I may be a nineteen-year-old girl, but I'm still Russian. Also, the way my life is going, I'm going to have to get used to drinking the roughest of alcohol."

Dooley nodded in surrender while he picked up the other cup. He watched the woman as they both took long sips. Her eyes slammed shut when she took that first swallow. Waiting for her to speak first, he pulled the cup away from his lips.

She swallowed the wine in her mouth and took a deep breath before speaking. "I think this year needs a proper decanting," she said as she investigated the cup's contents.

"I'll have to trust you on this one," Dooley answered, "since most of the stuff my father ever brought home was bottled in Geppetto's backyard. Never had much of the good stuff."

The countess leaned forward slightly while wrapping both hands around the cup. She lifted her eyes from the wine and place them on Dooley's eyes. "Sergeant Thomas Dooley, I think there are a number of things you did not do before this week, but I've watched you. You are a good soldier, and I know you are a good man. What are you doing here?"

"Just giving you wine," Dooley responded while returning her gaze.

"No," she retorted. "What are you doing here? An American? On a Russian submarine? In the Sea of Japan? Off the coast of Siberian Russia? Trying to rescue my cousin who is a member of the Tsarist's inner circle? Why are you here? You're young and handsome. With teeth such as yours, you should be home with a wife starting a large family. Not here risking your life for a worthless cause or money."

Using his tongue to feel grit on his teeth Dooley searched his wine for an answer. "I asked the same thing myself when I drove my blade into a man's guts tonight." He looked up at her. "Do you really want to know?"

"Yes, I do. Please start from the beginning. And my name is Zeta."

"Well, Zeta," Dooley said after taking another sip of his wine, "I grew up in Brooklyn, New York, and when I wasn't going to school, I helped my father fix wagons that hauled beer barrels, milk cans, and sacks of coal and potatoes. And delivered the same on occasion."

"Is that where your tomahawk axe came from?" she asked.

"I grew up on a good street, but we often made deliveries to areas not so nice. My father and his father always kept the axe under the seat, and I've seen both use it more than once. My older brother worked for my father full time, and it would have been passed to him, however, soldiers were writing home requesting roofing axes and ballpeen hammers. You know, for the trench fighting. Since my brother was married and with kids, he couldn't be drafted, so my father thought it would be put to better use with me. That is once he found out I was in the Army."

"You didn't want to help carry on the family business," Zeta asked, "as a good man should?"

"I did help for a while but got tired of the constant arguments between my brother and dad. If it wasn't about the future of the shop, it was about politics, socialism, unions, and Pinkertons. My thoughts, though, were always about other places and other times, so I ran away from home and lied about my age and joined the Army. I was only seventeen at the time and ended up on a training camp in Michigan. After our training, my regiment shipped out to France in late summer of 1918. President Wilson, at the request of the British and French governments, ordered my regiment, the 339th Infantry, to Russia to guard supplies while the Limeys and Frogs did the real fighting. However, we ended up in combat, against Wilson's wishes. After months of fighting alongside White Russians, my regiment was ordered home, but were shipped out unit by unit in late spring and the units that saw the hardest fighting were shipped out first, including my company. We docked in England for resupply before heading back to my father's repair shop."

"But after serving abroad," Zeta said interrupting him, "the Brooklyn skyline had lost its appeal?"

Dooley smiled. "I mustered out in England, and with money in my pocket. I thought that a slow boat back to the States would be just the cure. Then, it would be time for me start a family and help with the shop. So, I left most of my army-issue with a friend on the ship and bought a beat-up suitcase, one big enough to hold my Thompson, and filled it with used civies and what other weapons I could keep without the Army's knowledge. I made my way from England, halfway around the world, and ended up in Shanghai, which is where Major Utkin found me."

"Brooklyn," Zeta repeated. "Home of the Brooklyn Dodgers."

"You follow baseball?" Dooley asked but then paused for a second. "Your English is pretty good. Have you been to the States? And are you related that famous author, Tolstoy?"

"No, I just share the last name with a famous Russian author whose writings, if found with them in Russia, would have you sent to a labor camp. But, as far as my English, no. My father said the States was no place for a lady as it was full of illiterate street toughs and rowdy adventurers." She paused as she looked at Dooley with a sly grin. "I have the feeling that you are part of what my father warned me about."

Dooley's eyes twinkled. "Keep going."

"We usually went to England to visit relatives, and I attended an international girl's school in Berlin. That was before the war, of course, and when I could have access to American novels. I am fond of mystery and detective stories."

"You're an educated woman?" Dooley asked.

"It depends on what you call an education. Being fluent in other languages, learning about every major artist since Leonardo Di Vinci, how to discuss classic literature, dance like a lady while listening to men brag about themselves with a smile, and, playing tennis, badminton, and . . ." Zeta paused for a second. "And learning how to tickle the ivories?"

"Learning how to play the piano," Dooley answered as he looked at the row of books above her head. "Any valid works of literature up there?"

Zeta turned her eyes to look at the bottom of the shelf. "They're mostly about marine salvage, engineering, and diving birds. Although that philosophical essay by your president was a bit enlightening especially on what it takes to embrace human behavior. But, to my 'education,'" Zeta answered as she removed one hand from her cup and brought it to her collar, "you can have it. As females, we couldn't discuss or learn anything about politics, which is why that essay provides one redeeming quality aboard this submarine."

She dropped her eyes to look at Dooley as her shaking fingers fumbled with the top button of her army blouse.

Dooley watched her trembling fingers push the fat, wooden button through the buttonhole.

"My mother was an 'educated' woman," Zeta continued, "and ended up marrying my father, who dealt with precious stones and metals in St. Petersburg."

"The basis of the rumors for a cache of gems hidden on the estate?" Dooley asked.

"Yes," Zeta answered. "I found this all out after the Bolsheviks toppled the Tsar's throne. My father was tasked with amassing the wealth for his master who saw the clouds of the Revolution building on the horizon years ago. Ideally, when it came, my father's employer would have time to escape Russia with enough wealth to live on. He hid the diamonds my father accrued for him, but my father's employer faced a firing squad before anybody took the time to ask him where the diamonds were hidden."

"How close were you to the duchess? Familywise."

"The reasons why Olga's father allowed my father to work for him was not only because he was a renowned gemologist and jeweler. My father's employer was also attracted to my mother, who ended up becoming his mistress. An arrangement my father tolerated. Some say that I and Olga are, or were, stepsisters."

"So," Dooley asked, "you're next in line?"

"No," Zeta answered. "I am nothing more than the illegitimate offspring of a mistress. No true Tsarist Russian would have me anywhere near the throne."

Zeta paused to sip some more wine.

"Where are your parents now?" Dooley asked.

"They're in Shanghai, which is where Major Utkin found me as well," she answered, looking up at Dooley. "Like many Russians who supported the Tsar and had some money, my father immigrated us to Shanghai with the idea of starting over. During his employment, he was able to . . . how do you say . . . 'skim a little off the top.' He secretly posted his 'earnings' to various financial institutions around Shanghai for safekeeping. Unfortunately, he trusted the wrong men. When we arrived, most of his secret postings had been stolen. He used what little he did recover to open a shop where he still deals with precious stones and jewelry. It is a small shop, and to survive fiscally, he learned to deal with less than a reputable clientele who also insulted my mother's sense of status. Instead, she used her 'education' to remind herself that she is a woman who men still want. However, most of those men have worthless family names and little wealth in hand. That's why she is normally seen in the company of other Europeans.

"My father tolerated my mother being his employer's mistress back in Russia, but he could not accept her living in the past by being a whore. While they are still together, it is not a home anymore. All he does is shuffle about his store and complain about the men who stole from him. We live above the store, and I helped with the business when I wasn't earning crumbs giving music lesson to snotty kids. My mother, on the other hand, spends his paltry income living a life that no longer exists."

Listening, Dooley could not help but think of Mary Pickford dramas.

"Like my home, Shanghai is not a hospitable city," Zeta continued. "It is a home for ex-soldiers looking for employment that suits their education. Is that why you ended up there?"

Dooley sipped his wine before answering. "Partly. I did end up running into some White Russians I knew in Archangel, but I guess it was the idea of visiting an Oriental city of mystery that intrigued me. Maybe I read too much."

Zeta listened as she took another sip of wine. While doing so, she reached to undo a second button. Her hand still shook. "My mother was no saint, but she did want me to maintain my 'honesty' at least until a man with prospects presented himself. However, I now feel any effort to maintain my 'honesty' is a useless endeavor."

Dooley now saw that her cheeks were flushed. He also saw fear and uncertainty in her eyes, along with anticipation. Like her, he too was a young adult, although he'd had a number of sexual encounters including the months he spent in Russia. When his regiment was in garrison outside Arkhangelsk, or Archangel, Russians, including women, would hang around off-post offering shoe repair, laundry, and haircutting services. Other women offered sex for money and other commodities that were in great demand. While the regimental canteen did sell basic items, the commander ordered the rationing of those same items. Therefore, mail call was important for care packages sent from home filling in their needs. But along with them came books and notes sent by religious and charity organizations, admonishing the soldiers to avoid immoral women and strong drink, and to focus on living virtuously while keeping up with their reading.

Fortunately, the regimental surgeon, the one who died in the mortar attack, was literally on the front lines acting as a referee between the prostitutes and the soldiers, as he realized it would be impossible for military regulations to keep young men with money or chocolate from women who wanted them. As it turned out, he did his job well in terms of reducing the number of soldiers showing up for sick call with venereal disease. Although there was no direct cure for syphilis, the surgeon had been practiced in controlling its spread and mitigating its effects.

Dooley never took to the Russian prostitutes, but there was one woman a bit older than Dooley who ran a bookstore, albeit with mostly empty shelves. He stopped by her shop one day hoping to trade books and struck up a conversation. It turns out they had similar reading interests including early romance literature and later mystery stories, so that one conversation led to an amorous relationship. She never asked for payment, but she did like his cigarettes. The Army believed smoking helped with alertness and night vision, but Dooley had no problems with either and saved his rations for her. The woman also appreciated the small cans of Folgers Dooley received in his care packages.

Now, sitting in a stateroom, aboard a Russian submarine with a vulnerable young woman, Dooley saw her trembling hand and intent. "There is no need to reach for that third button, Zeta."

She flushed even more while taking her hand from that button. "I guess I am not as practiced as other women you've known?"

"Zeta," Dooley said slowly, "there will be a proper time. No need to hurry it."

Zeta's eyes twinkled before she took a deep sip of wine. Pulling the cup away from her lips, she spoke. "You said you traveled on your own from England to Shanghai. I did not know army sergeants were paid that well."

Dooley took another sip of wine before answering. "Despite regimental orders, a lot of guys blew their pay on whores outside of camp or on hooch. Also, guys gambled behind the latrines or sent their money home. I never saw fit, or had a need, to do any of those. Also, we could only buy so much at the regimental canteen, and because of the War Prohibition Act, the canteen couldn't sell alcohol. Our regimental commander did manage to get a hold of a beer shipment or a few cases of wine now and then, which he ordered the supply officer to ration out from the canteen for pennies. Therefore, saving up money was not an issue. Anyway, when I arrived in Shanghai, I went through my stash faster than I thought I would."

Zeta paused to think before speaking. "So, you were prudent with your money when forced to and footloose when the occasion arose."

"That's about it," Dooley answered. "In order to have enough money to pay for passage on anything heading east, I ended up fighting for a Chinese warlord, but after a month of that mess, I went back to Shanghai. Utkin found me sitting in a cheap hotel bar with a warm Tsingtao beer in one hand and a ragged detective novel in the other, a beat-up suitcase with second-hand clothes sitting in a shitty hotel room above my head, and fifty-two dollars and twenty-eight cents in my pocket. He said I could earn enough for an eastbound passage aboard any liner I wanted."

Zeta listened to Dooley's words. "So, you are not fighting for any principle? Ideology?"

"I did at first," Dooley said as he sat back into the chair a little more. "I ran away from home to join the Army and fight the evil Hun threatening civilized Europe. You know that hooey. But we ended up in Russia and, from what we were told, an even greater mission."

"What do you mean?" Zeta asked.

"A lot of the guys asked why we were fighting in Russia, with White Russians against Red Russians, especially since the Armistice was signed last November, and the war in France about to be officially ended any week now," Dooley said. "So, why risk our lives? In Russia. For no reason. At one point, doughboys from I Company mutinied against their officers. It was called the 'Bolshevik Syndrome.' The mutiny was quelled after several soldiers were executed. Afterward, HQ made it a habit of sending an officer by the name of Captain Rodham to give each company weekly briefings when we were in garrison. I don't know why I remember his name, but maybe he had that kind of face. Anyway, Rodham said if we didn't stop them in Russia, we'd be fighting them in Manhattan. And we were getting letters from home, which backed up what Rodham was saying. Once I turned eighteen, I sent a letter home and told my parents where I was and what I was doing. At first, they were darned mad, but after events like Anarchist April, they said I was doing the right thing. That's when Pop sent me the shingle axe."

"Anarchist April?"

"Yeah, Anarchist April," Dooley answered. "There's been quite a few immigrants into the US since the 1890s, totaling over fourteen million to be exact and growing. And we're not talking about the Irish, Scandinavians, or Germans. We're talking about Serbs, Armenians, Turks, Bulgars, Greeks, Slavs, Jews, and Asians. People Americans weren't used to seeing, languages Americans weren't used to hearing, and names Americans weren't used to pronouncing. Anyway, couple that flood of immigrants with German spies in Latin America, the Bolshevik Revolution, and the infiltration in the States of leftists. President Wilson signed the Espionage Act into law two years ago and the Sedition Act last year, which was not well accepted by a great deal of people, including loyal Americans."

"What were, or are, your feelings?" Zeta asked as she looked at the wine in her tin cup.

"Didn't really have any. Still don't. I grew up in a mixed neighborhood in Brooklyn, and never had truck with any of the colored kids there. Even after joining the army, bunking with Slavs and Jews, and fighting in Russia, I still don't. All I have to go on is Pop's letters."

"What does your father say now?"

"According to him, since 1917, many of these immigrants became disrupters with the idea of creating anarchy in our society and political system. One method by a small group of them was to send out mail bombs to a select group of targets, which they did in April. A good number were sent through a post office in Georgia and literally blew up in the faces of their recipients. It would have been worse, but a postal clerk in Georgia realized what was going on and was able to stop most of them from being sent out. That clerk was alert enough to stop one tragedy, but the anarchists are not stopping there. The anarchists, the disrupters, the radical leftists, the socialists, the Bolsheviks, whatever you call them, are out to invade America. The Red Scare is real, which was reason enough for us to fight the Reds in Russia, not in Brooklyn."

"I will have to take your word for it as I was never allowed to discuss politics," Zeta added as she turned her eyes up. "I'll go over Wilson's essay again, but can I ask you something?"

"Go ahead."

"What does Comintern mean?"

Before Dooley could answer, the sudden scrape of the curtain rings across the brass rod stopped him. Both he and Zeta looked up to see Major Utkin. Now changed into a pair of pressed slacks, polished leather cap-toed shoes, and a long-sleeve cotton shirt, he held out a small glass of red wine in his hand. "I am glad you two young people finally had an opportunity to get to know each other, but it is now time for sleep. I also appreciate you bringing the young lady some wine, which should help her sleep. However, I believe this is a bit more suiting."

Dooley took the glass from the major and handed it to the young woman. She put her cup to her lips and drained it before exchanging containers with Dooley. Their fingers touched.

Utkin continued. "I am also sorry to have to bring this topic up, but we must prepare the duchess for our arrival in Shanghai. Countess, if you wish to see her one more time, please finish your wine and do so before you go to sleep."

Zeta looked at the wine in the glass and nodded.

Dooley also nodded as he brought his tin cup to his lips. Finishing the wine, he stood and turned to squeeze past Utkin. With their chins almost touching he looked at the man. Along with a change of clothing, the Russian major had also washed his face and combed his dark hair. Like all his men, he was a non-smoker, handsome, and a well-built man who wore confidence like a custom-made silk shirt. Even the scar across his cheek added to his legitimacy. But, unlike his men, he was older. In his late thirties, he looked like a man who could run a multi-million-dollar corporation from the saddle of a thoroughbred or from the end of a long table.

"Major Utkin," Dooley said, "once we arrive in Shanghai, I will take the other half of my five hundred bucks and move on, but I'd be grateful if you looked after Zeta."

Both men looked down at her. She looked up with a Mary Pickford face. Utkin smiled. "No worries on that account, Sergeant Dooley. Countess Tolstoy will be taken care of."

Dooley nodded as all three of them lurched slightly forward as the bow of the submarine's diesels pushed them through another wave. Nodding goodbye to Zeta, he turned to leave them alone. He walked and stooped through the confines of the submarine but paused long enough to stop next to the table where the duchess, with her stocking feet sticking out from under the blanket, still lay. As Dooley said a silent prayer, he thought about her miraculous survival from the machine pistol's blast to her back, only to die a few moments later by falling off the staircase.

Before walking forward, he looked at the table where Gorki operated on his fellow submarine raider. The table was empty and spotlessly clean.

Dooley continued forward, bending his body to enter the crew's quarters and torpedo room. It was dark as the sailors and submarine raiders finished their wine, cleaned up as best they could, and crawled onto their stretcher-like canvas bunks, covering themselves with scratchy wool blankets. One man snored, and another man farted. Dooley also saw that Mashka was now lying in his own bunk flat on his back, sound asleep and covered with his blanket. Using the light that came through the bulkhead hatch from the crew's mess, Dooley did the same to prepare himself for sleep. Stowing his uniform and weapons in his narrow stand-up locker, he pushed aside the canvas-wrapped gun cleaning kit and boxes of rounds for his machine gun and grabbed his beat-up Dopp kit along with his last clean undershirt and placed them on the compartment's center table. He unbuckled the leather strap of his trench watch while noting the time. It was well past time for him to get some sleep. He ran his tongue across his gritty teeth while placing his watch under the pillow, exchanging it with his comb. The trip from Shanghai to Siberian Russia and back was to last little more than one full week, so he did not bring much in toiletries. With items in hand, he returned through the hatchway to the forward toilet.

Squeezing himself into the water closet, Dooley started to clean himself by squeezing out the last of his toothpaste on his toothbrush. As he started to brush his teeth, he recalled the conversation with Zeta and her questions, including one about what he was doing on this submarine.

Minutes later, as he rinsed soap from his face, he thought about the five hundred and fifty-two dollars he would have in his pocket. Running his wet fingers through his hair, he reached for his almost empty jar of hair oil. Rubbing the few droplets into his black hair, he reminded himself of one thing: *To be so young with some money in my pocket, the options of world travel will be limitless.*

CHAPTER 8

"**A**RE THEY ASLEEP?"

Gorki looked at the two officers sitting in folding chairs squeezed into the officer's stateroom. He held a pair of forceps in one hand and what appeared to be a kielbasa partially wrapped in a piece of gauze in the other hand. "Yes, they are, Major. Although Dooley earned his slumber, the sedatives I put in the wine helped. The wine that he gave the countess along with the wine you gave her most assuredly also put her to sleep."

"Now we can get to business without being overheard," Captain Vostok said as he sipped his wine while looking at the tube-like item in Gorki's hand. He saw the knot at one end. "Do I dare ask where you found it?"

The handsome, black-haired officer looked at the items in his hands before answering. "Let me just say I was curious and decided to look up her chemise." He leaned over to place the items on the blanket-covered mattress, next to the shoe that the duchess wore. The shoe, with its heel removed, lay next to a small heap of cut diamonds. "How did you know?"

Utkin sipped his wine again before answering. "As I imagined this operation, I found it my responsibility to not only become an expert gemologist, but also to understand every facet of the industry, including smuggling. I found my research quite rewarding as it consisted of well-documented crimes in novels, historical narratives, and legal proceedings. If one is given time, understanding human behavior is easily predictable. Therefore, determining how the duchess was going to finance herself after rescue was also predictable."

Gorki nodded with a smile. "No wonder you differentiate between poker and gambling. Anyway, I hope the diamonds inside that Ramses are of matching quality. And I hope you do not mind where they came from."

"As uncomfortable as it must have been for the duchess to have that inserted in her anus, I do not mind the addition to our coffer as the quality of the diamonds from the heel of her one shoe alone is enough to pay for a new submarine." Utkin sighed while peering into his wine. "It is a shame about the missing shoe, though."

"I am sorry," Gorki apologized as he reached for a wine glass next to the decanter sitting on the stateroom's desktop. Grabbing a glass, he continued. "I can only assume that the shoe must have popped off when she landed, and we were quite busy at the time."

Utkin smiled as he twisted the stem of his wine glass. "No matter. As the special action operators that we are, we will always find means to collect and repurpose assets along the way."

"Like charging forward into the teeth of fire while picking up the weapons from those who had fallen before us?" Vostok said as he peered into his glass of wine.

Utkin countered with a wry smile. "Or from those who fell under the weight of our onslaught. Either way, the fact that we did not recover that shoe is not as irritating as what will happen to it. Knocked about by time until the heel separates and spreading the diamonds like grains of sand. Or to be picked up by an oaf walking the beach and discarded as trash."

"Yes," Vostok continued, "but look at what other items we have at our disposal."

The men looked at the toilet seat that the duchess wore around her neck. It crushed the pillow under it. Some of the white paint had been scraped away.

"No wonder the Revolution occurred," Gorki commented. "While millions starved to death, the Tsar had the luxury of shitting while perched on a solid gold seat."

"I agree," Utkin joined in. "While it once supported somebody's arse, it will now support the next step of Operation Crossfire."

The men paused to sip their wine. While appreciating their bounty, Gorki reached into his pocket, pulling out something pinched between his thumb and index finger. He held it up to the stateroom's overhead light for all to see.

"I found out why she survived that pistol fire into her back," Gorki said as he rotated his hand. "Sewn into her dress are layers of diamonds. I left a few strewn about the beach."

Gorki dropped the fingernail-sized diamond in Utkin's open palm.

"I must say that the workmanship is beyond reproach," Utkin said as he hefted it in his palm. "They will be able to provide enough hard currency to fund the placement of our teams into the American public including you, Lieutenant Gorki. A residency at a prestigious New York City hospital awaits you. And you, Captain Vostok, you should be quite settled in your new future."

Vostok answered with a wry smile of his own. "Running a multi-million-dollar alcohol smuggling operation will become quite an enjoyable occupation since I will be operating from the comforts of my hacienda perched on the bluffs of the Baja Peninsula outside of Ensenada, and with vineyards and orchards stretching behind it as far as the eye can see."

"And while being a recently displaced Bavarian by the name of Wilhelm Hanover. An ex-patriot who is a landed gentleman with stature within the Mexican government," Utkin added.

"Thank God for the bombardment of Vera Cruz by the US Navy," Gorki said, chiming into the conversation. "And followed with Pershing's Punitive Expedition into Mexico in 1916 and 1917. The Mexicans have only ill feelings toward the American government, including Wilson and his moral diplomacy. Sentiments that will stand us in good stead."

"Do not forget about the feelings of the Cubans and Puerto Ricans and thank God for the Americans passing the Prohibition Amendment," Captain Vostok said with a grin. "With the funds that I will raise while smuggling Mexican liquors into ports along the California coast, we will have enough to create clean money. With crime comes opportunity."

Gorki raised his wine glass in salute and took a large swallow, almost emptying the glass. As he pulled the glass from his lips, the submarine surged as the bow drove itself through another wave. Gorki reached up to grab a pipe. "That said, what about the hatboxes?"

Utkin replied, "So much unrest has been fomenting for decades, and if one reads the tea leaves exactly, or makes sure the tea leaves fall into the right alignment at the bottom of the cup, the opportunities will be limitless. Prohibition, and the subsequent lawlessness; the Jazz Age and Negroes being appreciated by white people for their music, which will result in the open rise of the KKK and the competing rise of the NAACP; Wilson's Espionage Act and Sedition Act and his violations of constitutional rights; shifting diets to processed food; women getting the right to vote and smoke in public; and the battle between workers' unions and capitalism. Imagine the depthless chasms that await our exploitation."

"Just like crime, with confusion comes opportunity," Vostok said while sipping his wine.

"Yes," Utkin continued. "The Twenties are projected to become a decade that will allow our movement prospects we cannot afford to waste. Through this wealth, along with the procurement of more, our commandos will be sitting pretty when America's economy collapses leaving millionaires destitute as orphaned street urchins. I, myself though, would prefer to enjoy golf and female companionship while watching our movement grow during that time of sorrow. And relishing the best of wines while doing so."

The two men sipped their wine and reflected on Utkin's prophesizing.

"The task of this vessel," Utkin continued, "or any single member of our special action commandos, is to place an implied threat where there is none. Even something as simple as a well-placed snippet of an overly loud conversation in a crowded bar. We have before us the opportunity to create such a witches' brew. One where the recipe calls for the most hallucinogenic of toadstools. What greater pleasure to enjoy, through guile, misdeed, and misinformation, watching the resulting mayhem? To have the means to watch the American public, and politicians, behave as ship captains, deranged from distrust, anger and madness, to dash their vessels repeatedly against nonexistent rocks. The means to create such a matrix not only rests with what is on this bunk, but other means as well." A smile overtook Utkin's face as he paused to look at Gorki. "Did you inspect the nicely tied-up bun of her hair?"

Gorki smiled as he reached into his pocket again. Pulling out his hand, he dropped a brilliant dark blue gemstone in Utkin's palm.

The major held it up with a pleased smile. "Gentlemen, behold the Romanov Sapphire. Six hundred carats of royal greed."

The shape and size of an egg, they appreciated the world's largest cut sapphire. Even under the yellowish light just over their heads, the beauty of the stone was not missed.

"Too bad it will not see the light of day. Or at least for the next four decades," Utkin appraised, "but at least it will never grace the neckline of a royal."

The other men nodded silently before sipping their wine.

After a long minute, Vostok spoke up, "Shall I dispose of the duchess now?"

"Yes," Utkin answered, "but allow Gorki to inspect the body one more time and bring me the dress. Captain Vostok, have your radioman send a message to our asset in Shanghai. Tell him to go ahead with the cell meeting. Also, radio Buyan to let them know of our arrival."

Both Vostok and Gorki straightened their shoulders and sipped the last of their wine. As Gorki leaned forward to place his glass on the small desk, his eyebrows furrowed slightly.

Utkin finished his wine as well and noticed Gorki's expression, "Question?"

Gorki responded as he pursed his lips. "What of our passengers? I know you explained your reasoning for recruiting the American, and the presence of Countess Tolstoy was necessary for our mission, but what future use would both still be to us? Or would they be a detriment?"

Before Utkin answered, he reached for the decanter. "Let me refill your glasses."

The men held out their glasses.

"Gentlemen," Utkin continued as he tilted the bottle, "we have entered a new century, and along with it, the requirement to think in new ways when it comes to warfare and subjugation. The days of dreadnoughts slugging it out with each other at sea while artillery barrages bang away at regiments hiding in trenches, followed with thousands of men storming into rows of barbed wire only to be mowed down by Maxims. All ordered by generals and admirals ensconced in villas and lavish staterooms, are over. Our mission exemplifies such a new way of warfare. Combat where squads, even individual men, facilitated with intelligence, thought, intellect, purpose, focus, and pluck can navigate barbed wire as if it were an invisible gate in a picket fence. An innocuous statement overheard in a café over morning coffee can affect the outcome so an entire campaign, trump the designs of a general staff, or cause the collapse of a sovereign government. This submarine is an example of such action. With the advent of undersea warfare, the historical strategies that have directed maritime campaigns for centuries changed overnight as Captain Vostok can attest."

Utkin paused to sip his wine before continuing.

"The ability to be force multipliers is our focus as special action operatives. With audacity and the skill to use the ignorance of others, we shall be successful. I argue that both the countess and Sergeant Dooley are such assets that must be utilized as force multipliers. Our young lady is a simple girl, cloistered under sheltered circumstances her entire life, who will, I believe, prove to be quite a flexible foil at our disposal when needed. Unthinking in its own form, but a valuable weapon when manipulated by the right hands. The American, on the other hand, is quite conscious and aware, but still an asset when deployed properly. He's a romantic who ran away from home to chase the adventure he read about in his childhood. He still holds that wanderlust. I can tell. I can also tell he is a man of character, and men of character can be unbelievable assets, especially if romantics like him do not know that they are assets. Just moments ago, we listened to them, and at no time did Dooley tell the young, vulnerable countess of his exploits to bed her."

"Is that why you selected him from the foreigners clogging the bars of

Shanghai?" Gorki asked as he looked at his glass. "Because of his bravery in battle?"

Utkin answered. "Although a seaport home to millions, Shanghai is still a community where everybody knows everybody else's business, especially when it comes to foreigners, mercenaries, and interlopers lounging about its bars, lobbies, and brothels. Dooley arrived in Russia in the fall of 1918, a private soldier but earned his corporal stripes, along with a wound badge during his first engagement. A fight where he charged a fortified machine-gun nest and took it out with two hand grenades and his Thompson. His second engagement, where he used that hunting knife and shingle axe against dismounted Cossacks while saving the lives of his fellow soldiers, earned him his sergeant stripes, a second wound badge, and the Silver Star. Even after his arrival in China this spring, at the Battle of Wuhan, his bravery was noted by the White Russians fighting there. I understand your concern, Gorki," Utkin continued, "but let us see how we can use the American. He can be processed at any time."

Gorki and Vostok nodded to Major Utkin's sage advice. Vostok raised his glass in salute. "Who dares wins."

CHAPTER 9

THE BOW OF the USS Decatur plowed through a wave, then dropped into the trough on the other side. The drop jarred the men sitting around a wooden table bolted to the steel deck of Lieutenant Hillary's stateroom. Two open portholes, each guarded by a pair of blue curtains which fluffed with the incoming morning breeze, bathed them, and the sparsely furnished cabin, with early morning sunlight.

The cabin was furnished mostly with what the government deemed necessary to keep the captain of a torpedo boat destroyer in relative comfort. While a door pierced the forward bulkhead, a desk with the corrugated top rolled up was fixed against the aft bulkhead. Above the desk was a shelf with a row of books mostly filled with technical manuals. Above that row of books was a framed chart of Far East Asia. A chronometer accompanied the chart on one side while a barometer evened out the setting on the other side. Working to offset the room's austerity, several framed photos of families, lady friends, and previous and current shipmates were mounted to available bulkhead space.

The three officers, Hillary, Kermit, and their guest, who now wore khaki uniforms like the other officers, sat at the table. However, the uniform worn by the ship's guest was so heavily starched it crinkled when he moved. Chief Boatswain's Mate Fowler, wearing clean, but faded, dungarees sat with the officers, and all waited for the fifth person in the room to complete his duties. Wearing a white serving jacket, the slightly built Filipino poured sweet tea from a sweating steel pitcher into glasses. When he filled the last glass, he placed it on the table. "Will there be anything else, sir?"

Lieutenant Hillary reached for his tea. "No, Fabio, that will do. But I hope you don't mind me asking I hear that you and Demby finally found a location for your restaurant."

"Yes, sir. Just outside the Intramuros. We signed the lease last week and will start on our building when we get back from this patrol."

As Lieutenant Hillary brought the glass to his lips, he replied, "All I can say is that I can't wait to be your first patron. Now, go ahead and help Demby with lunch."

"Yes, sir," the Filipino replied as he nodded his head and turned for the door.

The men reached for their glasses as they watched the door close behind the steward.

"Isn't refrigeration a wonderful thing?" commented the ship's captain as he pulled the glass from his lips. "Our unit was just installed, and what a godsend."

The new officer pulled the glass from his lips and looked at its contents while shrugging his shoulders. "The tea is good."

Both Hillary and Kermit looked at each other.

Chief Fowler, who noticed the man's wristwatch, also looked at the academy ring on the officer's finger. Fowler also remembered the rings of his two officers and noticed that all three graduated two to three years apart from each other. "It's fine, Skipper. I'm sure the officer here doesn't mind roughin' it."

The new officer turned his youthful, clean-shaven face toward the chief petty officer and narrowed his eyes. Chief Fowler countered with a blank stare.

Seeing the exchange, Hillary jumped in. "This ship's been in the Far East since its commissioning two decades ago, so we never waste a chance to enjoy the little things. Anyway, I hope you don't mind us being busy, but getting a beat-up torpedo boat destroyer underway takes a bit of care. I also hope you don't mind bunking with the engineer."

The officer turned his attention from the chief to the ship's captain. "The stateroom is fine, and I have yet to meet the engineer, but it's nice to be underway again."

Fowler gave the young officer and the item in front of him on the table a leer.

"Let me introduce myself and my men," Lieutenant Hillary said, tilting his head to his right. "Lieutenant JG Caldwell Kermit, my executive officer and navigator."

The two officers nodded their heads at each other as Kermit spoke. "I go by Kermit."

"To my left," Hillary continued, "is Boatswain's Mate Chief Petty Officer Fowler. And I'm Lieutenant Rance Hillary. Now if you don't mind, could you fill us in on the secret? We're supposed to be two days into our two-month patrol but were told to wait for a passenger. Even my flotilla commander doesn't know what's going on. All we know is that the orders you handed me gave me your name and rank as Lieutenant Junior Grade Burton D. Harrison, a statement that you are on special assignment for the admiral of the Asiatic Fleet and the governor-general of the Philippines, that I'm under your direction, and you will have access to my radiotelegraph as you see fit."

The officer looked at Hillary before glancing at the fine-grained, leather portfolio in front of him. "I apologize for the delay as I had to finish gathering information, but the start of your patrol coincided nicely with a piece of information that fell into our laps."

"Well, Lieutenant Junior Grade Burton D. Harrison," said Chief Fowler as he noticed the initials embossed into the leather of the portfolio. "What might that information mean to us?"

The officer ignored the chief. "I'm with staff intelligence, and my commanding officer received a communique from our British counterpart in Hong Kong who asked a favor of us."

Everybody paused to look at the finely made office trapping in front of Harrison.

"Since your responsibility, Lieutenant Hillary, is to provide an American maritime presence in this region, I'm sure you've heard of the Lassiter Brothers and their gang."

Hillary scoffed. "Digby and Otter Lassiter, and the Black Badgers, have been the scourge of the China Seas since the turn of the century, and on the front of more newspapers than I can count. They're all white, all British, and all mean. Some say the only reason why none of them has entertained an audience by doing the hempin' jig on Gallows Row is that even the Devil won't take them. But despite their notoriety, we've never had the opportunity to run into them in international waters while they were in the act. And they usually have any number of disguised vessels and hideouts to operate from. They are also well regarded by local communities from Saigon to Shanghai, which is why, even though the Crown has had a one-hundred-pound reward for each of the Lassiter Brothers, and ten pounds for each of the Black Badgers, nobody ever ratted on where their hideouts are and when they'll be at those locations. In short, they've been elusive, and yes, they're blood-thirsty pirates, but the British government is temperamental when it comes to foreign nationals molesting British citizens even if they're murderous scum."

"That was until now," Harrison offered as he took a breath. "A prominent British citizen and his wife were sailing back from Indochina to Hong Kong when their yacht was boarded by the pirates. The crew was dispatched, and the couple was tortured. It seems, according to the Bamboo Telegraph, there was a rumor of a cache of Siamese gems onboard, and the couple ended up being murdered in the process. However, according to what is known, all that was loaded aboard the vessel was a cargo of expensive French wines. And before you ask, the British know all about the event because a cabin boy, who managed to crawl into the forward bosun locker and stay hidden during the boarding, was able to jump ship when the pirates sailed by an island near Macau in the middle of the night."

Chief Fowler asked, "What about the reward?"

"What about the reward?" Hillary replied.

"I mean, how much did the reward get increased by?" Chief Fowler asked. "The murder of a well-placed British man and wife must have increased the reward."

"It did," Harrison said as he lifted his glass of tea. "However, you shouldn't waste time dreaming about filling your pockets with reward money. As a uniformed member of the United States Navy, you are fulfilling an assignment for the government of the United States, therefore, nullifying any legal claim to any reward. Also, even if you could collect such a reward, then it would have to be divided between the ship's officers and crew. That means you would end up with only enough money to pay off your tab at the Bull and Bear. In other words, you'd be better off clipping your shipmates in a mess deck's poker hustle."

"Hey, Harrison!" Chief Fowler said while sitting straighter. "I don't cheat at cards!"

"Well, being good pirates," Hillary said, "fencing a cargo of wine shouldn't prove too difficult. That said, what of the yacht? Any pirate worth his salt knows how to repurpose assets, and a yacht owned by a millionaire could be a nice addition to their fleet, especially since they simply can't just sail it into any port and hang a 'For Sale' sign from the main mast. In other words, they're stuck with it and that is something of more concern to me than a cargo of French wine."

Harrison returned his attention to Hillary. "The raid occurred about a month ago, and the Admiralty publicly charged the Lassiter Brothers and the gang members who were with them with murder, which means, when captured and convicted, they will be executed. Their death certificates have already been filled out and signed. All that is missing is the date that the trap doors drop out from under their feet. So, knowing that the hangman's noose will be waiting for them at the British naval station in Hong Kong, HMS Tamar, they took the yacht and the vessel they used to track down the yacht in the first place, a vessel called the Grim Reaper . . ."

"The Grim Reaper?" Kermit expressed with interest and appreciation.

"You've heard of it?" Harrison asked.

Kermit leaned back in his chair as he replied. "Forty-foot, sloop-rigged, custom-built racing yacht in the 1890s, which has graced the covers of numerous magazines and journals. Now, it has a hull painted black and is out-fitted with a 400-horsepower, twelve-cylinder Liberty aircraft engine. It has smuggled more opium and eluded more Royal Navy ships than you can shake a stick at. Shallow draft which allows it to be operated in inland waters and hidden in mangrove swamps, but stout enough to take the roughest of seas. Where are they now?"

"They fled with both vessels to the Babuyan Islands. A group of islands off the northern end of Luzon. A group of islands that—"

"Are in American territory," interjected Hillary, "and where the British would be violating international law if they landed forces to capture him or fired ship's guns against their hideout. I can also assume that the reason why everything about this operation was communicated strictly through select officers was because of the native Bamboo Telegraph. All it would have taken was for one slip of the tongue and our quarry would be hightailing it to God knows where. And, yes, we've been to those islands before."

"Good," Harrison said as he ran his thumb along the edge of the portfolio while sitting straighter in his chair. "I realize that you are the ship's captain and how you command this ship is up to you. Also, I know the men aboard this ship are your responsibility and that you are senior to me, but since I put everything together, my commanding officer designated me the officer in charge of this operation from start to finish, which includes the delivery of our captives to Hong Kong, dead or alive. Also, the governor-general of the Philippines has a great deal of interest in this international partnership. All of which means I will need access to your radio on occasion."

"I can have my senior radio operator at your disposal," Hillary added.

"I know how to operate your set," Harrison stated. "And I will be using a non-standard code, so no need for him. In the end, I hope you realize the need for your cooperation."

The men facing Harrison knew what he meant, and they knew that the officer and the governor-general of the Philippines shared the same name.

Hillary leaned back in his chair. He paused to look at the tea in his glass. "Like I just said, we've operated in those islands before, and that knowledge, along with the pirates' reputation, will dictate how this operation will be carried out. I'm talking about the simultaneous use of the three-inch deck gun, our six-pounders, and an armed landing party to prevent escape into the interior of the island. Correct?"

"You are," Harrison replied as he checked his wristwatch. "Everything is in my portfolio including the latest map of the island, which was updated in 1905. The island's name is Bagay Alto. Along with all the information and naval intelligence we could lay our hands on, including specific members of their party. I was hoping we could go over the plan and map together. After which, Chief Fowler can muster my landing party for their briefing. I believe the Babuyan Islands are twelve hours away at this point, and we could have both forces in place by dawn. It stands to reason that, with the hangman's noose waiting for them, there should be plenty of gunplay."

Kermit looked at his commanding officer, and Hillary returned Kermit's look with a nod before answering Harrison. "Excuse me, Mr. Harrison, but you seem to presume quite a bit."

Taken slightly aback, Harrison replied, "I'm just being practical."

"Yes," Lieutenant Hillary responded, "presumptive and practical because you've taken time to do some research."

"How so?" Harrison asked again with the slightest strain of uncertainty in his voice.

The ship's men turned their attention to the staff officer.

"First, we know you and the governor-general share the same name," Hillary continued as he slowly sipped his sweet tea. "Second, you've looked up regulations and know that anytime the ship is in a combat operation, the captain must be on the bridge and the main deck gun must be under the direct control of a commissioned officer or most senior noncommissioned officer with documented qualifications relating to their ability to command such a weapon. However, our chief gunner's mate just retired after thirty years and is running a bar down in Zamboanga. There was no replacement ordered since this ship, with its keel having been laid in 1899, is sentenced to a Philadelphia scrap yard."

"This patrol will be the ship's last patrol, and the addition of that refrigeration unit was only a personal favor from an engineering officer at the Cavite shipyard. After our return to Manila, my crew will be mustered out in the Philippines at their requests, reassigned to other ships, or left aboard to steam it back to the States. This ship will be stripped of the five six-pounders and two eighteen-inch torpedo tubes, which have only been left onboard as a display of force during this patrol. Now, the only ammunition onboard, other than one hundred rounds for the six-pounders, are shells for the deck gun and bullets for two Lewis guns meant for the bridge. I also have two BARs, a dozen bolt-action rifles and sidearms, and a score of fifty-year-old cutlasses and pikes meant to repel boarders."

Hillary paused long enough to sip his tea again.

"However," Hillary continued, "what's most curious is that you never asked about the chief gunner's mate or our gunnery officer. Since this vessel is an armed vessel of the United States Navy, there is a billet for each. That means you already knew about the gunner's retirement, and that my gunnery officer was stricken with something and removed from this ship late last week. Even now, the doctors are still trying to figure out what's wrong with him."

As Hillary spoke, he briefly settled his eyes on one of the framed photos mounted to the bulkhead.

"Without a gunnery officer or chief gunner's mate, the duty of overseeing the deck gun in action would fall to my executive officer who has the documented qualifications, or he wouldn't be my executive officer. However, that duty could also fall on the shoulders of Chief Fowler as he is qualified to captain that deck gun. But you assumed that I would assign the most senior, and experienced, enlisted man as your second in command, which leads to my third assertion. That being you want Chief Fowler to be part of the landing party. In fact, you need him as part of that landing party. With him along nothing could go wrong, and with the potential of gunplay, it would be the perfect landing operation. Attacking a pirate redoubt, bullets whizzing by your head, and cementing an international appreciation, all which occurred while you were the officer in charge."

"I am sorry, Rance," Harrison said dismissively. "But I just assumed you would assign a senior petty officer with some experience."

"Fine," Hillary said while turning his head slightly. "So, you have no knowledge of the chief's experience?"

"None."

"Well, to set your mind at ease," Hillary continued, even though he knew Harrison was lying, "Chief Fowler's service started with being part of a landing party that took out a gun position in Subic Bay, a full day before the first shots were fired in the Spanish-American War back in 1898, also known as Admiral Dewey's Battle of Manila Bay. After that war, Chief Fowler fought in the Boxer Rebellion in 1900. He was one of two thousand Americans who marched from the coast and fought through two Boxer armies to reach Peking. After rescuing Americans and others trapped in the city, he spent the next seven months supporting the western legations and fighting the Boxers until they were defeated. After returning to the Philippines, he fought in the Insurrection, the Moros in Mindanao, and the Huks throughout the islands. Since then, he's rescued more shipwrecked persons and has broken more barstools over the heads of Royal marines than you can count."

Although Lieutenant Hillary seemed to have taken a bit of wind out of Harrison's sails, the staff officer still managed to keep a degree of assertiveness. "Rance, it seems you are perceptive, but I just want to remind you that I was placed in charge of this operation by the admiral in charge of the Asiatic Fleet and the governor-general of the Philippines who, was himself appointed by the President of the United States."

Hillary and Kermit seemed surprised by Harrison's assertiveness.

After a tense moment of silence, Lieutenant Hillary placed his glass on the table and reached for the still-sweating pitcher. As he did, his eyes sought out those persons who looked back at him from framed photos of his family, lady friends, and fellow shipmates. After grabbing the handle, he leaned forward to fill everybody's glasses. He spoke slowly as he did.

"Yes, Lieutenant Junior Grade Burton D. Harrison, I am quite perceptive, and that is the reason why I, a 1913 graduate of the Academy, am a lieutenant almost thirty years old and in command of a beat-up torpedo boat destroyer. Since a grounding that nearly broke its back in 1902, it has survived ten typhoons and twenty years on the China Station. Now, while the boilers are literally eating their own guts, my classmates from the Academy are either corporate executives or poised to be captains of modern warships."

He turned to fill his own glass and looked at the steel pitcher. "This pitcher may not be a crystal ball, but I can still use it to read the future."

He placed the pitcher in the center of the table and looked into Harrison's eyes. "We are going to finish our tea before you, I, and Kermit will adjourn to the wardroom to enjoy Wardroom Steward Demby Brown's beef stew and biscuits and go over the plan. At two p.m., Kermit will muster the gun crews for live-fire drills. It will be a good opportunity to exercise both the deck gun and men preparation for what will be a ferocious battle. I mean that, during the assault on a formidable pirate hideout, we will be confronted by with a sizable, and determined, force requiring us to expend an extraordinary amount of ammunition to determine the outcome of an uneven battle."

As Hillary outlined the upcoming battle, Harrison developed a thin smile.

"While Kermit is exercising his gun crews, Chief Fowler will be mustering his landing party at the ship's armory for their gear issue."

"His landing party!" Harrison exclaimed. His thin smile disappeared.

"Yes, his landing party," Lieutenant Hillary said slowly. "Like you said, I am the commanding officer of this vessel, which allows me to interpret orders and situations to best complete my mission and maintain the property of the American government and lives of American citizens, including my men. Since we're going up against the Lassiter Brothers and the Black Badgers, there will be fireworks aplenty, and I can already read the commendation I will write for Kermit. One that that will stand him in good stead when it comes time for a new command. Also, while Chief Fowler has enough medals to fill a seabag, he will oversee that operation because I want every one of my men to come back to my ship tomorrow all in one piece."

Harrison sat looking at Hillary with incredulous eyes as the officer continued.

"You will meet Chief Fowler at the ship's armory when he musters his landing party. You can draw your sidearm then."

The officer looked confused. "I already have my sidearm. And my expeditionary kit."

Hillary continued. "Chief Fowler will be the officer in charge, and you will follow his orders to the letter. Also, your being part of that force is up to Chief Fowler. If he says no, you will assist Kermit with the deck gun, where you will receive notable mention in my report to my commanding officer. You know, the fact that you were diligent in assisting my executive officer in the execution of his duties while withstanding murderous gunfire from shore and from attacking pirate vessels. If the chief allows you to accompany him, the same blurb will appear in my report to my commanding officer. Your choice."

* * *

Moments later, after watching the others file out of his stateroom, Hillary still sat at his table. It felt to him as if he was sitting at a witness stand in a courtroom and the men who walked out were witnesses who were dismissed after offering verbal testimony. Now, the tea in his hand was the Book of Life, the pitcher the unbiased judge, and the framed photos of friends and family a biased jury. While the witnesses were now gone, and their testimonies still pointed wagging fingers at each other in his head, the jury sat silently around him. None of them though, looked down their noses in predestined findings. Instead, their smiles seemed approving of his transgression.

Lifting his glass of tea, he stood and looked at the jury members in those framed photographs. He silently offered his own testimony in defense.

His service started out promising enough. Upon his graduation from the Academy, he received orders to Naval Intelligence in Washington, D.C., but with the youthful wanderlust urging him on, he requested flight training, which was approved. Halfway through his training though, rumors of an affair with an instructor's wife surfaced. Too naïve to disentangle himself from that affair, he was dismissed from flight training, and ended up on a minesweeper. All went well until the ship collided with a merchant vessel in San Diego Bay. As the officer of the deck at the time, he was assigned the blame for the mishap. At the official inquiry, he accepted the blame, but he stated that he was only following the specific orders given to him by the ship's commanding officer who had just left the bridge. The findings of the inquiry resulted in the dismissal of any official charges, but the stain remained.

Now, six years later and after postings that led his career nowhere, he sighed as he stopped in front of one photo. It was a photo of the officers from this ship, wearing their dress white uniforms while attending an official function at the Manila Hotel. The officers sat around a richly furnished table while having their arms around their wives or girlfriends and glasses of champagne in their hands. The man sitting next to Hillary was the ship's gunnery officer. He is, or was, a handsome young man with a pretty wife. Now, the gunnery officer lay bedridden in a hospital at Fort McKinley fifty pounds lighter. Starting with a slight case of mental confusion two weeks before their deployment, the gunnery officer was physically stricken just before their departure.

Hillary's eyes left the photo. He looked at the brown wooden door leading out of the stateroom while thinking about their passenger. He also thought about the timing of the events from the last week and three words came to mind: coincidence or conspiracy.

After an exceptionally long second, he muttered aloud to himself. "Impossible."

CHAPTER 10

DOOLEY WOKE TO the smell of brewing coffee. His eyes opened slowly, and the only light and sounds came through the hatch from the crew's mess. Dooley brought the heels of his palms to his eyes and, as he moved, he realized a slight headache and the soreness in his muscles. Rubbing his eyes, he also realized how hungry, and thirsty, he was. He sniffed at the aroma of brewing coffee again and, although everything on this submarine, including the water, smelled, or tasted like grease, oil, or brass polisher, he looked forward to a cup of it. Yawning again, he heard the missing sounds of marine diesels and the surface water rushing past the hull. He reached under his pillow for his trench watch. As he looked at the watch face, he remembered the questions he asked himself as he went to sleep.

How did the duchess survive machine pistol fire straight into her back, and why did she have a toilet seat hanging around her neck? Why was she wearing those god-awful shoes? What was in those hat boxes? And why did Mashka have a college-level textbook printed in English? Lastly, what was that one question from Zeta? Something about Comintern?

He thought back to the briefings that the regimental staff officer Rodham gave them in Archangel. Still groggy, his mind returned to the coffee.

Throwing his legs out of the bunk and half sitting up, Dooley reached down for his athletic shoes, and socks stuffed into them. After shaking out sand and slipping them on he stood and stooped through the open hatchway into the crew's mess. The subdued white lighting from the overhead fixtures illuminated two men reading, two men playing chess, and two others sharpening their knives. All of them, though, had wine glasses in front of them, and most wore trousers, undershirts, and canvas shoes.

Of the men reading, one man sat alone while holding a magazine published in French. Dooley looked at the cover and saw an image of a man wearing coveralls and a leather helmet, sitting on a motorized bicycle with what looked like an umbrella handle sticking up from behind him. The spokes of the umbrella were spread over the man's head. The contraption looked dangerous as hell. Sitting at the other end of the table, Morda, still wearing his college varsity attire, was occupied with his own reading. They all looked up to give Dooley a nod and a smile.

Dooley heard a noise and saw the cook through the serving window of the galley. Wearing the same clothing from the night before, but now with a white apron wrapped around his waist, the cook finished filling the cup and held it out the window for Dooley. Stepping over, he accepted the cup while looking at the photo of the Waldorf Astoria Hotel.

Dooley sipped the coffee while asking himself why he was not back in Brooklyn. But then he remembered the snooty cooks at the hotel's service entrance. Returning the cook's smile, he turned and looked at the men, who returned to their amusements. Now, he noticed what Morda was reading. The title of the book in his hands was Russian, but he recognized the man on the front cover. He was a grey-haired, stern-faced man with a trimmed mustache of matching grey. The man was Fredrick Taylor, a businessman and a proponent of the "Gospel of Efficiency," or Taylorism. Its root concept was to turn human workers into "autobots" to maximize efficiency and reduce waste in material, time, and money.

On the table in front of Morda was a closed, hardcover book. Again, he could not read the title, which looked Greek, but he recognized the image printed on the cover. A background of solid red and black cut diagonally in half. Over that was a black image of the world with white grid lines. Above the globe were the letters IWW stacked in pyramid shape. The image was that of the Workers Union of the World, or Wobblies, a union accused of being infiltrated with radical socialists, and one that provoked many arguments between his brother and father. While he learned about Taylor and the Wobblies through dinnertime disputes, he learned more about Taylor through a correspondence course he took after shipping out. One other book was also present in front of Morda. It was a smaller paperback. Once again, he couldn't read the title, but he did recognize the image. It was a muscle-bound gladiator holding a *gladius*. The victim of that sword laid at the gladiator's feet. Finding a spot, Dooley sat to enjoy his coffee.

Twenty minutes later, he exited the forward toilet and stepped back to the galley for a refill. Curious as to their progress, it was time to visit the control room. Passing the wardroom, he saw lunch on the table. Although hungry, he continued to the control room. On the way, he saw the curtains to Zeta's stateroom were still drawn closed. He stooped again to enter the control room where he saw four men—two men sitting at their stations with hands on their controls, and two others: the junior submarine officer and Captain Vostok. Bent over the chart table, they appeared to have heard Dooley.

"Have a good sleep?" Vostok asked as he straightened up.

Thinking back, Dooley couldn't remember the last time he slept that soundly. "I didn't know sleeping so well could work up such an appetite."

"My apologies," Vostok offered just as Utkin stooped into the control room from the aft quarters. He held a folded sheet of yellowed paper in his hand.

Utkin stepped over to the junior submarine officer and handed him the paper. He said something to the officer before turning to Dooley. "Good morning, Sergeant Dooley. Would you like something to eat?"

"Only if you're eating," Dooley said as he brought the coffee cup to his lips. He sipped his coffee as he turned and looked at the gauge panel in front of the helmsman. He centered his eyes on the compass and almost choked on his coffee as he did.

"Something wrong?" Vostok asked matter-of-factly. "Coffee too hot?"

Dooley turned to face Utkin and Vostok. "The coffee's fine, but while you don't owe me a meal, you do owe me an explanation."

Vostok looked at the gauge panel, and the gyrocompass. After a second, he held his hand out toward the hatchway leading to the officer's quarters.

Minutes later, sitting around the officer's table three men looked at each other. Although Dooley somehow knew they were not going back to Shanghai, he still had to ask, "So, we're not going back to Shanghai?"

"How did you assume that fact?" Utkin asked as he sipped his wine.

Dooley held his cup of coffee while reaching for a piece of white cheese.

At the same time, Vostok grabbed a bottle of wine. "One should never enjoy good cheese without good wine," Vostok said as he poured a glass for Dooley. "A combination that promotes a healthy gut and a mindful curiosity."

Dooley responded as he reached for the glass. "And no one should enjoy good wine without good conversation, including discussing a time when we will arrive at our destination."

Vostok nodded as he put the bottle down. Sitting back, he smoothed down his distinguished mustache and beard.

Dooley looked at the cheese as he spoke. "Although I grew up in Brooklyn, I've been an infantryman for the last year, and a noncommissioned officer for most of that. I've led men into combat, attended briefings, and spotted for artillery, so I know how to read map and compass. I can also tell time. According to what you said last night, we should've exited the Sea of Japan by now, which means we should've turned to a heading taking us roughly two-seven-zero degrees, or west. We're on a heading of one-two-zero, which means we're still heading southeast away from China. Into the Pacific Ocean."

"You are an astute young man," Captain Vostok said as he reached for a slice of brown bread. He picked up the knife and dipped it into the horseradish. Bringing out a dollop he spread it on the bread and brought it to his mouth but stopped to ask a question. "So, can you posit a reason as to why we are heading into the Pacific Ocean?"

"Perhaps two full hat boxes?" Dooley answered.

Captain Vostok bit into his bread and chewed slowly, allowing Utkin to answer.

"Sergeant, it seems we will have quite a reception in Shanghai, as those rumors of diamonds were well founded. After our rescue, diamonds were found scattered about beach. Surviving soldiers from the cliff and the patrol boats witnessed our departure and reported such to Vladivostok. In turn, red agents in Shanghai were notified. The problem: Shanghai is rife with intrigue where both Red and White Russians, and any number of associations are dancing circles around each other while trying to figure out what the other side is doing."

"And don't forget the Japanese, British, and Americans as they too have an interest in what the Reds and Whites are up to and who is in possession of such mammon. The same holds true for the French in Indochina, the Portuguese at Macau, and the Dutch in the East Indies. The bottom line is that the Reds want, need, to have those hatboxes of diamonds in their possession. Since disposing of the Tsar in 1917 they still find themselves fighting us while trying to establish an economically viable government. Also, they cannot afford the Whites to have that wealth at our disposal. The Reds, rightfully so, can fear a global filibust by the Whites. By us."

Utkin paused to sip his wine. Both he and Vostok looked at the sergeant. Dooley returned their looks while biting into his piece of cheese.

After chewing a couple of times, Dooley responded. "I, like most of my fellow soldiers, have been in contact with my family. I've also kept up with the news while traveling to Shanghai, so I know what we're facing at home. You know, a Red infiltration into American society and government, and the Third International or Comintern."

Dooley paused for a split second as he remembered Zeta's question. "I also appreciate what you and your comrades can do with that money to help save my country from the Reds. I can also appreciate the fact that you want to reinstall the old Tsarist monarchy. Right now, though, I'm not in Brooklyn. Instead, I'm on a Russian submarine traveling through the East China Sea, in the middle of the typhoon season, heading to places unknown. Other than the uniform on my back, a worn-down bar of Ivory soap in a beat-up

Dopp kit, weapons I 'borrowed' from Uncle Sam, and a duffel holding smelly BVDs, everything I own is back in Shanghai, including the two hundred and fifty dollars you paid me before leaving Shanghai, along with the fifty-two dollars and twenty-eight cents I had before you showed up. So, what am I to do now?"

Utkin smiled as he sipped his wine again. "Sergeant, you have demonstrated your abilities since embarking on this journey. Such talent is worth more than whatever used belongings you left in the backroom of a shabby Shanghai hotel or what is on deposit in a safe behind a reception desk, if it is still there."

Dooley listened as he popped the last of the cheese into his mouth. He chewed slowly. "Sounds like you're about to replace my belongings and my five hundred and fifty-two dollars and twenty-eight cents with something more substantial, but I'd like an explanation."

"Explanation to what?"

"A lot of things. Starting with your scar. How you ended up with this submarine. What the hell was the duchess doing with a toilet seat around her neck? How was she able to survive a machine pistol blast into her back, and what did you do with her body? How come nobody aboard this submarine smokes? Lastly, if we're not going back to Shanghai, and since Hong Kong, Japan, Macau, Formosa, Saigon, Manila, and Jakarta are not options, where is this submarine taking us?"

"Let me start with saying," Captain Vostok declared, "that you will be compensated for any items you left in Shanghai."

* * *

The two bottles of wine on the table were now empty along with the bread and cheese plates and jars of horseradish and gherkins. All that remained were glasses of wine in front of the men.

"Now you see where we are at. This naval weapon taken in the heat of war and the political turmoil that continues, an untold wealth, and our purpose. All three of which will be put to good use. An end that you will appreciate."

Dooley lifted his glass and looked at the remnants. "Sounds like you are offering me a job, Major. Why are you so certain I would accept a position within your organization? After all, I do have a family back in Brooklyn. One relying on me to carry on the family business."

"I did not recruit you from a bar in Shanghai out of hand," Major Utkin answered as he fingered the rim of his wine glass. "I always do my research, and I also have a habit of listening in on other people's conversations. Such as the one between you and the countess from last night. I hope you will forgive me."

"It's a small submarine," Dooley responded as he held his hands above his shoulders.

"Very well," Major Utkin said. "Let me simply state that you left Brooklyn, a seventeen-year-old runaway who forged papers to enlist. The reasons could be that you grew up reading of adventure. Or you wanted to save the civilized world from the evil Hun, or just wanted to escape a future of fixing wagons, hauling potatoes, or staring at the asses of draft horses. Or it could be all those reasons. No, Sergeant, you left Brooklyn to enter a fantastic world you knew only through Sir Arthur Conan Doyle, H.G. Wells, Edgar Rice Burroughs, Jules Verne, and pure characters such as Tom Swift. However, you walked into a world created by Thompson, Fedorov, Browning, Lewis, and Maxim and killed real men like the ones last night. You entered a world sutured together with barbed wire and lorded over by gore-stuffed ravens. Sergeant, you stepped from the nineteenth century and walked into the twentieth."

Utkin stopped to lift his hands above his shoulders. "Since your baptismal outside Archangel, you have been ordained into a select clergy. A coronation you must endure. You are trapped in this world, so you must accept being a native of this public."

Dooley's eyes followed and looked at the curved hull and piping over Utkin's head. "I'm ordained now. Huh. Although I've gambled some, I would hate to sit across the felt from you."

"Ah," Utkin responded, "but gambling implies lack of knowledge and a degree of uncertainty. I entertain neither. I play poker, and am always aware of the outcome, which is why I am placing a bet on you."

"*Caveat Emptor*," Dooley replied.

Both Utkin and Vostok tilted their heads slightly. After a second, Utkin spoke up. "A Latin phrase that boils down to the understanding 'buyer beware.' How does that phrase fit in here?"

"I could understand it as winner beware if I so chose, Major," Dooley replied. "You may not know as much about me as you think you do. I would remind you that there is a difference between a confident poker player and an arrogant poker player."

Utkin smiled. "I have seen the cards you have been dealt so far."

"Yes. So far," Dooley responded coyly. "Anyway, I see that my translator is in his bunk. Is he gonna be ok?"

"I told you, Gorki is an excellent doctor. Mashka woke earlier today and told us how you saved his life," Utkin said as he leaned his head out into the aisle and said something in Russian. He brought his head back inside the wardroom.

"He would've done the same for me. They all would've," Dooley responded as he saw the red-haired cook bring another open bottle of wine. They all waited until the cook placed the bottle on the table and left. Captain Vostok reached for the bottle to refill everybody's glasses.

"I see you suffer from an age-old malady that has claimed the lives of many victims throughout history," Utkin said as he watched his glass being filled.

"What malady is that?" Dooley asked as Vostok turned to fill his glass.

"You are cursed with a sickness that can be listed under any number of descriptive terms such as chivalry, romanticism, or idealism. A disease that has proved fatal to many a noble man. Mashka said that you went out of your way to not kill men at the barracks, but then you stood in front of what could only be described as a firing squad and killed several men in one swoop to save his life. Just like I said, you are a romantic." Utkin said as he picked up his glass. "Anyway, what we hope to accomplish with this submarine, my men, Vostok's men, and the diamonds, is to create a counter-counterrevolutionary force to combat the Reds in my home country and to stomp out the spread of

Bolshevism abroad wherever it may raise its ugly head. And not with just this one submarine and the men on it. I am creating units that can operate either overtly or covertly and independent of each other. We are now in the twentieth century and need to have new ways of combating such insidious activities before they metastasize. In doing so, I refer to the world's greater teacher: history. Only within the last few years we have witnessed the waste of a generation who, at the orders of generals ensconced inside a chateau, charged, en masse, into fire-spitting Maxims and walls of barbed wire. The result: rotting corpses dangling over strands of wire and becoming the bill of fare for crows. Now, going back a few decades I will refer to the Boers Wars of South Africa and the concept of commando warfare. Have you heard the term?"

Dooley sipped his wine before answering. "Commando. It's a Boer word that means obey or order, but what it infers is the reason why farmers, armed with hand-me-down rifles, were able to take on the British Empire. In other words, small, mobile units."

"Good. And such units in my plans will be called special action commandos with each commando specially trained—submarine raiders, intelligence detectives; espionage operatives, and air assault specialists—but with the ultimate combined mission to thwart the spread of Bolshevism wherever its foul presence reveals itself. I would like you to be part of one of them; perhaps part of the submarine raider commando?"

Dooley leaned against the padded leather bench seat as he heard the clang of metal. Looking up at a pipe just above him, he reached to feel a bump on his head. "I don't mind spending a week on a submarine, but the scenery can be a bit painful."

A smile broke out on Utkin's face. "So, you are thinking about my offer. Albeit not as a submarine raider."

"Thinking about it yes, but where will I end up?" Dooley asked. "And what would I be doing when I'm not tracking down Bolsheviks?"

Utkin cleared his throat slightly as he lifted his wine glass. "I sense you still have wanderlust controlling those heels of yours, so I can, indirectly, steer you toward employment that will satisfy your longings while providing a clean income meaning no connection with my effort, and giving me an experienced and well-positioned asset I can rely on at the same time. To help thwart the Red threat. I hope you understand my goal?"

"Can you be more specific?"

"Good with weapons, fit, and know how to use both a submachine gun and a spanner. I also sense that you like the sun," Utkin surmised. After a few seconds, he asked. "I saw how you watched the cook as he fished during our transit north. Have you ever fished before? Sport fishing. With charter boats."

After a pause while looking at the pipes above his head, Dooley smiled. "A charter boat captain in Havana?"

Before Utkin could reply, the cook stuck his head into the wardroom. He said something to Vostok while looking at Dooley. The captain replied to the cook before asking Dooley. "He asked if the lunch was satisfactory."

Dooley smiled. "I've been aboard this submarine for a week with every meal centering around red wine, cabbage, beets, onions, gherkins, dark bread, cheese, canned sardines, and horseradish. A diet my mother would be proud to have watched me eat, however, if he's thinking about a job at the Waldorf Astoria, he should think about expanding his bill of fare."

Vostok and Utkin smiled while something clicked in Dooley's head. A minute ago, Utkin had referred to one of his commandos as composed of intelligence detectives. It did not take but a second to connect that comment with what his Puerto Rican friend said about secrets in the Waldorf Astoria. Continuing, Dooley finished. "I just thought back to when I was a kid, and my mother kept trying to get me to eat my beets. My brother ate his, but I was a steak-and-potatoes kid, just like my old man who always took my side. It led to a lot of fights between him and my mother. Anyway, tell your cook the food's fine, and my mother would be proud of my morning movements these last few days."

Utkin said something to the cook, and the young man's face broke into a smile as he wiped his hands on his apron and withdrew his head from the cubicle.

"Your mother was right as everybody should eat their greens and the proof of one's constitution is in the morning stool," Vostok chimed in. "I fear though that the adulterated foods becoming popular in the United States will prove to be their downfall. All which rot the mind, body, teeth, and soul. Such fodder will keep Americans lined up at the trough and have severe future effects on the American system of moral fiber and even present a national security issue."

"In what way?" Dooley asked, even though he knew the answer. He remembered the bitching his fellow soldiers voiced after having to sit under the glare of army dentists.

"Dental issues lead to poor physical health, which reduces the pool of qualified recruits available for national emergencies," Utkin responded as a smile came to his face. "Leaving those most sound facing the dog of war and those lesser qualified alone with the gentler sex. The result? A pollution of the following generation. While women want different things from men, a healthy set of teeth is universally in demand. So, intermittent fitness assessments will be a requirement to remain in my employ."

Dooley responded slowly. "I can understand why you and your men do not smoke as it is bad for the wind, but how does wine fit in? You guys drink it like water."

"You are correct that smoking is bad for the lungs," Utkin explained, "but a nonsmoker with a trained nose can smell heavy smokers yards away. Especially in the bush. At night. As far as wine, specifically red wine, that drink has enjoyed prominence throughout many cultures for many centuries for a reason. Wine provides both blood and heart health and provides for mental vigor and extends that vim into old age. It is, in effect, the intellect's aide. Now, will you need more time to think about my offer?"

"Major Utkin. Captain Vostok," Dooley said slowly, "I am an American mercenary locked up on a Russian submarine in the middle of the East China Sea and headed to God-knows-where, so all I have time to do is to think. But to give me something to think about, tell me more about our destination and your plans for Countess Tolstoy. Lastly, tell me more about this air assault commando."

CHAPTER 11

"THAT STUPID SON of a bitch," muttered Harrison as he walked down the passageway to his stateroom. "He has no idea who he's playing with. None of them do."

The morning proved painful. To find out he would be under the charge of an enlisted man was painful enough but doing so while on an operation he put together was galling. Especially since combat against notorious pirates was in the offering along with the potential of valorous recognition. However, he reminded himself of the real reason he was on this ship.

Harrison stopped in front of the grey metal door and reached for the brass knob. Turning the knob, he pushed the door open. Like the captain's cabin, this stateroom was small and sparsely furnished, but furnished enough to allow two men to sleep and relax in relative comfort. The washstand, just like the one in Hillary's stateroom, was simple enough, but was also in use. A man wearing baggy overalls smeared with wet rust and holes worn in the back pockets was bent over washing his face. He stood at the sound of the door closing and turned to face Harrison while grabbing at the white towel hanging from the side of the washstand. Water dripped from his bushy red eyebrows as he brought the towel to his face.

"I'm McIntyre, the engineer. Sorry we didn't get a chance to meet earlier. Had to babysit a condensate pump. Anyway, I hear you're going to be on the chief's landing party?"

Harrison winced as he stepped to one of the wardrobes. "Word gets around fast."

"It's a small boat," McIntyre said as he wiped his chin with the towel.

"Burton D. Harrison. From the admiral's staff," he said as he reached for the wardrobe doorknob. Opening it, he clasped the shoulder strap of the musette bag along with his encased officer sword under the hanging uniforms. Turning, he closed the wardrobe door with his knee while placing the bag and sword on the lower bunk. "I hope you don't mind?"

"Go ahead," McIntyre said, drying behind an ear.

"Thanks," Harrison said as he bent over to open the flap of the canvas bag.

McIntyre finished wiping behind that ear and switched to the other ear. As he did, he saw Harrison pull out a booklet and place it on the grey wool blanket. His huge eyebrows furrowed. "You a Wilson man?"

Harrison looked at the booklet while reaching back into the bag. "Didn't have much time. Grabbed that at the last minute. Why?"

"I'm a Republican. Find Republicans a bit more predictable and practical, like good solid machinery. Anyway, Wilson, since he's been in office, has been the greatest violator of the Constitution. Maybe even the first president to do so."

"Sorry, Mack," Harrison said as it almost seemed like the ire in the engineer's eyes started to match his flaming red hair. "I guess this stateroom is too small and this voyage will be too long for such discussions. I do apologize."

McIntyre held the towel in one hand while inspecting his fingernails in the other. He uttered "huh" in response.

Harrison returned to his musette bag and pulled out a brand-new pair of khaki leggings, a box of cartridges, and a khaki-painted doughboy helmet. Placing them on the grey blanket next to the bag and Wilson's essay, he reached in again and pulled out another brand-new piece of military equipment—a cartridge belt with a canvas-covered canteen on one side and two conjoined canvas pouches containing full magazines for the .45 caliber pistol next to them. The pistol was encased in a polished leather holster with the letters US embossed on the holster's flap. The butt of the pistol, with a magazine inserted into the handle, poked out from under the flap. Unsnapping the flap, he withdrew the pistol.

The engineer whistled. "That's not normal issue."

Harrison grinned as he held it in one hand while pulling back the nickel-plated slide with the other. He pulled it back far enough to see brass in the breech. "It's a custom-made Colt .45. My father had it made specifically for me. Just got it in the mail."

"I'm trying to not be insulting," McIntyre continued, "but are those real ivory grips? And are those initials filled with real gold?"

"Yes, and yes," Harrison said matter-of-factly as he re-holstered the pistol.

McIntyre held the towel by two corners as he shook it out. "Well, just don't take any paper money for it."

"What do you mean?" Harrison replied perplexed. "I'm not selling it."

Just then, the shrill of a bosun's pipe screeched from the speaker mounted in one of the corners of the stateroom. The piping was followed by a distant, scratchy announcement. "Gun crews to your stations. Landing party muster at the starboard quarterdeck. Again, gun crews and landing party to your stations!"

Harrison lifted his arm to check his wristwatch while reaching out to untie the string securing the flap of the sword's leather casing.

"I'm going for stew," the engineer continued. "And I wouldn't take any paper money for that watch either."

* * *

Now, alone in the stateroom, Harrison finished putting on his expeditionary outfit and stood in front of the mirror mounted above the wash station. He positioned the steel helmet, and chin strap, so they were just right. Next, he adjusted his cartridge belt and touched the butt of his pistol poking out from under the leather holster flap. Reaching over, he checked the belt fasteners for his sword. Taking one last look to admire himself, he reached for the doorknob.

A minute later, he stood on the main deck looking at the almost empty South China Sea. The only thing he saw, other than blue sky and even bluer water, was the column of spiraling black smoke pouring from a floating smoke pot. He heard Mister Kermit's voice bark an order and turned to look forward. Just at the edge of the superstructure two men manned the forward starboard side six-pounder: a swivel-mounted gun. One man pulled a foot-long shell from the wooden case at his feet and another man stood by with the gun's lanyard in his hand.

Just past them, he saw the muzzle end of the ship's three-inch deck gun swing into view. The gun roared as a burst of flame and acrid smoke shot out from the muzzle. He immediately turned his eyes back to the floating smoke pot, just as a volcano of water exploded feet into the air as the shell struck the water near the floating smoke pot.

Suddenly, his nostrils were assailed by the acidic taint of cordite which was just as quickly replaced by fresh sea air. Next, one man on the six-pounder inserted a shell into the gun's open breech and slid the breech slide forward. He then stood aside to let the man with the lanyard bend over to take aim. At the same time, he heard a high-pitched voice speaking Tagalog. It was followed by several chuckles.

Turning right, he saw the source of the voice. Nine dungaree-clad men were strung out along the narrow deck and further aft, two more men manned the aft starboard six-pounder. While eight from the landing party stood grouped in pairs, Chief Fowler stood by himself next to the open metal doors of the ship's small-arms armory. He looked up from the clipboard in his hands and at the man who made a comment. It was the Filipino steward. That man stood next to the starboard boat davit and under one of the ship's two motorboats. Along with dungarees, he wore a white gob hat perched on the back of his head, like the other seamen. Fabio, who saw the chief's glare, returned his attention to the bolt-action Springfield in his hands. But the smile stayed on his face.

Harrison turned his attention from the smirking Filipino to the equipment at the feet of the four pairs of men: grey-painted helmets, leggings, cartridge belts, ammo pouches, magazines, canteens, and foot-long, sheathed bayonets, all of which looked like they had been well used. There were also boxes of cartridges and, at the feet of the Filipino and the black man next to him was a grey canvas musette bag with a white circle painted on the large flap. Centered on the circle was a bright red cross. Harrison also noticed, that among each team, was a folded white towel on top of the landing gear.

Harrison looked down at his crisp khakis, brand-new cartridge belt and holster, and polished weapons and shoes.

The deck gun roared behind him again, and the aft six-pounder belted out a round. However, nobody in the landing party paid attention to where the shells landed. Instead, the men lined up along the deck focused on their own weapons. The men, most of whom had cigarettes dangling from their lips or pinched between their fingers or were chewing gum, ranged in age from late thirties to the early twenties. They checked the sights, wiped the barrels with oiled rags, or cycled the bolts. While one man in each pair held a bolt-action rifle, the other man held either a Browning Automatic Rifle or a Lewis gun. One man holding a BAR was the strapping black man who Harrison recognized as Wardroom Steward Demby Brown, and he stood next to his grinning Filipino lover. They were both about forty years old, but the Filipino weighed a hundred pounds less and stood two feet shorter.

"Listen up," Chief Fowler bellowed as he dropped his clipboard to his side.

The men stopped handling their weapons and stood them on their stocks while holding onto the tips of the barrels. They continued to smoke cigarettes or chew gum while the deck gun and six-pounders fired again. The acrid smell of cordite tainted the air again.

Seeing he had everybody's attention, Fowler continued. "This here's Lieutenant Junior Grade Harrison. He's from the admiral's staff, and he's the reason for the landing party. He'll be coming along as an observer."

Observer! Harrison placed his hand on the custom-made holster. His fingers caressed the leather flap.

"We're headed to the Babuyan Islands, specifically an island called Bagay Alto," Fowler continued. "We're gonna row ashore just like we did in the Visayas last fall. This time, though, we're not gonna mix it up with gin-drunk natives. We're going up against Lassiter Brothers and the Black Badgers."

The men reacted, still holding the barrel tips of the weapons. A pair of eyes widened, a pair of lips spread into a smile, and a wad of gum flew from its abuser's mouth and over the handrail.

"All the information you'll need is on a chart that Mister Harrison brought with him. It's secured to a table on the fantail. Now that everybody that has their issue, I want each man to fire one magazine through their weapons then switch out with their teammates and fire another magazine through their partner's weapons. Afterwards, make your way with gear and weapons back to the table to sign for them and to study our target. Each team has a specific position, which is marked on the chart, along with your field of fire. Once satisfied, fill as many extra magazines as you can carry. Our job is to make sure they keep their date with a neck stretcher in Hong Kong. But if they don't want to be the obliging type, don't skimp on the ammunition. Any questions?"

The men looked at Fowler, then at their guest. Their assessments ranged from disinterest to amusement. The only verbal answer Fowler received came from the deck gun.

"Good," Chief Fowler said. "We'll muster at our boat stations at three a.m."

The eight men nodded and returned their attention to their weapons, Camels, and teammates. Meanwhile, Fowler turned his attention to Harrison. After an up-and-down appraisal he spoke.

"Looks like you're ready to take on Pancho Villa," Fowler commented as the men started exercising their weapons, "and his entire gang of banditos."

The forward six-pounder behind Harrison belted out another round as he squared his shoulders and ignored Fowler's comment. "What did that Filipino say?"

With a smirk, Fowler answered, "Look at the cowboy."

Harrison returned the chief's look but waited for Demby Brown to finish firing his twenty-round-capacity magazine. "Listen, Chief Fowler, I know you've been fighting in these islands since John Paul Jones was a cabin boy, but you need to remember that I am a commissioned officer in the United States Navy, and that you are an enlisted man."

"Mister Harrison," Fowler said as he lifted the clipboard and pointed it at the officer's chest. "I've never kneeled before a ring in my life, and I am not going to start now, so if you want to get some girl bait on that chest then you do exactly as I say, starting with losing that Captain Standish extender of yours. It may be useful for cutting cake at an officer's wedding or getting a horny bridesmaid into a linen closet, but it's nothing but a trip hazard in the jungle. 'Sides, if you're that close to an opponent then you're better off fighting like an enlisted man: use your helmet to smash in a face, use your boot heel to stomp on a hand, or use a pistol butt to crack an eye socket. Hand it over."

Both men looked at each other, but after a long second and sporadic fire from the bolt-action rifles, Harrison looked down and unclipped his sword sheath from the cartridge belt. After unsnapping the brass fasteners, he grabbed the sword by the sheath and held it in front of him. "Which boat am I on?"

Fowler grabbed the sword and pointed the hilt at the boat just aft of them. "And you stay right on my ass every second we're on the island."

"Anything else?

"Is it all that store bought?"

"Straight from the Mills Woven Military Equipment Catalogue. Why?"

Fowler leaned the sheathed sword against the bulkhead next to the open door of the armory, tossing the clipboard onto the countertop inside. He then turned and held out his hand.

The young staff officer smiled inwardly as he reached for the flap on the holster.

Unsnapping it, he grabbed the butt and pulled the weapon from the holster.

Fowler thrust his hand out slapping the weapon to the side as Harrison offered it to him muzzle first. "Dammit! The first thing you need to learn is to know how to turn over a weapon. Get your booger-picker off that trigger."

The officer, still smiling inwardly, nodded while removing his finger from the trigger and pointing the barrel away from Fowler.

The chief grasped the weapon by the slide. Readjusting in it in his hand he spoke again. "Real ivory grips, huh?"

Holding it close to his face, he used his other hand to pull back the nickel-plated slide. Fowler looked sternly at the officer while bringing his nose closer to the chamber. "Second lesson: never walk around with a bullet in the chamber unless you're ready to shoot somebody at that particular moment."

Just then both starboard-side six-pounders fired again. Their salvos were followed a long burst from a Lewis gun.

He solidified his statement by pulling the slide all the way back. The round in the chamber arced out of the weapon and landed on the deck where it bounced over the side. Locking the slide back, he used his thumb to push the eject button and the magazine dropped into the palm of his hand. "Eight rounds in the magazine?"

"It's an eight-round magazine!"

"You've never fired this thing?" the chief asked while pointing the full magazine at the officer's pistol.

"I just got it in the mail. My father had it custom made for me," Harrison offered questionably. "But I've used other forty-fives at the range at Fort McKinley as late as last week."

"Should've brought one of them. Third lesson: you never take an unused weapon into a fight. Especially if it's not government issue. Also, a shiny sidearm like this one will draw the attention of any pirate with at least one good eye, which tells them that the holder is somebody of significance and a bonehead, which means you will draw fire. And since you'll be standing next to me the whole time, I don't want to get shot because you feel like playing Admiral Farragut storming into Mobile Bay. Also, any pirate worth his salt would love to have that weapon strapped to his hip."

Before Harrison could respond, the firing of the deck gun, six pounders, small arms, and automatics ceased. Harrison and Fowler stopped their verbal exchange long enough to see the men bending over to collect spent brass casings. As Harrison returned his attention back to Fowler, he saw the chief pocket the magazine and stick the pistol in his belt. "Hey! That's mine!"

"Not now it isn't," Fowler said as he stepped into the small-arms locker. "You can get it back tomorrow morning. After our mission."

"What if it turns up missing?" Harrison asked with exasperation in his voice.

"How much did it cost daddy?" Fowler asked.

"With the handmade holster, cartridge belt, magazine pouches, and a box of handloaded cartridges, thirty-six dollars and seventy-six cents. Why?"

"If it gets lost, then I owe you. I've got two twenty-dollar notes in my locker."

Now Harrison knew what the engineer meant about paper money, but he also realized that the pistol was nothing compared to his reason for being on that ship. He had to stay focused. Taking a deep breath, he followed the chief into the closet-sized armory. On either side of them, pails were hung and, in front of them, against the bulkhead, was a wooden-topped workbench with brass-knobbed drawers and a pegboard for tools, brushes, and bottles of gun oil.

On either side of the bench stood grey metal lockers with drawers at their bases. Everything was stenciled, including the pails. Fowler pulled open a drawer under the workbench top and reached for one of the Colt forty-fives, two magazines, and a box of ammunition. At the same time, pairs of men cycled past the buckets and emptied their hands of spent brass. The last pair, Fabio and Demby, emptied their hands and, as they turned from the gun locker, Fabio made another comment in Tagalog.

Harrison looked at the Filipino's back but didn't ask the chief what he said.

"Like my men, I want you to cycle through two magazines," the chief continued while opening the cartridge box. Picking up one of the magazines, he started to insert bullets into the magazine with his thumb. "Once you've gone through them, keep the .45 I've given you, and sign for it on the fantail."

After inserting a fifth bullet into the magazine he handed it to Harrison.

The officer snatched up the magazine while looking into Fowler's eyes.

"Only five bullets? These magazines hold eight rounds."

"You only need to shoot a few bullets to get familiar with the weapon," Fowler continued as he began inserting bullets into a second magazine. "Also, too many bullets too often damage the spring inside the magazine. A failure you don't need while getting shot at."

Fowler finished and handed the second magazine to Harrison while grabbing a third empty magazine. "Step to the side and exercise your weapon. When you've gone through two magazines, come back and get a third magazine. That one will have three rounds."

"What am I supposed to do with three rounds?" Harrison exclaimed.

"Not shoot me in the back by accident, for one thing," Fowler responded slowly. "Fourth lesson: without having gone through a combat situation before, extra rounds mean extra chances to shoot a shipmate by accident and is a waste of ammunition. Limited access to ammunition forces fire discipline."

The officer looked at the chief. "Where's your gear? Your weapon?"

Fowler smiled slightly as he reached for another drawer. Pulling it open, Harrison saw the largest revolver he had ever seen. It had a six-inch barrel and a cylinder that looked big enough to hold rifle rounds. Next to it was a leather belt, brass buckle embossed with the letters *USA*, a leather holster, and a box of forty-four-forty caliber rounds.

"That pistol better be government issue," Harrison stated while looking at his own pistol in Fowler's beltline.

The chief replied as he reached for the revolver, "1872 US cavalry revolver, and it's taken down more horses, buffalo, and Sioux than you can count. It saved my uncle's ass at the Little Bighorn, and it got me through two Boxer armies."

"And that shotgun?" Harrison said he returned his eyes to the drawer.

Fowler looked back into the drawer and at the shotgun lying diagonally on more grey felt. "Winchester Model 1897 twelve-gauge pump-action shotgun, and before you say anything, yes, it's store-bought. Purchased by Uncle Sam and shipped here to fight insurrectionists in the jungles of Mindanao. Now, Mister Harrison, it's time to tend to your own weapon."

* * *

Dooley watched Vostok and Utkin leave the room, which left the ex-sergeant alone to ponder his future. He did, indeed, have quite a bit to think about. What started out as a week-long contract that would've netted enough money to get him back to, at least, the Western Hemisphere was now turning into something he had never imagined. He was so into his thoughts he failed to see the countess stick her head into the wardroom.

"Morning, Dooley. Or should I say afternoon?"

"Sorry, Zeta," Dooley responded as he turned to the voice. "Guess I was lost in thought."

"I should say so. I said your name twice. Anything important?"

Dooley paused before answering. "I had a conversation with our hosts, and it appears that we're not heading back to Shanghai."

"Oh," she said as she looked down at the items in her hands. "What about my cousin?"

"Go ahead," Dooley said as he looked at her Dopp kit and white face towel. "I'll ask the cook to get you something."

Zeta turned but stopped. She looked at Dooley. "Will you be here when I get back?"

"Don't forget to wash behind your ears."

Twenty minutes later, Dooley was still in the wardroom but now accompanied with a bottle of wine from her stateroom, two glasses, and a plate of dark bread and sharp cheese.

Zeta was dressed like Dooley with her oversized army trousers and a white male undershirt engulfing her. The short sleeves were rolled up, revealing thin, but shapely arms. Dooley also noticed that she didn't wear any sort of undershirt. Her face was a pinkish tinge, and her wet blond hair was brushed back and tied into a ponytail with a dark blue ribbon, both of which highlighted her big, blue innocent eyes.

They ate slowly while sipping Vostok's wine.

"I wished I could have had one more time to say goodbye to Olga," Zeta said with downcast eyes, "but I understand. So, if we're not going back to Shanghai, where are we going? And what about you? Where are you going?"

"Don't worry. I am not leaving you. At least just yet."

That statement caused her eyes to lift while bringing up the corners of her mouth.

Dooley continued. "The major told me that news of our raid and the acquisition of diamonds has reached Shanghai and other Asian port cities, which means there will be Reds waiting for us. Instead, we're going to an island where they have a base. We're supposed to stay there until other transportation is available."

"You're being like the major," Zeta said, lifting her glass.

Dooley lifted his wine glass in salute. "The island we're going to is out of normal shipping lanes, which is why the major and the captain selected it. As for me, Major Utkin offered to find me employment in the Caribbean. I tried to include you. Hope you don't mind."

"You are concerned about me?" she asked softly. The corners of her eyes revealed her appreciation.

Dooley also noticed that her appreciation was showing under that white undershirt. "Let's just say I am concerned about you starting on the right foot."

After lunch, the two idled away the rest of the afternoon and evening together by taking care of mundane tasks and enjoying small talk centering around baseball and mystery novels. At sunset, the submarine surfaced to recharge the vessel's batteries while driving itself further into the Pacific. At the same time though, the two were asked to remain inside the submarine. The seas were becoming a bit unsettled, and Vostok did not want to lose anybody overboard. Inside her stateroom, Dooley and Zeta braced themselves as the submarine's bow cleaved through another wave.

"It seems strange not to have the nightly landing drills," Dooley said as he sat in the chair at the stateroom desk. His black hair was neatly combed, and he wore his athletic shoes, army trousers. and a white undershirt, still damp. During the afternoon, Zeta did her best to handwash that undershirt as well as pieces of her own clothing in the forward head, using up the last of Dooley's Ivory soap as she did. On the desk in front of Dooley was an open atlas of the Pacific Ocean. Dooley inspected the open pages as Zeta sat on the edge of the bunk.

"I agree," Zeta said while folding one of her undershirts. "It was quite the show to see you demonstrate your shooting, swimming, and paddling skills."

"I wasn't the only man out there," Dooley said as he turned his attention from the atlas to her. He saw her shaking hands tamp down her undershirt.

"You were the only one I saw," Zeta said as her cheeks became flushed.

Dooley nodded as he turned back to the open atlas. He closed it.

CHAPTER 12

BURNING PIECES OF rust lofted from Number Two boiler stack and into the night sky as the torpedo-boat destroyer reversed its propellers. The ship slowly backed into its own wake and the darkness behind it while leaving the men in front of it to row the next half-mile themselves. Though equipped with inboard diesels, the engines remained unused.

As the boats neared the V-shaped beach, two men from each boat jumped over the gunwales, landing in the thigh-deep water. Holding weapons over their heads, they waded through the water and threw themselves into prone position on the sand. The barrels of the Lewis guns, propped up by the bipods, provided cover while the other man in each pair held their Springfields in one hand and boat anchors with lengths of rope in the other. While forcing the flukes into the sand, they heard the prows of the boats grind into the sand behind them. They also heard the dull thumps of wooden oars being stowed. The men in the boats slid over the gunwales joining their men already on the beach, leaving the boats canted over at the water's edge.

A minute later, nine men grouped around their leader.

"Alright," Fowler said quietly as he adjusted the canvas cartridge belt slung across his chest in Mexican-bandito fashion. "We've got a quarter mile to go and twenty minutes to get there." Without another word, Fowler, holding the barrel of his shotgun in front of him, turned into the trees lining the beach and headed west. The landing party fell in behind.

As outlined on their charts, the island was shaped like a fat baby's foot but was a mile in length. And, while the ball and the heel were elevated to a height of about fifty feet, they were heavily wooded, which would provide excellent cover for the Lewis guns and BAR teams. The arch though, while the lowest part of the island in elevation, provided a route in the form of a well-worn path created hundreds of years ago by transients who either visited the island or were cast upon its shores. That path between connected the island's two beaches. While the path was easily walked, there was a sharp rise at the beginning, but after one hundred yards, they reached to highest point. From there, the path trended downhill at a shallow decline. Alongside the path, the sailors heard water bubbling out of rocks on either side of them and run downhill. As the men walked, they also heard the scurrying of lizards and the chirping of birds. Island residents waking to a rising sun just now peeking over the horizon behind them. Alert to any foreign sounds, everybody saw the path widening, a result of the island's two hills funneling seasonal monsoon rainwater to the western beach. After following the downward slope another two hundred yards, the path flattened out.

At its end, the path widened to several yards and the island's forest grew with tree branches reaching out to each other, as if to hold hands. The result was a shaped panorama encapsulating, being blessed by a waking sun, a scene fit for the imagination of any first-rate novelist. The landscape centered in that panorama was built by the Spanish colonial government a decade before the Spanish-American War as a way station for its ships and shelter for storm victims. The view consisted of two brick-and-mortar buildings with a chimney poking out from the thatch-covered roof of the larger structure. Wispy smoke wafted from its top. The rear wall, the only one visible from this aspect, was pierced with two glassless windows, each missing one wooden typhoon shutter. The windows were closed off with bamboo vertical blinds. A stout wooden door occupied the space between the two windows.

Remembering the charts, Fowler envisioned the short wharf extending from the beach on the other side of the structure.

The other brick-and-mortar building, also with a thatch roof, was about two yards in length and situated closer to the stream that exited the jungle and cut through the smooth sand as it emptied into the sea. A bit higher off the ground and with no windows or back door, the two small apertures at the base of the building, with wooden tubs inside it revealed the building's purpose. The only other structures were two thatch canopies held up by wooden posts with one between the brick buildings and sheltering a picnic table strewn with wine and liquor bottles. The other canopy sheltered a u-shaped pile of collected driftwood. That canopy was just south of the larger structure.

Fowler pulled up to the tree line and stopped. He looked at the crescent-shaped beach and its shelters before looking down at his wristwatch. Turning, he surveyed the well-equipped landing party. Like him, they were prepared for the upcoming battle. While most of the men held their weapons by their hands, the men with the Lewis guns had slung them over their shoulders. Also, one man from each team carried the folded white towel in their cartridge belts while the other man in each team wore a bedroll bent over their shoulders with the ends tied together at their hips. Demby, however, did not have a blanket or towel. Instead, he carried his musette bag stuffed with first aid supplies and extra canteens. The cook also wore his old cavalry campaign hat. Brown, with years of sweat staining the felt, the wearer gave it a brushing before leaving the ship along with polishing the crossed sabers pinned to the front of it.

"The skipper will be bringing the ship into view by 5:15, which is when he'll notify the island's residents of our presence. Remember, every one of those pirates has a date with a hangman in Hong Kong, so if anything happens to me, Demby's in charge. Got it?"

He received eight nods as a response and a muted cough from Harrison.

"Good, and don't forget to mark your positions with your towels," Fowler said aloud but quietly as he looked Harrison over. The officer looked like he was getting ready to sit for a portrait instead getting ready for a fight where men were about to die.

"Urbach and Speranza, take your Lewis gun and set up your position on the north hill. Make sure you keep anybody from getting those boats underway and remember that we have to sail those things across the South China

Sea and return them to the Brits. Kozlowski and Olsen, take your positions on the south hill and do the same," ordered Fowler.

The men nodded and disappeared into the trees to their sides.

Fowler turned to the first of the BAR team. "Schneidmiller and Rheingold, take your BAR to the north side of the creek and set up at the base of the hill. Stop anybody from getting into the woods or up this path."

"You got it, Chief," Rheingold replied as he and his teammate turned into the jungle. Fowler then turned to Demby and Fabio. "You two, set up at the base of the south hill and keep an eye on me. Be ready to back me up if I need to breach that building."

"Where you gonna be at, Boss?" Demby asked.

Fowler looked at the canopy-covered stack of driftwood. It was about five yards to the south of the main structure. "I, and Mister Harrison, will be behind that firewood. It'll be close enough to talk to the pirates if they're willing to listen and provide us cover if not."

Like the others, Demby and Fabio seemed to melt into the jungle off to their side. Now alone, Fowler turned an eye to Harrison. "Ready to get your store-bought khakis dirty?" Not waiting for an answer, Fowler stepped out from the cover of the path. It took thirty seconds to cross the stretch of sand and plop down behind the stack of wood. Harrison was right behind him.

Once behind the stacked driftwood, they took time to view the scene around them. To the south, halfway up the tree-covered hill, a white towel hung from a branch. At the base of the hill, where the curved beach ended, he saw the towel marking Demby's and Fabio's position. Fowler turned his attention to the north and looked past the brick buildings. Harrison's eyes followed.

Seeing his men in place, Fowler's eyes settled on the brick building. Fowler, looking at the building from its side, could not see the front of the building but assumed the front was just like the back. Close enough to shoot down anybody stepping from the building, he turned his attention to the two vessels tied up to a dilapidated pier. Fifty foot long and held together by pairs of chipped concrete pilings and rust-eaten iron beams topped with thick wooden planks only two feet above the placid, early morning water, the whole structure would have been better served being torn down and replaced. Tied up to the rickety pilings, with their bows pointed seaward, were their targets.

On the south side, the black hull of the Grim Reaper, with its name painted on the transom in gold lettering, scraped against the concrete pilings. The forty-foot, sleek-hulled vessel had a wide-open deck, interrupted by the low roof of a cabin centered under the boom of a raked mast. The vessel's cockpit, with its spoked helm, occupied the space aft of the cabin, and an upside-down dinghy was lashed to the deck behind it. Built as an Atlantic racer in the 1890s, it enjoyed the limelight for a few years before being replaced with newer racers. After its racing days, the original owner sold it, and the new owner hired a crew to sail it to the Far East. Just after its arrival though, its crew crossed paths with the Lassiter Brothers, and it had been in their hands ever since.

On the north side of the pier, the millionaire's schooner-rigged yacht dwarfed the Grim Reaper in length, height, and ostentatiousness. While it appeared to have all the trappings of a man who traveled in style, they also saw the radio antennae rigged to the top of the main mast. They saw the name Bristol painted across the top of two French windows that pierced the vessel's white-painted transom. Hanging over the transom and from the bent arms of a davit was the vessel's equally well-constructed lifeboat. At one time, the yacht's white hull, polished brass portholes and deck fittings, and raised, teak-trimmed deck structures must have captured the awe of many seamen. However, now the vessel was in dire need of a paint brush and polishing cloth.

"Mister Harrison," Fowler said quietly as he leaned his shotgun against the driftwood and reached for the towel in his belt. "All we have to do now is to wait. Any questions?"

"Chief?" Harrison said as he watched Fowler drape the towel over the top of the wood pile, "why are we marking our positions? So that the pirates will know where we are?"

Fowler did not answer immediately. Instead, he pulled his revolver from its holster, blew nonexistent sand away from the rotating cylinder, and placed it on the towel. Sitting down and leaning his back against the stacked wood, he reached into his shirt pocket and pulled out a pack of Camels, a box of matches, and a package of Juicy Fruit. He tilted the items toward Harrison.

Harrison shook his head.

"Anyway," Fowler said as he placed the gum back into his pocket and jerked the packet of cigarettes up and down with his hand, "when the skipper brings our ship around that corner and puts his guns into action, he'll have to know where we are. Also, if those pirates are going to organize and charge a position, we'll be able to kill them quicker instead of taking potshots at each other from cover. You can use your pistol to shoot at anything you want to, but just be careful where you point that thing."

With that note, Fowler lit a cigarette and said, "You'll never know if this one will be your last."

Harrison leaned against the firewood as a thin smile crossed his face.

Fowler, tossing the match into the sand, looked up at the man's smirk. "Something I said?"

* * *

The dull, yellowish light from the ship's compass lit the undersides of faces of the two men who stood behind them. That same light illuminated the backs of Hillary and Kermit, who stood at the front of the bridge looking through the glass windows. Each holding a cup of coffee they glanced at the chronometer mounted next to the starboard-side door. They saw the island, one hundred yards beyond the railing of the bridge wing, scroll past them. They both turned to look back through the windowpanes and down at the deck gun. In the growing daylight, they saw two men leaning against the breech with one on either side and behind the splinter shields. Two other men sat on a stack of grey-painted crates right behind the gun. Each crate contained six arm-long rounds, with one crate already opened and sitting next to the closed ones. The men smoked or chewed gum while waiting. Slowly, the tree-covered hill at the south end of the island turned from black to grey. Soon, it would turn to green.

"It's been twelve hours since you radioed the flotilla commander and ten hours since he gave his seal of approval, so I guess we're still a go," Kermit said as he sipped his coffee.

Hillary sipped his coffee as well. "Well, I don't think he'll turn us around since he finally found out what happened to one of his destroyers. And he'll be even happier when he sees the after-action report. You know, a ship from his own flotilla eradicating the scourge of the seas and recovering valuable property for the British Crown, all while fighting off a pirate force of over-whelming magnitude. A force not seen since Blackbeard's siege of Charleston. Every letter in that report will warm the cockles of his heart and enhance his service record at the same time."

Hillary turned to face Kermit. "I know you coached the academy's sailing club when you were there, but I hope you didn't mind my assigning the chief to take the two vessels back to Hong Kong. I need you onboard."

"I understand," Kermit replied with a smile. "Although I wouldn't have minded spending a couple of days sailing a millionaire's yacht across the South China Sea, reading a good book while at the helm, sleeping in his bed, and crapping on his toilet. That said, I'm willing to not say anything about the validity of the after-action report as long as I get a chance to see what's left of the wine the pirates hijacked."

Hillary smiled in return. "You're starting to sound like Fowler."

"Is that necessarily a bad thing?" Kermit replied as he reached to put his coffee cup on the ledge. "However, I suggest that once we've captured or killed the pirates and have the vessels in our possession, we take an inventory of everything."

Hillary smiled. "I see your point. I'll bet that Chief Fowler has already thought of a way of squeeze every extra knot he can in order to get to Hong Kong before us."

Kermit looked through the bridge door and at the island and finished his captain's thoughts. "And anything worth a shilling, and is the least bit porta-ble, will end up in a pawn shop or in the hands of a fence in the Wan Chai District before you can say Kowloon."

"Well, we've gotta get them in our possession first," Hillary said as he placed his coffee cup on the ledge in front of him. "And that was only due to the unwavering and fearless efforts by you and your gun crews that we were able to thwart their evil intentions and cause the force to disband. In doing so, most of the pirates fled on other vessels while abandoning the Lassiter Brothers and their most loyal crew members. The same rogues we were dispatched to collect in the first place."

Kermit smiled at his commanding officer. "Have you ever thought of writing novels?"

"I'm working full time just trying to keep this tub afloat, but if you like, go ahead and use it in your writings. I'm only gonna use it for my report."

"I dare say such a report will land you on the bridge of any ship you choose, Skipper."

"Or with you in the next group of officers classing up at Naval Air Station Pensacola," Hillary said. "Just stay away from other officers' wives. But that's in the future. Right now, you've got to extract us from the threat of being overrun by a force of extraordinary magnitude."

"And don't forget, my efforts to protect this ship from a formidable pirate force was only possible by the aggressive actions of Chief Fowler and his landing party."

Hillary smiled as he looked from the gun to the island sliding past the open bridge door. "Get to your men, as I am predicting that when we come into view of the pirates, we'll come up against a fortified blockhouse threatening the lives of my landing party, and British property."

Kermit smiled back. "You mean a brick shithouse?"

CHAPTER 13

"THEY SHOULD BE coming into view any minute now," Fowler said quietly as he flicked away his cigarette butt and turned to peek over the wood pile. The western horizon was quickly filling up with billowing clouds piling up on top of a flat, dark blue sea. "Any questions?"

Harrison answered quietly, too, as he peered over the wood pile. The muzzle of his pistol, right next to his head, sniffed at the air in front of them. "Not a question . . ."

"Thought so," Fowler said with a smirk. "Only ensigns and admirals fail to ask questions, as one thinks he knows everything, and the other should. But you are neither."

Ignoring the chief's comment, Harrison continued, "but a statement. "You're a veteran with years of service out here, so I will give you that, but I find it insulting that you think I should entertain the idea of obeying orders from a Negro. And a gay one at that."

"Why do you think you'll be taking orders from Demby?"

"You just said it: if something happens to you, he'll be in charge."

"I always say that, and for good reason," Fowler answered, "but it sounds like you know something I don't?"

"I'm just saying."

While keeping his eyes on the bay's entrance and the structure in front of them, Fowler retorted, "Only fools see skin color here, Lieutenant Junior Grade Burton D. Harrison, and the only good officers are the ones that are color-blind."

Harrison, hearing the experience in Fowler's voice, remained silent.

"While I was fighting the Spanish here in the Philippines," Fowler continued, "Trooper Demby Brown rode with the Tenth United States Colored Cavalry Regiment. A regiment that helped end the Indian Wars on the Plains, and the same regiment that saved Roosevelt's ass, and the rest of the Rough Riders, from annihilation on Kettle Hill in Cuba. Demby and the rest of his regiment then turned around and supported Roosevelt's charge up San Juan Hill. They then continued to fight across Cuba where Demby distinguished himself at the Battle of Las Guasimas. After mustering out of the Army, he went to Paris to learn how to cook, and guess what? They don't care about skin color in Paris. Since France, he's been trying to find another place where he can settle without segregation, racism, prejudice, and fear of being lynched. The Philippines is that place, and it is where he'll finish out his twenty with the Navy. And with Fabio as part of his new life. I don't care if he's a Negro, gay, or a Cajun. He's the best sailor, fighter, cook, and medicine man I've ever run into, which is the reason why he's my backup. If the pirates charge our position, or if I have to go in and knock down the front door, I prefer none other than that gay Negro and his Filipino lover to have my back. Demby's the man you'll never be."

"Damn you!" Harrison bellowed, loud enough for the men inside the brick shelter to hear. "I'm going to place you on report when we get back to the ship for insolence."

Before Fowler had a chance to tell Harrison to keep his voice down, a ship's deck gun bellowed from seaward. An explosion followed that roar of gunfire. Fowler and Harrison turned to look south just in time to see the trunk of a palm tree crash backward into the tree-covered hill behind it.

"Why the hell is he firing at a palm tree?" Harrison shouted.

"I don't know what you're looking at, but I just saw an armed, sloop-rigged, pirate ship getting dismasted!" Fowler exclaimed as he reached for his shotgun while standing. "And you can whine about gay Negroes later. Right now, we've got a fight on our hands."

Both men turned their attention to the sea. The USS Decatur rounded the southern hill of the island and its sharp bow cleaved through the dark-blue water creating a creamy, frothy wave on either side. They also saw the gun crew on the ship's foredeck reloading the deck gun along with the men on the six-pounders who searched for targets themselves. At the same time, voices erupted from inside the main structure. They also saw the circle of light escape from a porthole on the Grim Reaper and from behind the blue curtains covering the portholes aboard the Bristol as well. As the camp came alive, a white man, wearing a pair of long-john underwear, jumped from the front door of the building and ran toward the weather-beaten wharf.

Fowler raised his shotgun and pushed the stock against his shoulder. He squeezed the trigger, and sand at the man's feet exploded. The man bowled forward, screaming and clutching his bare feet. Fowler pulled back on the pump action of his weapon, while pointing the barrel back at the front of the building. Another man jumped from the door. Fowler pulled the trigger and the weapon roared. Lead shot chewed into brick and the man's torso. The man fell back into the building, screaming. Frantic voices, along with the shrieks of the wounded men, exploded from the open windows of the building.

The deck gun roared again and, a split second later, an eruption of dust, brick and wood shot into the air behind the roof of the main structure. The man that Fowler shot in the feet, half-hobbled, and half-hopped back to the building. Two seconds later, the Lewis guns entered the fray. Quickly rotating their heads, Fowler and Harrison saw lines of tracer bullets from the north- and south-hill firing positions arch toward the two sailing vessels. The bullets chewed into the sterns of both vessels near the helm wheels. At that time, Fowler leaned his shotgun against the driftwood and reached for his revolver.

The back door of the main building opened, and another white man, with a revolver in each hand, jumped from it. Pointing the pistols at the wood pile, he ran toward the forest almost sideways.

Fowler raised his right arm and took aim at the running man. He pulled the trigger, and the huge pistol recoiled in his hand as the slug tore into the side of the man's chest, knocking him over. Fowler lowered his pistol and looked at Harrison with a smile, "It's no sport with a shotgun, but with a pistol you have to lead your target. That's called shooting."

Before Harrison could say anything, a voice from inside the building bellowed out through one of the back windows. "Bloody hell, mate!"

But that voice was interrupted by the roar of the ship's deck gun and the crack of two six-pounders, which was followed by the spouts of water erupting just in front of the decrepit pier.

"I'm listening!" Fowler yelled.

After a moment of raised voices escaping the building, the man spoke again. "Any reason why that ship had to bugger up the shitter?"

"My captain was just trying to get your attention!"

"By blowing up a shitter! What kind of pagan is he? And who the fuck are you?"

"Don't worry about my skipper. I'm the man you have to worry about. I'm going to kill you right here. Or I will escort you to the gallows. It makes no difference, but it's too early in the morning for me to drag your carcass across that sand. And I haven't had my coffee yet. So, it would be much easier on your skull for you walk across this beach on your own accord. How this morning ends is up to you!"

"Bugger off, mate!" The voice yelled, but then stopped for a second before adding. "Oy, do I know you?"

Fowler looked out of the corner of his eye. He saw Harrison narrow his eyes. "Yes!"

After a few seconds of muted argument, the man spoke again. "Fowler? Is that you!"

"Hello, Otter," Fowler responded. "Haven't talked to you since the last time we played cards. How's Digby?"

"You cheeky bastard! You just blew his foot off! Why'd you do that?"

"Because he was running!"

"You bastard! You don't know how lucky you were to survive that last night we played cards. To leave the Wan Chai District on your own feet!"

"There was no luck in me surviving that night, but if you want to survive today, throw out your weapons!"

Otter Lassiter went silent again, but the mumble of voices continued. In the meantime, the ship's guns found other targets, including a rock sticking out of the sand at the north end of the beach where it joined the slope of the north hill.

"You're not going to tell me you know those men?" Harrison asked as he peered over the driftwood.

"Weren't you just listening? Christ! No wonder you're an officer!" Fowler responded scornfully. "Anyway, I was on liberty, and not in uniform. And it was an illegal joint, which means I wasn't there."

Shaking his head, Harrison watched as the ship's deck gun fired another round. The round exploded against a tree at the north end of the beach. "Are they going to make a break for it?"

Chief Fowler, looking at the bloody footsteps in the sand in front of the building, was about to answer but was interrupted. They heard the engines on each of the two yachts fire up. The exhaust bubbled out of the overboard discharge pipes along with seawater that cooled the engines. With his eyes on the vessels, Fowler answered. "There's at least one man on each vessel, and they've been able to fire up the engines without exposing themselves to the Lewis guns. There's two badly wounded men inside the building. They also know that there are at least three gun positions along with my ship. They could charge our position since we have only a revolver and a shotgun, then make for the vessels and fight their way out of the bay. They'll convince the wounded men to stay behind to offer a distraction with gunfire while the rest of them run for it, firing their weapons as they do."

As Harrison returned his attention to the main building, a shot rang out and a piece of driftwood next to his head exploded. Harrison fell back, dropping his pistol at the same time.

Fowler looked down at the officer. "Lesson Number Five: never drop your weapon in the sand! Pick it up as they're breaking for it!"

Harrison pushed himself back to his knees and stood while recovering his pistol. In doing so, Harrison felt liquid running down the side of his head and onto his khaki-clad shoulder. Harrison reached up to touch it, and when he looked at his hand, he saw blood.

"Congratulations! Looks like you just earned a Purple Heart!"

The officer ignored the chief and waited. A few seconds later, just as Fowler predicted, men spilled from the front door, firing wildly in all directions. Fowler and Harrison raised their weapons and were about to fire but stopped as blasts of machine guns erupted from behind them. They turned to look over their shoulders. As they did, they saw something incredible.

CHAPTER 14

THE FLOORBOARDS CREAKED, and the disjointed sounds of rusty bedsprings created an irritating melody that serenaded the slow conversation going on in the squalid room below. Sawdust knocked from the floorboards above filtered through the thick layer of tobacco smoke before settling on eight men and the table they sat around. The sooty flame of a brass lamp on the table flickered as particles landed in the oily flame.

"I do appreciate your inviting me to a second meeting with your cell, Comrade Captain Borodin, and as a proper Frenchman and devout communist, I would never show any ingratitude, but wasn't it possible to have our meeting elsewhere?"

The man who voiced his concerns spoke English while holding an upside-down aperitif glass above his left shoulder. He waited for a bent-over Chinese man with mutated hands to shuffle his way around the table as he filled everyone's glasses from a bottle. "The last time we met here, it was some drunk's piss leaking on us, not sawdust."

The complainer wore a light grey suit like the man he addressed but was not as well kept. The dark circles under his eyes, scuffed black leather shoes, and cigarette ash caked into the thighs of his trousers, revealed his night along Shanghai's fashionable Hengshan Street. He looked at his wristwatch as smoke from a cigarette swirled past his face. "It's six a.m. I know a place over in the French Concession. It's just now opening for breakfast. We can beat the drunks and office workers if we hurry."

The floorboards above ceased the creaking, but it was replaced by the muffled sound of boot heels thumping against the floorboards and coinage hitting the floorboards.

The man addressed as Comrade Captain Borodin sat opposite the complaining man. He leaned back in his wicker chair as he picked up his aperitif. He was one of two men who was not smoking. He took a second to appreciate the fortified white wine as best he could in the dim lighting before answering. His lips parted, but he was interrupted by the vibrating blare of a ship's foghorn, which penetrated the backroom walls. Outside those walls, a ship followed the black waters of the slow-moving Huangpu River, which divided Shanghai into two parts. Above them the boots stomped out of the room.

"Well, Henri," Comrade Captain Borodin replied slowly. "As a proper Russian, and communist myself, I would never insult my guests as I, too, can think of other places that I would rather be at this time of morning. And yes, this fine bottle you brought to this meeting should be immediately followed with hot coffee and warm pastries with good butter and sweet jam, but . . ." He paused as he leaned toward the flickering light from the oil lamp. "None of us have the luxury of making such choices this morning. I was only awakened an hour ago myself, and to a specific piece of news."

Henri, still holding the glass above his shoulder, now right side up as the Chinese man turned the bottle to fill the Frenchman's glass, blurted, "Is it the Romanov Sapphire?"

Borodin narrowed his eyes at Henri.

The Frenchman saw the silent rebuke and coughed while turning his attention to the now-filled aperitif glass as he brought it before his eyes. "I'm only saying this because of rumors that started floating around Shanghai since yesterday."

The other men in the room leaned toward the flickering oily flame. At the same time, the Chinese man, having filled the last glass, leaned forward to place the half-empty bottle of sherry on the table. After doing so, he shuffled to a wooden door just as beaten up as the rest of the room. Reaching it, his shaky weather-beaten hand, missing two fingers, pushed down on the patina-stained brass door lever.

Comrade Captain Borodin watched the old man pull the door closed behind him. When shut, Borodin glanced at the line of light at the bottom of the door and saw the shadows of non-moving feet. He pursed his lips as he looked up at the men around the table. "I received an official communication, and it seems that we have answers to mysteries that started to trouble us a week ago and that are confirming rumors we started hearing yesterday."

The men remained silent as they all looked over the lamp and into his eyes.

"While Countess Zeta Tolstoy's parents continue to live in that run-down flat off Huashan Road, and her mother continues to lift her chemise for any white man with a pound note crumpled up in his pocket, their daughter disappeared last Monday. A disappearance that coincided with the timely vanishing of Major Utkin, the once again, sudden arrival, then departure of Captain Vostok and his White Russian scum, the submarine they stole from the People's and Workers' Navy a year ago, and an American they collected at the last minute."

Another man, one sitting next to Henri and the only other man who did not smoke, interjected, "I have argued we could have taken that submarine at any time, especially two weeks ago when they showed up again on the other side of the Huangpu River with only a third of its crew. A submarine manned by a dozen White Russian scum is much easier to take than a submarine crewed with thirty-three of those bastards. I could have hired Chinese street rabble to board that submarine, dispose of its captain and crew. Given the opportunity to cut off a European's testicles and stow them in his own mouth while he bleeds out, the lowest street soldiers from the Green Gang would've done it without pay."

The man who spoke wore clean dungarees and a sun-faded captain's hat perched jauntily on his head. His clothing revealed his occupation and the emblem on the crumpled captain's hat distinguished him as a ship's captain for the Mersk-Alba Shipping Company, a Russian-owned company operating beat-up steamers along the Chinese coast. While the clothing revealed his occupation and cap noted his rank, his build and sunburnt forearms denoted his ability.

"I agree, Comrade Captain Lagos," Borodin said while lifting his glass. "The opportunity for a Chinaman to castrate a European with a rusty razor and to turn his scrotum into a coin purse would be good sport, even if those testicles were attached to a White Russian traitor, a Red Russian patriot, or a French tourist. That said, while Vostok's men are submariners and not fighters, and such a takeover could have been easy, I argue that such a preemptive move would have been foolish. Vostok, his men, and the submarine, disappear for weeks, only to reappear intermittently here or other Oriental port cities to purchase all manner of oddities like foodstuffs, petrol, tools, machine parts, metal stock, and even bolts of silk, spools of silk thread, and bicycle parts."

"He is off his nut," stated a man holding a pipe. "One of my contacts said his men bought a dozen percussion cap firing locks from his antique store. The last time they were used was when they were mounted to rifled Enfield muskets while putting down the mutiny in India seventy years ago."

"Yes," Borodin continued, "and while paying occasionally in English pounds or American dollars, they usually pay with small bars of gold or silver, uncut gems, or pearls. Which is why many assume that the White Russian submariners happened upon a cached wealth of gems including the Romanov Sapphire. A wealth that we've been looking for since the start of the Revolution and one that belongs to the workers and peoples of Soviet Russia. The question has been about that source of revenue, and that question is why I called this meeting. For the last few months, there has been speculation as to their whereabouts and purpose, and every time a discussion about the Romanov Sapphire and a cache of diamonds crops up. That wealth must be held by Bolshevist Russia and not scum who will use it against their own culture. To take that submarine and its crew before we've ascertained the location of the wealth would have been foolish. At least up until yesterday."

"Forgive me," Henri spoke up. "I have been informed of the countess and her family and the story of the diamonds since my arrival from Paris, but please explain to me the significance of Captain Vostok, Major Utkin, and the

American to this saga."

"Very well," Borodin said as he picked up his wine glass again. "However, it would be more fitting Comrade Captain Lagos inform you of Captain Vostok."

Captain Lagos answered as he reached for his wine. "We started out as classmates at the Kuznetsov Naval Academy in 1880, and often served together since then. Even at the Battle of Port Arthur, when the Japanese attacked our fleet in 1904, both of us were wounded aboard the Pallada. After the war ended in 1905, I remained with the Baltic Fleet, becoming the captain of a cruiser. Meantime, Vostok took on new interests. The newly invented airplane and submarine technologies seemed to command his every thought. Even hornets and wasps competed for that same thought space. Eventually though, I started to become dissatisfied with the Tsarist government. When the Revolution broke out in 1917, I had no choice and have had no regrets."

Captain Lagos paused to sip his wine before continuing.

"I thought Vostok held the same ideals as he, too, was part of the Revolution from the beginning. However, about a year ago, he seemed to have a change of heart, gathered a crew of White Russian ex-submariners and engineers, absconded with an American-built submarine purchased by the Tsar's navy before the war and was sitting in Vladivostok awaiting repairs. They even managed to kill comrades aboard the submarine. Since then, he and his crew have been men without a country wandering the Western Pacific with no real mission."

"Seems a strange ending for man so promising to socialism," Henri said as he emptied his glass and reached for the bottle. "What of Utkin? How does he fit into this scene?"

Borodin spoke. "Utkin, like Comrade Captain Lagos here and Vostok, though much younger, started out in the service of the Tsar himself, but with the Army. He had some education and enlisted in 1900 as a cadet. And he, too, fought in the Sino-Russian War with an artillery unit and fought with distinction and was wounded in battle in 1904. That action resulted in a facial scar, which he wears with pride. He completed his service as an officer and returned to the Crimea where he reentered university engineering studies. However, he was drawn to another way of life by becoming a police officer."

Adjusting the seam of his trouser leg, Borodin continued.

"From what I understand, he was quite the street detective in Sevasto-pol, and when the War broke out in 1914, he was recalled. By 1916, before the Revolution, he found himself in an armored vehicle development group and was doing quite well, but the Revolution came along in 1917, where he became a member of the Bolshevik Secret State Police or Cheka. And, just like Vostok, he, too, seemed to have a change of heart, and a bit more than a year ago disappeared for a brief time, but only to reappear with a cadre of hardened killers. At some point, he teamed up with Vostok, and they have been White Russian treacherous filth ever since."

Borodin stopped as he leaned for the wine bottle. "Now, about the American."

While waiting for Borodin, they paused to sip their wine, knock the ashes off a cigarette, or tap an upside-down pipe bowl against a table leg. As Borodin placed the bottle back on the table, he looked at the crack of the door. The shadow of feet was still there. With a pleased smile Borodin continued.

"Sergeant Thomas Dooley, of Brooklyn, New York, fought in Russia with the United States Army 339th Infantry Regiment where he distinguished himself in battle on more than one occasion. But since then, he made his way to Shanghai and ended up in the employ of a Chinese warlord along with White Russian mercenaries where he was able to build creditable references. But when Utkin found him, Dooley was a discouraged mercenary with just over fifty American dollars to his name and, like so many others idling about the streets of Shanghai, looking to earn enough money to book passage anywhere else. Why they recruited him for this mission is beyond us. However, his presence is irrelevant to this meeting. We need to get back to the reason why we are in this room. It seems that the whole clutch of them have reappeared. Around midnight the night before last. At an estate outside of Vladivostok, where they were successful in rescuing the countess's cousin and a wealth of precious stones, including the Romanov Sapphire. The same precious stones that we have been trying to put back into the coffers of the People's and Workers' Party of the Soviet Union for two years."

Captain Lagos interrupted by asking, "How do you know that they were able to escape with a wealth of gems?"

"A group of submarine raiders landed by boat on a beach below the estate, and that is where they made their escape," Borodin answered. "Survivors found diamonds strewn about the beach."

The men either leaned back in their chairs, inhaled on a cigarette, or quaffed their wine as they absorbed the information.

Borodin continued, "They attacked the estate and killed many comrades, but the survivors were able to identify Utkin and Vostok, along with a man wearing an American army uniform and carrying a Thompson submachine gun. They radioed headquarters in Vladivostok who, in turn, transmitted a message to Moscow, which ended up in our hands."

"Do you think they will come back here to Shanghai?" Henri asked.

"Possibly," Borodin answered while fingering the stem of his glass, "as there are few marketplaces for such a cache. And hanging onto such wealth would be useless. Gentlemen, I suspect they will arrive here in Shanghai within days to sell their gains. If not here, then Hong Kong, Macau, Saigon, Manila, or Taipei. Cells in those cities have been made aware of the submarine raiders actions and have been tasked to keep alert to any arrival of the submarine and to capture the submarine before diamonds start flooding the markets or traded for a whore's attention. Such is our task. I would ask that when we leave this room, you go about your daily business but keep your eyes and ears open to any rumors of Vostok's impending arrival, and discreetly inquire about any potential of the diamonds arriving here. If you do hear of any information, you may use the same drop-off for any communications."

Borodin paused for a second to look at the men around the table, stopping with Captain Lagos. "However, it appears that I have been given other commitments for the near future. If I do not respond to your submissions immediately, just continue to gather information and follow up on any rumors floating about. Wait for my return."

The men all looked at Borodin over the rims of their aperitif glasses, while tobacco smoke hovered above their heads. He responded to their looks.

"Remember that Utkin and Vostok and their White Russian scum followers cannot be allowed to keep such a vast hoard of wealth in their possession. It must be in the hands of the people and workers of Soviet Russia."

To signal the end of the meeting, Borodin stood, pushing his chair back with his legs and bringing the glass to his lips. The others followed suit. As the first of the men stepped for the door, Borodin looked down at the bottom of the door. The shadow of the feet was gone. Borodin smiled as he watched one of the men push down on the brass lever.

Borodin was the last to leave the dingy room and into a hallway just as grimy and beaten as the room they left. The hallway led past a staircase and to the building's front door. The paint was faded and scarred with patches of missing plaster. Narrow wooden doors, just as traumatized as the plastered walls, stood like sentries marking his departure. At the bottom of the staircase, and in front of the door, the aged Chinese man who served the wine to the men in the room now stood hunched over holding a bucket of sawdust in one mutilated hand while sprinkling sawdust on a puddle of vomit with the other. The man looked up, offering a brown-stained, gapped-tooth smile.

The Russian did not return the smile. Instead, Borodin continued to the door. A few seconds later, he joined the morning pedestrian traffic and walked, but only for a few yards. He stopped and pretended to be interested in a curio in a storefront window. He pretended to be interested in the curio just long enough to see the broken-down Chinese man who poured their wine exit the four-story, redbrick whorehouse. Inside the building, he was an aged and crippled Asian. Now, he ran from that door, spry as a game telegraph boy.

Borodin smiled as he turned to continue his walk down the street through the throng of pedestrians, street hawkers, and street orphans busily starting the day. Borodin was well known in this part of town, so the orphans and ware hawkers did not harass him for coins or purchases.

He approached a red-and-black rickshaw parked at the next intersection. He walked up to the vehicle from behind and saw the puller sitting on a street curb in front of the rickshaw pinching a hand-rolled Chinese fag between his fingers. Seeing Borodin out of the corner of his eye, the rickshaw puller stood and flicked the butt into the street. A street urchin swooped in and snatched up the butt before it hit the brick pavement.

Borodin did not step up into the vehicle. Instead, he fished into his pants pocket for a coin. Throwing it to the rickshaw puller, he said something to the man in Mandarin. In turn, the man snatched up the flying coin as his face broke into a broad smile. Borodin watched him turn and meld into the teeming pedestrian traffic.

"I see our Chinese server ran down the street spry as a gamecock."

"Which means, Issak," Borodin said as he turned to face the speaker, "that, within an hour, the leader of the Green Gang will know about the prospect of a wealth, now in the hands of White Russian trash, landing in his territory. A wealth that he would not want to slip between his fingers and go to a rival gangster."

"Or the coffers of a sovereign government, or the vaults of some banker."

"Aren't all three the same?" Captain Lagos said with a wry smile.

Borodin returned the wry smile with one of his own. "Yes, they are, Issak, and all the agents of rogue gangs, western governments, corporate gangsters, bankers, financiers, and mercenary groups from here to Saigon will all know about the vast wealth in the hands of country-less White Russians leaving the Red Russians poor and destitute with no ability to mount an international socialist movement."

"How long do you think it will take before we start seeing the results of our efforts?"

Borodin looked at his wristwatch before answering. "I think our friend has just now contacted a man of means and has his broken palm out for coin. At this same time, I believe Friend Henri has already stumbled into a café to place his hand on some tart's knee and brag about being a detective on the hunt for the Romanov Sapphire."

Captain Lagos scoffed. "That damned Frog. He's not a true communist. He's a foolish ideologue seeking pompous glory."

"I agree," Borodin said as he saw his rickshaw puller return through the pedestrians with a newspaper in one hand and a packet of Chesterfields in the other, "as the French communists are nothing but womanizing idealists, but never discount the ability to mold idealists into any tool or weapon you need. One should always keep useful idiots close. Anyway, I have a meeting scheduled at Foucault's. Please meet us there at 11:00 a.m."

"Are you meeting a brother, sister, a close or distant friend, or an acquaintance? And does that meeting have anything to do with our concern in the Philippines?"

"Let us just say a friend for now," Borodin answered, "and yes, but indirectly."

CHAPTER 15

ILLARY SAT IN his chair on the bridge wing, enjoying the early tropical morning along with more coffee. He looked at the billowing silvery clouds piling up on the western grey-blue horizon. Turning his attention to the three-inch gun crew he watched two men remove binding clamps from a second ammunition box as a third man inserted the last arm-long shell from the first case into the open breech of the deck gun. Five spent brass casings rested inside the first ammunition box. The fourth man stood on the other side of the breech with the lanyard looped around one hand, his other hand on a hand crank, and an eye pressed against the rear sight. Kermit stood next to that man holding a pair of binoculars against his eyes. Both men panned the shoreline seeking another target. Suddenly, their attention was interrupted by automatic gun fire, but not from the island. Like the men on the deck gun, Hillary turned his head to look aft and saw a line of incendiary bullets slamming into the ship's fantail, which threw chunks of paint and rust into the air.

Dumping the cup over the side and jumping out of the chair, Hillary hurled himself through the open door and inside the bridge. He looked at his bridge watch who now wore shocked looks on their faces while waiting for their next order. They both cried out simultaneously, "What the hell was that?"

"I don't know, but we've got company!"

Hillary stood and peered around the corner of the door frame looking aft at the source of the machine-gun fire.

"What do you see, Skipper?" the helmsman asked.

Hillary answered by bringing his head back inside the bridge. "Schmidt! Turn to port until you see our attacker! Krivor, maintain our speed!"

Both men obeyed their orders as Hillary stepped back out onto the bridge wing and yelled down at Kermit. "Kermit! Pump as many shells into that ship as fast as you can! Have the six-pounder crews do the same! Our asses are on the line!"

As Schmidt spun the helm wheel, everybody watched as the bow of the destroyer followed suit. While still receiving bursts of machine gun fire, the attacker came into view. Dead ahead of them was a ship, which rounded the southern end of the island just as the Decatur had done only minutes ago, and everybody on the bridge or on the deck saw a ship without any navigational lighting. About three hundred yards to the south, they could see that the ship was like any other beat-up tramp steamer they had seen plying these waters for years. It had a high forecastle with a small crane mounted to the deck of the forecastle. At the other end of the ship, the two-story, white-painted super-structure topped with the bridge.

On the side of the bridge superstructure, visible to the Americans, was a lifeboat cradled in the arms of a davit. In the center of the ship and taking up most of its length, was the main deck, where cargo that could not be lowered into the confines of the cargo hull could be stacked up for shipment. In this case, though, there was no cargo stacked on the deck. The red-painted hull was cut with severe lines of rust much like the suture lines holding the human cranium together. However, what Hillary did not see was a name painted on the bow nor a flag flying from the stern or the mast above the bridge. But he did see three machine gun positions: one on the forecastle, one above the bridge, and one on the main deck, and they were all busy firing bursts at his ship.

The men aboard the Decatur watched from their protected hiding spots as white water started to pile up against the bluff bow of the mystery ship. The vessel was increasing to a rate of speed unheard of for these steamers. Suddenly, the window on the portside of the bridge blew out, and bullets punched through the aft bulkhead of the bridge. Schmidt and Krivor ducked but still worked the helm and the EOT.

"Damn it!" Hillary yelled as he ducked as well. After that burst of gunfire, he stood and looked over the bridge wing's railing. The men on the deck gun were gone. "Kermit!"

"We're down here!"

Hillary leaned over the railing further and saw that his men took shelter under him and along the starboard side of the superstructure next to the starboard six-pounder gun crew. "You guys okay?"

"We're fine. Just not used to getting shot at by a mystery ship. I hope you don't mind?"

"You're taking care of your men, and that's your job. When you can, you've got plenty of rounds available, so make them count. I'll get the black gang to break out more ammunition."

He didn't wait for Kermit's reply but stepped into the bridge as he thought to himself, *I sure could use those Lewis guns right now.*

Hillary uncapped a brass tube, letting the rubber cap dangle by its lanyard as he placed his mouth against the oval opening and blew forcibly into it. He pulled away his mouth and listened for a second.

"What the hell's going on up there?" a muffled voice answered.

As Hillary heard the distant Lewis guns from the beach joining in on the fight, he responded. "Mack! We're being attacked by a ship that looks like it can match us in speed! Be ready to answer any bells at a second's notice! Also, send four men to the ship's magazine to break out more ammo for the deck gun, and have four more go to the armory! Have them grab whatever small arms are left and report to the bridge! Tell them to keep their heads down!"

Hillary replaced the cap into the voice tube without waiting for a reply and turned his attention to the attacking ship, which changed course and tactic. It now concentrated its fire on the south hill of the island, sending three lines of incendiary bullets arching toward the two white towels hanging from tree branches. Neither gunner ashore responded in kind. Hillary prayed for the lives of his men as he watched in amazement as the mystery ship, with an unheard of-rate of speed, inserted itself between the Decatur and the beach and continued firing at the beach.

Hillary, watching the fight, started to recognize the machine guns. The automatics were fat-barreled, water-cooled, swivel-mounted Maxims. Each automatic was manned by a gunner who stood behind the weapons and another man who stood to the side and helped feed belted ammunition into the ravenous weapons from a box of ammunition at their feet. Aside from the machine-gun teams, Hillary saw a man standing on the bridge looking back at him though the bridge windows. From what Hillary could see, the man, just like the others visible to him, was a white man wearing civilian clothes. Suddenly, he heard Kermit's deck gun fire a round as well as both six-pounders on the starboard side and watched as black dots appeared in the white-painted steel under the ship's bridge and under the lifeboat on that side. He looked back at the man standing on the bridge. Smoke billowed inside the bridge, and men inside reacted. The man watching, though, did not seem to be perturbed.

That's gotta smart, Hillary said to himself as he saw the men manning two of those machine guns swing their weapons back toward the Decatur. Hillary ducked as he heard the bullets slam into the steel of his ship.

The deck gun fired again, and Hillary saw the round punch through the side of the hull under the bridge and into what should have been an engineering space. Smoke immediately poured out of that hole. The man standing on the bridge, though, seemed more interested running his ship and the crewed automatics. Two of his machine guns kept their fire going into the torpedo boat destroyer's deck guns while the weapon on the forecastle continued firing wildly at the shore as the speeding mystery ship followed the curve of the beach.

As the ship approached the north end of the curved beach, Hillary looked at the rounded stern of the mystery ship. He saw no name painted across the stern, but he did see smoke stream out open portholes and out of the holes created by his guns.

Just then, four engineers carrying rifles and cartridge belts appeared at the top of the stairs leading up to the portside bridge wing.

"Thanks, men," Hillary said, "but a bit too late."

"What the hell was all that about, sir?" One of them asked.

Hillary replied as he saw the last part of the ship vanish behind the island, leaving a boiling wake to mark its departure. "I don't know Schwartz, but it looks like they're gone for now. Strap on those cartridge belts and shoulder those rifles. We're going to nose up to the end of the dock and put you ashore."

"Aye, aye, sir," Schwartz replied as he turned to the others. "Alright guys. You heard the skipper!"

Hillary leaned over the rail of the bridge wing, "Kermit, secure your guns and ammunition, but have your men remain on the guns in case that ship returns. We're gonna nudge up against the wharf, so get your men to sling a Jacob's ladder over the bow."

"Yes, sir," Kermit replied as he lifted the strap of the binoculars from around his neck and over his head, hanging them from the gun sight.

Hillary stepped back into the bridge. "Schmidt, I'll take the helm. Go aft and standby the stern anchor. Drop it when we're about twenty yards out from the wharf."

The man saluted as Hillary replaced him on the helm. Between Hillary and Krivor, the men expertly brought the bow of the ship against the dilapidated structure. As they did, Hillary, like everybody else, saw his landing party, with weapons held at the ready, leave the safety of trees and head toward several bodies sprawled across the beach. The bodies, laying in different configurations, wore a variety of clothing, but his eyes fell on one body in particular that lay on the sand and next to the pile of driftwood. It wore a uniform. His heart sank.

* * *

Minutes later, with the stern anchor deployed, the bow of the torpedo-boat destroyer was held against the end of the wharf with mooring lines secured to the concrete pilings. A rope ladder dangled from the bow. At the other end of the decrepit wharf, Hillary stood on the beach with Kermit next to him, while speaking to the senior survivor of the landing party. Fabio and Demby stood next to the senior survivor. They held their head gear in their hands, along with their weapons. Hillary, although looking at the man directly in front of him, saw that Fabio was on the verge of crying. Next to him, Demby, rubbing the brim of his Stetson in his hand with his fingers as if it were rosary beads, also looked distraught. The rest of the landing party and the newly arrived engineers busied themselves by collecting sidearms, wine and liquor bottles, and wrapping bullet-ravaged bodies in the navy blankets each pair carried. Off to the side of the activity, two white men wearing rags for clothing and with sand-coated, foppish hair, sat with their hands bound by rope.

"Now tell me how Harrison earned his Purple Heart the hard way?"

"Well, sir," Fowler started to say as he hung his helmet by its chinstrap from his holstered revolver, "we had 'em just where we wanted them. Two wounded pirates were providing cover fire from inside the building, and the rest of them made for the boats while shooting. Suddenly that mystery ship swooped in and mucked up the works."

"Was the ship shooting to help the pirates?" Hillary asked as he reviewed his men.

"Sorta, sir," Fowler replied as he wiped his forehead with the back of his hand. "They shot at our towels, and anything else they felt like. It was as if the gunners on the ship were trying to create confusion and distraction. I don't think they were here to help the pirates directly. Otherwise, they could have brought the ship against the wharf or beached it to let the pirates jump aboard. They had the firepower and horsepower to do both. Any idea who they were?"

"I agree," Hillary chimed in as he turned his attention to the north end of the beach, "as it appeared that way to me and, no, I have no idea who they were. No flag flying from the mast, no name painted on the bow or stern. And I have no idea how a beat-up island tramp streamer was able to swoop in like Eddie Rickenbacker behind the wheel of a Packard Speedster. Anyway, it doesn't look like they're coming back. So again, what happened to Harrison?"

Hillary noticed the pause and turned his attention from the north end of the beach to Fowler, who stood straighter. Hillary also looked out of the corner of his eye and saw tears leaking from Fabio's eyes. Demby looked at the sand, while crushing his Stetson in his huge hand.

Fowler spoke up. "Well sir, I think Harrison was just a bit too eager to get some girl bait on his chest. As soon as the pirates broke for cover, Harrison stood and exposed himself. He was about to shoot at the pirates when one of the gunners from that mystery ship took a particular interest in him. He must've taken at least a dozen rounds through his chest."

Hillary nodded slightly as he heard Fowler's explanation. He also noticed the fact that Fowler was splattered with blood. "Is that Harrison's blood?"

"Yes, sir," Fowler answered haltingly.

"That's pretty good shooting with a Maxim from that distance. From a speeding ship. Harrison was supposed to be on your ass the whole time. Yet, you don't have a scratch." After pausing for a second, he turned to Demby. "Wardroom Steward Demby Julius Brown, do you have something to say?"

The huge black man, with the BAR in one hand and his crumpled Stetson in the other, looked up from the sand. His lips parted, but Fowler interrupted him.

"Sir, it's just like I said," Fowler said firmly while looking directly at Demby."

Hillary kept his eyes on Demby. He also saw Fabio make a cross with his hand. "Chief Ernst Fowler, since I've known you, I can count the number of times you have referred to me as sir, and each time you did you were on the wrong side of not guilty. I believe this last 'sir' makes Number Nine. Wardroom Steward Demby, I'm still waiting."

Finally, Demby spoke. "I'm sorry, sar. I didn't mean to kill the officer."

"Demby, I told you to keep your fat mouth shut!"

"Chief Petty Officer Fowler!" Hillary bellowed. "Let the man finish!"

Fowler tightened his lips but kept his eyes on Demby.

"Sar, I didn't mean to kill the officer," Demby pleaded again, "but he was going to shoot the boss in the back of the head, and I couldn't let that happen."

With disbelief, Hillary slowly restated what he had just been told. "You mean to tell me that you shot and killed a uniformed officer of the United States Navy because he was about to shoot and kill a uniformed noncommissioned officer of the United States Navy?"

"Yes, sar," Demby replied as he looked at his captain. "That's the God-honest truth, sar! The boss stood to use his shotgun against the pirates right when that mystery ship was shooting at our positions on the hill. But I was obeying my orders, and they was to keep an eye on the boss and the officer. Fabio and I took cover behind a tree, and we watched as the officer stand like he had the debil inside him. He stood behind the boss and put his pistol to the back of the boss's head. I unloaded my BAR into him."

Hillary looked at Fabio. "Is that what happened, Fabio?"

"Yes, sir!" Fabio replied with a firm nod. "Yes, sir!"

Hillary, taking a breath, saw the fear on Fabio's face. He thought for a long second and was about to speak up when the ship's radio senior operator, Petty Officer "Sparks" Bassinger, yelled something as he climbed down the rope ladder. He held a slip of paper in his hand as he did. Everybody standing at the beach end of the wharf watched as Sparks quickly stepped down the wharf toward them. As he passed the millionaire's yacht, the radio operator slowed long enough to appreciate the yacht, specifically the main mast, along the way. Pulling up next to the officers, he spoke. "Skipper, we just got a message from the flotilla commander."

The sailor, a tow-headed young man with wire-rimmed spectacles offered the message to his captain.

Hillary accepted the piece of thin paper and read the words. After a few seconds, he nodded to himself before looking at his men. "Sparks, draft a reply. Have it go like this: 'Mission complete. Have two surviving pirates in custody, along with two vessels of British registry. Will return both pirates and vessels to Hong Kong as planned. Pirates suffered eight men dead, including both Lassiter Brothers. Their bodies will also be returned to Hong Kong aboard

USS Decatur. We were also attacked by a steam-powered vessel armed with three Maxim machine guns during the landing and suffered minor damages along with one fatality. Regret to report the death of Lieutenant Junior Grade Burton D. Harrison, who died of injuries received during the combat operation. Will take body and personal belongings to Hong Kong for transfer to the American Consulate, along with an official after-action report.' Got it?"

"Got it," Sparks replied.

"Good. Type it up and have it waiting for my review. Also, look at the yacht's Marconi. Being a millionaire businessman, I can imagine he's got quite a rig."

"Yes, sir," Sparks replied as he turned to obey his orders.

Hillary returned his attention to the three men in front of him, who seemed to have relaxed slightly. "It looks like you understand. Harrison died because of injuries suffered during a combat operation, and that is what will go in the official record. Got it?"

Both Demby and Fabio cracked smiles and Fowler reached into his shirt pocket. "What's next, Skipper?"

Hillary reached out to pull two cigarettes from Fowler's sweat-soaked pack. Passing one to Kermit, he put the other one between his lips while answering. "We will follow our plan but with a couple of changes the flotilla commander doesn't need to know about just yet. Demby and Fabio, place your weapons and gear aboard the Grim Reaper and conduct an inventory of stores. Then go aboard the Decatur to get cleaned up and grab whatever you'll need for a four-day transit to Hong Kong. You'll be feeding four men. And draw more ammo."

"Yes sir," the two men replied as they hurriedly saluted their commanding officer. They stepped past him and toward the Grim Reaper.

Hillary looked over his shoulder to watch them leave before returning his looks at the chief petty officer. Fowler, pinching an unlit cigarette between his lips, held out a lit match. The officers bent forward to light their cigarettes. After lighting their Camels, Hillary issued more orders. "Chief, have one Lewis gun team place their weapons and gear on the racer before they get a change of clothing and toothbrushes as well. Have the other half of the landing party do the same and board the Brit's yacht. Have everybody draw more ammo. They can keep their BAR and small arms but have them take their Lewis gun and ammunition back to the bridge."

Kermit exhaled before he spoke. "All sounds good, but the maximum speed between us and the two sailing vessels is quite different, and we're going to have some badly chopped-up bodies onboard with no morgue facilities. And there's that mystery ship we still have to worry about."

"You're correct, Kermit. A slow transit to Hong Kong without morgue facilities would be quite unhealthy for all concerned. And that mystery ship could show up at any time, so having a Lewis gun to back up our deck gun and six-pounders would help." Hillary paused and turned to look at the British yacht. "While we'll have to speed ahead, which means I'll have to listen to Mack's wrath, the two sailing vessels can stay together. The Grim Reaper, having a BAR and Lewis gun along with small arms, will provide quite a base of supportive fire for the yacht. On the other hand, we can dismount one of the six-pounders and, along with three cases of ammunition, have it transferred to the foredeck of the yacht. I don't think the Brits would mind a few holes drilled through that teak deck. Especially since we've already put a few bullet holes into the stern."

Kermit nodded as he inhaled on the cigarette. "While our six-pounders pack a helluva punch, the one bolted to that foredeck will only be as useful as its crew. I've drilled Seaman Schnabel and Petty Officer Molatoff on the six-pounders before. They're able to fire and reload thirty rounds a minute and all with well-placed shots. I'd recommend them to board the yacht."

"I guess that sounds like the plan then," Hillary replied.

"Sir, you still want me to sail those vessels to Hong Kong?"

Hillary spit a piece of tobacco from his lips before answering. "First, Demby's out of the woods for shooting Harrison, so stop the 'sir' crap. Second, you and I need to figure out why Harrison tried to kill you. Also, with the potential of further combat, I can't leave my men and two recovered pieces of valuable property in the hands of an enlisted man. Mister Kermit has expressed interest in having the opportunity to take a crap on a millionaire's yacht, so he can sail them back. Agree?"

Kermit and Fowler nodded slightly, but Fowler had a questioning look on his face while Kermit took on a pleased smile as he turned his head to look at the masts of the two sailing vessels.

Hillary looked at both men but spoke to Kermit first. "Kermit?"

The officer exhaled with a smile on his lips. "Oh, nothing, Skipper. It's just that I brought along some reading material for our patrol and had planned on starting with Don Quixote's *Man of La Mancha*. Now, it looks like I'll have the proper setting to enjoy such a classic work."

Hillary nodded in agreement. "Excellent choice to idle away a couple days at sea."

"Skipper," Fowler said interjecting himself. "Are you sure the Navy stopped awarding prize money? I'm only asking because retirement's comin' up, and I don't relish livin' off a measly government pension."

"Chief Fowler," Hillary spoke up with a little glee in his voice, "the Navy stopped awarding prize money back in the nineteenth century. The consensus was that military personnel earn enough to live off and awarding prize money was another form of piracy—something civilized nations tend to look down upon. Besides, you're going to die in the Philippines an old man, and your pension is chump change compared to what you've got stashed in banks around Manila."

"What do you mean?" Chief Fowler asked with a quizzical look.

Kermit chimed in with a smile of his own, "We've calculated that you have enough paper money and specie on deposit to take care of a dozen retirees for the rest of their lives."

He looked back at the two officers and responded, "I'll see to getting those bodies wrapped up and onboard, and I'll get the surviving pirates to sickbay for a check out."

"Good, and store the bodies in the steering compartment," Hillary replied as he turned his eyes to his executive officer. "Kermit, inspect the vessels for seaworthiness including their lifeboats. Also, inventory any wine that the pirates didn't drink up, and any liquor or beer they brought with them. Then divide all wines and liquors between the mess and the wardroom on the Decatur and the two sailing vessels. As far as I'm concerned, the pirates drank it all up."

"What about the pirates?' Fowler asked. "They survived the fight and have nothing to look forward to but a date with a neck stretcher in Hong Kong. The least we could do is get 'em a little tight."

"Fair enough," Hillary replied, "but just enough to keep the edge off. Also, Kermit, after Sparks has determined what kind of radio setup is aboard that yacht, go ahead and work out a communications plan with him."

Just then, the three of them heard a distant buzzing sound. They looked around them, but the only noise they could really hear was the sound of the Decatur's internal machinery escaping through its smokestacks. They looked into the early morning dark blue sky.

"There it is, Skipper," Fowler said while pointing with the barrel of his shotgun.

The two officers looked to the north. The sun glinted off something shiny but with a greenish tint.

"Is that an airplane? Doesn't sound like any airplane I've ever heard," Fowler said as he pulled the smoke from his mouth and exhaled.

"It's 1919, and aircraft have only been around for the last sixteen years, and you've been out here that entire time. So, exactly how many airplane engines have you heard?"

"Enough to know that they normally do not sound like that."

"Well, I've never heard an airplane engine sound like that before either," Hillary replied, "and I've never heard of an airplane this far out to sea. On its own."

The three men watched the daylight star slowly move across the distant sky before Hillary gave another order. "Well, whatever it is, it's no concern of ours. Let's get to work."

Kermit and Fowler nodded as they flicked their butts into the sand, leaving their commanding officer to his thoughts and his cigarette. He was thinking about whatever that was in the sky. There's no way an airplane should have been out this far. They were in the middle of a group of islands with no known landing fields. To the east was the Pacific Ocean and thousands of miles of open sea. To the north and west were Hong Kong and Formosa: both at least two days away. The closest air facility to the south was on the Philippine main island, Luzon. Even still, the facility was hundreds of miles south and out of range.

There should be no airplane out here, Hillary reminded himself as he flicked his butt into the water while thinking about their recent encounter.

CHAPTER 16

I'M NOT MUCH of a connoisseur, Skipper, but this stuff ain't bad."

Hillary brought the glass away from his lips while appreciating the red wine. Even the bright, mid-morning sun entering through the stateroom's portholes highlighting its rich hue seemed to enhance its taste. "This 'stuff' is a Gruaud Larose, and you could have sold it for twenty dollars a bottle at any wine shop in Hong Kong if you had beaten us there. And no, we cannot pour the wine back into the bottle and recork it."

Fowler, appreciating the color of the wine as well, replied, "Well, all I can say is, having Kermit sail those ships to Hong Kong was a good idea."

Hillary smiled as he glanced at the ship's barometer mounted above his desk before turning his attention to the items strewn across his bunk: the sheathed sword and open steamer suitcase. Hanging from the hook on the open wardrobe door was Harrison's blood-stained landing gear issue, musette bag, and holstered pistol. "Somehow, after looking at that fancy pistol belt and holster I don't think he came aboard this ship with that government-issued sidearm."

Fowler sighed. "I'll log his personal weapon into the ship's armory when I can."

"Better," Hillary said as he turned his attention to the table. He saw a naval academy ring, a Rolex wristwatch, and an open leather billfold with its contents spaced next to it: a photo of a pretty brunette wearing a ball gown while standing on a grand staircase, a Massachusetts-issued motor vehicle license with an expiration date of December 1919, a navy identification card with a commissioning date matching the year on the Academy class ring— 1918—and a folded piece of white paper the size of a postage stamp.

He picked up the motor vehicle license card and reviewed the photo. It matched the face wrapped in canvas in the steering compartment. He put it down and lifted the identification card. Unfolding it, he saw that the information typed on the left side and the photo on the right side also matched the body and vehicle license. He put that portfolio on top of the driver's license and spoke. "In order to keep everything aboveboard and that we turn over the right body to the American Consulate in Hong Kong, I sent the flotilla commander Harrison's name according to his IDs, orders, and a physical description. Everything says Harrison is who he said he was."

"And the laundry marks in his uniforms and underwear," Fowler added, "and the initials embroidered on his handkerchiefs and portfolio are a match, too. Who has monogrammed underwear? Really?"

Hillary paused before continuing. "So, if he's a stiff-ass officer, why did he not have any cash in his wallet? A naval officer from a well-connected family and the recipient of steady pay who could afford a watch like that one always walks around with some cash. Even just a couple of fins. What? A missing watch was too obvious?"

Fowler looked past his wine glass and at his commanding officer. "It's a fake."

"How do you know?" Hillary asked. "It looks legit to me."

"Doesn't have the right kind of serial number. And don't feel bad. Most men couldn't tell it was a fake," Fowler replied with a grin. "I guess his daddy got a little cheap."

"I'm still surprised it didn't find its way into your pocket. But that's for later. Right now, we have to figure out why he tried to execute you."

"Yes," Fowler said, "but we happen to be out of Pinkerton badges."

Hillary raised one eyebrow and looked at his chief petty officer.

Fowler looked down at the table. "I don't know why. I haven't done anything wrong."

Hillary continued to remain silent while looking at the enlisted man.

Chief Fowler looked up from the table. "Honest, I haven't done anything that bad."

Hillary smiled slightly and started to finger the stem of the wine glass.

Fowler looked back down at the table. "I haven't done anything that bad recently."

Hillary pinched the stem of the wine glass between his fingers and lifted it.

Chief Fowler restated, "I haven't done anything worth being executed over."

Hillary brought the wine glass to his lips.

"Honest, sir, I haven't slept with married woman in over a month, and, no, I don't recognize the girl in that photo. All I've done the last month is bury my face in books."

Hillary sipped his wine while surveying the man in front of him. After a long sip, he answered. "Chief Petty Officer Ernst Willard Fowler, you're a man who would steal from the dead and cheat at cards."

"Hey," Chief Fowler objected. "I just happened to be better than others at cards."

"And are," Hillary continued, "a pickpocket, a womanizer, an opportunist, a purveyor in counterfeit currencies, ill-gotten jewelry, and fake pearls, an all-around scoundrel cursed with a selective memory, but I never thought you would do anything so heinous it would require an execution by a naval officer."

"Thank you," Fowler replied with a tilt of his glass. "And I don't cheat at cards."

"But you've done something out of the ordinary."

"All I've done out of the ordinary is conduct more research on the Manila Galleon, Ching Shih, that shipment of British gold coins, and the mystical island watched by old wise men."

Hillary sighed as he put down his wine glass and looked at Harrison's possessions. "There has to be a clue somewhere, something that will tell us why he tried to kill you."

"And poison the gunnery officer," Fowler added.

"I suspected the same," Hillary surmised. "Everything was too damned convenient."

Fowler did not answer but reached out with his free hand and started to poke through the items on the table. He picked up the photo of the smiling lady in the photo and flipped it over. He read the sentiment, which was written in ink and in a woman's hand. At the same time, Hillary pushed the ID cards aside and picked up the folded paper. The paper crinkled as he unfolded it, and flecks of dried blood and flesh sprinkled the tabletop.

"What do you see, Skipper?"

Hillary turned the paper over for Fowler to see. The paper, now the size of a palm, had lines of numbers hand printed in pencil. Some numbers were smeared by the blood that soaked through the thin paper, but most of the numbers were still legible.

Fowler looked at the paper. "Alright, I see numbers, but what do they mean?"

"I don't know," Hillary said as he laid the paper on the table and picked up his glass of wine. "But, we have at least two mysteries on our hands and fine merlot to assist us."

"How's wine supposed to help?"

Hillary held his glass to the light coming in from the portholes. "As you mentioned the night we left Manila, I did take a cryptology class, and did so well, my instructor contacted the Office of Naval Intelligence, but I turned those orders down for flight training instead. Anyway, I remember quite a bit including two items the instructor always pounded into us. First, he was a nut when it came to word problems and number cryptograms. He even made solving parlor word games and number puzzles part of our curriculum as warm-up exercises. He also challenged us to pick up a musical instrument. The idea was to exercise the brain while learning how to spot patterns. The second item was, whenever faced with a challenge, problem, mystery, conundrum, or a code, its best to relax and find something to take your mind off the issue at hand."

"What do you mean?" Chief Fowler asked as he sipped his wine.

"You know. Spend early Saturday morning horseback riding. Early to rise for fresh air, physical exertion, application of strategic thought, and in proximity with other persons of mental dexterity themselves, which all combines for a good night's sleep."

"Point taken, but how does wine fit in?"

"My instructor was not only a puzzle devotee but was also a wine aficionado, which means he appreciated patience and good wine, and with those two come good company, and with good company comes relaxation and conversation. Something about how wine thins the blood, which allows for more blood flow through the brain. Anyway, riding horses is an example." Hillary continued as he sipped his wine, "Playing golf, taking in a ball game, a game of chess, or playing poker in a neighborhood saloon with friends and decent cigars. Activities that involve relaxation, association, conversation, and simulation, which result in realization."

"Wait a minute!" Fowler exclaimed as he sat straight in his chair and placed his near-empty wine glass on the table. "Harrison said something about me being a good poker player."

Hillary reached for the bottle of wine on the table. "Now we're getting somewhere."

"Don't mind if I do," Fowler said as he lifted his glass for Hillary to refill it.

With full glasses, the men appreciated the soft morning breeze entering through the portholes and the feel of the ship's turbines vibrating through the deck at their feet.

"Let's start from the beginning," Hillary said as he rotated the stem of the glass in his fingers. "Independent of each other, we both assumed that somehow our gunnery officer was incapacitated. Either by Harrison or someone associated with him. Correct?"

"Which," Fowler replied, "allowed Harrison to be a member of the landing party where he could kill me in the confusion of battle while earning a commendation."

"Good," Hillary said, "and the fact that he knew you are a 'good' card player and that you kept running out on your bar tabs in Hong Kong says he conducted research on you, which means he knew that you were looking into a lady pirate from a hundred years ago and a mythical island guarded by old wise men. It can also help explain, if somebody really wanted you dead, why they waited to do it in combat and not on some dark street while on liberty. You said it yourself; he wanted to be involved in an operation that would put hair on his chest and a commendation in his record."

"Good so far," Fowler said, "which bulks up the fact that I wasn't targeted for sleeping with a man's wife. My research into treasure and a mythical island set something in the works for somebody somewhere. It also explains a gut feeling I've been having."

"Which is?"

"While conducting my research, I felt as if I was being followed," Fowler continued. "I even got the feeling that somebody was checking the books I was reading."

"Books are at libraries for a reason."

"I know, but I wasn't reading just any books. Sometimes I would go back to update my notes, and the books I looked at before now smelled of perfume. I started to leave books markers at certain places in certain books I checked out. Sometimes closer to the spine and sometimes closer to the edge. When I went back, I would find that they've moved."

Hillary paused for a second. "Did you start any new romances? Recently?"

"I've always got a couple of dames on the hook," Fowler said as he pursed his lips. He was about to say something else but stopped for a second. After a pause he continued. "There was this woman. From California. A typist for a shipping line. She said she liked my dancing."

"It looks like we're getting caught up," Hillary accepted as he finished the wine in his glass. He saw the chief reach for the bottle. He waited for the chief to refill both of their glasses. "Now we have what we can assume to be a coded message with the possibility of it containing instructions from whomever to complete a future assignment."

"Why a future assignment?" Fowler asked. "Couldn't it be the instructions to kill me?"

"I'm just assuming because Sparks said Harrison used the radiotelegraph last night," Hillary replied. "Anyway, why would he keep a message he's already read? He couldn't be that stupid."

"He got himself killed by a man he thought was subhuman."

"Touché," Hillary said as he looked at the bloodied paper. "Digit-based codes are common and can be in all kinds of variations as long as the sender and receiver are on the same page. Literally. Our numbers are grouped into threes, but with no obvious organization or pattern."

"Did you have similar codes to break in that class of yours?" Fowler asked.

Hillary reached for his wine glass. "This one reminds me of the Ottendorf code: a straightforward cipher with a simple key that both the sender and the receiver have access to. And I remember the instructor stressing the destruction of any messages once decoded, but Harrison carried a coded message on him. That tells me he's a novice and somebody's dupe. We can compare the handwriting from the note to anything he has on his person. Perhaps a letter he wrote or a personal diary. Don't know what it will tell us, but it's a start."

Fowler brought his glass of wine to his lips. "I agree that he's somebody's puppet, and I also agree that since he was stupid enough to keep a coded message on his person, he might be stupid enough to have the key somewhere here in his baggage, but what exactly is a key?"

Hillary smiled deviously. "A novel, a collection of poems, a pamphlet, or an essay. Something a person could carry without arousing suspicion or found in any library, newsstand, under the arm of a pedestrian, or even a living room coffee table or bedside nightstand."

"What about a newspaper?"

"Yes," Hillary responded, "and that would make deciphering it by an opponent challenging as most newspapers are reprinted daily with new information. Magazines and journals would also work as they're reprinted weekly or monthly, making the message that much more difficult to decipher. That leaves both forms of print material safer and better for the senders and receivers, but any miscommunication of which edition is being used can cause confusion. Also, a person walking around with an out-of-date newspaper would be a giveaway to any good Pinkerton."

Hillary paused long enough to look at the paper with the numbers. After a second, he turned to look at the items on the bunk.

"And how do the numbers work?"

"The numbers, grouped in three in our case, can represent the page number, the line number going down or up, and the letter or word number going across from either right or left. And . . ." The ship's captain leaned over to pick up the sheathed officer's sword from the bunk. Using it to poke around the folded clothing in the suitcase, he spoke at last. "No books or newspapers in the suitcase, but let's see what's in that musette bag."

Hillary used the tip of the sword to lift the canvas field bag off the hook and bring it to the table. Placing the sword on the table, Hillary lifted the flap and looked inside. A broad smile spread across his face as he looked up at Fowler. Hillary inserted his hand into the musette bag and withdrew a booklet. One authored by their commander-in-chief. "Even the most inexperienced spy can't be that stupid."

Minutes later, the noon sun shined through the portholes and landed on the faces of two stunned men. The sunlight also landed on a second piece of paper. Both men continued to look at the words on the note: "Friend, process CPO Fowler for termination. Do so during anti-pirate efforts ashore. Prevent USS Decatur from visiting Buyan at all costs. Repeat: at all costs."

"You stepped into something this time, Chief," Hillary said.

"Something alright," Fowler replied. "But why? All this malarkey for a chest of coins. They're worth a fortune, but it's not like the crown jewels were inside that thing."

"It's not about a chest of gold sovereigns," Hillary said as he reached for the bottle. Refilling their glasses, he continued. "It's about much more. But to figure that out we have questions that require answering. Why would a commissioned officer in the US Navy try to kill you? Who's controlling him? For what reason would somebody in our chain of command want to keep us away from an island we know nothing about? Lastly, who in our chain of command is involved, and are they monitoring our radio traffic?"

"I don't know the answer to those questions, but we have a couple more," Fowler said as he sipped his wine. "I know we have two pieces of identification and a guarantee from our commander that the body in the steering compartment is Burton D. Harrison. So, the question is, why did an educated man with the right family name decide to do what he did? Is he a Red?"

"Calling him a Red right now seems like quite a jump, but let's go there," Hillary replied. "Not all Reds are out-of-work factory workers. Also, those workers must be organized and led by somebody with wherewithal. While some of those leaders are true believers, there are others who simply have too much time on their hands, and perhaps Harrison was part of the latter. I think Kermit mentioned something about reading Don Quixote."

"How does that book fit in here?"

Hillary paused to sip his wine before answering. "Our young man, just like the character in Don Quixote, may have read stories of the downtrodden and of knights in shining armor coming to their rescue. Mostly fiction of course, but what I'm saying is that Harrison, an impressionable man of means, has set out to right the wrongs of others as a way of achieving that fictious and classic glory."

"Okay," Fowler replied. "But what about the rest of the chain of command? The flotilla commander? The governor-general? Who do we tell about this?"

Hillary paused to sip his wine before answering. "Or should we?"

Chapter 17

THE SUN WAITED patiently at its zenith in the clear June sky as if to enjoy the view. Under it, motor-powered, and animal- and human-drawn vehicles shuffled persons and cargos over worn paver stones. On either side of Huashan Road, pedestrians powered themselves along the sidewalks. Mixed in with the foot traffic, European men in suits looked for seats at open-air cafes and enclosed bars to have lunch, while European women, in their gaily colored dresses dipped in and out of quaint shops in the search for needed household items or to browse. There were also British marines, Japanese sailors, and French aviators strutting in twos or threes. At one of those street-side cafes, Borodin, still wearing his suit from the morning meeting, sat at the end of a line of round tables along a waist-high wrought iron fence. He was intent on his newspaper.

"Mind if I join you, brother?"

Borodin looked up and saw that the brim of the Panama hat blocked out the noon sun poised behind the man's head. "Please do, brother."

Captain Lagos pulled out the metal-framed chair while turning to a Chinese waiter tending to a table with European women. The waiter saw Lagos point to Borodin's coffee cup and bowed.

Lagos returned his attention to Borodin, who folded the newspaper and placed it on the table. He set his coffee cup on top of it.

"Any new news?" Lagos asked as he sat and pulled on the pressed creases of his trouser legs. He removed the Panama hat from his head and placed it on the cloth-covered seat of the empty chair to his right. His thick, grey hair, damp from his morning bath, was neatly combed.

"Yes," Borodin said with a confident smile. "First, it appears the British and the Japanese have announced they will officially end their cooperative search for the Busan One as of today, which will allow the owners to file their insurance claim. After weeks of searching for such a valuable ship with its cargo of ores and modern foundry and factory machinery onboard, and its crew, they declared the ship lost at sea with no survivors."

"That is good news," Lagos replied with an equally confident smile.

"Whoever heard of making vehicles out of aluminum anyway?" Borodin continued. "But, as it turns out, the Japanese efforts to enter the automobile industry worked well for their aviation industry. And for us."

Lagos listened as he turned his attention to the approaching waiter and waited for the man to place a cup of coffee and saucer on the table. The waiter stood and walked down the line of tables to the other end where a man just sat down. The new arrival was a white man wearing a linen suit appropriate for the seasonable June weather. Lagos continued his conversation with Borodin. "But it is a shame that captain, crew, and technicians spent the entire winter mining aluminum along the Manchurian coast, only to disappear on their way back to Tokyo for a fine payday. And the Japanese motor company, Tokyo Motor Vehicle Works, Ltd., invested so much into constructing a vessel capable of going anywhere in the world to mine, process, and convert ores into metal stock and plate, only to succumb to unknown forces."

"Yes," Borodin said as he lifted his coffee cup. "Quite a shame for somebody."

"Agreed," Lagos said as he tasted his coffee. "And what of the second item of interest?"

As Borodin pulled the coffee cup from his lips, a broad smile highlighted his eyes. "It seems, with a little nudging on our part, along with well-placed names, Anarchist April in America has succeeded. Groups of disparate idealists have taken to barroom pulpits, backroom printing presses, and street corner audiences to do our bidding. Blessed are the ones who accept misinformation so willingly."

"So, the effects of the mail-bombing campaign are falling into place," Lagos stated as he lifted his coffee cup again.

"Yes. Enough packages left the post office to cause quite a bit of consternation among the American populace and within the halls of government. The populace is calling for a crackdown on lawlessness and the arrest of anarchists with last names they cannot pronounce, which, if applied improperly, will result in a violation of civil liberties."

"Good," Lagos said with a smile. "Which means that we should be able to start inserting more operatives over the next year with ease. While yellow-press jobbers prey on the ears of those less nimbly minded, our operatives will be able to slip in behind those herds and into desks with bowties and sharpened pencils."

"A skilled accountant with a sharpened pencil, a bit of perseverance, and a streak of guile is more powerful than any baton-wielding police force in America, but speaking of sharpened pencils," Borodin said as he placed his coffee cup back on top of the newspaper, "I need some names for my Camelot List as I am planning on transmitting the list to Agent Cranberry during our transit south. It seems Agent Cranberry has moved up within the Department of Justice and is a step closer to the newly appointed attorney general."

"Ah, Attorney General Mitchell Palmer," Lagos said with a smile. "What an opportunity. With timing we should have such a governmental overreach of arrests and deportations that even law-abiding Americans will take to the streets and to the editorial pages. By this fall, the secretaries from the Departments of Labor, Commerce, Treasury, and Justice should be at each other's throats fighting over jurisdiction and departmental intrusion, leaving the average American confused. Meanwhile, our operatives slide quietly through the fracas and into vacant positions of weight. I am reviewing the membership rolls of American maritime unions, and there will be a number of names that will readily, and unknowingly, lend themselves to undue attention from the attorney general when it suits our purposes."

"Very good, Issak," Borodin said. "Unfortunately, though, while we have progression in the States, it appears we may have an issue closer to home."

Lagos tilted his head. "How so?"

"After our meeting this morning, I received word of our concern in the Philippines. It seems our concern was not liquidated properly, and we suffered a loss in the family."

Lagos leaned forward and lifted his coffee cup. "I am sorry to hear such disconcerting news. Was he a close friend of the family?"

"Not really," Borodin answered. "He was a recent introduction to a brother of ours and had not attended any family reunions. Our friend was the son of a Boston family, and our brother met him through the US Naval Academy and had him posted with the Asiatic Fleet after graduation."

"Do you think he left any dirty family laundry hanging out for others to see?" Lagos asked.

"Hard to tell, but one can only hope he emptied his pockets before he did his wash," Borodin stated as he shooed a fly away. "That said, our concern is still in need of attention. It seems that after the operation where our friend was supposed to handle the concern, our target was placed in charge of two vessels of sail, and they are on their way back to Hong Kong, separate from the naval vessel he was part of. Not to worry, though, as our maritime asset will approach the sailing vessels when they are far behind the torpedo boat destroyer and process the men onboard. That should be sometime a little after sunset or later. We will then see how we can convert those vessels into assets for us."

"Good," Lagos continued, "but what is the purpose of our meeting? It seems that it was arranged before you found out about our concern."

"You are correct," Borodin said as he placed his coffee cup in front of the folded newspaper. Straightening up in his chair, he slid the newspaper over to his right before relocating his coffee cup in front of him. "I called this meeting as an addendum to the plan we had in place."

Lagos nodded and both men sipped their coffee. After a few seconds, they were interrupted.

"Excuse me friend, do you have a match?"

Both men looked up. It was the same man who sat at the other end of the line of tables moments ago. He appeared to be just as tough as the two Russians but younger by about thirty years. He had a handsome face topped with wavy black hair neatly combed and parted in the middle. His eyes were a striking dark blue. He held a pack of Chesterfields in his right hand.

"I'm sorry," Borodin responded. "For cigarettes, I use a Victory Pocket Lighter. Only cigars deserve the respect of a fine wooden stick match."

"I agree," the man said as he shifted the packet from his right to left hand.

"Do you care to join us, Mister?" Borodin asked as he revealed the palm of his hand.

"Don't mind if I do, and the name is Rodham. Hugh Rodham," the man said as he turned to search out the waiter. Spotting him, the new arrival pointed to the coffee cups on the table. He sat down and placed the Chesterfields on the table in front of him. He waited for the Russians to speak.

"My name is Mothershed, and my companion is Mayberry," Borodin said.

"Nice to meet you both," the new arrival said.

"Likewise," Borodin said. "And I am glad you found time to meet at my request."

"My pleasure. So, what is it you require from me?" Rodham asked.

Borodin was about the answer, but he saw the Chinese waiter holding a tray walk to the table.

A minute later, after the waiter reserviced the table, Borodin continued speaking. "As it turns out, more than I thought I would. First, I've been hearing rumors concerning the arrival of a cache of gems, including the Romanov Sapphire, along these shores. Have you heard the same?"

Rodham answered, "I started hearing talk yesterday, which strengthened into something substantial this morning. The talk now centers around the White Russians coming here to start selling them or place them on deposit. Since their value is beyond comprehension, I notified my superiors in a coded telegram only a half hour ago. I hope that was satisfactory?"

"Oh, yes. And I would ask that you keep your ears and eyes available for any further information concerning such wealth and to make sure the US

Army is also kept up to date."

"Understand," Rodham replied, "but wouldn't the U S Army be more concerned with the gems in the hands of the Reds, specifically Comintern? And not the Whites?"

"I see your point as I too would rather see that wealth in our hands and not the Whites," Borodin replied. "But it is appropriate for the US Army to always be aware of any factors that might upset the balance of power in the Far East, including a group of White Russians with a submarine, a compliment of torpedoes, and a wealth of gems at their disposal."

"Point taken," Rodham said as he flicked away a speck of dust from the tabletop. "Was there something else?"

"Yes," Borodin said. "It seems a friend of ours has failed in an errand."

"Sorry for your loss," Rodham said. "How can I help?"

"Condolences accepted," Borodin said with a nod. "What we have is a US Navy torpedo boat destroyer from the Asiatic Fleet that just deployed on a two-month patrol. Onboard is a person who appears to have conducted research into a fabled pirate treasure buried on a China Seas Island, which indirectly connected him to an island that, let me say, should remain off limits. Our goal was to have that person processed before he convinced his captain to visit the island. While trying to figure out how to best to liquidate our concern, American naval intelligence was informed of British pirates hiding out on American territory, so we asked a friend to take charge of that opportunity and involve himself. It would allow our friend to process our target while involving himself into a minor combat action as a means of establishing the basis of a rewarding career. Unfortunately, quite the reverse occurred. That said, while we have plans for the concern, there is still the ship and its captain. The bottom line is that we cannot have any interference with that island. At least for the next few weeks. What we would like you to do is to contact your headquarters in the Philippines through your normal channels and have them work with the US Navy to have that naval vessel, which is now enroute to Hong Kong, redirected after their port stop to meet you somewhere halfway between here and Hong Kong to save time. A passenger liner, the SS Mongolia, is due to depart from here later this afternoon for the Keelung in Formosa. It should not take too long for that naval ship to depart Hong Kong and collect you there. Tell your supervisors you have information about pirates threatening American lives or property somewhere along the Chinese coast. Whatever you can conceive as your mission is to make sure that that vessel goes nowhere near our facility. We have no idea what kind of bee was put into that captain's bonnet, and we are completing Phase Two of our effort."

Rodham smiled. "I am to provide a ball of yarn and the destroyer is the cat."

"That is an astute comparison," Borodin surmised.

"I can have a message to US Army headquarters in Manila within thirty minutes through routine channels, and I can book a ticket aboard that liner at the same time, but there are issues: what plans I come up with will probably require assistance from your assets, and it appears that, since I am going on a sea voyage, I will need up-to-date reading material." He looked down at Borodin's newspaper. "Is that out of date?"

Borodin looked at the paper while reaching into his suit coat. "Yes, but I am sure you will find this piece of American literature quite enlightening."

Borodin pulled his hand from under the suitcoat. He held out a paperback book.

Rodham accepted the book and reviewed the cover. He smiled. "Ah, like good wine and cheese, nothing pairs better than a thoughtful read while spending time on the high seas."

"I've enjoyed this classic myself. I hope you do as well."

"The Adventures of Huckleberry Finn," Rodham reflected as he opened the cover to look at its publishing information including its edition number. Satisfied, he inserted the read inside his suitcoat. "The other issue, still, concerns the ball of yarn and how to use it."

"That would be no issue," Lagos said, speaking for the first time since Rodham sat at the table. "We will monitor your communications with the US Army while you are aboard the destroyer and I, through the Mersk-Alba Shipping Company, can provide any sort of rolling toys to toss down the hallway."

"Fair enough," Rodham said with a nod. "What about the island I'm supposed to keep them from? What is its name?"

"The answer to that question depends on which chart you are looking at and the date of that source. Let us just say, on any modern US Navy chart it will be called Langkawi," Lagos said, "but we call it Buyan. The Russian version of Atlantis."

Rodham looked at Lagos, then at Borodin. "Atlantis? Sounds like we have a plan and will look forward to our next meeting whenever and wherever that may be."

Borodin spoke as he lifted his coffee cup. "I am looking forward to it. Also, once this operation is secure, you may have the means to ask for a new posting. Any notions?"

"This may surprise you, but I've given thought to resigning my commission and returning home to apply myself toward a new career: textiles."

"Textiles?" Borodin asked before sipping his coffee.

"More specially, drapes and curtains. After all, everybody needs a little privacy."

Borodin pulled the cup away from his mouth. *"Persona."*

Rodham tilted his head slightly. *"Persona?"*

"Yes*, persona*. It means mask or façade and is the root meaning behind personality. All people have personalities which are merely masks, and quite often many more than just one. The point is that whatever a person presents to the public is just a mask. I guess what I am saying is that we all live behind curtains, and the key is to make sure the audience does not realize that."

Rodman thought for a brief second before making an effort to stand. "That is sound advice."

Borodin offered a nod of acceptance, and he and Lagos both watched Rodman stand. The American collected his belongings and pushed them into his trouser pocket. When he withdrew his hand, he had an American twenty-five cent piece pinched between his fingers. Dropping the silver coin on the table, Rodham looked at the men one last time and spoke before turning away from the table. "I think the next ten years should prove quite interesting, and I hope to see you at the dinner table sometime. Perhaps at a family reunion?"

Both nodded as they watched Rodham disappear into the undulating pedestrian traffic.

"Textiles?" Lagos asked as he finished his coffee. "And where is he from?"

Borodin lifted his cup to finish his coffee as well. "He is from Chicago, and I can understand his decision. Manufacturing drapes and curtains is a sound and innocent industry. An occupation that will fill out enough yearly tax records for any curious persons to be satisfied. I mean now that the American government has created the graduated income tax, there will be one more government agency created to oversee its people, and the collection of revenues."

"And another agency for us to infiltrate."

"Very good, Issak. Anyway, Chicago, like Detroit, is located along the Great Lakes and in proximity to Canada."

"I see your point since Prohibition and the resulting lawlessness will soon consume America," Lagos said as he reached into his pants pocket. "What of his army experience?"

"He apprenticed an American-Marconi wireless office before his university studies. It was there, at the university, where he met a sister of ours. That meeting was quite difficult since American academia is a bastion of conservative thought. But we will give it time. Anyway, the relationship began with our sister who was prospecting. She saw Rodham reading an illicit copy of Antonio Gramsci's Prison Notebook in the back of a barroom off campus one day. Starting a conversation about imprisoned Marxists, she began a year-long relationship, which ended up with her encouraging him to apply for a commission in 1917 as America entered the war. They were married before being assigned to the 339th Infantry Regiment and sent to Camp Custer in Michigan for training. Because of his apprenticeship, he started out in the regiment's signals section, but eventually reassigned to the intelligence section after their arrival in Russia. Both billets served us well."

"The 339th Infantry Regiment?" Lagos asked. "The same regiment as the

American who is with our brothers at this moment?"

"Yes. Rodham was a staff officer with regimental headquarters while the sergeant served in a rifle company, which means that if they do end up meeting during this little junket of ours, it could prove very advantageous for us. I mean by him taking the soldier under his wing."

Lagos paused to finish his coffee. "Is Rodham still being chaperoned? And how did he end up in Shanghai now?"

Borodin smiled again as he fished in his pocket. "I foresaw a need for Rodham's presence, so, through coded messages to Manila, we told him he was needed in Shanghai. He gave his chain of command a story about information concerning a spy network and asked for permission to come to Shanghai for further investigation on the pretense that he was going on leave to enjoy Shanghai as a tourist. His chain of command 'authorized his leave,' and here he is. As far as him being chaperoned, yes. Although I have full confidence in his loyalty, we still have to vet him."

Both men paused for a minute as Lagos fished in his pocket as well. Finding a coin, Lagos continued, "It seems that the office in Vladivostok has contracted with a phosphate mining company for us to transport stores to a mining operation in Micronesia. Our return here to Shanghai is still up in the air."

"A phosphate mining company, huh?" Borodin noted.

"More specially, guano," Lagos replied as they both pulled their hands from their pockets. "You know, bird shit."

The men smiled as they laid coins on the table next to their cups as well. "Are your tabs paid off here in Shanghai?" Borodin asked while picking up his newspaper.

Lagos, bending over to pick up his Panama hat himself, answered. "Yes, my accounts are up to date, and our transport awaits."

CHAPTER 18

TWO PEOPLE SAT on the wooden slats in between a set of metal tracks bolted to the foredeck of the submarine. The tracks ran from the base of the conning tower to the bow but not being a submariner, Dooley did not know their purpose. Somehow, though, they reminded him of something. After looking at the tracks for another second, he returned his thoughts to sea rushing past him and the person pressing against his left shoulder.

He and Zeta reclined against the base of the grey-painted conning tower with their legs stretched in front of them. At the same time, fresh sea air rushed at their faces as the submarine pushed its way through a placid, dark-blue sea. The smell outside the submarine was quite the elixir. The view to their right was also just as pleasing. A flat sea stretched to join the horizon many miles away, and the bulging silvery clouds piled on top of each other as if they were trying to reach heaven. A hoard of clouds so heavy one could almost imagine that side of the world was under threat of being tilted over. A bright yellow sun hung just above that towering bank of clouds. It promised to be a beautiful sunset, especially since they were not headed toward a life-threatening raid and were out of Japanese waters. Several feet above them, Captain Vostok and Major Utkin leaned over the forward edge of the structure. They too were enjoying the late afternoon sea air along with hot coffee.

Zeta looked past her eyebrows and at the men standing over them. She smiled briefly before returning her attention to Dooley, who seemed to be occupied by the water sliding past the hull. "I can't but hold the feeling we are like a young couple sitting on park bench with chaperones literally standing over our shoulders."

"Well," Dooley said as he turned his eyes from the sea, "if they've been paid to be chaperones, someone needs their money back."

Zeta grinned back at Dooley and said, "Too late. The damage has already been done."

"And speaking of money," Dooley continued as he returned his gaze to the rushing water, "I'll get enough out of this picnic for a passage home, and a decent suit along with a hat and a pair of good wingtips."

"So, you will return to Brooklyn?" Zeta asked as her heart skipped a beat. "Wearing a suit? What about your shingle axe? Will you be able to accessorize properly?"

"The suit is for my mother's sake," he said with a sigh. "And if my mother has her wishes, I'd be facing a life of fixing wagons, making grandkids for her, and spending my days looking up the ass ends of Alice and Betsy."

"Alice and Betsy?"

"My dad's horses. They're good animals and can pull the heaviest of loads, which means they'll never die."

"So, what about joining Utkin and Vostok? To fight Bolshevism?"

Dooley again paused as he looked at the books in his lap, which came from Vostok's stateroom. The top book was a paperback written by aviator and war veteran, James Doolittle. Under it was a book about submarines and written by marine engineer and treasure hunter Simon Lake. "Utkin's right, and he's playing on my wanderlust including treasure and flying."

"What do you know of either? I mean outside those books?"

"Not much practical experience about treasure hunting, but I do know something about flying," Dooley said before pausing. He sniffed the air rushing at them. "When I joined my regiment, we were shipped to Camp Custer in Michigan for training. During that time, on the weekends or after retreat, I spent my time at the camp library, which was next to a training airfield. One day, I was standing outside the library watching the airplanes take off when an officer, a qualified pilot and instructor, noticed me. He asked if I wanted to become a pilot. I told him I've never been around airplanes before. He said he checked out my reading list with the NCO at the library and asked me if I had completed any higher education. I lied and said I completed high school. I guess he saw something in me, as he gave me a short, thirty-minute lesson. After the lesson, he said I would need to complete required officer assessment examinations, which would qualify me to become a student pilot. All I had to was to submit a request that he would endorse through my chain of command and complete those exams. I would then have to transfer from my regiment to flight training, but—"

Zeta finished, "Your officers would find out that you were a seventeen-year-old high-school dropout who ran away from home and forged your way into an army."

Dooley turned his head to face Zeta. "I told myself I could take high school correspondence courses, which I did, and apply the credits toward my diploma. When I turned eighteen, which became the minimum age to join the army after they lowered the enlistment age from twenty-one, I could then request a commission and a transfer, but by the time I turned eighteen there was no way I could leave my regiment since we were getting ready to ship out."

"Well," Zeta said slowly, "you had your combat, earned your stripes and medals, and left the army with your dreams accompanying you, but again, what are your plans?"

"Utkin asked me to join his submarine raiders, but I said no. However, he also offered me a position with a flight group of his," Dooley said as he turned his eyes up to watch the sun, which started to surrender to the beguiling of the far-off billowing clouds. "I guess I'll wait and see what is waiting for us there and let Utkin know that I've made up my mind."

"About the flight group?"

Dooley turned from the oncoming night to look at Zeta. She still wore the oversized Russian army uniform, and at the end of her outstretched legs and cuffed-up trousers, were a pair of round-toed leather boots. The boots reminded Dooley of the big-shoed clowns he laughed at when his father sprung for a day at the circus. But instead of wearing a stupid hat with hawk's bells and white make-up on her face, she wore blond hair pulled back and tied into a ponytail with a piece of blue ribbon. Her eyes were such a sparkling blue and so bright and wide the innocence in her face could not be subdued. He still remembered those eyes when he looked down at them during the previous night. The night when she became a full woman. Suddenly, as if struck by a lightning bolt, he felt the guilt of bragging about his future while realizing that her future was in the hands of the men leaning over the ledge of the conning tower above them.

"I'm sorry," Dooley said as he reached over to pat her hands, which she immediately snatched up and forced into her lap. "What about you? What do you want to do?"

Zeta looked at Dooley's hand, which she clasped between hers before turning to gaze at the ocean around them. "I've been trying to think of a quote. I may not get it right, but here it is: 'The world is your oyster, so it is time to sharpen your knife.' I may have gotten it wrong, but I think you know what I mean. I just wish I could hold and sharpen that knife. To be a man."

"Again, I'm sorry," Dooley said as he felt her heartbeat through her fingers. "I guess I come from a different world."

"You come from a world where women are about to get the right to vote, and Negroes have had the right to vote. And, while you have families like the Vanderbilts, you come from a world with no monarchies or aristocracies. The question should be what can I do?" She paused to look at Dooley's hand clasped between hers.

"My mother taught me that all women only have one thing we can control and that is the same thing most men want. To her that one thing meant control, however, she ended up being under the control of any man with a pound note in his hand. She now lives in a fantasy world where she drops her Gibsons in the back of a bar just as easily as she steps into them in the morning. She pretends she is still that twenty-year-old on a ballroom dance floor with a last name that still means something and with men lined up to dance with her. Men who had pedigrees that once meant something as well. I have that control, but it is temporary just like the smell of a rose garden you pass while on a trolley. Such attempts at personal control for women like me are like fleeting attempts to grasp at snowflakes in a flurry."

She stopped to look at Dooley who was looking at her. While his eyes acknowledged understanding and compassion, they also revealed some distant, unknown, thought.

"What are you thinking about?" Zeta asked.

"Oh, nothing," Dooley answered softly. "But I suggest that you can still pick up that Boston shucker. What I mean is, once you realize all the assets at your disposal and have a goal in mind, you have control. Physically, you were born with one, and mentally you've developed the other through reading, languages, and the arts, and how to manipulate those that stand in front of your goals. You know, to get them to react the way you want."

Dooley again paused, allowing Zeta to think. "So, what if you had that sharpened blade in your hand? Or in other words, the means at your disposal? Like a handful of diamonds to build upon. What goals do you have? What do you want to do?"

Zeta smiled to herself as she rubbed Dooley's fingers with her own. "I would assume, creating an account in the right bank with the right connections and the right dupes running it. To avoid what happened to my father."

"See. You learned from another's mistake. What's next?"

She paused while continuing to massage Dooley's fingers. "From what you said, I need to focus on something. What about being a Pinkerton? An international reporter? An adventuress?"

"You know about the Pinkerton National Detective Agency?" Dooley asked.

"Only from what I've read and what I have heard. My father's friends talked about the Reds and how the Pinkerton Agency was hired by the US government to break up workers' strikes in the States. You know, like the Molly McGuire Coal Miner strikes. I was more inclined to read about their exploits when it came to uncovering assassination plots and closing in on counterfeiting rings or train-robbing gangs like Butch Cassidy and the Sundance Kid."

"Very good," Dooley said. "You've focused on a strategic target, which allows you to understand the obstructions in front of you and forces you to think ahead. Just like a game of chess or billiards. See what I'm getting at?"

"Yes," she said with a distant look in her eyes.

To Dooley that distant gaze filled her voice with calm. "Good," he said with a nod, "but I suggest, if you want to be a Pinkerton, you need to set up an intelligence component. You are well read and can speak several languages and have been taught how to tickle a man's fancy but learning how to gather information properly will add to your ability as a Pinkerton. You need to establish a base of operations in a strategically located crossroads such as Cairo, Madrid, Havana, or New York. Anywhere that will suit your future goals. But once established, create your intelligence component."

"What kind of intelligence?"

"Books to start with and ones that will serve a purpose, starting with that essay or pamphlet by President Wilson. The same copy that's in Vostok's stateroom next to these books. The title sounds appropriate. Second, learn to use your senses, including ears and eyes. Third: create a system of runners using shoeshine boys, waiters, or telegraph runners for example. No one suspects an illiterate street urchin who can barely speak English. In fact, the Pinkerton Agency, which was started in 1850, was the first to hire females and blacks."

She smiled as she looked into Dooley's eyes. "It all sounds like a dream. Like I'm a character in an intriguing novel."

"I'm glad," Dooley said with a smile of his own, "but life should be a novel where you, as the protagonist, control the blade of the oyster knife, the haft of a fountain pen, or the keys of an Underwood Number Three. So, where do we start?"

Zeta paused as she looked past Dooley and at the disappearing sun. "I am thinking of Chicago, at Weeghman Field, watching the Cubs with a Pabst and a red hot with mustard. Or walking through Istanbul's Grand Bazar, sampling figs and shopping for oranges while following a suspect. Or being at the helm of a yacht sailing across the Bay of Biscay in the severest of storms to deliver a secret message. Maybe in the cockpit of a Sopwith Camel crossing the Sahara."

"Those are some narratives, but you're going to have to build up some experience."

"Like you?" Zeta said with an admiring smile. "Although we're both nineteen, somehow, I get the feeling that you're much older."

"Well," Dooley answered slowly, "dodging bullets while freezing my ass off in a Russian winter and operating a Thompson submachine gun at the same time has put on some mileage."

"I see," Zeta answered with a smile, "but it looks like the miles have treated you well."

Chapter 19

THE VIEW FRAMED by the bridge windows was a view that those same windows photographed thousands of times before. A blue-black flat sea topped with far-off clouds ballooning into the heavens. Behind those clouds, an exhausted sun surrendered to the gravity of a turning world like a child trying to stay awake long enough to see Santa Claus but failing in the futile effort. Only the rays of the sun escaped to greet the arrival of night. Inside the bridge, the helmsman stood with hands on the spoked wheel. Behind him stood another man holding a half-empty fifth of Scotch whiskey in one hand and glasses, pinched between his fingers, in the other.

"Krivor, make sure you split this whiskey evenly with Sparks and his striker. They're in the radio shack now," Fowler said as he placed the glasses on the chart table. Now free, he used that hand to uncork the bottle and pour drinks for himself and the seaman.

"Thanks," Krivor said as he kept a hand on a spoke while reaching behind him.

Fowler nodded as he recorked the bottle and handed Krivor his whiskey. Leaving the bottle and other glasses on the chart table, he joined his captain, who was enjoying his own bottle of whiskey on the bridge.

"Thank God those pirates didn't drink up all that wine, and God bless them for the whiskey," Fowler said as he lifted his glass in salute.

"I don't know how much you know about history, but pirates weren't always after Spanish doubloons," Hillary said as he brought his glass to his lips. "Medicines, alcohol, ship's tackle, and arms were just as valuable as gold. Even Blackbeard lay siege to Charleston demanding only a chest of medicines, including laudanum and mercury."

"Mercury? Quicksilver?"

"Yes. Starting with ancient Greece, it was viewed as a cure for certain illnesses, which, over time, was thought to be a cure for syphilis. It was taken in various forms including with laudanum or alcohol, and through injection up the urethra in metal syringes."

Fowler closed his eyes slightly. "That sounds painful. But isn't mercury poisonous?"

"We can't judge what people thought before us," Hillary said, "and yes. It results in brain disease and physical issues. Ever heard the phrase 'mad as a hatter'? The phrase came from the fact that heated mercury was involved in hat manufacturing, and the people exposed to the vapors developed irrational behavior. Just like the gunnery officer did before he got sick. Remember when he started talking about mules riding elves?"

"Well," Fowler said with a smile as he reached for the whiskey in the binocular holder. Pulling it out he looked at the bottom of the clear glass bottle. "Mercury is a heavy metal that puddles like liquid silver and, since I don't see any quicksilver at the bottom of the bottle, I assume this whiskey wasn't used to cure syphilis, so I'll drink to that."

After a pull each, they turned to appreciate the coming of night and to sniff the sea air pressing at their faces.

Behind them, at the ship's stern and inside the ship's steering room, were bodies wrapped in canvas and hemp rope. Somewhere, about one hundred miles behind the bodies, were the two sailing vessels and nine members of his crew. In front of the bow, on the far side of those clouds, was the historic seaport where they would drop off those bodies and resupply for a new mission, a mission that they were just informed of but knew nothing of its intent or perils.

Hillary placed his glass on the ledge of the handrail while reaching into his shirt pocket. He pulled out a folded piece of stationery from the radio room. Unfolding it, he looked at the handwritten words. He repeated those words out loud as if rereading them would reveal some sort of hidden message. "Your gunnery officer is recovering. Illness brought on by a suspected poisoning. Still determining cause. Proceed to HMS Tamar in Hong Kong and board American consulate and stores. Transfer bodies and Harrison's possessions, along with an official report of the action, and remain to wait for crews returning sailing vessels. Once together, proceed to Port of Keelung to receive a US Army intelligence officer. Major Hugh Rodham will be at Raphael's with further instructions. Excellent completion of a successful mission."

"My ass," Fowler stated as he inspected his whiskey glass. "Yes, we are returning two valuable sailing vessels along with two pirates. We also erased the Lassiter Brothers, and the Black Badgers, from the seas in doing so. And when we return to the Philippines, there will be enough commendations to go around, but we still have issues. A US Navy officer tried to kill me for some unknown reason. We decoded a message which was meant to keep us away from an island we know nothing about, and now we're going to Formosa to pick up another officer for God-knows-why. We embarked Harrison and look where it got us, and I just wonder if it was Harrison who poisoned the gunnery officer's chop suey."

The chief stopped talking as he looked at his commanding officer with widening eyes. The ship's captain returned the look with widening eyes of his own.

"Looks like we're getting old as we get older. We should've figured out how the gunnery officer was poisoned a while ago, or at least with what," Hillary said as he sat back in his chair. "The question is whether Harrison did it himself. To kill the gunnery officer or did he screw up just like with you? Or was he meant to take him out of the picture. Or did somebody else do it?"

"There seems to be quite a setup behind the scenes, but who? Why?" Fowler answered thoughtfully. "I like your idea about keeping everything under wraps."

"I agree. If we were to send a message back to headquarters and tell them to check the gunnery officer for mercury poisoning, then somebody'll wise up we're getting wise. It's best to not say anything. 'Sides, if he's no longer exposed, then he should have no long-lasting ill effects. I'm writing everything in my own logbook, so when this is over with, whatever it is, I'll have written testimony that will suffice as the official record. Something the Navy or the government can use to bust up whatever is going on. Or use it as evidence in my court-martial if we overthought whatever this is."

"Or evidence for some sort of infiltration of foreigners into our government," Fowler said with the wink of an eye, "but which foreigners?"

"That's a damned good question, and we can start with the Japanese," Hillary said. "Ever since the war with Russia in '05 the Japanese have been the supreme Asian military and naval power in Asia and Pacific. They also resent the presence of British colonies and enclaves stretching from India to Shanghai and us in the Philippines. Any future war in this region will be between us, the Brits, and the Japanese. The Chinese feel the same, but they're too busy fighting each other to have any influence."

"I'm going out on a limb, Skipper," the Chief said. "But I don't see Harrison working with Asian spies to take the Philippines or Hong Kong over. I can think of two other possibilities, starting with it's an inside job. You know, Americans themselves on some sort of revolution or coup. Or it's the Bolsheviks: the Reds."

Hillary paused before answering. "An American coup against their own government to create their own country might be a stretch, but not out of the realm of possibilities. And the Japanese still have a way to go before they can take on two modern Western powers, and we're not even talking about the Dutch and the French. The most probable assumption is an effort by the Reds, or even the Whites."

"Why the Whites? I know a lot of them migrated to China and elsewhere to form organizations to raise money and support," the chief said. "So, I would think that they would just want to retake Russia, not an island in the South China Sea?"

"I wouldn't discount the motives of the White Russians too soon,

but let's look at the Reds, and persons such as Harrison. Socialist rhet-
oric has been around well before the Bolshevik Revolution in 1917. The
American Eugene Debs is a most recent example, and the German Karl
Marx is a more distant one, but the point is that Bolshevism has had
time to attract quite a gathering. Also, while the Reds are trying to sta-
bilize their own government in Russia, they're trying to export socialism
as well. Think about it: the Dutch in the East Indies, the French in Indochina, the Portuguese at Macau, the Americans in the Philippines,
and the Brits in Hong Kong. And that's just here in the Orient. There's
Africa and South and Latin America. Places rife with imperialism, sub-
jugated populations, and resentment. I've been keeping up on current
affairs, and the Reds have a group: The Third International or Comintern, and it's their job to sow seeds of discontent, to use the resentment
many Asians, and others, have against their Western masters. To rise and
throw off the stranglehold of imperialism and to seek sovereignty, albeit
under the surreptitious control of the Reds. And the Reds also have secret police they call the *Cheka,* a force that I've heard is not very sociable."

"Well, Professor Hillary, I guess you have been keeping up on current
affairs," the chief said with a sideway look. "Of all the possibilities, the ones
that sound the most likely include the infiltration of the American military
and government by American anarchists and foreign socialists. Which means
we don't know who to trust."

"Again, I'm going to write everything down," the captain said. "And I'm
going to cross every T and dot every I, and I'm going to keep that log a secret
until we can find somebody to turn it over to. Somebody we can trust."

"Sounds like the best thing at the moment, but there is something else."

"What's that, Chief?"

"Mister Kermit's hobby is English, right?"

"He reads early classic literature," Hillary answered as he narrowed his
eyes.

"Thought so," the chief said with a nod. "Who knows when we'll be able to find somebody we can trust? Which means there will be quite a bit of mileage between now and then."

"And your point is?" Hillary asked with a voice dripping of skepticism.

"My point is that we keep track of every single little intrigue, and when this is all said and done, we can use Mister Kermit's skill as a writer, your logbook, and my . . ."

"Your what?"

"My personality to create a novel. Think about it. When shit hits the fan, it'll be the story of the century. American sailors thwarting a Red infiltration into the American government and military. A book, not written by a deskbound, bow-tied pencil neck, but a book written with pens filled with saltwater and blood onto pages smelling of brimstone and gunpowder. We'll be rich!"

"Damn it. Have you no shame?"

"C'mon, Skipper, think about it: Spies, intrigue on the high seas, pirate battles on blood-soaked beaches, mystery ships, coded messages, and shadowy islands being watched by sleeping wise men. Just think who could play us if they turn the book into a moving picture: Valentino could play you, and maybe Fairbanks play me. Now as far as Kermit—"

Hillary was about to answer but the door next to the chart table slamming open interrupted him. Sparks erupted from the open door. Krivor, Hillary, and Fowler all turned to see him race to the bridge wing. The look on his face was alarming.

"Skipper! Mister Kermit's being attacked by a flying one-eyed whale and a flying red-eyed, fire-breathing dragon!"

CHAPTER 20

STILL SITTING ON the deck of the of the submarine between the rails, but now with a bottle of Captain Vostok's wine between them, Dooley and Zeta watched the sunset still off to their right. The bottle itself was inserted into a two-foot-deep well in the deck. Dooley glanced down at the well and wondered its purpose. He thought back to when he was on the troopship that brought him to Russia. He saw, before they left New York and when they resupplied in London, holes where the sailors assembled and installed portable cranes to help lift smaller loads. Turning his attention back to the sunset, they enjoyed wine from proper glasses as they watched the setting sun illuminate the silvery clouds in front of it. Now that the mission was over, the wine tasted sweeter, and the sunset was more appealing. Dooley thought back to Utkin's proposal.

"This reminds me of the wine my father used to drink back when he could afford it," Zeta said, bringing Dooley back to the present.

Dooley heard her voice and brought himself back. He said truthfully as he took his eyes from the luminescent clouds to her innocent face, "And like my father used to say, when he sprung for good wine himself, it's all that much better when in good company."

"Thank you," she said as she tilted her glass in salute.

He tilted his glass then took a sip. After a pause, she spoke. "So—"

"I am sorry to interrupt your conversation," Captain Vostok said.

Dooley and Zeta turned their heads toward each other as they looked up.

Their lips were inches apart. They saw the two men with wine glasses in their own hands, smiling down at them. Vostok pointed with his glass of wine. "I suggest you finish your wine, but in due time, as a lovely drop such as this one should never be rushed. Once finished though, get below, and collect your things. We will soon have the opportunity to stretch our legs."

Both Dooley and Zeta followed the direction of Vostok's arm. So fixated on the sunset to their right, and their future, they failed to notice the island ahead of them, although they could be excused for missing the detail. Pressed under the weight of a darkening sky, they saw a thin, black line with a salient bump in the center.

* * *

An hour later, as the submarine approached the island's western U-shaped beach, Dooley absorbed his new surroundings. He was still on the foredeck of the submarine and still next to Zeta, who now grasped the hooped wooden handles of her carpet bag, which pressed against her bulky trousers. Dooley wore his pistol belt around his waist, with the wooden handle of his shingle hammer jammed through it. The strap of his musette bag rested across his chest, and the sling of his Thompson hung over his shoulder, held in place with his hand. A partially filled duffel dangled from his left hand. Between them and the bow stood two submariners, each holding a coiled length of the submarine's mooring lines in their hands. All stood between the sets of metal tracks bolted to the deck. While watching as they glided toward the electrically lit pier, Dooley thought about the hot steak and cold milk Utkin promised him. He also patted the musette bag and felt the heel of the Mary Jane, wondering why he still had it.

With the sun sequestered beyond the horizon and now, darkened clouds, and the stars having yet made their appearance, the only lighting came from the few electric lampposts outlining the wooden pier about fifty yards ahead. Under that yellowish lighting stood four shabbily dressed Asian men and two skinny dogs. The dogs' barking roiled off into the night air. At the shore end of the pier, where a narrow, rock-strewn beach backed by a short dirt-paved street stretched into the darkness on either direction, was a wagon with a pony tethered to it. On the other side of the wagon and pony was a row of two-story wooden buildings backing the dirt-paved street. Separating the row of buildings in half was a road that came from the island's interior straight to the pier. Dooley saw unlit advertisements decorating the front of the buildings, and the only lighting from the buildings leaked through slits in the window blinds on the second floors. Dooley looked down at the wrist holding the sling of his weapon on his shoulder. It was 8 p.m.

The Asian men on the pier waited for the ends of the mooring lines while the dogs kept up their barking. The only other sound was the rhythmic echoing of the diesels escaping through the exhaust ports aft of the submarine's conning tower. The sounds of the marine engines and the dogs blended while rolling into the darkness, and as Dooley listened, he thought about the salient mountain he observed while approaching the island during sunset.

Suddenly, Captain Vostok's voice joined the engines and the dogs. Dooley turned in Vostok's direction and saw him standing on the conning tower, barking into the open hatch at his feet. Almost immediately, Dooley heard a change in the diesel's rpm and felt the difference though the soles of his athletic shoes. The submarine's bow nudged past the end of the pier, and the submariners on the foredeck tossed the coils to two of the waiting Asians. With the ropes in their hands, two men on the pier kept pace with the submarine. The barking dogs followed as the men on the aft deck of the submarine threw their lines to the two other Asians.

It did not take much longer to moor the vessel, to secure the diesels, and for the submarine raiders to push their duffels and weapons out through the deck hatches with them following. One at a time, the raiders disembarked across the vessel's gangplank. Utkin, Dooley, and Zeta followed. The four Asian men, dressed in ragged, but clean clothing in styles that spanned several decades, remained on the pier. They continued their silence as they inspected Dooley and Zeta while their dogs were busy sniffing everybody's legs and wagging their tails.

"Now what?" Dooley asked Utkin while looking at the men inspecting him.

Utkin, standing next to one of the electric lamps lifted the duffel he held by a strap and handed it to a waiting Asian while saying something to Gorki in Russian. Gorki saluted Utkin and started to walk toward the end of the pier and a wagon and pony. The raiders followed, including Morda and Mashka, who paused long enough to flash Dooley a smile and a thumbs up. One of the Asian men walked with them. As Dooley returned Mashka's smile, he felt somebody tug at his musette bag. He turned to see another Asian, one with a brown-stained smile, wrap an even darker, brown-skinned hand around the strap.

"Hey!"

Utkin spoke. "He wants to take your kit to the wagon. It will end up at our quarters."

"I carry my own gear," Dooley said with a nod toward Zeta. "He can take Zeta's though."

The Asian man seemed to understand and reached for Zeta's carpet bag, which she readily handed over. The man accepted the bag and was turning to join his comrades, but Utkin stopped him long enough to hand over a pack of English cigarettes. Utkin then started out after his comrades. Zeta and Dooley and the two yapping dogs followed. When the men reached the wagon, the Asian stepped up into the bench seat as Morda said something loudly. The rest of the men broke out into laughter while dumping their duffels in the wagon.

"Where are they going and what are they laughing at?" Dooley asked as he and Zeta approached the end of the pier. He saw Zeta's cheek blush slightly.

"Their barracks," Utkin replied, "which is south of here. After a wash and a change of clothing they plan on visiting the Hog Pen. Morda was bragging about his sexual abilities."

"Hog Pen?"

"Yes," Utkin said with a smile that accentuated the scar on his cheek. "It's a club constructed by my men for after-duty hours where I allow limited access to ardent spirits. But there is plenty of the island-made wine and hard cider, which you will appreciate. The club has a piano, and my men are quite adept with string instruments. It also houses the island's brothel. The staff are not much to look at. In fact, they are the ugliest whores this side of the Himalayas, but through Gorki's diligence, they are the cleanest whores this side of the Himalayas. Guaranteed not to cause any casualties among my men."

Both Zeta and Dooley looked at Utkin's back questioningly while Dooley spoke up. "If you don't mind me saying, Major Utkin, this looks like a one-horse island, so I'm a bit surprised to hear it comes with its own cathouse."

Utkin smiled in return. "You are correct. This island is truly a one-horse island, however, that will change. The pony's name is Tin-tin, and the islanders asked if I could reward their hospitality with another pony. Tin-tin's mate was killed by a tree fall. The replacement is scheduled to arrive along with supplies. Once off-loaded, that ship will be your transportation away from this island as well. As far as the brothel, I can explain as we stretch our legs, but let me just start with saying that my men are young, fit, and virile. A side of nature I cannot ignore."

They heard the man in the wagon give an order in Chinese while snapping the reins. Tin-tin obeyed and started to turn left. Its unshod hooves pounded the dirt. The three of them, now standing side by side, watched the pony and wagon complete the turn and fade into the darkened road leading into the trees and away from the beach.

With Vostok and the submarine behind them, Major Utkin held out his hand. "Your cold milk and hot steak await."

Dooley looked at Zeta, who looked back. Dooley nodded and stepped forward.

"Excellent," Utkin said as he stepped forward as well. "Don't forget, though, you promised an answer to my proposal. However, let me be the gracious host as we walk. I'll give you a summarized history of the island, and how we ended up here, and hopefully, I will have your answer in three kilometers."

They stepped off the pier toward the storefronts on the other side of the narrow street. As they did, the last pair of weak, electric lamps marked their departure like uniformed royal yeomen outside the Queen's door. The buildings were what anybody would see along any waterfront, although they did not look like they had been too busy. Dooley noticed undisturbed sand on the planks in front of the building closest to him. He also saw sand piled in the lower corners of the windowsills. On the right side of the road were what looked like a barber shop and bathhouse complete with the striped barber pole, a saloon advertising Tsingtao Beer, and a tobacco shop offering the finest blends. On the left half were what looked like a butcher shop, an apothecary, and another saloon, which also advertised Tsingtao Beer. These buildings reminded Dooley of some of the older storefronts back home.

"Excuse me, Major, I can't help but be reminded of certain streets in Brooklyn, but we're on an island stuck between the Pacific Ocean and the East China Sea."

"You always seem to be so observant—a trait that will bode well in our effort to thwart the spread of Bolshevism around the world."

Dooley responded as they stepped onto the dirt road. "I haven't agreed to any contracts yet."

"Fair enough, Sergeant Dooley, and your statement about Brooklyn concerns the ending of our tour, so let me start from the beginning."

By now, they joined the road that led into the woods behind the waterfront road and buildings. As they passed between the buildings, Dooley saw the picnic tables, outhouses, and clotheslines in the small yards behind the buildings. "Go ahead."

"This island," Utkin started, "has a long history. It is also off the normal shipping lanes, which is why I selected this island to for my organization."

Now, on the road proper, which was paved with rough cut stones, it became extremely dark under the canopy of branches that tried to join from each side of the road. Though dark, Dooley recognized the trees as a mixture of tropical, semi-tropical, and temperate.

"The first of the island's visitors seemed to have been Chinese explorers. There has been speculation the Chinese followed the prevailing winds and currents of the North Pacific and traveled as far as North America, and islands such as this one served as stops for resupply and repair. There is circumstantial evidence that they called the island 'The Sleeping Brothers.'"

"You're saying the Chinese visited North America?" Zeta asked.

"Speculation," Utkin answered, "but there is enough evidence to assume the Chinese visited the Americas hundreds of years before Columbus, but the Chinese found only naked savages living in caves or animal-skin shelters. No economies, populations, or cites to trade with, which is why they turned their trading focus along the coasts of Africa, Persia, and India."

They walked up the slight incline to where the road leveled out. It was now a smooth dirt road, which continued into darkness with seemingly no end. However, they saw the occasional flash of a light through the trees to the south and could hear the slight hum of a generator coming from somewhere ahead of them. Utkin continued his verbal tour.

"For hundreds of years after the Chinese, no one needed to visit this island, but then Magellan found a way around South America by going under it and was able to conquer the Philippines on the other side of the Pacific. That conquest allowed the Spanish to begin trading in silks and porcelains from China, spices from the Indies, and pearls, gems, and ivory from Siam. The problem was the Portuguese controlled all trade between mainland Asia and Europe, meaning the Indian Ocean, and the routes around Africa and into the Atlantic. That meant the Spanish had to create a trade route going east to the New World, since going around Cape Horn was impractical. So, by the mid-1500s, the Spanish were able to map a good portion of the New World including what is now Mexico and the Isthmus of Panama. With the Pacific Ocean on the west side and the Caribbean Sea, the Gulf of Mexico, and Cuba on the east side, and plenty of pack animals in between, the Spanish conceived the trade system known as the Manila Galleon. What developed was an annual sailing of ships, starting in 1565, departing the Philippines with Oriental treasures onboard and following the prevailing winds and currents north from the Philippines. However, the Japanese closed off their islands, and any unfortunate Europeans who found themselves cast ashore in Japan were executed outright or worked to death as slaves."

By now, they walked a distance from the beach, and the unhurried exercise felt good. Suddenly, the trees that enclosed them seemed to disappear. Also, the hum of the distant generator grew slightly louder. Ahead of them, Dooley saw the outline of a building in the distance, out in the open, with hints of lights escaping it. Between them and that building, he also began to see the angular shadows of unlit structures. Dooley also saw that the trees did not disappear but were cut back by at least fifty yards either side of the road. He looked up and saw stars twinkling against the black sky. Those stars helped outline a central mountain that seemed to lord over the island. It was a perfect evening: a cool night, walking under the stars while listening to tales of Spanish treasure ships. They continued, and Dooley noticed track imprints in the road. The imprints were the same width as the tracks bolted to the deck of the submarine.

"Since traveling close to Japan was unadvisable," Utkin continued, "the ships had to stay further out to sea the farther north they went and, in doing so, ran into this island. Realizing the same thing the Chinese did, the Spanish knew it would serve them nicely before continuing the four-month long voyage around the North Pacific Ocean and down the coast of North America to the western coast of *Nueva España*. The island supplied fresh water and wood for fires and ship repair. There were also beaches for careening hulls. They recorded what they found including species native to mainland China, namely pork and fowl. Such evidence supports speculations about Chinese visitations. The Spanish also recorded the island's location as best they could, and with each new voyage of the Manila Galleon, the island was improved. So, with each stop, they planted a peach pit, an acorn, or a yam. And when they could afford to do so, they released a pair of goats or swine. The idea was that these animals would reproduce, keep the ground cover to a minimum, and provide meat, milk, cheese, and leather."

"Did the island become permanently inhabited by the Spanish?" Zeta asked.

"In a way. The island served as a place to bury anybody who died at the start of the voyage. Disposing of bodies over the side, although necessary, seemed sacrilegious to the Catholic Spanish, and carrying bodies onboard occupied precious space. Also, if anybody started to show signs of disease or illness, they were left behind to prevent the spread of disease onboard, which is the reason why the Spanish, after their first stop, built a church to conse-crate the dead and to provide shelter and religious solace for those left behind. Also, leaving a person behind meant more rations, water, and space for those left aboard."

"Were any persons left behind voluntarily? What about the clergy?" Zeta asked again.

"No 'volunteers' were recorded as being left behind," Utkin answered. "Anybody traveling with the Manila Galleon was intent on reaching Spain, or at least Mexico or the Spanish Main. Remember that anybody leaving the Philippines was traveling with personal fortunes that would provide enough wealth to set them up for life. As for the clergy, while men of cloth did take their vows seriously, piety went only so far. If a clergyman was left behind, it was because he contracted some sort of illness himself. And to answer a fur-ther question, there was no extended or continuous lineage established by the Spanish castaways on the island as it was physically not possible. According to the Spanish records, anybody left behind was found dead by the subsequent Manila Galleon. Their bodies were usually locked within the wooden struc-ture of the church. I guess they knew they were about to die, so, when the time was near, they fortified themselves inside so that their bodies would not be ravaged by feral swine or seabirds. Their remains were buried in the graveyard behind, or under, the church."

Utkin paused to appreciate the night sky.

"It is possible to assume that the reason why nobody was ever found alive after, at minimum, a year's solitude, despite the island's restorative qualities, was a simple one: Nobody wanted to be left behind, so if they started to feel the effects of their disease at the start of the voyage or even before departing the Philippines, they would hide any symptoms until a point where symptoms could no longer be hidden from passenger and crew, and the diseases had done their damage. Anyway, those left behind were told to maintain the church and graveyard and wait to be picked up by the next fleet. And that is the reason why the earliest Spanish records identified the island as *Isla de la Muerte*. However, the name 'Island of the Dead' was not well received by those who were or would be left behind, so, because of the appearance of the island, the Spanish started to call it 'The Twin Saints' or 'Sleeping Saints.'" Anyway, the system worked well until the Spanish Empire collapsed itself. The last Manila Galleon to depart the Orient for Mexico sailed in 1811. At that point, the island again was abandoned."

"The island may have been abandoned by the Spanish," Dooley conceded, "but I have a question about those left behind and their goods. Even the lowest seaman had some sort of 'treasure' and if they were banished to the island because of disease or for whatever reason, what happened to their goods?"

"Good question," Utkin answered after a slight pause, "but we never thought about trying to answer that question ourselves. However, the Spanish did not simply abandon persons standing on the beach naked. They were allowed clothing, diaries, ink wells, personal religious texts, crucifixes, and rosary beads, but not the bulk of their goods as they were consigned to trusted signees. But it is possible to assume that the persons probably secreted what they could: a handful of pearls, a few gems, a gunpowder apostle filled with nuggets, or pieces of jewelry."

"If the island provided so much over the centuries, why was it left abandoned?" Zeta asked. "Why did nobody remain on this island permanently? Even after the Manila Galleon?"

"Good question again," Utkin said as they continued their easy gait under the growing number of bright stars against the wide black sky. "While the location did fit within the necessity of the Spanish to avoid having its subjects and treasures to be cast about on Japanese shores, that does not mean it sufficed the needs of other mariners, especially since the advent of steam-powered vessels and navigation technology improved over the decades. Even to-day, no matter how many lines you draw on the map, none of those lines come within two days sail, or steam, of this island. For that reason, it did attract its next resident, albeit only for a short time, and that being the famous Chinese lady pirate, Ching Shih. She operated from this island, as well as other islands, for a span in the 1820s as a base of supply and shelter while darting out to shipping lanes and attacking shipping. Something the pirates in the Caribbe-an did expertly. However, this particular island proved not worth the effort, so she abandoned this island."

Utkin stopped speaking as they walked. He, like the others, looked up into the incredibly beautiful night sky. "Is it not a brilliant night sky?"

Both Zeta and Dooley looked up in agreement before returning their eyes to their front. They saw an open, grassy field. On the right, or south side of the road, there were two single-story buildings offset from the road by about fifty feet or so and widely separated from each other. They appeared to be made from sheets of corrugated tin and had slanted roofs. The fronts were closed off with what looked like sliding doors. On the left were two other similar buildings set back off the road by about fifty feet as well. The setup reminded Dooley of another place and time, but he couldn't think of when or where. At the other end of the two buildings on the north side, Dooley saw a two-story building, with slits of light leaking through window curtains.

They walked the last kilometer past the rectangular tin sheds and stopped in front of that two-story house, which was situated off the road just like the tin-covered structures. It welcomed them with a wide porch and two large front windows with intact glass panes on both floors. The lighting sneak-ing out from behind the draped windows on the first floor accentuated the white-painted door between the two windows, and the porch columns made from stacked stone slabs and mortar. In front of the left-side window, four wicker chairs surrounding a square wooden table presented a solace that the submarine never could. Also, while the buildings at the waterfront reminded Dooley of Brooklyn, this house reminded Dooley of his uncle's farm in Up-state New York. During family reunions he played with his cousins while the adults spent the afternoons sitting on the porch, drinking beer, playing cards, and gossiping about the black sheep in their families or arguing over politics and unions. Appreciating the view, Dooley saw a plate-sized Coca-Cola logo mounted to the wall between the window and the door. It had a thermometer in its center just like at his uncle's house. A brass-ringed barometer hung from a hook under the Coca-Cola placard.

Unlike his uncle's house though, this one was powered by a generator. He could hear the muted hum coming from somewhere behind the house. Dooley looked to his side and saw a metal flagpole, again just like at his uncle's house, where flying the American flag was a duty. While there was no flag hanging from the pole, Dooley did see a weathervane with the silhouette of a dragon with what looked like a plowshare in front of it. Looking at the implement mounted to the top of the pole, he noticed, despite the darkness of the night, it was painted a bright orange. His thoughts were disrupted by the front door opening with the red-haired cook from the submarine filling the space. He wore clean, pressed slacks and a white cotton shirt. He said something in Russian.

Utkin responded and the cook nodded as he stepped through the open door and down the two-step staircase. He stopped in front of Dooley and held out his hands.

Utkin spoke to Dooley. "He'll take your kit to your room and clean your laundry."

"It shouldn't take him too long," Dooley said as he held out his partially filled duffel. "I'll take care of the rest."

"Good," Utkin said before saying something to the cook in Russian. Turning his attention back to Dooley he stated, "Your milk is on its way."

Dooley nodded and moved to turn over his duffel, weapons, web gear, and musette bag. He looked over the cook's shoulder and through the open door into the first floor. He saw a staircase and a full bookshelf under it. Further back was a brick fireplace with a thick, wooden mantle.

The Russian major continued to speak. "Since you are the lady of the house while on this island you will have primary access to the indoor water closet. While water is piped into the house, it still must be heated, so give us time to finish preparing your bath. Also, the cook was able to collect suitable clothing for you to wear as your personal effects will be laundered by morning. In the meantime, would you join us for some milk?"

She turned to look at Dooley. "That would do nicely."

"Good," Utkin said in English before turning to the cook, who had all of Dooley's kit in his hands. Utkin spoke in Russian to the man who nodded while turning to step up to the door. Utkin followed him onto the porch but turned to sit at the table on the porch.

* * *

Anybody looking at the ship from a wharf or from another ship would have dismissed it as just one of thousands of tramp steamers plying the Orient. A hull painted over so many times it was as if only those thick layers held the hull together. The high forecastle, with its rusting anchor windless and beat-up derrick and enclosed bosun locker underneath seemed to want to push the bow of the of the ship underwater. At the other end of the ship, the equally high, white-painted, two-story superstructure, topped with an enclosed box-like structure, also seemed to work at sinking the stern. In between was the length of the ship's rust-streaked hull. Though the hull appeared to be severely deteriorated, and the weighty ends seemed to almost snap the ship in half, the ship pushed itself south through the waters of the East China Sea.

Inside though, the setting differed. Borodin and Lagos, wearing casual linen clothing, reclined in padded wooden chairs in the ship's roomy salon. The men faced each other over a fine white tablecloth topped with an excellent merlot and two half-filled glasses all of which topped a stout oaken table. The dozen framed photos of islands and other ships mounted to the white-painted bulkheads listened to their after-dinner conversation while the open portholes admitted a cool, early evening breeze. The portholes piercing the starboard bulkhead also provided a viewing for another amazing Oriental sunset an hour ago. Now, after enjoying a pleasing dinner, the two men indulged their wine while waiting patiently for an updated radiotelegraph.

The first message, received just after sunset, indicated their targets, with their running lights switched on, were about to be attacked.

"I am beginning to appreciate why you seamen are drawn to a life at sea," Borodin said as he patted his stomach with one hand. "And the food aboard this vessel solidifies that sense of adventure along with singing me a lullaby."

Captain Issak Lagos patted his stomach as well. "She might not be much to look at from the outside but like any good whore, she has it where it counts, and from both ends."

"Speaking of which," Borodin said, "What of the damages to our asset?"

Lagos answered as he lifted his wine glass. "Three shells exploded in the airplane engine repair shop under the bridge but fortunately, everybody was on deck, so we lost no men. And another couple of shells exploded in the engine room. Feeling he had done enough to facilitate the action, the captain withdrew to wait for an opportunity. Now here we, and they, are."

Just then, the dark brown wooden door at the aft bulkhead of the salon opened. A studious looking man wearing pressed dungarees and a pencil behind an ear entered from the radio room behind him. He held a piece of yellow note paper in his hand.

Both men looked at him. "Ah, it looks like we have news," Lagos said with a smile.

However, the man holding the paper was not smiling.

CHAPTER 21

MINUTES LATER, BUT hundreds of miles away, three people sat at the table with their military blouses unbuttoned and holding glasses of cold milk in their hands. An electric lantern hung from a thick beam above them. A brass stand with an assortment of reading material stood under the windowsill. As they relaxed, Dooley looked at the magazine on top of the pile. It had a photo of man wearing a racing uniform and standing next to an expensive-looking bicycle on the front cover. Dooley quickly remembered the magazine he saw on the submarine. The one with the motorized bicycle and overhead propeller blades.

"Major Utkin," Dooley said while listening to the generator drone on, "I can see some European influence on the island, including this house."

"After the lady pirate abandoned her efforts, the island went fallow for two decades. Until a British subject named Brooks realized no country documented ownership of the island. Brooks made his fortune with real estate in London, New York City and, in the Far East. He took legal possession of this island through the British courts with the notion of turning it into a profitable way station for shipping. He imported workers, including women, from the mainland and built the pier and the waterfront we landed at."

Utkin took another gulp of milk before continuing.

"There is a similar beach on the east side of the island where he constructed a facility so boats and smaller ships could be drawn from the water and onto a covered railway to complete hull repairs as needed. He also imported cattle adding to the swine and goats rooting around this island. They all provided meat, milk, and hunting for ship's crews that he hoped would soon be stopping by. He also piped water to the pier and added to the fruit trees planted by the Spanish along with vineyards to produce a variety of wines and ciders. To construct this house, Brooks included stonecutters among his workers. They excavated into the bedrock and built the house over the excavation while using the stone from the excavation. The cellar became a ready typhoon shelter with a constant temperature of sixty degrees Fahrenheit. Excellent for the short-term storage of perishables and the long-term conditioning for wines and ciders. The house itself has withstood any number of tropical storms over the decades. The scheme was to have so much to offer captains would not mind sailing out of their way. Especially, if a ship ran into a storm and needed repairs or needed to restock food or water. He advertised this island in the shipping columns as Brooks Landing. His idea was sound but not his timing."

"What happened to disrupt what sounds like a good plan?" Dooley asked.

"Good old Yankee ingenuity," Utkin continued. "While Brooks was constructing this facility in the early 1840s, the American public grew more in need of Oriental products, so maritime architects developed their famous clipper ships. Sailing vessels renowned for their speed, they became the ultimate in the transportation and shipping technology. That introduction killed any opportunity for Brooks to be successful in his efforts, even after the heyday of the clipper ship, which ended by the 1850s. Brooks gave into reality and left the island but legally held onto it. In fact, his family still owns it today, but there hasn't been a Brooks family member on this island in years. While most of his workers left with him, some forsook the slums of Nanking and Shanghai. The men you saw on the pier are their descendants. There are three dozen or so islanders spread about the island who maintain it for the Brooks family."

"Now that we are caught up on the island's history," Dooley said as he enjoyed his milk, "you can explain your presence."

Utkin leaned forward to grab the glass pitcher of milk. As he lifted the container and topped off everybody's glasses, sweat dripped from the pitcher and landed on the table. Setting it back on the table, he explained. "When I, and others of a same frame of mind, wanted to organize an effort to stop the spread of Bolshevism, and restore Imperial Russia, we realized the assets we could use, including the submarine you spent the last week on. While we probably would not use it to attack Bolshevik shipping, at least not yet, we did plan on using the submarine as a platform for clandestine operations. However, the sovereign nations in Asia, namely Japan, and the Europeans and Americans who either control the rest of Asia directly through colonialism or indirectly through imperialism, would not tolerate a military submarine armed with torpedoes and submariners lounging about its ports. Also, we had to covertly build a cadre of multi-faceted fighters to complete our missions and, just like the submarine, there are few places with which to do so. We needed a secure place to solidify my effort. I did my research and here we are."

Utkin paused long enough to hold up his hands before continuing.

"Since the 1850s, the island's residents have lived in solitude, created an extended family of sorts, and welcomed the odd ship needing repairs while offering a butchered beeve or a keg of cider at the same time. I, and Captain Vostok, among a few others, arrived several months ago on a tramp steamer with 'mechanical difficulties,' which forced us to remain on the island for a good number of days. We befriended the island's residents and used our time for 'sport hunting' and saw that it would suit our needs. We 'repaired' the steamer and left but returned with that steamer and the submarine, and between both vessels, started to import men and supplies needed to construct our operation."

"What did they ask for in return?" Dooley asked as he brought the glass of milk to his lips once more. "And could you trust them not to say anything after your departure?"

"Good question," Utkin said as he fingered the rim of his glass. "They are an innocent lot who have had the fortune to not get caught in modern world-ly affairs. Although they would not turn their eyes away from the occasional newspaper, book, or periodical donated by a visiting vessel. There are perhaps five celebrated men here who can read either English or Mandarin Chinese. When a new piece of material is available, these men become the island's thespians who act out what they are reading to a captive audience as if they were characters in a Shakespeare play, and the end of the pier becomes the Globe Theatre. We added to that bookshelf under the staircase. The whole island came to watch their performance as they read a copy of Stephen Crane's classic novel. I never thought that the reading of a young man's involvement in a single battle during the Civil War could be so moving."

"What about money?" Zeta asked as she wiped milk from her upper lip.

"Countess," Utkin offered, "they are not enslaved to the hegemony of specie or the sorcery of bank notes. Instead, their currency consists of a pair of scissors, a spool of thread, a bar of soap, a packet of Camels, or a bottle of rum, a pound of Folgers, or even the tin it came in. A rusty tin full of bent nails is worth more than a chest of gold sovereigns. But since we are on the topic, I would keep an eye on your knife and shingle axe of yours."

"So, what about your submarine?" Dooley asked. "I can't imagine you would just have it tied up to the pier on any given day. You know, just in case the odd ship does stop by. Perhaps one from the Bolshevik Navy? And Bolshevik marines?"

"True enough, Sergeant Dooley," Utkin answered with a nod. "As we laid the groundwork for our operation, we discovered a shallow cave at the southern end of the island, under a lengthy hill that you will see in the morning. Among my cadre are sappers, so with the proper use of explosives and simple pioneering tools, we were able to create a niche large enough. The barracks for my submarine raider commando, and the Hog Pen, are within steps of the hill."

"What about the air assault commando? Where's their base?" Dooley asked as he brought the glass of milk to his lips. It was almost empty.

"Their barracks is in the forest behind us. It is at the base of the island's central mountain."

"Do they have their very own off-duty clubhouse?" Dooley asked.

Utkin smiled, "Their barracks is a simple structure providing for indoor

sleeping and outdoor eating and toilet areas, like the other commando barracks, and is their base for training and mountain climbing exercises, so no.
However, since they and members of my other commandos remained behind,
and with the fact that I have only seven whores, they have their place at the
back of the queue. My men, including the air assault commando volunteers
understand."

"Volunteers?"

"Yes," Utkin replied. "While all my operatives must meet exacting health
and physical stamina requirements, being a member of the air assault commando entails more risk. All my men volunteered, including Gorki, Morda,
and Mashka, but I must be judicious in my selections. Like you have alluded
to, with my ability to play poker, I pride myself on being able to read people
and abilities, and to place the right person in the right place at the right time."

"Which is why you enlisted Sergeant Dooley?" Zeta asked with a proud
smile.

Utkin answered with a confident smile himself. "Basically, I matched
best talents with the right commando to maximize our efforts to combat the
Reds wherever they may appear. And do not forget I have noticed Dooley's
attributes. You both shall see my wisdom tomorrow morning. I have had the
concept of a new type of delivery vehicle swimming about my head for some
time and sketched out rough diagrams for my engineers to fabricate over the
last number of weeks. They, along with my air-assault operatives, were tasked
with finalizing the creation of special delivery vehicles and to have them ready
for testing upon our return."

Dooley paused to finish his glass of milk. While doing so, he thought back
to Utkin's futuristic-looking silencer for his revolver and the canvas-and-rub-
ber frogman fins for his men. Lastly, he thought about the athletic shoes that
they used while wearing the fins and conducting the raid. "Looking forward
to it."

"I am glad to hear of your interest," Utkin said as he too finished his milk.
"So, do you have an answer to my proposal?"

Dooley looked out of the corner of his eye and saw Zeta's apprehension.

"You were a bit sketchy on certain details the last time we talked."

"Understood," Utkin continued with a nod. After a pause he continued. "I would ask you to divest yourself of this operation and take the transportation off this island when it arrives. After your transportation deposits you in Formosa, you need to walk off that jetty and fall into a waterfront gin joint, spend your hard-earned pay, and befriend others of your ilk. If anybody asks, you completed a job for some rogue White Russians in order to earn enough money for a passage to Latin America, where you will seek your fortune through other means. Perhaps as a fishing charter captain with a penchant for flying. Since the end of the war, there will be quite a number of persons looking at spending their time and money at fishing. There will also be quite a few trained, and unemployed, pilots languishing about in bars and hotel lobbies; therefore, your presence would not be an anomaly. There are also fleets of surplus airplanes in need of use, and since the Caribbean consists of islands and shorelines where communications through mail and other means is quite important, I foresee aviation becoming integral to the region and part of your future. Correct so far?"

"So far," Dooley answered, "but I am not an experienced seaman, nor a pilot."

"You are right," Utkin replied. "But what you are is a young, ex-soldier looking for a little adventure, which include flying instruction. To pay for your instructions you will take day labor matching your abilities."

"Are there any other reasons," Dooley asked, "that would require me to become familiar to the region, the culture, and the lingo?"

"Yes, yes, and yes, Sergeant Dooley. Along with becoming a fixture as an experienced pilot who can be called upon when needed and one that anybody can learn to trust whether you are sitting in the cockpit of an airplane, idling the afternoon away in a neighborhood cantina, or spending the weekend fixing up a worthless fishing boat for your own use. Just like there are numerous populations throughout Asia the Reds would like to exploit, the same holds true with Latin American and the Caribbean. Your job would be to spend a few years in the area, to become part of the local scenery."

"Like a flowerpot?"

"A flowerpot ferrying humans and mail via airplane or charter boat into a rundown Mexican seaport village. But also, to keep your wits about you, and to support our operations when the need arises. It is close enough to Brooklyn for the occasional visit home via passenger ship or a Pullman from Miami if you are tired of the sea, but far enough away to satiate your wanderlust. After all, a squandered youth creates a bitter old man. Anyway, having a person such as you in place would be of great benefit to your country, especially since America shares a long border with Mexico, and Cuba is ninety miles from Florida. Both locations populated by citizens who take umbrage with America's perceived colonial presence. Lands perfect for Red exploitation."

"I see your point," Dooley said, "and I agree about the threats to my country."

Major Utkin leaned back in his chair and his face broke into a broad smile, which stretched his scar. "So, you will accept my offer?"

Dooley, though, could not see the same enthusiasm on Zeta's face. "What about Zeta?"

Both men paused to look at Zeta. She looked back with confusion and concern.

Dooley saw her uncertainty. "While she is left only with the family name, you are literally holding the family jewels. The same jewels that you will use to fight a Red threat to the world. You've offered a niche to an unemployed ex-doughboy who started out with fifty-two dollars and twenty-eight cents in his pocket while taking the long journey back to Brooklyn, USA. The same soldier who is a high-school dropout and speaks only one language, although I've learned to curse in Russian. I believe you can find a position for Countess Zeta Tolstoy, an educated woman who is knowledgeable of the arts, well read, and multilingual. As a member of your intelligence detective commando? A Pinkerton?"

Dooley noticed, while speaking, that Zeta sat straighter in her chair.

Utkin paused while he looked at both and after a few seconds, replied, "You are correct, Sergeant, and I have given thought as to how Miss Zeta here can continue to be an effective member of our organization. And I do like how you used the term Pinkerton in the positive. An excellent reference to the birth of detection as a profession and the formation of counterintelligence agencies." The Russian major paused long enough to turn toward Zeta. "A Pinkerton, huh, and a lady one at that."

"I would not be the first," Zeta answered firmly.

"Ah, you know your American history," Utkin said with appreciation. He paused again, but only for a second. "I dare say, though, going back to Shanghai would be problematic. Too many interested persons who know of your involvement in the raid. Instead, you might be best situated elsewhere. As far as your parents, we can provide overseership to prevent any sort of distraction."

Zeta's eyes brightened as she sat straighter in her chair. "A Pinkerton? In the Caribbean?"

"Possibly," Utkin said, stopping long enough to sip his milk, "but if anybody saw you together while Dooley was operating as an innocent boat captain or pilot ferrying who knows what in and out of Caracas, it might reveal his identity. Or yours. Let me think on the issue while we are on this island. Your transportation off the island will be here soon, and I will have a proposal for you then. That said, you strike me as a person who is continental in nature. Perhaps posing as an art student in Madrid?"

Utkin retuned his attention to Dooley.

"So, Sergeant Thomas Dooley, what is your answer?"

"It appears that you think of me as a bit less 'continental,' but you are correct in your assessments," Dooley answered while lifting his glass, "as I am partial to idling my afternoons away in shithole cantinas."

"Then shithole cantinas it shall be," Utkin replied with a huge smile that further accentuated the scar on his cheek.

"I will hold you to your word," Dooley responded, "but will we have direct contact with you or your operatives?"

"In our modern times, there are any number of communications methods available. Do you know anything of radios?"

Dooley answered, "I was a member of the American Marconi Radio

Club sponsored by the public library in my neighborhood, and that experience almost got me assigned to Regiment's signal section, but I wanted to be a field soldier. I also saw radio operators up at Battalion or Regiment during briefings."

"It is a start," Utkin answered. "However, any need for a communications plan is in the future. But for now, let us see if the air-assault commando fits your wanderlust."

"Fair enough," Dooley answered, "as I want to do my bit to keep the Reds out of Brooklyn and am willing to work with your men. But will that include Gorki? He seems so perfect, and I can see his wavy black hair and chiseled good looks disarming quite a few females on the dance floor or in their beds. The only problem is that I don't think I've heard him speak more than a dozen words in either English or Russian. In fact, your men tend to be tight lipped."

"You are right in that he can be useful in so many areas, but I have detailed him to our intelligence detective commando," Major Utkin said as he picked up his glass of milk. "I'm recalling an old proverb: 'those who speak the least tend to hear the most.'"

"And I can think of another proverb, Major, and it goes something like, 'the best doctors are those that are the best listeners.' Something about bedside manner. I'm saying that because I have been made to understand the right doctor with the right patients can gather the right information. You know, those who have, what some might consider embarrassing 'maladies.'"

"Again, you are correct, Sergeant Dooley. Strategic control and knowledge are vital assets in our business, hence, the prostitutes. Like you said, Gorki has several attributes, but being a physician specializing in venereal disease and gynecology is one such trait. One that well-placed patients, including Red agents who can get VD or request abortions will appreciate. While I imported these women for the benefit of my men, I also imported them from the most wretched streets of Nanking and Shanghai for Gorki."

"You scrounged up a gang of scab-ridden whores for your men's, and Gorki's, benefit?"

"Well," Utkin said with a grin, "while I needed sexual releasers for my men, I was given an issue. I could have started with good-looking, white whores, ones with clean health cards, and from prominent establishments along Huashan Road, but they surely would be missed. And ones that might be smart enough to use their knowledge of what they have seen here on this island. Also, if I were to dispose of them permanently after the completion of their tenure, then that would invite attention I would not care for."

"And you would not have had guinea pigs for Gorki," Dooley stated.

"Yes, and I could have rounded up some Euro-trash main street trollops or even some back-alley owls. Ones that may have not had their health cards updated or ones that may not be missed as readily. Even still, I went the exact opposite track. I contracted several Chinese 'employees' that were in dire straits. Women in need of money, human compassion, decent housing, and good medical care. Upon completion of their services, they are promised lucrative compensation, and in exchange for continued compliance, and silence."

"Your reasoning is sound, but do you think your efforts will make sure they hold up their end of the bargain?"

"Sergeant Dooley, they are literally holding up their end of the bargain as we speak."

Both men looked at Zeta. She brought her eyes to the table with blushing cheeks.

"I am sorry, Countess," Major Utkin apologized. "Sometimes boys will be boys."

Just then, before she could reply, the submarine's cook opened the front door and popped his head out. He said something to the major.

After listening, the major nodded his head. "Countess, you heard him. Your bath is drawn, and clothing has been laid out, so please. Sergeant, you will be next, but in the meantime, what cuts of beef do both of you prefer, and how would like your beef prepared?"

CHAPTER 22

JUST LIKE SO many mornings in the Orient, this morning was brilliant and soul heartening, but it failed to lift the spirits of the men aboard the USS Decatur, including those of Lieutenant Hillary and Chief Fowler. Like the men not detailed for other duties, Hillary, and Fowler, standing on the bridge, searched the seas for their missing shipmates. They hoped for the best but feared the worst. Hillary, with binoculars hanging from his neck, so much wanted to see bulging sails racing toward him. Once under the security of the ship's guns, they could all continue to Hong Kong safe and sound. However, after receiving that spine-chilling radio message, the best he could hope for was to see a dinghy, overloaded with nine bedraggled seamen, bobbing in the blue sea. He didn't want to think about the worst.

"Captain, it's well past dawn, and we've been searching for hours. I don't want to be the one to say it, but . . ."

Both men fell silent. After a minute, Hillary continued, "Ernst, I can't give up."

"I know you can't, Rance, and I don't want to either, but we've got to face reality. We're where they should be, and we've been looking for hours. The only thing we've seen here is that beat-up tramp steamer just before sunrise. And the only thing the captain of the tub said was that the bridge watch woke him after midnight where they reported what looked like some sort of gun battle going on to the south, over the horizon. Maintaining best speed, they spent the rest of the night getting to and searching this area. That was until we showed up, and neither one of us spotted anything. Not a single kapok or paddle. Maybe the currents carried off what was left. Who knows? They could be dead, or they could be adrift in an overcrowded lifeboat. Or they could end up on a deserted island somewhere. But your commanding officer's breathing down your neck, and there are chopped-up bodies in our steering room, and it's June. I've also been watching the barometer. And don't forget that we have to explain to the Brits about missing property. Lastly, our men were attacked by air machines that shouldn't even exist."

"Just like that ship and airplane at Bagay Alto," Hillary said. "Somehow they're connected."

Both men paused to look back out to sea.

After a few seconds, Fowler continued the conversation. "So, the governor-general of the Philippines is a bit put out that his nephew's dead?"

Hillary scoffed quietly. "Can you believe it? The man wants a full report as to how his nephew died, and he wants to know if his nephew's actions warrant a medal."

"Told you. That stiff-ass ring knocker was in it for the medals. Now his family wants something they can put on the fireplace mantle to display to friends and family during holiday dinners. That's one for the books."

"I know it is, but his death is the least of my worries," Hillary said with sorrowful surrender in his voice while looking at his wristwatch. After a brief pause, he finished. "We'll continue this search pattern for one more hour. At that time, we'll turn the helm to get us back on track for Hong Kong. At flank speed we should arrive by tomorrow evening. To hell with burning up fuel unnecessarily. They can keep my pay. I'll put together a report in the meantime."

"Are you going to put into your official report the exact words we received from Mister Kermit?" Fowler asked. "About the flying one-eyed whale and the flying fire-spitting dragon?"

"I'm inclined to keep the exact description to ourselves, Ernst. We'll just add it to a list of mysteries we need to solve on our own."

"Speaking of mysteries," Fowler asked, "is there any need to suspect that beat-up tramp steamer? I mean it just happened to be in the area where we lost our shipmates."

"I don't know about that, Ernst, but I do know that the only thing holding that tub together was fifty years of paint and rust, and it was flying a British merchant marine flag, and its registry on the stern indicated Hong Kong. The captain said he was enroute to Jakarta with a cargo of machine parts and two steam locomotive engines, which explained the items under the tarpaulins on the main deck. Both of us have seen hundreds of ships like that. Why?"

"Just wondering. It's been a tough last couple of days, which all centers around Harrison trying to shoot me in the head. We don't know who to trust. Or who would believe us?"

"I agree since our only witnesses are, or were, a gay Filipino and his Negro lover."

"Huh," Fowler replied. After a minute of thought, he spoke. "Do you think Harrison's family knew or knows that he might have been tied up with the Reds? If that's what he's doing?"

"I don't know about his family's wishes concerning his valor in battle or if they knew he might be tied up with the Reds, or might have been part of the plot themselves, but we can't worry about that now. We've got other issues."

"Yeah, like that guy Rodham."

* * *

The mechanical coughing of an engine woke Dooley from a deep sleep, but he only heard that ruckus briefly before it went away. Somehow, that riotous sputtering was familiar to Dooley, but still groggy, he couldn't place the sound. Although he did recognize the following din, and that was from a boastful rooster asserting his dominion over the backyard. With his eyes still closed, he enjoyed the noisy fowl, the softness of the covered mattress under him, the warmth of the covers over him, and the sun shining through the window next to the bed's headboard. He inhaled deeply, relishing the smell of laundered underclothes, and the aroma of brewing coffee and baking bread snaking through the crack under the door. He opened his eyes.

The sparsely furnished room, with its white, plastered walls, was at the back of the second floor. Other than the bed, there was a squat wardrobe in one corner and a four-drawer bureau next to it. On top of the bureau, he saw a ceramic wash basin and pitcher, along with an array of toiletries including a new bar of Ivory soap. A framed mirror mounted to the wall lorded over the toiletries. Next to his bed on the side opposite the window was a nightstand with an electric lamp and a candle stick in a brass holder.

He yawned while giving himself a long stretch. After rotating his wrists above his head, he pushed himself into a sitting position, letting the covers fall away from his chest. Now upright, he realized that the generator from last night was no longer running. He saw its little, doghouse-like covering last night as he bathed on the back porch. The small cast iron bathtub, with cold water piped to it, was situated only feet from the kitchen and enclosed by two blankets strung along a rope.

He turned his head to the right and looked out the window into the backyard. The setting would have been seen on any farm in any decade. He saw a garden, enclosed by chicken wire and wooden stakes, along with an out-house fronted by a covered porch. Craning his head some more, there was a table with a wash tub and a scrub board, and metal poles with lines strung between the two. A few pieces of laundry wafted in the breeze.

Behind that rustic setting, and in front of the forest, fat brown cows grazed contently. Behind the cows started the forest, which shrouded the island's mountain slope almost all the way up to its summit. Dooley's eyes followed the green-cloaked rise and stopped at a harsh façade staring down at him. Now he knew why the Chinese and the Spanish referred to the island as The Sleeping Brothers or The Twin Saints. A weather-beaten rocky face glared back at him, and the harsh regard seemed to be enhanced by the shadow created by the rocky outcropping that capped off the mountain. The glare reminded him of clergy members with their long coats, stern looks, and wide-brimmed hats, but his thoughts were disturbed by the door to the outhouse opening and a man filling the framed void.

The man looked like the men Dooley spent the last week with. However, this man seemed to have an additional quality. His sturdy face and eyes exuded confidence. Even the way he stepped from the door and tossed the folded newspaper onto the seat of the chair to his right projected sureness. Also, his clothing was different from the loose-fitting army blouses and trousers the submarine raiders wore; instead, this man wore a pair of green coveralls buttoned to the neck. The coveralls were festooned with huge pockets closed off with flaps. Also, short patches of yellow, brown, and blue cloth hung from the coveralls. The legs of the coveralls were tucked into high-top, laced-up leather boots, which he recognized as being popular with pilots and other officers with money. The man's head was also covered with what looked like an American-style leather football helmet with goggles resting on the front of the helmet. He stepped to the washstand setting on top of a small table and rinsed his hands before stepping off the porch.

Then Dooley thought about his own gear. He turned from the window and looked beyond his feet to his gear piled on a cedar chest. Lifting the covers to the side, Dooley swung his bare legs from the bed and planted them on the cool, wooden planks. He stepped to the end of the bed and looked down. His Thompson was still wrapped in canvas strips and had not been cleaned since the raid, nor had his hunting knife and axe been oiled. He also thought about Olga's shoe still among other items in the canvas shoulder bag. Then he got another whiff of the coffee and bread.

Stepping over to the bureau and pulling the drawers out one at a time, he saw his uniform along with his worn underclothes and the duffel: all washed and neatly folded. Along with his clothing, he saw neatly folded slacks, cotton shirts, and fresh undergarments. The same type of civilian clothing Utkin and the cook wore after the raid. With the bottom drawer still open, Dooley lifted his eyes to the mirror and rubbed the stubble on his chin and ran his fingers through his tousled black hair.

Thirty minutes later, Dooley, now smelling of ivory soap, wore grey slacks, socks, leather shoes, and a short-sleeve shirt. After a visit to the outhouse, he stood on the front porch enjoying a second cup of coffee. He also enjoyed the morning air while watching chickens peck away in front of the house. He also waited for Zeta, as the door to her room was closed when he left his room. He thought about the other night on the submarine when they made love. It was her first experience, and it was a good one, though neither one of them had bathed in a week, and the enclosed bunk offered little freedom of movement. Last night would have been a good night but having just arrived and sleeping in another man's house seemed too forward. His thoughts were disturbed by a breeze touching his freshly shaved cheek.

He looked to his left at the orange weathervane. He then turned to the right and looked at the two tin-covered buildings to the north of the road before turning to look to the south. The meadow was situated in a valley running east and west with the island's central mountain behind the farmhouse. In front of the farmhouse, beyond the east-west running dirt road, and the other two tin-covered buildings south of the road was a tree-covered hill also running west and east. While thinking about the submarine cavern under that hill, Dooley thought about the island's name and envisioned the island's salient profile. In his mind, he saw an image of two men sitting with their backs against each other and their knees drawn up while sharing a wide-brimmed hat and sleeping away the afternoon. His thoughts were disturbed by movement in front of him.

A sliding door covering the front of one of the tin-sheathed structures was pushed to one side by two men, who not only wore the same clothing as the man at the outhouse but were also outfitted with flat canvas backpacks. They also wore white scarves around their necks. Once open, Dooley saw a large biplane inside the structure. The biplane had one engine on each side of the fuselage and mounted on the bottom wings. He now knew why the scene seemed familiar. He was at an airfield. Inside, the two men joined six others who stood in front of one of the wing-sets of the biplane. Except for one person, they all wore the same clothing and kit. The one man that was dressed differently was Major Utkin. He wore the same clothing as Dooley.

Dooley's observing was disrupted by the sound of squeaking hinges behind him. He turned to see the submarine's young cook standing in the doorway and holding a tray. Seeing that his breakfast was ready Dooley sat at the table and waited as the man refilled his coffee cup from a porcelain coffee pot. As the cook set out their breakfast, Dooley enjoyed more coffee while looking at the stand under the large window. The magazine with the image of the bicycle racer was still there, but now a pair of German-made binoculars on top of it. He also saw the plate-sized Coca-Cola display with the thermometer in its center mounted on the wall between the door and window. The red line stopped at eighty degrees on the graduated scale. He looked at the barometer under the thermometer and saw where the needle pointed. *A bit low,* Dooley thought to himself.

Just then, the door opened again, and Zeta stepped out onto the porch.

Her face glowed from a fresh scrubbing, and though barefoot, she wore pink slacks and a short sleeve white blouse edged with blue piping. She looked so innocent; he couldn't wait to make love to her again.

"Did you sleep well?" she asked while sitting in front of her coffee cup.

"The bed was a bit big for my taste," Dooley responded as he uncovered the biscuits.

Smiling, she reached for a biscuit with one hand and the butter knife with the other.

As they enjoyed the moment along with coffee, biscuits, butter, peach preserves, and fresh strawberries, they saw Utkin talking to his men. It seemed like he was giving them instructions. Halfway through a second tasty biscuit they saw Utkin leave the shelter of the hangar and walk across the grassy field. He waved at Dooley and Zeta with a hand holding a book or notepad.

Behind Utkin, the men lined up behind the bottom wings of the biplane and started to push it from inside the structure. As the men pushed the airplane across the grass and to the dirt road where they turned it to the east, specific details became apparent. In shape or form, it was just like any other biplane Dooley had seen or sat in, but its size and what covered it was a different matter. It reminded him of the covers of technology magazines: namely that of recently invented three- and four-seater airplanes built by both the Allies and the Central Powers.

The craft was at least forty feet long and with a wingspan of at least fifty feet. Dooley saw an extended nose with a single-barreled machine gun mounted to a track surrounding the open cockpit. Behind and above that position, above the robust landing gear system and sandwiched between the upper and lower wings, was the pilot's exposed cockpit. Several feet behind that cockpit was the rear gunner-slash-bombardier cockpit with its own track-mounted, single-barreled machine gun. Another gun barrel poked out from the bottom of the machine. Under the rear gunner's position, Dooley assumed the rear gunner could stand to operate the upper weapon and lay prone at the bottom of the cockpit to operate the lower weapon. But Dooley remembered his readings and knew that the person in that position had the main responsibility of releasing bombs attached to the bottom of the airplane between the landing gear and the rear gunner's position. While Dooley saw the machine guns and no bombs, he noticed other interesting items.

The skin of the flying machine was not canvas; instead, the aircraft was sheathed with silvery metal that glinted in the morning sun just like Martian spacecraft he read about as a child. The metal sheathing was devoid of tail numbers, national flags, or squadron logos. On the lower wings, one on either side of the fuselage, were fourteen-cylinder, inline engines with wooden propellers. The propellors were mounted to the rear of the engines. Under the wings and under the engines were two sets of landing gear with two large pneumatic wheels each. The widely spaced landing gear looked stout enough to handle the roughest of takeoffs or landings, while carrying quite a load. Lastly, he saw what looked like wheelchairs mounted to the side of the fuselage, on either side of the rear gunner's position. Around the airplane, the men seemed to ready themselves for a flight. Dooley looked at the runway.

While the open field centered in the narrow valley itself was a little more than one hundred yards wide, it was about a mile long. Regularly spaced along one side of the road, starting with the house, were waist-high wooden stakes with red ribbons flickering from their tops. At the base of the stakes, he saw Mason jars. The scenario started to come together in Dooley's mind as he thought about the flat packs strapped to the backs of the men. He smiled in understanding.

He didn't know much about parachutes, but he knew that the American government, like most nations throughout most of the war, did not issue parachutes to their airplane pilots or aircrews. So, most of those who did want to use them had to purchase the parachutes on their own through civilian outlets. Dooley had seen pictures of them in magazines, and the types he saw were not strapped to the backs of pilots but were sat upon instead and had a tether tying them to the aircraft. Remembering what he knew of parachutes while focusing on the side-mounted wheelchairs his interest intensified.

Dooley saw that instead of having wire-spoked wheels on both sides, there were two wheels mounted together on the outboard side of the chairs. The inboard side was pressed against the metal sides of the plane with one chair just forward of the rear gunner's position and one aft of it.

Watching with interest, the couple continued with their breakfast as Utkin, stepping past the odd chicken, approached the steps to the porch. A minute later, Utkin placed a notepad on the table and pulled a folded handkerchief from his back pocket. Reaching for a strawberry, he sat down. "I hope you've slept well and that your beef was satisfactory?" he said, as he bit into the strawberry while wiping the back of his neck with his other hand.

"Major," Dooley answered after swallowing a piece of buttered biscuit. "I can't speak for the countess, but don't think I'll be able to face another steak like that again for some time."

"Glad to hear it," Utkin said as he placed a damp handkerchief on the table next to his notepad. "I hope this breakfast was sufficient as you will have an interesting day ahead of you."

"Well, it's starting out promising enough," Dooley said with appreciation, "including seeing that airplane. Did it grow up on beef steaks, too?"

Utkin smiled with appreciation as he pointed the half-eaten berry at the biplane. "You are witnessing the advancement of the air assault commando and the innovation of aviation technology as a necessary part of that special action group. The concept is based off the German Gotha GV bomber. A pusher engine type of aircraft designed to carry over one thousand, five hundred pounds of bombs and a crew of three while armed with four machine guns. However, there is always opportunity for improvement."

"Well, it seems like you've taken advantage of those opportunities," Dooley said, as he reached for a strawberry, "only four short years ago pilots were shooting at each other with revolvers or dropped simple hand bombs."

Utkin smiled at the compliment. "The Gotha design included three cockpits, a landing gear system, and motor and wing attachments built around a steel frame. It proved strong enough for the fields of France but too rigid and prone to fracturing under less-than-ideal operations elsewhere, and too heavy for our purposes. Also, the rest of the airplane's frame, the wings and empennage were made from wood, but all of it was covered with canvas and coated with paint and shellac varnish. A volatile combination. Also, having a multiple component frame required the presence of skilled metalsmiths, carpenters, and woodworkers. To assuage difficulties, we created a structure made entirely from aluminum piping and tubing and covered with aluminum sheathing. Fortunately, I've had access to quite a quantity of aluminum and the ability to machine parts necessary for my needs."

"All-metal flying machines," Dooley mentioned out loud. "Who'd have thought?"

Utkin smiled as he continued. "In doing so, we have an airframe that is extremely lightweight but robust and flexible. The machine is also less flammable, and one that does not require a varied maintenance crew. Instead, any crewman capable of reading a schematic and using an adjustable spanner can repair that frame in the field, and while under duress. In fact, that crew, armed with a simple tool bundle, can have the entire aircraft disassembled and stowed in the hold of a ship as an innocent shipment of machine parts in a day. Such a design also allowed us to incorporate more powerful engines."

"Sounds impressive," Dooley said as he lifted the strawberry to his lips. "A futuristic, all-metal airplane carrying both crew and parachute soldiers. Impressive, but what about those wheelchair-looking things?"

Utkin smiled as he also finished his strawberry. "You will see their value in a few minutes but let me provide more context. I asked you to join my effort as I could always use good men to check the spread of Bolshevism. As part of that front, I require pilots who can do more than fly in and out of humble airfields with cases of untaxed rum. I expect our pilots to have spine, to be excellent gunners, and capable of deploying our air assault commando under any form of duress; hence, the reason for those wheelchairs. While I designated the unit 'Air Assault Commando,' they jokingly call themselves the 'Armchair Commando.'"

Dooley, Zeta, and Utkin continued to watch from the porch as three of the men climbed up the side of the airplane and took their flight positions. Of the men left on the ground, two split off and went around the tail of the plane to the other side. The two men on the side visible to the people on the porch moved to sit in those attached wheelchairs. Facing forward, the men sat behind the propeller and buckled themselves in. Once secure in their chairs, they reached up to pull their goggles over their eyes before wrapping their scarves around their lower faces.

Dooley watched as the pilot finished his preflight checklist and yelled something to the men. The port engine coughed grey smoke from its exhaust ports, but it caught immediately, and the propellers blasted prop wash and exhaust straight into the faces of the men behind them. The odd chicken nearby suddenly scurried away with their wings flapping in the air.

"Before you say anything," Utkin spoke up, "we realize that breathing engine exhaust is not healthy for my parachutists. Respirators will arrive on your transportation off this island."

Dooley nodded as they all watched the pilot start the other engine. Once the engine caught, Dooley asked, "No need to walk the propellers?"

Utkin responded. "You only do that with rotary engines to scavenge oil out of cylinders."

The pilot started to increase the engine's rpm.

"No need to hand crank them either," Dooley said loud enough to overcome the engines.

"Totally electric start. All it takes is the turn of a key and the push of a button," Utkin responded. "Advancements in aviation are coming along quite nicely. It dispenses with having to complete awkward tasks at inopportune times or in inappropriate places."

A minute later, with both engines running smoothly, the pilot and his aircrew lowered their goggles and wrapped their scarves around their faces like the men in the chairs. Once the engines had the time to warm up, the pilot increased the rpm of the engines, but the machine remained in place. Dooley thought back to his lesson at Camp Custer and assumed the pilot was pushing down on his brakes while testing his engines.

As if to read Dooley's thoughts, Utkin spoke up. "He's testing his engines and getting ready for a short field take off," Utkin stated as he spread peach preserves on a piece of biscuit. "The machine is based on a design capable of taking off from large fields while carrying quite a payload, but we need machines that can carry the same loads while being able to extract men or equipment from restrictive areas."

"Like mountainous jungle dirt roads in Cuba or something?" Dooley asked.

Utkin smiled in response. "The pilot is experienced, and the airplane has received recent technological developments, especially with its wings. So, we shall see how my ideas will work out this morning."

Dooley remained quiet as they sipped their coffee and finished their breakfast while watching. As they did, Dooley noticed that a piece of metal along the trailing edge of the airplane's wing moved. It remained down as the pilot continued to stand on the brakes and increased the engine's rpm to its maximum. The thunderous noise erupting from the exhaust ports roared across the island's central field, and Dooley could almost hear the window-pane behind him rattle in its frame. After one minute, the pilot finally took his feet off the brake pedals, and the plane leapt forward.

Dooley expected to see the plane to start bouncing off the ground like the nimble little trainer he flew at Camp Custer. Instead, the airplane's tires remained in contact with the dirt as the huge, bomber-designed machine tore down the road, building speed and airflow over the wings. It sped past the first several stakes, but then everybody saw the crack of light under the large pneumatic tires. And that crack of light suddenly became a chasm as the plane bounded off the ground. Now, with momentum, the pilot seemingly leveled out his airplane, but only slightly. At a shallow angle, the plane remained in line with the road as it cleared the trees boxing in the valley. The roar of the plane's engines dissipated into the clear, dark blue sky as the airplane flew away from the island.

"What was that? Three hundred feet?" Dooley asked as he reached for the coffee pot.

Utkin paused as he finished a strawberry. "As I said, he is a good pilot. And he will now be circling around the island and approach from the west."

At that moment, two other men walked out from the airplane shelter. While they wore high boots and green coveralls with patches like the others, they did not have the leather helmets, goggles, scarves, or parachutes. Instead, each man carried a bolt of white cloth under their arms as they walked toward the first set of wooden stakes.

"Markers for the parachute soldiers?" Dooley asked.

"The idea of parachutes has been around since da Vinci," Utkin said, "and in use in the last several decades starting with the advent of human-carrying balloons. However, I am in the need for specific parachutes that can be used to insert men into areas where airplanes cannot operate. Back in 1907, a French bicycle mechanic assembled an engine-powered vehicle capable of rising and landing vertically, but that flight lasted only twenty seconds. Eventually, there will be aviation technology available to allow man to take off and land vertically in the space of a parked motor car. But until that day arrives, parachutes are a technology we can use."

"Understandable," Dooley said while he thought back to the front cover of the magazine on the submarine.

They watched the two men step onto the road and bend to unroll the cloth. After making a huge X on the road, they anchored their efforts with nearby, hand-sized rocks. After reviewing their work, the men returned to the shade of the hangar.

Dooley continued, "But I thought most pilots or aircrewmen didn't or couldn't wear them because of their weight and bulkiness, and a thing called honor."

"Yes," Utkin said with a smile. "Before 1918, the military leadership gave little thought to parachute technology and safety, and what they were made from. It wasn't until 1918, when the leaders realized having experienced, and breathing, pilots was more valuable than having a fleet of wood-and-canvas airplanes flown by short-lived recruits. So, when the leadership did employ parachutes for their crews, they provided parachutes that were heavy, which stressed single-seater fighters with struggling engines. The bulkiness also presented entanglement hazards when exiting stricken machines and occupied space better used by extra machine guns, magazines, or bombs."

"You've addressed those issues?" Dooley said as he investigated his coffee.

"I have," Utkin replied. "Since the fighting stopped last fall, developers have had the time to look at previous designs, starting with creating parachutes worn on the backs of pilots instead of having to sit on them. Doing so limits extra strapping, which reduces entanglement hazards and reduces weight. Another step is that most parachute canopies were made from inexpensive, but heavy, cotton. Silk is an alternative, but an expensive one. And although my parachutes are made of silk, there must be a synthetic medium made available. While the fighting stopped last fall, a treaty is now being solidified and because of that, treaty corporations are lining up to steal patents from German corporations, including their chemical industries. Ideally, researchers should be able to create a lightweight material that will be useful as military-grade applications."

Dooley remained silent but thought back to the chemistry book under Mashka's pillow.

Utkin finished by saying, "But let us watch what will happen this morning."

CHAPTER 23

LIKE THE MORNING view from the deck of the torpedo boat destroyer and from the porch of the Brooks House, the vista from the fantail of a dilapidated steamer chugging over a brilliantly blue sea was just as welcoming, but the concern differed. Borodin enjoyed his coffee while inhaling the sea air and watching the boiling wake trailing behind the ship's propeller. That said, he still had the radio report from last night on his mind. He turned from the view and looked at that message held down by the coffee pot. The message detailed the results from last night's action. Two men wounded with one severely injured and one aircraft slightly damaged. Once the two aircraft pounced on the sailing vessels from above, the dilapidated tramp steamer moved in and deployed a squad of raiders who subdued the survivors and took control of the sailing vessels. He brought the cup to his lips while thinking about the next twelve hours, and the failure of their main objective. His thoughts, though, were disturbed by Captain Lagos, who stepped around the corner of the superstructure. He held a folded piece of paper in his hand and wore an intriguing look on his face.

"Good morning, Issak," Borodin said as he lowered the coffee cup and reached for the pot on the table. "Please, sit and explain that unsettled look."

Reaching for a chair, Captain Lagos sat as Borodin filled his cup. Lagos accepted the coffee while placing the folded paper on top of the first message before Borodin put the pot back on top of the messages.

After a long sip, and a sigh, he answered Borodin. "It appears that since

SERGEANT DOOLEY AND THE SUBMARINE RAIDERS

the intervention at Bagay Alto, our friend was able to reconfigure his asset's appearance to a point where it was not recognized by the captain of the destroyer. Our friend remained in the area long enough to greet the American vessel and keep him occupied while the sailing vessels put distance between them and the naval vessel. Our motorized asset is now approaching Buyan, and the sailing vessels are not far behind."

"Very good, Issak," Borodin said with a smile. "But that is the good news. Of the bad news, I already know that our target, the man called Fowler was not among them, so I was just thinking how well our acquaintance Rodham can assist us in that matter."

Captain Lagos sighed. "Agreed, but we have a matter closer to home. The Americans, with their variety of arms, put up a formidable resistance, and we just suffered a fatality. The gunner should make it, although without a leg. Unfortunately, the copilot died thirty minutes ago."

Borodin turned his eyes back to the boiling wake while Captain Lagos continued.

"Among that variety of weapons, the Americans had a six-pounder, which they put to good use. The gunners landed a shot that went through the nose of one of our aircraft, through the copilot's chest and the leg of the standing gunner behind him before exiting the stern section of the craft without exploding. While I lament the loss of one of our own, I appreciate that the weapon fired an explosive round capable of piercing the steel hull of a ship before exploding inside but was not designed to be set off by a thin sheet of aluminum and the flesh and bone of a human chest and a thigh. If that round exploded, we would be short a well-trained crew and a necessary piece of inventory."

"Neither of which we could stand to lose," Borodin replied. "However, we now have two additional assets that will play a valuable part in the Latin American operations, especially with the creation of the Prohibition Amendment. I only wish that we could have seized that American destroyer. Its deck guns would have been welcome supplements to our mobile assets."

Lagos smiled in return, "Yes, they would have been, but we also don't need their attention at this point. However, with the treaty about to be signed any day now, there will be plenty of surplus weapons piling up in scrap yards, and we can thank the American industrialists for that. The Merchants of Death reaped in astronomical profits by overproducing arms and ammunition at the cost of an entire generation of humanity. A surplus about to be made available to the public right at the beginning of Prohibition, and just in time for an economic disparity that will raise the ire of an indignant younger generation."

Borodin smiled as he looked up from the wake. "What's that phrase? The world is your oyster, so go sharpen your knife?"

* * *

Utkin reached for the binoculars on the stand and placed them on the table next to the notepad before reaching into his pants pocket. Dooley and Zeta looked at the top page of the notepad. It was full of writing, in Russian, along with a sketch of a gear or wheel in the lower left corner. Utkin finished digging in his pocket and pulled out a shortened pencil. Flipping the top several pages over, Dooley saw the major had already taken several lines of notes and added to them as he glanced at the weathervane, the thermometer, and barometer. Utkin's eyes paused on the barometer for a second longer.

After recording the weather, Utkin laid the pencil on the notepad and picked up the binoculars. He followed the silver specter as it turned and flew over the Pacific Ocean, following the coastline of the island's southern half. Dooley's and Zeta's eyes followed as the airplane turned to fly along the lengthy rise harboring the submarine cavern inside.

Utkin broke the silence while keeping his eyes on the airplane as it passed the rise and made a wide turn to come in from the west. "The pilot is at three thousand feet and will be settling on a pass over the island in line with the road. The idea behind testing at such a height is so that the vehicles will have the altitude to deploy their canopies, and if there are malfunctions, the men will have time to detach themselves from the chairs and deploy their own parachutes. Something that they will do anyhow. Anyway, this is our first deployment with humans, so having altitude to work with allows us to fine tune our methodologies."

Utkin paused again. "There will be times in the future where altitude and daylight will not be our brothers-in-arms. I need quick-witted men under those parachute canopies."

Dooley understood the invitation just as he saw the look on Zeta's face. "You've had malfunctions before?" Dooley asked while watching the silvery glint far off to the west line up along with the island's main road.

"Yes," Utkin answered while lowering the binoculars onto the table and looking at Dooley. "My idea was years in the making, but, while we were accomplishing our mission to the north, my technicians completed the final touches here. They made eight sorties deploying these same four deployment vehicles weighted with sandbags. So, out of thirty-two individual operational tests, there were three parachute failures. A failure rate of ten percent, which is acceptable."

"I understand acceptable losses after having been in the Army," Dooley threw in, "along with the need for not sitting in those things while landing. That'll crack a man's back for sure. But what the hell are they going to do with wheelchairs in combat? Attack an old folks' home?"

Just then, they all heard a slight change in the rpm of the airplane's engines. The change focused their eyes on the silvery airplane as it crossed over the forest just as the back two chairs fell away from airplane. A second later, the front two dropped away from the fuselage. Dooley saw the chairs tumble in their angled descents as two things happened almost simultaneously. A bundle of green ballooned from the backs of each chair. Also, packages dropped from the bottoms of each chair, but only fell about twenty feet or so before bouncing at the ends of ropes.

"You see, the chairs and men are not aerodynamically stable, which is why they tumbled upon their release," Utkin started to explain. "Each deployment vehicle, once free of the aircraft, is still attached by a forty-foot static line, which is meant to pull the parachute open and allow it to catch the air, not the airplane. After becoming taunt, the weight of the parachutist and chair caused the buckle to detach the parachute tether. Once the parachutes are deployed, they release the kits under their seats to help steady their descent. Those kits are their field packs. The last purpose is so that the weight of the package is not either on the backs of the soldiers or on the chairs upon landing."

Utkin paused as they watched the next phase of the operation. As if on cue, all four of the men rolled out of their chairs, which were now just over the middle section of the road and at about a thousand feet of altitude. Once clear of the chairs, the men's parachutes also exploded, leaving them dangling under the parachutes.

"Good so far," Utkin said with appreciation as he took his eyes off the men and watched the airplane continue to fly back out to sea. "The airplane has done its job and will land once the men are on the ground and have cleared the runway."

Now, the parachute soldiers were a few hundred feet above the ground, dropping at a slight forward angle. They also raised their arms and pulled on the parachute strings.

"They're getting ready to touch down. I've had a section of each parachute canopy cut out so, as they descend, the air inside the canopies will spill out the back. That feature, along with the men pulling at the shrouds, will allow the canopies to be steered to a degree."

As Utkin described the operation, the parachute soldiers seemed to be listening. They were, indeed, steering themselves toward the white cross on the road. Yards behind the parachute soldiers, the wheelchairs, with the drop packs, floated downward under the control of the wind and gravity. They were the first to land. First, the drop packs, then the chairs, then the canopies, which collapsed on the dirt. Next were the parachute soldiers who all landed within a second of each other. Two of them landed in the center of the cross, and as their feet touched ground the men ran several steps while unbuckling their harnesses, freeing them of the parachutes. The other two men landed between them and the chairs and tumbled to the ground in a controlled roll. They stood immediately and unbuckled their harnesses as well.

"This is when parachute soldiers will be most vulnerable," Utkin explained as he jotted down more notes. "Assuming they have been spotted by the opposition, the parachute soldiers must disengage from their trappings, then race to retrieve their packed automatic weapons to defend themselves. Speed and coordination are what is needed now."

Even as Utkin explained, the men closest to the wheelchairs, were already free of the harnesses. They pushed their goggles up to their foreheads and pulled the scarves down around their necks while running for the packs and setting upon them like starving lions on a stricken gazelle, gutting it with their claws. Meanwhile, the two men who landed on the cross unbuttoned their coveralls and reached in. They withdrew large-caliber, short-barreled revolvers and took a kneeling position facing east. The barrels of the revolvers sought out targets, which were glass jars at the base of the flagged stakes about fifteen yards away. Each man fired two shots, shattering four glass jars. The loud report of the pistols echoed hauntingly across the meadow. The men, while still holding their pistols, reached back into their coveralls and removed hand grenades. Using one hand to hold the hand bombs, they pulled the safety pins with the other and threw them with skill. The exploding grenades threw up clouds of road dirt. Concussive waves chased the haunting reports of the pistols across the meadow.

"The men with the revolvers and hand grenades," Utkin continued, "provide firepower while the other men retrieve their automatic weapons. And before you ask, they all carry revolvers inside the coveralls. The idea is to prevent entanglements while descending."

The men who set upon the packs retrieved automatic rifles from the packs. As they inserted magazines into the weapons, Dooley saw these automatics differed from the ones the submarine raiders carried the other night. These rifles seemed to have much shorter barrels and longer box magazines. After arming themselves, they threw the packs onto their backs and dropped to the to the sides of the roads into prone positions while pointing their barrels at the surviving Mason jars. Meanwhile, the other two men stood and ran to their wheelchairs where they set their revolvers on the ground and repeated the field maneuvers. Once the extended magazines were inserted, the men laid the weapons on the ground and reached back into their coveralls, removing adjustable wrenches.

"I am sure you have noticed their weaponry by now," Utkin continued. "They are armed with short-barreled revolvers and automatic rifles, proven weapons with stopping power. Parachute soldiers are about shock and awe."

By now, the two men who remained with the wheelchairs made great progress with disassembling them into separate parts. Some pieces were long sections of tubing, while others were shorter. Other pieces were angled. Once disassembled, the men each picked up two of the longest pieces of tubing and threaded them together with joints of tubing bent at an angle.

As Dooley continued to watch, the men picked up a third piece of tubing just as long as the first two and attached them as well by using the threaded joints. As they tightened the assembly with their wrenches, Dooley glanced at the wire-spoked wheels still lying on the ground, then back at the triangular-shaped frame. He next threw his eyes over to the stand under the window.

"I see you understand what is going on," Utkin said as he turned to look at Dooley. "Parachute operatives are an expeditious lot who will be called upon to insert themselves into areas where rapid movement is essential. Even if rapid movement is not essential, the bicycles can be used to transport heavy loads while the operatives push and walk beside them. Lastly, just like the airplane, the bicycles are assembled from simple aluminum tubing and piping and can be easily disassembled and packaged when needed. Just like my aircraft."

As the major spoke, Dooley, Zeta, and Utkin watched the two parachute men complete the assembly of their vehicles. And sure enough, in what seemed to take no more than three minutes, they were inserting the last wheel into the forks of the bicycles and tightening down the wheel fasteners. Once assembled, the two men left their bicycles and switched places with the two men guarding the group. That second pair of men took just as long, and before Dooley realized it, he watched four men with their packs and weapons slung across their backs, pedal down the road and away from the Brooks House.

Dooley turned to Utkin, who went back to taking more notes. Dooley let him finish. After writing a few more lines on the notepaper, Utkin nodded to himself while laying the pencil on the table next to the notebook. He returned Dooley's look.

"I hope you are impressed with my efforts. Such audaciousness will be needed to thwart any Bolshevik intentions, especially in Latin America."

"I've been impressed with everything you've done so far," Dooley responded honestly before joking, "The next thing I know you'll be inventing flying submarines."

Utkin leaned back in his chair while replying with a wry smile, "The world is my oyster, and I have already sharpened my knife. Now it is time for you to show me your whetstone."

CHAPTER 24

THIRTY MINUTES LATER, Dooley, still wearing his civilian clothing, now held a leather helmet with goggles in his hand and wore a silk scarf around his neck. He and two other people stood in front of the same hangar that housed the all-metal airplane; however, the double sliding doors were opened in reverse. They looked at the single-engine biplane in front of them. It was a wood-and-canvas, two-seat trainer.

"Quite a letdown after seeing your all-metal bomber drop those parachute soldiers," Dooley said, keeping his eyes on the vintage machine. He heard chickens clucking behind them. "How much chicken shit did you have to scoop out of that thing to make room for me and the pilot?"

"I apologize, Sergeant," Utkin answered, "but I have only one physical result of that concept, so risking it in the hands of a trainee wouldn't be prudent. I hope no offense is taken."

Dooley paused. "None taken, but I see what you have in this hangar, so I can't imagine what you have stowed in the others."

Utkin was about to respond but a man walked around the corner of the door, interrupting him. All three turned to look at a man wearing patch-covered green coveralls with the legs tucked into laced-up leather boots, and a leather flying helmet and goggles on his head. A man of average height and trim build, he had a strong face with dark brown eyes. He smiled at Dooley.

"Sergeant Dooley, I am Sergei Popov, your instructor while you are our guest."

Dooley turned his head to look at Utkin and Zeta. Both smiled encouragingly. Dooley nodded and turned back to Popov and asked: "Which part is the wing?"

The instructor answered with a chuckle while stepping forward.

An hour later, Dooley found himself five hundred feet above the Pacific Ocean with the control stick in his hand, rudder pedals under his shoes, the leather helmet on his head, goggles over his eyes, and the silk scarf wrapped around his lower face. The short ends flowed behind his head in the rushing air.

After walking a lap around the airplane while giving Dooley a lecture, the pilot got the airplane off the ground and over the water south of the island. Once over water, Dooley took the controls while sitting in the front seat. Popov yelled instructions from the rear seat and Dooley followed through.

"You are doing well!" Sergei Popov shouted. While the engine was loud, the instructor had no problem communicating with the student pilot. "Now, I want you to perform a square pattern while following your compass! Head straight north past the island! Then west! Then south! Maintain five hundred feet! Line up on the western end of the runway facing east!"

Dooley nodded while following through with his instructions. Dooley banked the aircraft and turned north. Keeping his eyes on his gauges and compass as much as possible, he took the time to view the sky and island while he came up to the island's eastern coastline. The sky was a clear, brilliant blue dotted with fluffy clouds, and the air, although tainted by the engine exhaust, was refreshing. The island, with its central mountain, reminded him of the fantastical islands he read about as a child.

As he passed the south valley to his left, he looked at the dirt road, the hangars, and the house with all of it surrounded by forest, which was pinched in by the island's central mountain and long-running rise to the south. He craned his neck over the leather-padded cockpit coaming and looked down. He saw the marine slipway Utkin mentioned earlier. Although he did not see the cradle that boats and small ships could be drawn up on, he saw the peaked, tin-sheathed roof that covered it. The structure started where the island's central road ended and ran the width of the beach ending out over the water. On either side of the covered structure, he saw two single-story wooden buildings covered with the same rust-stained tin as the slipway. He also saw two men walk across the clean sand from one of the buildings and to the covered slipway. The men walked alongside what looked like a set of tractor tracks in the sand, which led from one of the buildings to the water's edge at the side of the covered slipway. He saw something else. Lying on the beach, on either side of the covered railway were what looked like four dark brown rib bones. Ones that looked like they came from the ribcage of a dinosaur.

Looking ahead, he judged that the forested island was about five miles long north to south, and about three miles wide from east to west. Rising sharply from the island's center and shrouded under a cloak of trees, sat the island's Siamese twin patriarchs. He remembered Utkin's statement about the air assault commando using the mountain for climbing exercises.

As he flew past the conjoined saints, the north valley came into view. While heavily wooded, the valley was scarred by the scab of an open, grassy meadow at its center. At first, he saw only brown dots against the rich, green grass. But once used to what he was looking at, he saw the outline of a building's foundation in the center of the meadow, along with what looked like a worn path leading to the outline from both the east and west sides of the meadow. To the south of the meadow, he saw three large rocks nestling with each other.

Lastly, his eyes seemed to focus on what appeared to be rectangular dots both inside rocky outline and in the grass around it. Continuing, the airplane passed the long-running, tree-covered rise at the north end of the island. He looked down at the eastern end of it where it sloped to the water's edge. That end of the hill was bare of trees; instead, the incline was covered with short grass and tuft bushes. Looking at the incline, which reminded him of the angled double door tornado access to his uncle's cellar, he thought he saw some sort of movement. Grabbing the flowing end of his scarf he wiped his goggles before looking down again, but everything was still. Dismissing it, he turned his eyes to look ahead, and at the broad expanse of ocean.

It was flat and dark blue marred only by a single ship a few miles ahead. The V-shaped wake aft of the ship marred the smooth water behind it. Dooley remembered what Utkin said about his transportation off the island. Curious, he continued his northbound leg to overshoot the ship. Craning his neck over the right side of the cockpit and looking ahead, he saw a rust-stained hull, a weather-beaten superstructure, and a lifeboat secured in davits on either side of the bridge superstructure and under the bridge wings. It looked like any other island steamer he saw populating Shanghai harbor while he sat along the waterfront drinking beer or eating lunch. And, just like many of those ships in the harbor or steaming down the rivers leading to the harbor, this one had canvas-covered items strapped to the ship's central deck. As he neared the ship, Dooley felt a tap on his left shoulder.

* * *

Pleased with the landing, although Dooley knew Sergei also had his hands and feet on the controls at the same time, Dooley taxied the airplane to the front of the empty side of the hangar. Turning off the engine, he climbed out of the cockpit and dropped his feet heavily on the ground. Stretching with his hands on his hips and bending backward, he listened to Sergei's comments about his flying while looking at the all-metal airplane. Now abandoned after its post-flight maintenance, he wondered if he would ever get a chance to pilot that thing.

Satisfied with Popov's remarks, Dooley turned toward the porch while pulling his leather helmet and goggles from his head. As he walked, he unwound the silk scarf from his lower face. With the items dangling from his hands, he walked past chickens pecking at gravel while looking at three people sitting on the porch. They were enjoying drinks, which made him realize how thirsty he was. He also tasted exhaust on his tongue.

A couple of minutes later, he stepped up the wooden stairs to the porch, where he saw Zeta filling a glass from a stoneware jug. Once full, she put the jug back on the table and lifted the glass for Dooley.

"It's hard pear cider," Zeta said with a smile.

Dooley straddled his helmet and goggles and scarf over the handrailing and reached for the glass. He returned Zeta's smile before taking a long pull. Although his mouth still tasted like engine exhaust, he enjoyed the cool, soothing taste of the cold cider.

"How was the flight?" Major Utkin asked as he lifted his glass. "And how is the cider?"

Dooley looked at his half-empty glass and smiled. "Somehow, I see a future of flying tourists hell bent on fishing into remote fishing villages and my aunt could do no better with her cider."

Both Vostok and Utkin raised their cider in salute. Zeta raised her glass, but she wore a muted smile, a look that Dooley noticed over the rim of his glass.

"Excellent," Utkin said as he pulled his glass from his lips, "but please finish your cider, then get ready for lunch. We shall be right here where we can talk further of how we will use your talents to protect the American shores from Bolshevik infiltrators."

Dooley lifted his glass to finish the cider but stopped mid-lift. "What about Zeta?"

Utkin nodded. "Scrub well. Oil has a way of sticking."

After a visit to the outhouse, he walked back into the house through the kitchen. As a child, when visiting his uncle's farm, it seemed like, when she wasn't on the porch drinking beer, she did nothing but cook food on the wood-burning stove, roll out dough on the table, or bottle homemade alcohol on the back stoop. Conversely, the only time his uncle ever stepped foot into the kitchen was to get something out of the icebox or to pass out in the pantry when he was too drunk to climb the stairs to his bedroom. His aunt modified the walk-in pantry to include a foldaway shelf that doubled as a bunk.

Looking about the kitchen, Dooley saw seared tuna steaks and fried potato wedges mounded on a plate. Nodding to the smiling cook who sprinkled salt on the food, Dooley walked past the cook, and noticed that the door to the pantry behind him was open. Lo and behold, the pantry was just like his aunt's pantry: stocked with canned and dry goods and complete with a stretcher-like canvas bunk. At one end was a folded sheet and blanket. At the other end a pillow. Stepping out of the kitchen, he started up the steps to his room. While doing so, he again thought about his future, that of Zeta's, and his childhood readings of the Allan Pinkerton and his exploits in the mid-1800s. It was then when Pinkerton employed spy tactics and special operatives unheard of at the time. Pinkerton was heralded as a virtuous nativist warrior, even though he was a Scottish immigrant himself, fighting both international and domestic evil.

Reaching the top of the stairs, Dooley walked the short hallway and stopped in front of his door. As he entered the room, his thoughts shifted to nights at the dinner table when his father and brother argued about, among other issues, the Pinkerton Agency's subsequent roles in infiltrating labor unions and the strong-armed tactics used to put down strikes and intimidate workers. His brother contended that the Pinkertons were only gangsters hired by corrupt politicians and corporate criminals to violate the rights of Americans.

Reaching the bureau, Dooley poured water from the pitcher into the basin. He unbuttoned his stained shirt while asking himself why Utkin and Vostok seemed to know about the American term "Pinkerton." He could accept Zeta knowing about America's first detective agency as she seemed to be enthralled with America, but Utkin and Vostok?

After pulling the shirt off, he wadded it up and used it to wipe his armpits before throwing it on the bed. Bending down to wet his face, he remembered the history of the Pinkertons. The agency came to prominence as the founder infiltrated a Southern successionist group and uncovered their plot to assassinate Abraham Lincoln in 1860. Using unassuming females and blacks, Pinkerton was able to infiltrate the group in Baltimore and thwart the plot. Since then, Allan Pinkerton never looked back.

As he soaped up his face, Dooley realized he now understood Utkin a little better. More relaxed, he thought about how the government began using the Agency's operatives as bodyguards for politicians. Such was the embryonic birth of government-sponsored counterintelligence operations and the

Secret Service. Although the Pinkerton Agency enjoyed a reputable public image at its conception, it was tarnished by the publicized and brutal involvement while being under the pay of railroad tycoons and senators signing pieces of legislation favoring corporate leaders.

After rinsing his face, he stood straight and picked up a folded towel next to the basin. Drying his face, neck, and forearms, he continued to think about the Pinkertons. Though maligned by the press and public opinion, the Pinkerton Agency, even after the death of its founder in 1884, still enjoyed a vibrant reputation, especially when it came to the unorthodox use of operatives and methodologies. Dooley finished by wiping his armpits with the damp cloth. Putting it down on the bureau, he picked up his comb and ran it through his wavy, black hair while realizing that Pinkerton Agency provided a playbook for Utkin to follow.

Laying the comb down, Dooley first smiled then opened his mouth to inspect his tongue. Picking up his toothbrush, he finished preparing for lunch.

* * *

Back at the table, Dooley enjoyed more cold cider and a tasty lunch.

"How did you like your fish steak?" Vostok asked as he lifted a piece of fish seasoned with pickled beet-and-onion relish. "Although it looks like my question was a waste of breath."

Dooley looked at his empty plate while holding his glass of cider. "Excellent, and that comes from a man who doesn't normally eat fish. I'll miss your cook's food."

Utkin smiled as he leaned back in his chair. "From what you indicate, you are accepting a position, and the locale for such employment: the circum-Caribbean region, where fish and poultry, along with rice, is a staple in any cultural diet."

"I only hope they have good cooks there as well," Dooley responded while sucking at his teeth. "But since we're on the topic, during my flight, I saw a steamer. Our transportation?"

"No," Vostok said as he reached for the second stoneware jug. Refilling everybody's glasses, he continued, "The captain radioed and said he suffered a fire and needs to stop for repairs and to collect a beef while here. He said that he can complete the repairs on his own. Since this island and its facilities have a singular purpose, we couldn't tell them no."

"How did he know to radio the island?" Dooley asked. "Do the residents have a radio?"

"No," Vostok answered. "They saw your airplane and assumed that there was some sort of modern European presence on the island. They hailed us through an open frequency, and we explained our presence as a temporary joint commercial and military effort and are expecting a return ship to pick us up in a day."

Utkin joined in to finish the conversation, "That transportation is en-route to this island and will be here perhaps by this time tomorrow. The captain will take you to Formosa, where there are liners departing for other ports. In the meantime, Captain Vostok has been watching the barometer, and it seems like we might be in for unsettled weather. So, we may curtail flight instruction, but Popov will avail himself for ground instruction. Please note the trap door in the kitchen. The cellar is stocked, and you may avail yourselves of the library under the staircase."

Dooley nodded while tapping his stomach. "I saw the bookshelf, and this lunch was quite satisfactory. He paused to look at Zeta. "I can understand pausing any training for the time being, but I don't think an afternoon walk would compromise your activities. This island looks interesting. It's like settings I've imagined in my readings, including the mountain that's staring down on us, and what I guess is the island's town at the western end of that road."

Zeta smiled as she turned to face the major and the submarine captain.

The two men looked at each other for a second before Utkin replied, "Fine idea, especially since the oncoming poor weather might keep you indoors until you leave this island. Enjoy yourself, but I would not spend time exploring 'downtown.'"

"Why," Dooley asked. "It's the middle of the day. Aren't any of the businesses open? Is it because today's Sunday?"

Utkin smiled, "Sergeant, unless there is a vessel at the wharf on the western side of the island, every day is Sunday. Now, I'll have the cook pack a snack for you. But let us finish this cider while we lay out plans concerning your employment. And I mean for both of you."

Chapter 25

WHILE DOOLEY REFRESHED himself and changed his shirt before lunch, Zeta still wore her pink slacks, sailor-like blouse, and the ribbon in her blond hair, but now along with sandals. With a canvas knapsack slung over Dooley's shoulders, the pair walked down the road as if they didn't have a care in the world.

As they enjoyed their surroundings, the young couple watched chickens pecking away along the road, cattle grazing on the north side of the road, and Tin-tin sauntering toward the grazing beeves. Dooley looked past the grazing animals into the woods bordering the meadow, where under the disapproving scrutiny from the mountain's southern saint, was the barracks for the air assault commando. He thought about the other commandos while asking himself what he got himself into. Just then, movement out of the corner of his eye caused the sergeant to look over his shoulder and at the tin-covered hangar furthest from the Brooks House. He saw Mashka step from a side door and wave with his good arm. The young couple slowed to let him to catch up.

"How's the arm?" Dooley asked as Mashka pulled up next to Zeta.

The Russian tapped his shoulder before answering with a thumbs up. Mashka then started a conversation with Zeta, in Russian. The two of them continued their conversation while all three enjoyed the weather, the fresh air, and the time away from the submarine. As they entered the western edge of the forest, they walked a little longer until they came upon two paths.

At that point, the two Russians stopped talking, but Mashka turned to face Dooley. He smiled and nodded firmly. "You a good mug, Tomas."

With that he turned and stepped onto the path leading south.

"You're welcome," Dooley replied with a smile.

"What are you thinking?" Zeta asked as they watched Mashka saunter down the path.

"I'm thinking he's way too young to be wrapped up in this mess."

"You're nineteen, just like he is, and look what you've been through."

He looked at her and surrendered with a wink. "Let's go."

As they walked, Dooley asked Zeta what she and Mashka talked about.

"You, for starters," she replied. "He kept going on about you being a champion soldier. I also asked him where he's from. He was a university student in Sevastopol. That was until the army drafted him. However, the Revolution occurred and was out of the war before he could fight. After his discharge, he returned to the university to study chemistry. That was where Major Utkin found him. But never mind. Let us enjoy this walk."

Walking through the forest they noticed that many of the trees were hardwoods like oaks and deliberately spaced about, which allowed sunlight to filter through the leafy branches and a breeze to refresh the forest floor. The sergeant noticed a variety of tracks in the loose sand of the path and thought about the free-ranging goats and swine. With no natural predators other than humans, the fauna must have enjoyed an idyllic existence.

As the two walked, they started to see human-built structures nestled in cleared patches of forest starting with a pair of exercise bars. The same type he had to climb over at an obstacle course at Camp Custer. The next structure they saw was a simple wood structure covered with tin sheathing and with a front porch and two windows in front. The windows were closed off with bamboo blinds instead of glass panes. On one side of the home was a garden enclosed with wooden slats and chicken wire, an outhouse, a clothesline with garments, and an outdoor cooking area with a lit fire. The path continued its curve, and as they walked, Dooley recognized another part of an obstacle course: an elongated pit filled with mud, and strands of barbed wire, raised one foot off the ground, stretching over it. They also saw, through the tree branches over their shoulders, a disapproving sideways glance leering down at them.

"It's as if we're being chaperoned again," Dooley observed aloud as he looked at the stone face. It reminded him of the down-the-nose looks he got from the snooty kitchen staff at the Waldorf Astoria. "Don't know what it's like, though."

"I do," Zeta said as she continued the walk down the path, "and it's a bit constrictive."

"I can imagine so," Dooley responded as he readjusted the straps of the knapsack.

After several steps, Zeta broke the silence. "How did you lose your virginity?"

"Damn, Zeta! Do you think that's a proper question to ask a man you barely know?"

She chuckled while walking. "You took my virginity while on board a smelly submarine, after a week of not bathing, and after conducting a raid on an estate to recover diamonds from Red Russians. A raid that resulted in the death of many men."

He sighed in surrender while reaching up to touch a tree leaf. "I was fifteen and she lived near my uncle's farm. Her husband was in town getting cattle feed. She took my virginity in the loft of a barn in full view of a dozen barn cats and a church steeple."

"Now, was that difficult to answer?"

Dooley smiled as they came under the full haughtiness of the north-facing saint. Finally, they stopped at the edge of the forest bordering the north meadow.

The grazing cattle Dooley saw during his flight were now canted over on their stomachs, after having done their best to keep the meadow manicured. They allowed their meal to digest while watching a human disemboweling an invisible opponent. Morda, now shirtless and covered with mud, swiped the blade of his entrenching tool as he lunged forward. It seems that they caught the muscular Russian as he finished his exercise. Recovering from his lunge, the wayward gladiator bent over to pick up his white undershirt. Using it to wipe his face, Morda turned back into the woods.

"Looks like he fancies himself a gladiator," Dooley commented while turning to face his companion. "Glass of wine?"

Minutes later, they sat on the grass at the base of the stacked boulders. Backs against the stone, legs stretched out in front of them, and a tablecloth spread between, the American and the Russian enjoyed their picnic and the view. Although they did not know what the church itself was constructed of, more than likely rough-hewn planks from the local forest now gone, both saw that the foundation consisted of cut stone slabs interlaid within each other. Dooley looked about the meadow and noticed the absence of anything he expected to see. He remembered one time, a tornado tore through his uncle's county and destroyed his barn, leaving behind scraps of boards, pieces of shingles, bent nails, and twisted iron hinges. There was none of that here.

"So, Madrid, huh?" Dooley said, reaching for a piece of cheese. He felt a raindrop on his hand as he did. It was early afternoon, and the western sky gained several clouds. "Do you speak Spanish? And will you fit in?"

"Not fluently," she replied as she lifted her wine glass to her lips. She smiled first. "But it will come back. And I will fit in as I am just one of thousands of struggling university students trying to study art while getting by after the destruction of war. Orphaned at seventeen with an accent hard to place and a name just as ambiguous."

"So, do you believe Utkin when he said Spain is set for a Bolshevik takeover? A civil war?"

"Yes," Zeta replied, "although not right away. Perhaps in twenty years, but don't ask me how or why I know that because I don't know myself."

"Well, Miss Eva Farna, late of Gdansk," Dooley replied as he popped the cheese into his mouth. Chewing it, he continued, "your cover is a bit more intriguing than mine. I'm supposed to be plain old ex-Sergeant Thomas Dooley. From Brooklyn. A decorated veteran working as a fish-gutting, beer-getting, white deck hand slaving for islander wages on charter fishing boats just to learn the business from the bottom up. What few pesos I still have in my pocket after paying off my tabs on Fridays is used to pay for flight instruction. Such activities will serve me well when it comes to battling Red infiltration and the Comintern."

"I've heard that term before," Zeta said. "Remember, I tried to ask you the other night."

"Yeah, I remember. Why?"

"The night of the raid," she replied, "I overheard the man that Major Utkin shot say that he, Major Utkin, was part of something called Comintern. Why?"

Lifting his wine glass, he stopped halfway up.

"Something wrong?"

Dooley recovered by sipping his wine. After pulling the glass from his mouth he asked, "Are you sure you heard the conversation correctly?"

"Yes," she replied with a hint of concern in her voice. "I didn't know what was going on in that room, and I guess Major Utkin thought I was busy calling out for my cousin and not paying attention to what he was doing. Why?"

"Oh, nothing," Dooley lied as he inspected his wine. "It just that there's been quite a bit going the last few days. I'm just trying to sort it all out."

Just then he felt another raindrop on his hand. He looked up at the sky and saw the far-off western sky filling up with more clouds. Swallowing the last of his wine, he continued. "I think we need to finish our walk, but I want to look at something before we leave."

Zeta nodded and followed suit. "What are you looking for?"

He leaned forward to pack their picnic while answering. "Not sure."

A minute later, with the knapsack across his back, the couple walked around the grave markers, starting with the ones within the church foundation. Dooley remembered what Utkin said about those with more status being buried under the floorboards of the church. The rest of the marked graves were outside the foundation and between it and the exposed boulders to the south. However, all the markers were simple slabs of stone laid into the dirt and surrounded by grass, which the cattle did their best to keep short. Zeta took the opportunity to read the brief words etched into each stone and pronouncing her Spanish by repeating the information out loud. As Dooley walked next to her and listened, he looked at the graves themselves and noticed again what he had seen from the air.

"I think this is the last one," Zeta said. "This one is marked 1811."

Standing next to her, he glanced back at the boulders. "Excuse me."

Zeta remained where she stood and watched Dooley step up to one of the lower boulders which he used to step onto the next higher one. Once on top, his eyes surveyed the meadow in front of him. After a minute, he slid off the boulders rejoining Zeta.

She saw a strange look on his face. "What's wrong?"

"Are you sure you heard that conversation correctly? The one between Utkin and the man he shot? The one about Comintern?"

Zeta did not answer directly. Instead, she narrowed her eyes while looking at the grave at her feet. After a second, they flew open in understanding.

"Yes, I think he's a Red," Dooley answered as he turned east and stepped forward with Zeta following. "Comintern, according to the staff officer back in Archangel, the officer I mentioned before, the one named Rodham, is an organization with the purpose of exporting Bolshevism from Russia, around the world through guile, infiltration, mistrust, and misinformation."

"But what about the men in the water? The barracks? The *dacha*. I heard and saw the gunfire. Are you saying Utkin ordered the deaths of dozens of fellow Bolsheviks? Why?"

"Any better way to create a cover for yourself? Your organization?" Dooley responded as he stopped walking and turned his shoulder. "Did you notice anything about the graves?"

She turned to back look at the graves. After a few seconds she responded, "I see now."

Dooley felt another raindrop. "I'm guessing, but I think I can put it together. Come on."

Straightening his shoulders while adjusting the straps of his knapsack, he continued walking. "I think Utkin, and the others are Reds and belong to Comintern. But if they're going to infiltrate America or another country, it would be best to not have anything connecting them to the Bolshevik government, including financial ties. Besides, from what I know, the Bolshevik government is dead broke anyhow. So, killing two birds with one stone, they concocted a scheme to find that wealth of diamonds and use it to fund their operation. Or at least get it started. You know, seed money. And somehow, I think Prohibition will fit into their scheme. I've also seen what some of them are reading, which means they'll find places within American society to make an honest living while doing so. You know, like the pencil necks on Wall Street or stiff suits in government. I'll also bet they're building a cadre of dupes like us to use for the future."

Zeta looked at the dirt in the pathway as they approached the edge of the forest. "So, I am responsible for my cousin's death?"

"Zeta!" he answered sternly. "You didn't push her off that staircase, and Utkin would've found another way to get ahold of those diamonds. We just made it easier."

She continued to look at the dirt in front of her steps.

"But that wasn't the start," Dooley continued. "After recruiting the right men, they probably stole their submarine in a grand fashion and killed a bunch of innocent Red Russian sailors or soldiers leaving them out like dressed deer for newspaper photographers. Utkin gathered his resources and came to this island to put all the pieces together, but that was before our raid. A time where they still needed funds to finance their operation. I'll bet while Utkin and Vostok conducted their research and realized this island would be a great place to create his force, they came across stories of the Manila Galleon and Chinese pirate gold."

By now, they reentered the forest.

"Remember: I asked if any of the persons the Spanish left behind held onto at least a handful of their goods, and he said that wasn't his concern. The first attraction was the isolation of this island, but since they're here, why not spend some time looking for a bit of treasure. I'll argue that every Spaniard left behind, whether a seaman, a priest, administrator, or passenger, held onto what they could, even if it was just a few pearls in a coin pouch."

"Doing so," Zeta added, "represented some sort of hope, some sort of life, by knowing that 'when' rescued the following year they would have some means of paying their way at least back to the Spanish colonies in the Caribbean where the rest of their goods would be waiting for them on deposit somewhere. At least in theory."

"Correct. Which is why you can see the outlines of the graves. While the grass over the graves has regrown, it doesn't match the grass around the graves. Utkin had his men dig up those graves within the last several months, and it's been the dry season up until a few weeks ago. After digging up the graves, they probably recovered enough to finance their operation until he could conduct the raid back at your old family estate."

They were now following the path that looped around the eastern side of the central mountain. As they walked and talked, Dooley thought he heard the muffled sound of an engine. After hearing it intermittently, he realized it was coming from the north. Glancing back over his shoulder, at the east-west running rise behind them, he thought back to his flight lesson, when he thought he saw the ground at the eastern end of the sloping hill move.

"It all sounds so fantastic but yet plausible," Zeta said. "But why didn't those Spaniards who buried the dead take the goods off the bodies before burying them? Why bury the goods with the bodies? Or even the persons who were left behind? Why wouldn't they dig up the graves and recover the goods? What about the islanders? Why wouldn't they dig up the graves? And what about the Chinese lady pirate?"

As they continued their walk through the forest, the sergeant continued. "I agree that there may have been the odd person that would risk internal damnation for stealing from a dead man or digging up a corpse, but the Spanish were, are, religious, Catholic, and superstitious, so no sense in inviting bad luck. They wanted to keep whatever chances they had of going to heaven or getting off the island. Especially if they're being watched."

Dooley paused to look up through the tree branches. He could still see the overarching, disapproving glare of the mountain face staring down his long, rocky nose.

"That covers the Spanish," Zeta said as she looked at the same censuring scowl from the mountain's face.

"Now as far as the Chinese lady pirate," Dooley continued as he stuck his thumbs through the straps of his knapsack, "the rumor of her burying treasure on this island is, more than likely, horseshit, as the notion of pirates and buried treasure is stuff of fiction. Most pirates raided for ready cash. That said, if you're going to bury treasure you need to bury it in a place that is easy to relocate, and what better place than a marked grave? I argue that if they dug up a grave to bury the treasure, they may have found goods with the body. The pirates could have realized the wealth at their feet and dug up all the graves, but that occurred one hundred years ago, and the grass would not be different like it is now. Also, every single grave has been disturbed. If the pirates did raid the graves, and Utkin came in after them, I doubt he would have wasted the time digging up every grave after the first few drew blanks."

Zeta answered as she looked at another homestead nestled among the island's trees. "I know you don't have all the answers. You're just surmising."

"I am," Dooley said as he looked at the same homestead. He also thought about something. "Just like the Spanish, the Chinese are a superstitious lot. They're big on ancestor worship, and they probably left the graves alone to avoid upsetting the island's spirits."

"Lastly, what about the islanders that remained behind after Brooks left?" Zeta asked.

"Of course, they could have, but why?" Dooley responded as they came upon what looked like a shooting range in a cleared area of forest: The range consisted of a weather-beaten wooden bench and three posts five yards in front of it. Shards of broken glass and stoneware jugs littered the ground. "Remember what Utkin said about the islanders? About a rusty can full of bent nails being more important than gold? Back where the church once stood, I didn't see any hardware on the ground. Not a single nail. I bet, by the 1850s, the islanders stripped what was left of the church, leaving only the foundation behind as they had access to stone. The church still exists but in those small homesteads we've been walking past."

Zeta looked back at the homestead. After a few seconds, she turned to face her companion as they walked. She nodded in agreement.

They walked south and saw another shallow mud pit with strands of barbed wire stretched over it. Noting the training implement, he looked south and through the thinning trees. They saw the beach, the marine repair facility, and the newly arrived ship. He saw that, before going up on the railway, the ship's crew lowered the ship's motorboat from the davit on the side of the ship visible to Dooley and left it canted over on the beach partly out of the water. Ahead of the boat, still lying in the sand, were the large rib-looking pieces. Looking back at the marine slipway, he realized where those sections came from. However, the boat on the beach and the large wooden pieces were not as interesting as what he did not see on the deck of that ship.

The two covered items he saw during his flight were gone. Dooley turned his head slightly to look behind him. He thought about that long-running east-west rise, the noise he heard some minutes ago, and the moving ground he saw during his flight. He turned and looked at the facility. The covered slipway looked just like he thought it would from this view, which was nothing more than a slightly angled, U-shaped wooden cradle where the bow of vessels would be pointed into. Once in place, and using winches and cables, and if the vessel's engines were operational, the vessel would be drawn up on the cradle, putting as much hull out of water as needed. While the keel of whatever boat or ship rested on the backbone of the slipway, the vessel was held in place by adjustable wooden timbers spaced along the railway. It looked much the dried ribcage of a dead animal poking out of the grass. In this case, though, a section of the wooden ribs was removed, and that was what he saw lying in the sand.

He saw men watching from the beach, including Utkin and Vostok. At the shore end of the railway, and under its the roof, were white men wearing coveralls and standing by an anchored metal windlass. A wire cable stretched from the bow of the vessel to the vertical drum and returned to the ship's own anchor windlass. Standing on the bow of the ship were other white men wearing coveralls, who used the ship's powered windlass to pull itself onto the cradle. Under the ship's stern, which was still in the water, the water boiled.

"Utkin said the ship's captain only wanted to use the repair shops," Zeta stated as they continued their walk. "So why is it powering itself onto the slipway?"

Thinking for a second, he then answered, "Let's get back before it starts raining."

Now that Dooley had a better idea of what was going on, they followed the path as it curved to the west. In a few minutes, they found themselves standing at the edge of the east-west running road. To their east, the road was scarred by treads like what Dooley had seen on farm machinery back home and on the armored vehicles he saw at Camp Custer. Those machinery scars also joined the wide path opposite them. The path, or road more like it, ran into the forest to the south. The tracks were also just like the ones he saw on the beach from the airplane. He also thought about the rails bolted to the foredeck of the submarine.

Zeta looked up at the sky. "What's next?"

Looking up at the building clouds as well, Dooley knew that by this evening, it would be storming. He smiled. Bringing his thoughts back to the present, he answered her question. "What we do is walk down this road and return with pleased, but tired, smiles on our faces. We are going to relax on the porch and have more of that cold cider while talking about our transportation off this island and our roles in combating the Bolsheviks. Then we will get cleaned up for dinner. Afterward, you and I will select something from the bookshelves under the staircase, but then feign tiredness and we will retire to our rooms."

"That's it?"

"Not exactly. After they think we've gone to sleep, I'll sneak over to your room as they are expecting it, but I'll bring a couple pillows that they're not expecting. We'll make loud, passionate love, then collapse into a long, deserved sleep. In the meantime, I need to go look at a couple of things. The only issue is that the cook has a bunk in the kitchen, and I don't know if he slept there last night or if he'll sleep there tonight. If I try to sneak out of the house through the first floor, he might hear me. I need to figure out a way to leave and get back in without getting caught. Anyway, after that, all we need to do is to wait for our transportation. Once we are away from here, I'm sure we will still be monitored for a while. You know, just to make sure we're legit, and we can play along with that. However, at some point we're going to have to let the authorities know what's going on, but we'll have to be smart about it."

"I understand," Zeta said, "but don't we have enough to tell the authorities? What if you're caught? And for what?"

"When I saw that ship earlier today, I saw two items covered with tarpaulins on the main deck. They're gone now. I also noticed other things, but if we're going to let the American government in on this operation, I need to give them as much information as possible."

Zeta looked at the sky. "What if the cook is sleeping in the kitchen? How are you going to sneak out of the room in the middle of the night without getting caught? What about me?"

Dooley answered with a smile as they approached the edge of the meadow. The Brooks House was ahead of them. "You'll be fine. As far as me sneaking out of my house and not getting caught, let me just say my mother never caught me when I snuck out in the middle of the night to visit Edna McGinty over on Hayes Street."

Zeta smiled. "You're a cad."

CHAPTER 26

THE YOUNG COUPLE sauntered toward the Brooks House while Dooley appreciated the late afternoon sky. Half an hour later, Zeta and Dooley, now refreshed, enjoyed cider while sitting on the porch. Each had a book in front of them on the table next to their glasses. By 5 p.m., the two Russian officers were also refreshed and enjoying cider at the table as well.

"On the way back," Dooley said after a long sip, "we saw the ship put itself up on the slipway. I thought it had a simple fire, so why did it need to go onto the slipway?"

"We were told that as well," Vostok said, "but it looks like the damage was more extensive than realized. Anyway, that ship is not your concern as your transportation will be here by tomorrow afternoon. You will depart the following morning for Keelung Harbor, and from there, you will be on your way to help us filibust the spread of Bolshevism."

Vostok finished his statement by raising his glass in a toast. The others followed.

"So, I can assume you enjoyed your picnic," Vostok asked as he leaned back in his chair while looking at the books. "Did you visit the church grounds?"

"Yes, we did, and found it to be a somber place," Dooley answered while wondering if he should mention seeing Morda playing gladiator. "And I can see that while the persons left behind were given decent burials by the next arrivals, their last few months on this island must have been idyllic. I find it hard to believe that no one survived."

"I, too," Utkin said as he looked at the book in front of the American. "With access to fresh air, water, fruit, meat, and goat milk, such luxuries should have cured whatever ailments that caused their deposition, so I find the irony poetic. Perhaps after realizing they had such illnesses, they refused to say anything to start or complete their voyage with their wealth. Much like your Captain Ahab in that book in front of you. A man of means, status, and skill but a man who drove himself to his own demise in search of evil in the form of a great white whale. It is a rough comparison, but it will work."

"So, you said this island still belongs to the Brooks family," Zeta stated, "Have they come back since the 1850s?"

Utkin answered as he too sipped his cider and looked at the book in front of Zeta. "As Brooks departed the island, he gave instructions to the persons who choose to stay behind, that the house and facilities remain intact for his return. The islanders followed his wishes, especially since the occasional Brooks descendant did arrive on a family yacht now and then. Along with the occasional Royal Naval vessel as the island is still British property. The house remained for them and to serve as an inn for captains and officers who stopped to service their ships. In return, visitors exchanged books or left some behind. Such as that one. Is it in Spanish?"

"It's a romance novel," she answered while looking down at the old paper cover. "Takes place in Cuba before the Spanish-American War."

Utkin cracked a smile. "I know there are pieces by Chekov, Nabokov, and even Tolstoy, your namesake, among others. Works of classic Russian literature outlawed by the Bolsheviks, so I would have thought those selections would have been more pleasing, but I am glad you are starting on your Spanish refreshers—"

But he was interrupted. The door behind him opened, and the cook popped his head out. He said something in Russian, and Utkin responded in Russian.

At the same time, Zeta pinched Dooley's thigh under the table.

"Countess, Sergeant," Utkin said. "Dinner is served. I hope you are in the mood for goulash with rye bread and butter?"

"Just as long as it's as good as Mother's," Dooley replied.

"I am sure you will not be disappointed," Utkin replied as he leaned forward. "Also, while the cook slept here last night, to prepare for our arrival, and to take care of us today, he will return to the submarine raider commando for other duties. He will decant some wine for you on the kitchen table along with sliced food."

"What about you?" Dooley asked.

Utkin answered. "I, too, will be with my submarine raiders. For a drill."

Dooley smiled as he looked at the two Russian officers, "Leaving us two alone? With a cellar full of wine and cider? Is that wise?"

* * *

Why did they leave us by ourselves? Dooley asked himself as he tried to see the fat raindrops assaulting the wooden shingles above his head.

Dooley, wearing his US Army uniform trousers and undershirt while lying on his bed above the covers, turned his head to look out the window. Water ran off the slanted roof in sheets. It started to rain a little after sunset, which offered Dooley and Zeta the excuse to retire to their rooms early. With the generator running in its little housing behind the kitchen, there was power for the reading lamp. After having muddled through the first twenty pages of Moby Dick, Dooley finally heard the front door shut. While Vostok departed soon after dinner, Utkin said he wanted to nap before the drill. Pushing himself off the bed, Dooley left his room and crossed the hallway. He knocked on the door, then opened it without waiting. Zeta, wearing a pair of pearl white pajamas, stood next to the window in bare feet.

"He's walking across the road to the south," Zeta said as she peeked through the blinds.

Dooley pulled up behind her and looked over her head through the crack in the blinds, just in time to see a black, oilskin slicker melt into the night rain. Once Utkin was out of sight, they both backed away from the window. Zeta turned as she sat on the edge of the bed. "Well, now what?"

Dooley backed up to an upholstered chair in the corner and sat. He lifted his forearm and looked at his watch. "It's almost ten now. He will need time to get to where's he's going . . ."

"That's if he's going there," Zeta commented. "Don't you find it strange that he left us unsupervised? Do you think they are trying to trick us? Maybe he's out there waiting to see if you're going to go do something."

Dropping his arm, Dooley leaned forward to watch his toes as he wriggled them. "Well, the first question is: why? Have we done something that raised their concern? Also, Utkin and Vostok do not strike me as men who make mistakes, although I do think Utkin has made a couple of misjudgments in the last few days. As far as Utkin waiting out there in the rain to see what I'm going to do, that seems a waste of time. That said, this is what we are going to do."

He took his eyes from his toes and looked up at Zeta. He saw a twinkle in her eyes.

"First, I'm going down to the kitchen and get wine along with cheese. We will enjoy our dessert and discuss the finer points of Melville's classic. Then we will turn the lights out. I think the rain will continue for a time but will slacken. Even if it ends, I think there'll be enough cloud cover, so I won't have to worry about moonshine."

"It'll be black as hell out there," Zeta said.

"I've operated in the dark before. You just need to allow your eyes to adjust."

* * *

Just as the centuries-old stone wharf at Cavite witnessed the departure of the USS Decatur only days ago, the scene at the stone quayside of HMS Tamar in Hong Kong witnessed the arrival of the same American torpedo boat destroyer. The somber glare of electric lamps lining the quay wall illuminated a string of lorries under them. Sitting in the front seats or on the cargoes in the beds of the lorries, the white drivers and Chinese stevedores watched the ship glide into place. The sailors lining the main deck tossed mooring lines to waiting dockworkers. The sounds of spinning turbines inside the destroyer escaping the exhaust stacks and the barking of orders from men on the quay bounced off the stone walls of the warehouses lining the other side of the quay. Above the American sailors, embers not only escaped from the Number Two stack but started to escape from the Number Three stack as well. On the starboard bridge wing, Hillary and Fowler watched their men secure the ship to iron bitts. As they did, both men noticed the British version of the American torpedo boat destroyer tied at the quay wall in front of them. The name painted across the transom was Krakatoa. Just as with Hillary's ship, lorries lined up along the quay, and men waited to load that ship as well. However, there were no armed marines or photographers waiting by the sacks of potatoes.

Hillary and Fowler looked at the royal marines who stood in the center gap of the lorries directly below the bridge wing. Four of the marines stood at attention with bolt-action Enfield rifles slung over their right shoulders. Wearing battle dress uniforms and cartridge belts, they waited just as patiently as the lorries. In front of the marines, stood their officer. He wore his uniform along with Webley revolver holstered at his side and carried a clipboard in his hand. Next to him stood two men wearing civilian suits and carrying bulky cameras in their hands.

The blue-painted, British-made Leyland lorries all had the same white stenciling on the doors, which identified them as property of the Royal Navy. Each vehicle, except for one, had open beds filled with refueling equipment, food stores, and cases of ammunition. The only vehicle that did not have an open bed was one with a canvas-covered frame, and it was at the end of the line of lorries and adjacent to the stern of the destroyer. The canvas was marked with a white circle and a red cross in the center, and it was occupied by white men who either wore western-style civilian suits or Royal Navy uniforms with Red Cross armbands on their left arms. They all carried items in their hands as well. The items ranged from leather satchels to bulky cameras to a metal-framed canvas stretcher one with a coil of rope tied to each end.

Minutes later, with three pairs of criss-crossed mooring ropes securing the destroyer to the iron bitts along the quay, Hillary finished giving orders to the man operating both the helm and EOT. Satisfied, he called out, "Mack, go ahead and begin refueling. Once your hose is hooked up go below to secure from sea. We're not going cold iron, though. Leave Number Two Boiler on the line along with the Number Two generator. It's almost midnight and I want to be underway before dawn."

"Aye, aye, Skipper," the Scottish-American engineer replied without looking up.

Standing on the foredeck with two members of his black gang and a coil of rope in his hand, he tossed the rope while holding onto one end toward a man standing by the first lorry. The man caught it as his mates started to uncoil a length of black hose from the bed of the lorry.

Seeing that the refueling was underway, Hillary turned to look over the aft side of the bridge wing and down at his quartermaster. "Busachek, strap on a pistol and cartridge belt, and get men to lower the gangplank. You got the quarterdeck."

The quartermaster saluted without looking up.

Hillary turned to face his chief petty officer, "Ernst, get our guests from the brig and escort them to the quarterdeck. Before you do though, give them each a belt of whiskey and a pack of smokes. Bring the hospital steward and another man with you. I'll get Sparks to gather Harrison's belongings from my stateroom and meet you on the stern."

"Sure thing, Rance," the boatswain's mate replied as he turned to leave.

After watching his chief enter the bridge and walk to the ladder leading down to the main deck, Hillary looked at his helmsman. "Krivor, announce that the smoking lamp is out. Then announce for all hands not on watch to muster with Busachek. After that, secure the bridge from sea and help Busachek."

"You got it, Skipper," Krivor said while reaching behind him for the handset.

Just then, Sparks opened the door leading from the ship's radio room. Wearing his glasses on his forehead again, he carried three envelopes in his hand. He stepped up to the ship's captain and held them out, along with a fountain pen. "I typed up the report just like you wanted and made three copies. One for the ship's office, one for the American consulate to mail to Manila, and one for the Brits. They need your signature."

"Very good, Sparks," Hillary said as he received the envelopes and the fountain pen. "Go ahead and get Harrison's stuff from my stateroom. Bring his baggage to the stern."

Sparks answered by dropping his glasses to his eyes.

With that last order, everything moved into action, including the medical personnel and civilian standing next to the last lorry in the line. They walked over and stood next to the stern of the ship, which was about four feet above the stone pavement of the quay wall. At the ship's gangplank, as the first of the supplies, a crate of eggs, was about to exchange hands between the sailors and the stevedores, they paused. So did the crewmen aboard HMS Krakatoa.

Fowler, still wearing his working dungarees and his chief's hat but now wearing a cartridge belt and holstered pistol, stepped out from an open doorway in the superstructure with the pirates following. He led them past the file of Americans who gave the pirates pats on their backs, words of encouragement, or cigarettes. The prisoners, who stumbled more than walked, wore American dungarees and shoes, and had their combed hair neatly parted in the middle. With untied hands, they followed Fowler onto the angled gangplank, reaching out for the rope guidelines to steady them. The marine officer came forward along with the cameramen. The enlisted marines unslung their rifles in unison and followed in step. As Fowler and the pirates stepped down the gangplank, they were greeted with the blinding flash of cameras, forcing the pirates to bring their hands to their eyes. Fowler, instead, squared away his shoulders, inserted his thumb into his cartridge belt, and looked firmly into the camera flashes.

"That's far enough," Fowler said to the pirates as he stopped at the end of the gangplank. The lead pirate bumped into Fowler. After looking over his shoulder Fowler stepped onto British soil and to the side allowing the marine officer to step up and face the pirates while bringing up the clipboard in front of him. The officer looked at the paper on the clipboard before looking over the top of it and at the pirates. He also inhaled deeply and, after shooting a look at Fowler, the officer returned his eyes to the paper on the clipboard. Clearing his throat, the officer spoke. "George 'Bones' Robinson."

The pirate in front brought his hands from his bleary eyes and smiled. He was missing his front teeth. "That's me, gov."

The officer coughed slightly before reading the second name. "Geoff 'Blackie' Ryan."

The other man, standing behind 'Bones' Robinson, answered by raising a thumb while turning his head to the side to puke. The officer took a half step back as the vomit splattered on the stone pavement.

The officer spoke again. "By law, I am required a verbal acknowledgement."

The pirate wiped his lips with the back of his hand while focusing his bleary eyes on the officer. "I'm Geoff 'Blackie' Ryan, you bloody Vic bastard."

Accepting the response with visible umbrage, the officer cleared his throat again before reading off the charges listed on the paper. Once finished, he looked up from his paper. His eyes focused on Chief Fowler's peaked hat. "There were no officers available for the exchange?"

"They're busy. You're going to have to put up with a crusty old China hand."

Though slightly taken aback, the officer concluded the change of custody. "Chief Petty Officer, I will now take charge of these prisoners."

The marines behind the officer stepped to the foot of the gangplank and turned to face each other. They held their rifles at the ready. The two pirates, bobbing and weaving one foot from British soil, waited for Fowler to tell them what to do.

"Bones, Blackie, go ahead. May God be with you."

Still standing on the gangplank the two men turned to face Fowler. Both reached out for his hand with Bones going first.

"I'm guessing my missus will read about this when the morning drunks roll into her place, but I doubt she'll spend a farthing to catch a ferry from Kowloon and see me off."

"Knowing Mavis, I think you're right," Fowler answered.

Bones sighed. "If you get the chance, could you go in and check on her."

"I'll see her the next time I'm in town."

"Don't forget to pay off your tab," Bones said as he let go of Fowler's hand and stepped onto British soil. Blackie grabbed Fowler's hand firmly while looking into the American's eyes. "I'm glad you didn't give us a chance to kill you after our last card game."

"You never had a chance," Fowler replied as he grasped the pirate's hand firmly. "Now go."

The three men looked at each other with sad eyes, and after a few seconds, Fowler spoke up. "If I pay off my tab, Mavis will just piss it away, so I'll do you mugs a favor. I'll buy you each a headstone."

The two pirates nodded their heads, but it was "Blackie" Ryan who spoke up. "Don't give these bloody Vics one more penny than they deserve. They're going to wrap us up together in the same canvas hammock after the hanging anyway, so put everything on one stone."

"Done," Fowler stated as he watched "Blackie" step onto British soil.

The officer stepped aside as his men escorted the stumbling pirates away from the gangway. As the pirates were marched away from the lampposts, the officer took a second to tug at the bottom of his uniform jacket. He spoke to Fowler while doing so. "Chief, for some reason I do not find it surprising that you knew those men, or even that man's wife, but even still, do you think it proper to allow those men to be drunk at such a time?"

Fowler looked at the officer's epaulets. "I don't know when they're going to be hung, but I assume it's going to be soon, so anytime to be drunk is a good time. Just make sure your damned neck stretcher does the job properly."

With that ending comment, Fowler tossed a salute at the officer before turning to walk up the gangplank. "Stiff-ass Brit," he mumbled while stepping back onto the destroyer's deck. Behind him, the pirates and the marines disappeared into the darkness, which signaled the men to start passing the stores. At the same time, the two cameramen who documented the transfer of prisoners joined the men at the stern. Meanwhile, two men who stood with the

British medical personnel walked forward to the gangplank. They were slight of build, in their fifties, and wore homburg hats, civilian suits, bowties, and pencil-thin grey mustaches. They also gripped the handles of leather satchels in their right hands. A couple minutes later, the formal transfer of the dead pirates started.

Fowler joined them, and others, on the stern while being accompanied by two seamen. Once there, one of them, who carried a first aid musette bag in his hand, gave out surgical masks and gloves. The personnel on the quay wall donned their own medical protective clothing as well.

"Why are you wearing a sidearm," Hillary asked as he donned his mask.

Fowler answered by standing a bit straighter and looking to the cameramen on the pier.

"Forget it," Hillary said as one of the cameras flashed. "Go ahead and crack the hatch."

Still looking at the cameramen Fowler, and the other seaman, lifted the main deck access to the steering room and, as they cracked the hatch, everybody gagged behind their masks. With a pause Fowler threw his feet into the hatchway and stepped down the ladder into the room. The seaman followed. One at a time, the two men in the compartment pushed the canvas-wrapped bodies out of the steering compartment headfirst. Everybody saw the fluid-soaked wraps. On deck, the hospital steward and Hillary accepted the bodies and placed them on the British stretcher, which lay on the deck next to the hatchway. They untied the lashings enough to expose the grey, puffy faces.

The British representative, who removed newspaper clippings and police photos from his satchel before setting it at his feet, sifted through the items in his hands until he found a match. Standing over the corpse, the representative held the photos in front his face and shifted his eyes back and forth until he was sure of the identification. The official then filled out a toe tag with a pencil and handed it to the hospital steward who tied it to the lashings after the canvas was closed. Hillary and the hospital steward then lifted the stretcher, with the ropes, over the ship's handrail lowering it to the waiting men on the quay wall. Thus, the process continued, documented by the flashes of cameras, until the last British citizen, Otter Lassiter, was processed. With the last dead pirate tagged, the British representative handed a blank tag and his pencil over to the hospital steward. Picking up his satchel, the representative placed it under his arm and stepped aside. The last body was pushed out of the steering room and laid on the stretcher. At this point the American representative stepped forward.

Hillary reached into his uniform pocket pulling out Harrison's driver's license, military ID portfolio, and the orders Harrison gave him upon boarding, and handed them to the American representative. Accepting the documents, the man stood over Harrison's corpse while the hospital steward removed the lashing exposing Harrison's face. The representative's eyes shifted from the two photos to the body on the stretcher. After several seconds, he looked up at Hillary and nodded. The hospital steward filled out the mortuary tag and secured it to the lashings before closing the wrap. Once done, Hillary and the hospital steward lifted the stretcher over the handrail and lowered it to the British.

After the British medical personnel on the quay wall accepted Harrison's body, the men on the ship's fantail removed their protective medical masks and gloves, which the hospital steward collected. Hillary reached into his back pocket and pulled out two envelopes. He handed one to the British representative. "This report explains the entire action."

"Good," the man said as he accepted the envelope and placed it in his satchel. "Sir, I now believe the transfer of the pirates is complete, and I would like to thank you for your efforts; However, there is one last detail." When he withdrew his hand from the satchel, the British representative, holding a folded sheet of paper, cleared his throat and held it out for Hillary. He turned his eyes to the deck as he did.

Hillary accepted the paper and unfolded it. He read the few words and list of numbers and the amount due at the bottom of the sheet of paper.

"No Lewis gun?" Hillary asked.

"I am sorry," the man continued, "but the Crown is quite particular in certain matters, so I am not authorized to supply weapons. Even the ammunition you requested put me in a spot. However, after what you did for us, I did what I could, but I am sorry for the bill." After clearing his throat again, he continued. "I would've had no problem with paying for the produce, tinned food, and the boiler parts from my budget, but I could not hide the expenditure concerning the ammunition. The Lassiter Brothers must have put up a prodigious fight."

"They did."

"Well, the Lassiter Brothers were quite an annoyance over the years, so having that bother discharged is a relief. And I am sorry that the effort cost the lives of your men. I am sure they were good men."

At this point, the American representative chimed in. "As far as your officer, he will be buried in the Stanley Military Cemetery until further arrangements are made. I also arranged for a service tomorrow afternoon. Although I do not think he was known by anybody in Hong Kong."

"Thank you, sir," Hillary replied as he held out the second envelope to the American representative, along with the bill the British representative handed him while keeping his eyes on the British representative. "I'm sorry that we lost your vessels and the property aboard them. We are not sure what happened as they seemed to be attacked by forces unknown to us. Everything is in the report, and, yes, they were good men."

The British man nodded slightly as he turned to leave. He stopped after one step and turned. Using his knuckle to smooth out his trimmed mustache, he spoke. "The pirates were obviously under the influence, but I thought the American navy was a dry navy. Where did you find the means to get them to such a state?"

Hillary looked back at the American representative before looking at his British counterpart. He cleared his throat. "I ordered they be given a bottle of medicinal brandy from my sickbay. It was the least I could do. I hope you don't mind since they are going to be hung soon."

"Quite right, Lieutenant Hillary," he answered with a sigh. "They're going to be hung at noon, or twelve hours from now. The issue is that, under British law, men condemned to death must be completely lucid and aware of their execution as it is being carried out."

"I understand," Hillary said, "I hope we didn't cross any boundaries."

"Young man," he said while straightening his shoulders. "There has been no indiscretion noted from my end and have a safe transit back to where you plan on going. In the meantime, there is a case marked for the ship's captain among the stores. It is the least I could do."

With that note, the British man turned his head and stepped toward the quarterdeck.

Everybody watched as the representative approached the quarterdeck and the British medical personnel loaded themselves into their lorry and started the engine. The cameramen also made their getaway by disappearing into the night to get their photos into the morning editions.

"What's next, Skipper?" Fowler asked.

Hillary looked at the hospital steward, "Go ahead and clean the medical clothing and tell the cook to bring up a gallon of vinegar."

The man nodded as he turned to obey his orders.

"And you," Hillary said pointing to the seaman who helped with the bodies. "I'm sorry to have to tell you this but get some clean rags and a bucket half full of potable water. When the cook shows up with the vinegar, mix the two and wipe down everything in the steering room. Leave the hatch open when you're done."

The seaman saluted as he turned to carry out his orders.

As Hillary, Fowler, and the American representative watched the seaman leave, Sparks, carrying Harrison's belongings, stepped out from the shadow of the superstructure. He stopped next to his commanding officer and set Harrison's property at the feet of the American representative.

"I, too, am sorry for your loss," the representative said as he lifted the leather satchel in his hand. Using the other hand, he unclasped the brass fastener and lifted the satchel's cover to insert the envelope with its official report, Harrison's identification papers, and the bill. He spoke while doing so. "I understand that you are being ordered back to Manila, so I understand topping off with fuel, but I don't understand the stores and ammunition. It's only a two-day transit back, and it is not likely you'll have to battle a nest of pirates again."

Hillary looked at Fowler, then at Sparks. "I have received orders to return to the Philippines by the governor-general. However, I have also received orders from my immediate commander to continue my patrol and to figure out what happened. Lastly, I received orders from the US Army Philippine Department to proceed to Keelung Harbor in Formosa to pick up a Captain Hugh Rodham and to inspect some sort of problem threatening American property owned by missionaries along the Chinese coast."

"I see your predicament," the representative offered, "and how you follow your orders is your prerogative. But all I know is that I've just been handed a bill that stresses my budget. Fuel, apples, and canned fish is one thing, but all that ammunition is another." Without waiting for a reply, he turned to leave as well but stopped to look down at Harrison's property. "I'll have my man bring up my auto. Have a man take Harrison's effects there."

Hillary offered a vague nod as the man turned to leave. After watching him walk toward the men handling stores, Hillary sighed and turned to Sparks. "What the hell are you doing standing there, you scurrilous knave! You heard his royal highness!"

Sparks smiled as he leaned to grab Harrison's property. Standing up, he spoke. "I can think of one American that should be hung along with those pirates."

"Hold your seditious tongue before I have you flogged," Hillary said harshly. "Be gone, and do not fowl my air no more!"

Sparks offered a shallow curtsy while holding Harrison's belongings.

Both Hillary and Fowler watched Sparks walk away with Harrison's belongings hanging from his hands. As they did, Hillary turned to Fowler, who pulled a pack of Camels from his shirt pocket and offered a smoke to Hillary.

"I'd say that was pretty bold," Fowler said. "We got their pirates for them, got our ship shot up, and lost nine men in the process, and they still hand us the bill. I bet they even charged Uncle Sam for Harrison's toe tag and that pencil. Told you; nothing but stiff-ass Brits."

Hillary smiled as he lit his cigarette. "Are you worried that the money they'll charge for that pencil will affect your pension?"

Half a cigarette later, the men leaned over the handrail while flicking their ashes into Hong Kong harbor.

"So, we're set?" Fowler asked. "What if the brass keeps radioing us?"

Hillary took a moment before answering that question. "Seaman Spivey is expecting, right?"

"Yes," Fowler answered. "His wife is due next month."

"Have Sparks write up orders for Spivey," Hillary said, "and have Spivey draw advanced *per diem*. Also, have Sparks check with the shipping offices for a liner heading back to Manila."

"What if he doesn't want to go?"

"It's not up for discussion," Hillary said as he looked at trash floating in the water between the hull and the stone quay wall. "Also, this tub should've have been turned into razor blades years ago, so can I help it if my radio keeps breaking down?"

"Screw the brass?"

"Screw the brass," Hillary replied while bringing his smoke to his lips. "Speaking of screwing the brass, I told you to give Bones and Blackie enough to keep the edge off. I didn't tell you to get 'em plowed. 'Sides you only had a minute."

Fowler smiled as he brought his smoke to his lips. "Lieutenant Rance Hillary, they've been plowed since being brought aboard."

Hillary turned to look at his chief petty officer.

Fowler responded, "They weren't no trouble. 'Sides, we had plenty of booze to go around, and I didn't have to pay for any of it."

"Chief, you're a cad."

CHAPTER 27

DOOLEY PAUSED TO look back at the bed. Zeta's pajamas were thrown over the footboard, and the countess was covered up to her chin. Her blond hair lay sprawled on the pillow around her head, and her face glowed under the lighting from the electric lamp on the nightstand. The face was an expression of both satisfaction and concern. Next to her, under the covers, were two pillows and a duffel stuffed with clothing and bed linens.

"Turn out the light," Dooley said as he looked at his watch. "It's just past midnight, and I'll be back before dawn. I'll knock quietly four times to let you know when I'm back. In the meantime, if you see that door crack open, pretend to be asleep. Any questions?"

"Just come back," she said quietly while inspecting the only man that had ever made love to her. He wore his army uniform, black watch cap, athletic shoes, and a length of rope tied around his waist. His shingle axe and leather sheathed hunting knife hung from loops. His weapons and web gear remained piled on top of the cedar chest in his room.

Dooley answered by reaching for the doorknob. At the same time, he heard the click of the lamp switch. Closing the door behind him, he stood motionless in the darkness, listening to the house and the rain outside. After a few seconds, he made his way down the hallway and stairs, and through the kitchen. The rain was still coming down, but it seemed to slacken. Stepping off the back porch he made his way past the outhouse and to the forest behind it. He stepped just into the edge of the forest and started walking east. Somewhere between him and under the hard-faced gaze of the island's southern saint, was the air assault commando barracks. But he was not worried about them as they should be asleep by now.

As he headed toward the path that would take him north, he tried to mentally file everything he knew, or observed, to date. Based on what he had been able to gather so far, he assumed there were perhaps thirty-five experienced submariners including Vostok and his officer. Stopping next to the trunk of a tree, Dooley listened for half a minute. The rain was now ending, and his ears paid attention to the new silence. Hearing nothing out of the ordinary, he stepped forward again. As he did, he felt cold rainwater run down the back of his neck.

Returning his thoughts to the commando units, Dooley totaled the number of men in the air assault commando, both pilots and parachute soldiers. Again, fearless men with special skills. As far as the submarine raiders, he spent a full week on the submarine with ten raiders, not including Utkin and Gorki. The sheer force of such trained men could not be discounted. He cringed at the thought of those he did not know about: operatives already buried deep in American society. Men and women of the espionage, intelligence, and detective commandos of which Gorki, Morda, and Mashka would become members. He thought back to the week leading up to the raid, and the firearms and sharpened blades they practiced with. He also remembered this afternoon, when they caught Morda finishing up his own private fight against unseen opponents.

Moving on, he came to edge of the dirt path. Ahead of him, and to his right, through the thinning trees of the forest, he saw glints of light and heard the metallic knells coming from the marine railway. Turning left, he followed the edge of the pathway to the north. Stopping every two hundred yards or so to look behind him he eventually made it past the north meadow and to the base of the north hill. Covered with trees and bushes, it disappeared into the night sky. Not really knowing what else to do, he stood there, thinking about his next move while the water dripping from the tree branches and leaves continued to soak his uniform. Going back to his flight lesson, he thought about the exposed sloping end of the hill as it reached the sea. About fifty feet high and almost as wide, his thoughts went back to what Utkin said about the cavern under the hill at the southern half of the island. After excavating it enough to house an entire submarine, he asked himself: "What the hell was under this hill then?"

Still standing there, listening to the first few bars of a building amphibian chorus, which started just as the diminishing curtains of rain were pulled aside by unseen stage handlers, he heard an engine. Dooley looked at his trench watch and noted it was just past one thirty, but his attention was snatched away by a sudden explosion of both light and sound. He instinctively threw himself against a nearby tree trunk. Looking toward the stage he saw the star of the show; a man, outlined by a weak light, standing in the frame of a doorway. "What the hell?" Dooley mumbled under his breath.

For several seconds, the man stood in the open doorway. Dooley saw that he wore the same patch-covered coveralls as the men from the air assault commando. The man seemed to be enjoying the night air and looking up at the black sky, and the doorway he stood in reminded Dooley of cowboy pictures he watched while in garrison: Western adventures with entrances built against the sides of mountains leading to gold mines. The man, and the door frame, were highlighted by a yellowish glow from somewhere deep inside the hill. Also, the sound of that engine Dooley heard earlier was more pronounced. After some more seconds, the man reached for the door handle and pulled it closed, leaving Dooley recovered in blackness and listening to the amphibian choir. Dooley waited for his night vision to return while thinking of his next move. So many directions tore at his thoughts and while trying to let the compass needle settle, he started to hear another sound. It came from the east. After listening further, he realized it was the sound of a boat engine.

* * *

"The engine room is back in order, Captain," reported the lanky, blond-haired man while stuffing a rag into the back pocket of his rust-stained coveralls. "But we did lose Number Two distilling plant. A three-inch shell punched straight through the hull and exploded in the distiller. Also, we lost two replacement airplane engines from the repair shop along with a lathe, but two other replacement engines were left unscathed."

"Thank you, Peter," Captain Bogdanovich responded as he looked over the engineer's shoulder, and at the chronometer on the bulkhead of the ship's wardroom. "It's one-thirty now. Make sure you and your engineers get cleaned up and have some wine before going to sleep but be prepared for changes in our plans."

The ship's engineer nodded as he stepped toward the door. Captain Bogdanovich and the other two men at the table watched him leave before continuing their conversation.

"Well, all I know is once we start on the hull we are committed," Bogdanovich restated.

"Being a submariner," Vostok interrupted with a smile, "I fully understand the idea of hull integrity, but at the same time, we can't wait for a lowly American navy lieutenant in command of a twenty-year-old ship to make up his mind."

Both Vostok and Bogdanovich paused to look at Utkin. After a second, Vostok asked. "What are the orders for that officer?"

"I dare say he has quite a dilemma on his hands," Utkin said. "He has orders to return to the Philippines by order of the governor-general. The captain also has orders from the US Army to go to Keelung Harbor to pick up Hugh Rodham with further orders to the China coast. Lastly, to continue with his patrol to find out what happened to his men, which means a possible visit to our little refuge."

"And an interruption with our schedule," Vostok finished.

"What do you think he'll do?" Bogdanovich asked.

"It appears that the captain has acknowledged receiving each message, but has not indicated which order he will follow," Utkin replied, "but we might be in for a fight."

Bogdanovich gave Utkin a questioning look.

Utkin continued. "He sent a message to the American consulate in

Keelung and asked to have a fuel barge available by 9 p.m. tomorrow night, or tonight. Since he is topping off on fuel, he is either going to the China coast or continuing his patrol with the intention of visiting us. He topped off with fuel in Hong Kong and would not need to refuel if he were returning to Manila. Also, it appears that the American consulate in Hong Kong is put out as he was handed a bill for ten thousand rounds of .303 ammunition, two hundred shells for their six-pounders, and an extra fifty shells for his three-inch deck gun. The consulate radioed the Philippines and wants the Navy to reimburse his office so he can finish the fiscal quarter in the black."

"I see your point," Bogdanovich said with a wry smile. "Why the fuel and ammunition if he plans on returning to Manila and, while he did expend some ammunition at Bagay Alto, he did not expend that much. It seems our young knight in shining armor feels slighted and seeks redress on the field of honor."

Vostok and Bogdanovich noticed Utkin's smile, but it was Vostok who responded.

"Dmitri, I see the wheels turning in your head and I agree with what you are thinking; however, we must be mindful of the bigger picture. And we can only accomplish that with patience. If he responds to any of those radio messages, then we will have an idea of our next course of action. In the end though, we still need to modify our departure plans by moving our schedule up, and to remove evidence of our presence, which include setting off charges to collapse our underground bases once they've been vacated."

Captain Bogdanovich spoke up. "I see preparing to depart this island with a clean slate as no issue. The real issue is our ability to insert our maritime assets into the next step of our plan without raising eyebrows. Individuals from your espionage and detective commandos can be, and have been, easily slipped into place intermittently across the entirety of the Western Hemisphere. And don't forget the men in your air assault and submarine raider commandos. Since the Armistice was signed last November, governments have been discharging veterans by the millions. While most are going back to farms, shops, and factories, there are those dogs of war who still seek to hold steel. These same veterans can easily take up residence in shitholes like Cara-cas working as security for Latin American despots or corporate hooligans. But on the other hand, our maritime assets are huge physical entities, and having them just show up is something American intelligence and Prohibition law enforcement agencies will have to notice. The arrivals of our assets will be viewed as preliminary steps in the smuggling of alcohol once the Prohibition becomes the law of the land."

"Forgive me for being a landsman," Utkin replied as he lifted his glass, "but that Japanese metal ore processing ship we captured months ago seems to have had no problems slipping into its new role after completing its mission here on this island."

"You are right," Bogdanovich replied as he also lifted his wine glass. "It proved successful as a test. To modify its physical appearance; to construct a history for the vessel starting with its creation as an ore-dredging and process-ing vessel made from the hull of an Argentinian cattle ship by a gold-mining consortium; and to insert it into Mexico's maritime registry under a Mexican flag and the official homeport of Ensenada. That effort proved to be success-ful as it did not create any untoward attention, but we had the luxury of time and obscurity on our hands. Now might not be the case especially since we have three vessels arriving tomorrow, including two renowned sailing vessels. Also, once we leave the Orient, your submarine, Captain Vostok, will surely be missed, and inquiring minds will want to know where you, your crew, and submarine disappeared to. And let us not forget about this lovely piece of asset," Bogdanovich finished, raising his wine glass above his shoulder.

"Understood, Igor," Vostok chimed in. "The disappearance of vessels from one side of the world and their sudden reemergence on the other side will be noticed. But while it appears that we may be rushed, there is no need to panic. What we must do is start our evacuation from this island now, to have our agents in Latin America do their best with preparing false documents and histories. At the same time, we need to prepare for an unwelcomed visit."

The room went quiet for a few seconds as the men peered into the wine in their glasses.

After a few seconds, Utkin sat up a bit straighter. He cleared his throat before speaking. "As I see it, we could let the captain of that ship arrive here and investigate our island while we remain undercover. If he discovers nothing of our presence, then we are good."

"We could," Vostok said, "but the chances of not discovering even something slightly suspicious is quite low, and any resulting gunfight would risk any future efforts for our mission. Also, since the captain is knowingly stepping into a fight, he will probably radio his superiors when he feels necessary, thus, bringing undue attention to this island."

"Or we could attack the ship before they approach this island," Utkin said, "and if they send out an SOS with their location, the US Navy would send their ships to that area and not here to this island. We know that the captain of that ship is resupplying and will depart in the next couple of hours. If he is coming here, via Formosa, then we could estimate his speed and direction and intercept him."

Vostok nodded. "We could, but the weather must be dealt with. However, my men are finishing up with the reinstallation of the torpedo-handling tackle aboard my submarine. Also, Sergei can drive his craft back to the submarine for us to load it onto the foredeck. Lastly, I can have my officer get it underway by dawn. Hopefully, once our friend is aboard that destroyer, he should be able to send a message giving us information we can use."

Utkin smiled slightly. "All sounds reasonable as the Americans are probably not suspecting an attack by submarine. Or a submarine plane. So, it should be easy to put four torpedoes into the hull of that thing once it is located." Utkin paused to look over at Captain Vostok. "What is the progress of our torpedo upgrade?"

"Well," Vostok answered, "before our departure to recover those diamonds, my engineers have been able to update the power plant and drive train of four of our five-year-old torpedoes in the submarine cavern, and Mashka was able to produce enough of his new explosives to rearm the warheads of those same torpedoes at his shop. Those torpedoes have been reassembled and are waiting to be loaded aboard the submarine. Since the destroyer is a lightly built ship meant to chase torpedo boats and is getting on in years, it should sink well before any Maydays are sent out. I will instruct my officer to machine-gun any survivors."

"What of the family friend on the ship?" Bogdanovich asked. "Should we notify him of the attack? So, he'll be ready?"

"I think not," Vostok answered. "If we radio him, he may unintentionally reveal our plans. But if he survives the torpedoing, he can identify himself in the water."

"Very good," Utkin spoke as he leaned for the wine bottle. "Igor, I can have my air assault bomber ready, but its range is comparatively limited, and its strike would not be as decisive as I would prefer so, its use would have to be of last resort. I would much prefer to have you and your asset," Utkin paused to raise his hands with one of them holding the wine bottle, "to redeploy with the same two seaborne air assault airplanes you just brought back. The air assault crews can reattach the wings and engines just as quickly as it took them to take them off. Also, with the speed of your ship, you can be away from this island and well ahead of Vostok's submarine even if it leaves first."

"Agreed," Bogdanovich said as he held out his glass for a refill. "The wings and engines are complete with their postflight maintenance aboard this ship, and I sent a boat to pick their crews. I'll let them sleep for a few hours, then have them get the machines back onboard and their engines and wings reattached. However, the destroyer will have time to radio out a Mayday if we attack them ourselves."

"Yes, they may, but any Mayday sent out needs to be timed for our benefit," Utkin agreed, "So, I would ask you, Igor, to act as a scout to find the destroyer but then just track it until Vostok's submarine can be brought into play, or the other way around if your officer, or Sergei, sights him first. A coordinated sub-sea, surface, and air assault would be best, but if we only had one asset available to destroy that ship. I would prefer Vostok's submarine, and those upgraded torpedoes, to carry out the assault. Such action will give us time to coordinate when needed and sink that ship as far away from this island as possible."

"I think your plans are acceptable, Dmitri," Vostok chimed in as he also held out his glass for a refill. "But what about your plans to modify the hull of your ship, Igor? After all, we put this ship on the railway for a reason."

"I know we did," Captain Bogdanovich responded, "and despite the damage to my machine shop, my men can continue with the internal modifications and installation of the secret compartments at the bottom of our hull. We can expedite the installation of the submarine doors upon our return as we will have no choice. We need to install those doors out of sight of ship repair or drydock workers elsewhere, and we need to do so in order to slip this vessel into the maritime landscape quietly. This ship has been scheduled to be a vital part of the Ensenada-San Diego Run as early as next year."

"Good," Utkin replied. "Let them have a few hours, as this coming daylight should prove interesting."

"In the meantime, though," Vostok replied, "I do realize that while my submarine can be armed with four upgraded torpedoes and underway by dawn, we still have four more that require an upgrade. You know, just in case they are needed in the future. And since you are already busy modifying the internals of your ship with a damaged machine shop, Igor, and the blacksmith shop at the railway is only good for hammering out bent nails, I would ask that when our next asset arrives tomorrow, that we put its machine shop to use. I know that Captain Lagos had only planned on staying for a few hours, but with the weather as it is, and the fact that the torpedo technicians and their equipment will have to be back on that submarine for its deployment, I would ask to have that ship made available. I can have one torpedo technician remain behind to restart his work on the remaining four torpedoes, and Mashka can restart his work on the remaining warheads. Theoretically, when my submarine returns, it can be rearmed with another load of upgraded torpedoes."

"Let us just be fortunate enough so that we will not need them," Utkin said as he raised his wine glass in salute. "At least for this mission."

Chapter 28

AFTER THE MAN closed the door, Dooley remained next to the tree listening as the motorboat engine got louder. Within five minutes, the engine was close by, somewhere to the east. He also heard the coxswain put the engine in idle. Dooley looked at his watch and saw it was just after two. The cloud cover continued to thin, letting more starlight leak through. Just at that time, the door opened again, and Dooley heard men talking as they filed out of the rectangular black hole. The light inside the cavern was now extinguished, and the sound of a running engine inside the hill was gone. The last man out pushed the door closed behind him and undid a roll of camouflage netting above the door. Aided by the growing starlight, he saw the men, carrying musette bags and bedrolls, snake away into the trees.

Several minutes later, he heard the idling motorboat engine come to life, but soon after that, the sound of the motorboat faded away leaving Dooley serenaded by frogs, toads, and insects. Stepping from the tree trunk, he walked toward the entrance. Stopping in front of it, he pushed the netting aside and reached for the door handle while thinking about what might be inside.

Once he closed the door behind him, he stuck his arms out to his sides. He felt planks along with upright timbers. Waiting a few seconds, his eyes adjusted. Stepping forward he started to feel the rocky wall of the cavern under the hill. Walking further still with his hands on the rocky wall, he got the impression that the tunnel curved to his right. He also felt the gravel on the tunnel's dirt floor through the rubber soles of his shoes. At first, the only real light came from the face of his luminescent trench watch, but as he stepped cautiously forward while following the bend in the tunnel, which now started to curve left, there seemed another source of light. It came from somewhere in front of him. After about fifteen steps the rocky wall he had his hands on fell away. At the same time, the source, or sources, of light became brighter, but not by much. However, it was enough to reveal a sight that caused him to take a deep breath.

Exhaling, he remembered the smells of the submarine he spent the last week on while he thought about the showcase with the flying insects in Vostok's stateroom. Also, just like standing in the control room of the submarine, he remembered looking up and into the hatchway that led to the deck of the conning tower. In this case though, he realized why he could see a bit better. Centered in the roof of the long, narrow cavern was a hole, perhaps two to three yards in diameter. Tree roots dangled from its edges and water dripped from them. The weak starlight that leaked through the hole revealed the shadows of three metal creatures floating inside that cavern. All Dooley could think of was the fantastic science novels he read as a kid. Focusing his eyes on the thing in front of him, he saw what looked like a metal hornet or wasp. This thing, however, was completely enclosed, about thirty feet long, and with a set of wings about twenty feet long each. The wings were mounted to a metal fuselage about two thirds up from the water. There was one inline engine, fixed with a wood propeller, mounted to the underside of the wing. Above the wing root, the enclosed machine had a windshield that wrapped around to the sides, just like the images he saw in magazines of futuristic luxury automobiles with gracious protruding engine hoods. Dooley looked through the side window glass and at a soft, greenish glow. While not much of a glow, there was enough to reveal the hint of an airplane cockpit. Above the roof area with the windshield was a slightly raised ring of a hatch. Right next to it was a small, round hub with a piece of pipe about two feet long sticking out of it. There was also another slightly raised ring of a hatchway about eight feet aft of the first one.

Taking his eyes off the metal thing he looked at his trench watch and re-alized the source of that soft glow inside the machine. Turning to his right he decided to inspect the rest of the cavern and the other metal creatures, which unlike the machine in front of him, lacked wings. He walked the length of a ledge about eight feet wide and saw three worktables along the curved wall of the cavern: presumably one for each air creature. There was also a single four-cylinder generator mounted on a wheeled metal frame and wired to a small switchboard. Next to it he saw an electrically powered, bench-mount-ed, metal-turning tool of some sort. To his left he also saw that each floating machine had its own square-nosed punt floating in the water.

Under the weak starlight leaking through the hole in the roof, he looked at the machines and saw each one had a soft, greenish glow coming from in-side the cockpit area. That illumination helped reveal what appeared to be combinations of seaplanes and submarines, but each in their own way. The middle one in the line, the one under the hole in the cavern's ceiling, was narrower and more angular in shape than the one in the back of the cavern, but ten feet longer. For lack of a better word, the term dragon came to mind as he pictured Jules Verne's drawings of Captain Nemo's Nautilus. He also remembered the weathervane outside the Brooks House and what looked like a plowshare on its front. This craft had two hatches located above the cockpit, above the greenish glow, and next to each other. Just like the machine behind it there was an extended pipe by the starboard hatch.

The hatches were above an area that resembled the windshield and side windows of an automobile. It had a place along the side of the hull, under the windshield, where it looked like a wing was attached at one point. In front of the windshield area, was long and sharp nose with a small, curved fin-like wing on the side of it. A few feet aft of the cockpit area was another closed hatch. The starlight entering through the hole in the cavern's ceilings enhanced the metal creature's mythical scourge.

The next one in line, the one at the front, had a hull shaped much like a whale and even had what looked like a slightly raised hatch where the spout hole would have been. Next to it was a pipe perhaps four feet high or so. Under those items the front of the machine had one centered oblong windshield. At the other end, the tail of the machine was a bit higher than on the other two machines and had a rudder like an airplane along with flippers like a whale's or fins like that of a submarine. Lastly, closer to the front, it had places where it looked like wings could also be attached. The wing attachment places were about midway down on the fuselage.

Wondering the purposes of these machines, Dooley approached the wall of the cavern's entrance. After he walked up to it and spent a couple of minutes feeling it. He found the cable and hand winches that operated the set of doors. He also felt a wooden frame covered with canvas. With increased understanding, he stepped back toward the last air creature in line.

Climbing into the punt, he undid the rope and reached up to grab the trailing edge of the wing. Using it to pull himself along, he made it to the side of the machine and tied the boat's rope through a robust footstep at the root of the wing. With intense curiosity, he stepped from the boat and onto the wing. He looked at the small, outer hub next to the hatchway above the cockpit. The hub was the size of a kid's wagon wheel with that short extension of pipe sticking out of it. He also saw that the pipe was fitted with a long piece of glass. Dooley looked at the hatchway next to it. Turning the handle wheel on top, he peeled the round hatch back. The starlight from the hole in the cavern's roof and the glow inside the thing gave Dooley cause to mutter to himself, *You slick bastard.*

Dooley looked at two seats, side by side, with a space between them. As his eyes adjusted further, he started to see gauges, brass labels, pedals, and a control stick. He also saw items that reminded him of being inside the submarine including a small helm wheel and the pipe with the glass that extended downward to the floor of the compartment next to the right-side seat. He remembered his comment to Utkin about him building flying submarines.

Slowly closing the hatch, Dooley knew it was time to get back to Zeta.

It was 4 a.m. when Dooley approached the crossroads where the north path joined the east-west running road. Opposite him was the start of the path leading south. Taking one last look toward the noise coming from the marine slipway and at the glint of several deck lights he was about to turn and follow the road to the Brooks House but stopped. Coming down the road he saw a pair of dim headlights. He also heard a soft mechanical clanking.

Stepping next to a tree trunk, he watched through the reappearing rain. The noise was becoming louder, and it sounded familiar. It sounded just like the tanks he saw at Camp Custer. He also saw the headlights were becoming a bit brighter. As he watched and listened, he had a hard time believing what was developing in front of him. Finally, the machine came abreast of him and turned from the road onto the path heading south.

The turn gave Dooley time to look through the rounded windshield and into the enclosed cab of the machine. All he could think of were the carousal rides he took as a kid when his father took the family to Coney Island. It was perhaps fifteen feet in length with a set of stubby wings about twelve feet long each. It had a tail like an airplane, but a boat propeller under the tail. Between the propeller and the airplane-like tail was a protruding pipe. Looking under the thing, he saw not a wheeled landing gear system but a pair of tracks just like a military tank. Looking up, above the cockpit, he saw a single engine and front-mounted propeller mounted by a metal framework on top of the enclosed cab. There was even what looked like the barrel of a cannon sticking out from the cockpit with its breech inside the thing and next to the pilot's head. He also knew the man sitting behind the windshield of that carnival ride.

Turning toward the house, his mind reeled at what he saw that night. He also remembered the writings of America's premier undersea explorer, Simon Lake, and his submarine with its tractor tracks, which allowed it to cross the seabed and ramp up onto a beach when needed. Thinking about the tracked vehicle behind him, he thought about the other hangars spaced along the road ahead of him.

* * *

Though the sun rose above the horizon just after five, it was unseen by those awake that morning. The sky was nothing but a dark grey, ominous-looking pile of clouds. Under the weighty blanket, the submarine raiders busied themselves winching open the slanted doors that closed off the cavern's entrance. They stopped hand cranking as Captain Vostok, standing on the ledge of the cavern, signaled they were open far enough. Locking the handles in place, the submarine raiders watched as the water behind the submarine boiled and the bow of the vessel pushed itself past the open doors. Everybody waved to the submarine officer on the conning tower and the pilot next to him. They also looked at the stubby little aircraft on the foredeck of the submarine, and the hand-powered crane hovering over it. The submarine, and its reconnaissance asset, drove itself into the low-hanging clouds, just as the clouds emptied themselves of their contents.

"Quite an ominous start to our little foray," the submarine officer said to the pilot standing next to him. Both men, wearing oilcloth rain slickers and hats with wide brims, stood on the deck of the conning tower. They braced their feet against the surging seas while holding the coaming of the coning tower with their hands.

Sergei Popov looked up as he wiped rain from his eyes with the back of his hand. "*Da*, but I think it should clear once we get away from this island."

The submarine officer took his eyes away from the pilot and looked at the three items on the deck in from of them. "Let us hope so, as I would hate to see you attempt a takeoff in these seas. And to recover your sub-airplane in the same."

Popov looked at those same items on the foredeck. The first item was the portable, hand-operated crane that the crew assembled once the bottom part had been slipped into place. The bottom of the singular upright pipe was inserted into the same hole that held Dooley's wine bottle earlier. Its upper horizontal arm extended over the second item on the foredeck. The same sub-airplane that Dooley saw last night, and the same one Popov was expected to fly as an extension of the submarine's reconnaissance capability.

"Nothing wrong with keeping skills sharp," Sergei said as he turned to look at the officer.

The submarine officer responded with a smile as both looked down at the third item fixed between the tail of the flying machine and the vertical pipe of the crane. It was nothing but a simple brass tube resembling an old-fashioned, hand-drawn field cannon from the Napoleonic Wars. Instead of wheels, though, the barrel was mounted to a frame inserted into the two tracks and had its muzzle fixed to the end of the aircraft. On its side, at the end closest to the conning tower was a firing mechanism and a pull lanyard neatly coiled and hanging from the firing mechanism. The last time that the percussion cap and trigger assembly was fired in anger, it was attached to a British Enfield musket during the Indian Mutiny in the 1850s.

* * *

"Sergeant Dooley?"

The voice at the door knocked Dooley out of his slumber. With his eyes stilled closed, he answered. "Yes?"

"Breakfast on the porch soon," the voice said through the door. "Coffee now?"

"Please," he answered as he yawned. With his eyes still closed, he heard the footsteps walk away. After a few seconds, he opened them halfway and looked around the room first at the footboard, where he saw that Zeta's pajamas, along with her Dopp kit on the bureau, were now gone. Yawning again he pushed himself up and rested against the headboard. Rubbing his eyes with his hands he peeked at his wristwatch on the nightstand next to the bed.

Just then he heard the porcelain doorknob turn. Looking at the opening door, he saw Zeta. She wore her pajamas and slippers and carried her Dopp kit and towel. Her hair was wet and brushed back behind her ears.

"The cook said you were awake," she said with a welcoming smile. "I went to the water closet and privy. I hope you don't mind."

Dooley yawned again while stretching his arms above his head. "No, I don't mind. I also hope Utkin didn't mind us sleeping together under his roof."

"He couldn't be that upset," she said as she placed her items on top the bureau. "The cook is preparing quite a breakfast."

Realizing his hunger, he asked, "Which consists of . . ." but stopped as Zeta started to unbutton her top. After the last button she pushed it from her shoulders and tossed it at Dooley.

He caught the warm nightwear and brought it to his nose. "Have you no modesty?"

"Are you not enjoying seeing me naked early in the morning?" She turned to smile at him. "Let me enjoy this moment. I feel liberated."

Dooley draped the top over his face as he leaned against the headboard enjoying the smell and warmth. "Let me know when you're getting ready to drop your bottoms."

Just then there was a knock on the door. Dooley grabbed the pajama top from his eyes and the covers from his body. Swinging his legs onto the floor, his feet landed next to his underclothing. At the same time, Zeta jumped behind the bureau. Dooley smiled while placing his feet into the underwear bottoms. Standing up, he threw the pajama top at her while stepping to the door. "Chicken."

She smiled while peeking around the bureau as Dooley opened the door.

"Thank you," he said as he accepted the tray. After closing the door with his foot, he stepped over to Zeta and held out the tray.

"What do you want me to do with that?" she asked.

He looked at her breasts. "You may find it liberating to parade around topless in front of your lover, but I find it spicy to be served coffee in bed by naked, blonde-haired Russian countesses."

She smiled as she pointed her thumbs into the waistline of her pajamas. "So, just how many times have you been served coffee in bed by naked, blonde-haired Russian countesses?"

"At least once," he answered as he saw her bottoms fall to the floor.

Thirty minutes later, Zeta, with Dooley behind her, stepped onto the porch. Dooley pushed the door closed behind him as he saw four men either sitting at the table or leaning against the porch railing. All held coffee cups in their hands and wore casual clothing just like Zeta and Dooley, although one

SERGEANT DOOLEY AND THE SUBMARINE RAIDERS

man wore a ship's captain hat. The men stood as Zeta stepped to the table. She wore a pair of grey slacks and a loose-fitting white blouse, and a blue ribbon tying her hair back. Dooley wore a pair of black slacks and a plaid, short-sleeved shirt.

Utkin was the first to speak. "Good morning. I hope you slept well."

"We did," Dooley answered, "and I hope you don't mind us sleeping in."

"Sleeping late occasionally is good for the mind and soul," Utkin answered as he looked over at Zeta. "I can also understand as to how your sleep may have been interrupted."

"Mind if I sit down?" Zeta asked as she blushed.

"Forgive me, and please do, Countess, Sergeant," Utkin said as he sipped his coffee. "We're just finishing ourselves."

"Thank you," Dooley said as he pulled out a chair for Zeta. Once she was seated, he stepped to the side of the table where he could face the four men. On the table was a ceramic coffee pot, two cups and saucers, a bowl of apple slices, and an envelope. Dooley pulled out his own chair, seating himself. "Are you from that ship on the slipway?" he asked as he picked up a coffee pot off the tray on the table and filled a cup for Zeta.

"Our apologies," Vostok said as he brought his coffee cup away from his lips. "It seems that those men have plenty to do, so no. However, I would like to introduce Captain Lagos and Mister Borodin. They arrived with the transportation that will take you off this island."

Dooley finished filling Zeta's cup and started to fill his own while looking out from under the porch roof. "And aren't you a bit early?"

"I must admit the weather is deteriorating, which is why I pressed my ship," the man addressed as Captain Lagos said while he stepped from the railing and held out his coffee cup. "But, from the radio traffic we've heard so far, it is a widespread, disorganized low front that could become a typhoon. How it develops, though, will dictate the time of our departure and our next port of call."

"Either way it doesn't look good, right?" Dooley said as he filled the man's cup.

"We'll see, but we came here for reasons other than just to drop off a pony and pick you two up," Lagos said as he withdrew his full cup. Turning his attention to the Coca-Cola thermometer and brass-ringed barometer, he said, "We will continue to off-load our ship and embark other items throughout the day. You can move into your staterooms after breakfast."

Borodin chimed in while lifting his coffee cup to point out at the meadow. "Although the ship is not like this very rustic setting I, from a landsman's point of view, found my time aboard that ship comfortable."

Dooley looked over at Zeta who returned his look. "When do you really need us aboard?"

Captain Lagos smiled. "Drinks at four and we will go from there."

Just then the door opened, followed by the cook who held two plates of food.

Utkin smiled as he stood from the table. "Enjoy your steak, eggs, and potatoes, and help yourself to whatever you need until you board the ship. And do not forget that envelope, as you were rather keen on its contents."

Twenty minutes later, after finishing their breakfast and Dooley pocketing the envelope, Zeta and Dooley enjoyed the last of their coffee and a slice of apple.

"I can't believe all of what you said," Zeta commented. "It seems so fantastical."

"It may be," he answered, "but it's real enough: the all-metal bomber airplane and flying all-metal seaplanes that look like they could submerge like submarines. And the fact that the men who created these machines are well-trained killers and have a wealth of diamonds in their possession. Think of the damage they can do in the States. It's beyond comprehension."

"Not to mention they have a submarine, and torpedoes somewhere, and at least two ships to transport all of their weaponry," Zeta said as she sipped her coffee. "It also seems like they don't make a move without planning it out to the last degree, so what about the stuff you saw in that last hangar from this morning? The one that Mashka came out of."

"It looks like a cross between Doctor Frankenstein's laboratory and my father's shop. I saw all kinds of scales, beakers, and books about chemistry, and right next to them I saw a lath to turn metal stock, and a machine to grind metal shavings into powder. It looks like Mashka is conducting experiments with explosives. There were cans of gunpowder and other chemicals."

"You said something about ground aluminum," Zeta said. "Why aluminum?"

"I don't know," Dooley responded, "but I do know that, since all their airplanes and bicycles are made from aluminum, there must be piles of aluminum shavings all over the place. I also know that gunpowder, by itself, is not a powerful explosive, especially for bombs and artillery. But, while people have been improving explosives over the last few thousand years, the Great War forced advances in chemistry and explosives in the just the last few. I think that Mashka's been experimenting with more powerful forms of explosives. I also saw various empty explosive shells and handheld aerial bombs on a workbench, along with what looked like the empty warhead of a torpedo. I wouldn't put anything past Utkin. And Mashka seems like one bright kid. Perhaps a bit too innocent for hanging around this mob, but still one hell of a kid."

"It sounds like you know what you are talking about," Zeta as she took in the island view.

"Also," Dooley continued, "aluminum is non-ferrous, meaning no sparks. Also, I saw a lot of brass tools. Also, non-ferrous. That said, it doesn't take no more than a few wayward grains to ruin your day."

* * *

"Demby's cornbread sure would help this canned stuff," Hillary said as lifted a spoonful of *chili con carne* to his lips. As he did, the destroyer's bow dropped into a deep trough, causing him to spill a drop of sauce on the table next to a chart. Hillary chewed as he looked at a line of islands strung between the north end of Formosa and the southern Japanese islands. The same islands that they would pass through after picking up the man called Rodham later that evening. After swallowing, he looked at his men. "Pass me the Tabasco, Mack."

The chief engineer grabbed the bottle of the pepper sauce and doused his lunch before handing the bottle to Hillary. "Remember the time Demby caught you putting catsup on one of his steaks?"

"Yeah," Hillary replied as he accepted the sauce. "But this isn't his chili, and that was one of the only times I remember him ruining beef."

The three men paused to smile at fond memories.

Breaking the silence, Hillary spoke, "Ernst, are you sure you want to do it this way?"

Fowler answered as he reached for his rum. The same rum the British consul gave them. "Yes, I do."

"Do you know where to start?" Mack asked after swallowing a spoonful of chili. "That island is more than fifteen square miles in size."

"Like I said at the start of this patrol," Fowler continued as he sipped his rum, "I've been researching this island and have a good idea of the lay of the land. Also, Mack, you need every one of your black gang to keep the ship running, and Skipper, you need Busachek, and every deck ape onboard, to help you fight this ship. We're better off with having only me on shore to run interference. And remember, we might have to fight flying machines."

"We have a three-inch deck gun, a Lewis gun, and four six-pounders, and are well stocked with ammunition." Hillary said, finishing Fowler's concern. "And all of which are useless since we've never trained for airplane combat."

"You are correct, Skipper," Fowler finished, "but even with training it means nothing without proper sights. All we have are iron sights meant to fight slower, surface targets. Not against machines flying at one hundred miles an hour and hundreds of feet above us. All I can say is just keep telling the men to lead their targets."

Hillary took another spoonful of chili. "Keep going."

"Well," the chief continued, "after all my studying and after what we've seen and heard so far, I think I know of a couple places to start looking."

"Well, here is what we know for sure," Mack said as he reached for his glass of rum. "Kermit and the others were attacked by a flying one-eyed whale and a flying fire-breathing dragon. Now, assuming such machines don't exist, there must be other options, including the ship we ran into after the attack. I didn't think of it at the time, but it did look a bit like the tramp steamer that attacked us back at Bagay Alto."

"All tramp steamers look after a while," Hillary said.

"Granted," the chief continued, "but it had several hours to alter its appearance."

Hillary put his spoon back into the bowl of chili and reached for his glass of rum. "Although I only saw the ship's captain through a pair of binoculars during a gun battle the first time, and only from a distance at night the second time, they could have been the same man."

"Also," Mack said as he put his glass back on the table, "don't forget that the ship that night had two items under canvas on its main deck. The captain said they were locomotives he was transporting to God-knows-where, but remember, I'm Scottish, this ship's chief engineer, and I know steam engines, including locomotives. The profile under those canvas tarps didn't resemble anything I would've recognized."

"Next," Fowler continued, "we've decoded a message that Harrison carried with him, and it concerned the island I've been researching a month before the patrol. Both that ship and island have a connection, and we, need to figure it out. We also need to pick up Rodham tonight and see what we can get out of him before we get to the island."

Hillary looked at Mack, and the chief engineer returned that look with a nod. Hillary nodded in return and looked over at Fowler. "So how and where, and what will you need?"

"When we get there," Fowler said, "lower the paint punt over the side and I'll paddle ashore. I'll take a couple of canteens of water, a bayonet, my shotgun and a bandolier of shells for it, my revolver and a fully stocked cartridge belt, Harrison's forty-five, and a musette bag with extra magazines for the forty-five, and lifeboat rations."

"Is that all?" Hillary chided. "I can have Busachek dismount a six-pounder for you to carry over your shoulder, along with a case of ammunition you can sling under your arm."

Fowler answered the quip with a smile. "The darkness will give me and you time to reconnoiter until morning when you can bring the Decatur into play."

"Do you two know when or where the little game will start?" Mack asked as he sipped his rum. "We're not exactly sure what's there and we'll have no communication with you."

Both Fowler and Hillary looked at each for a second, with Fowler breaking the pause. "Both of us should see about the same thing, the same threats or targets, so I think our reactions should coincide. Anyway, I've already marked my main pickup point and alternate pickup point on the chart up on the bridge in case things go south. But, if things go well, I'll be waiting for you mugs at the dock on the western side with a big, fat smile."

The men paused to look at the chart. Just then, the ship surged again as it plowed through another wave.

"Well," Hillary said as he looked at the blanket of clouds scudding past the open porthole, "you have things figured out once we get there, but the problem is getting there. They may also know we're on our way."

"How do you know that?" Mack asked.

Hillary said while holding onto his chili, "Sparks gave me a message from the flotilla commander just before lunch and he was carping about getting a bill from our consulate in Hong Kong. About an expense he didn't plan on, namely ammunition, and it also appears that the Brits may have overcharged as well. Anyway, our communications may be monitored, and it wouldn't take long to figure out that the extra ammunition was meant for a reason."

The other two men nodded in agreement.

After another sip of rum, Hillary spoke. "I'll have Sparks stay on the radio to monitor ship reports between Formosa and Japan. We'll figure out a way around this weather."

CHAPTER 29

AS CAPTAIN LAGOS said, the weather hadn't made up its mind. While leaden clouds smothered the island, occasional patches of blue were breaking out above the stone residence, giving some life to the dismal hour. Dooley and Zeta, still on the porch, looked under the clouds and saw a wagon with two horses pull into view from the forest on western side of the island. Sitting in the front seat was Mashka and another white man. As the wagon pulled closer to Mashka's shack, they saw that the pony harnessed to the wagon was not Tin-tin Instead, Tin-tin walked, unharnessed, next to the pony pulling the wagon.

"Isn't that cute?" said Zeta.

"They remind me of my dad's horses," Dooley said while flipping the bowl of apple slices onto a napkin. "Alice and Betsy don't go anywhere without each other. Time for a walk."

Leaving the crockery on the table, Dooley and Zeta stepped off the porch and walked to the tin-covered shelter. By the time they reached the shelter, Mashka and his mate, both wearing coveralls, were removing items from the structure. Mashka carried a roll of camouflage netting over his shoulder, and the other man held a can of powered aluminum in his arms. A bench-mounted lathe was already in the bed of the wagon.

Acting if he did not know about explosives, Dooley asked, "What's the aluminum for?"

Mashka looked at his partner's arms before answering. "Keeping up with my experiments."

Dooley smiled while opening the napkin in his hand. "Are you coming with us?" he asked as he held out a slice for Tin-tin. The harnessed pony nosed over for his piece of apple.

"No," Mashka replied as he placed the roll of netting in the wagon. "Not yet."

Zeta rubbed Tin-tin on the forehead as he licked the apple slice from Dooley's hand. "Looks like Gorki did a good job on the shoulder," Zeta said to Mashka. "Please be safe. We'll say goodbye later."

With a smile from Mashka, Dooley held out two slices of apple for the harnessed pony. Tin-tin nosed over for his next slice. Giving the last slice to Tin-tin, Dooley looked at his wristwatch, then up at the sky. "It's just past noon. Enough time for a walk."

Together, they turned and walked in the direction of the marine railway. Dooley pointed out the remnants of the tractor tracks in the dirt road and repeated some of what he told Zeta earlier. Minutes later, the young people approached the end of the road and the head of the railway. Just as a cloud from somewhere above started to empty its contents, they ran for one of those open-faced shops Dooley saw during his flight and last night.

Getting undercover just in time, they watched as the ship that pulled itself up on the marine rail yesterday disappear behind a rain squall north end of them.

"Why did they go through the effort of getting onto the slipway only to take themselves off a day later?" Zeta asked as the grey curtain consumed the stern of the ship.

"I don't know," Dooley said, but it's not like they had to replace an underwater part of the ship like the propeller. They must've used the propeller to push themselves onto this thing and to help take it off. The only thing I can figure out is that the ship is part of their operation and they're up to something."

After the stern vanished, Dooley and Zeta inspected the facility while dodging rain bursts. Looking about, Dooley imagined the facility was just like it was created in the 1840s. The only clue to its modern use was the tracks in the sand, which started from one of the open-faced sheds. After some minutes, Dooley and Zeta started back to the house.

The walk to the house was pleasant but wet and as they approached the porch, they saw that the wagon was gone. Dooley turned to Zeta. "Go ahead and clean up."

"What are you going to do?"

"I'll get us some wine," Dooley answered with a smile. "And since you're bent on being a Pinkerton, I'll show you how to clean my gun."

The afternoon passed pleasantly for the couple as they were accompanied by two bottles of wine, a plate of tangy cheese, and raindrops splattering against Zeta's bedroom windowpane. Dooley's uniform was still damp from last night's excursion. But now that it was not possible for the Russians to see his damp uniform, he took it from inside the wardrobe and draped the blouse and trousers over the posts of Zeta's bed. The rest of his clothing, and most of his weapons, gun-cleaning kit, extra box of cartridges, and canvas web gear, were spread across the bed on one side with Zeta's clothing on the other side.

The two young people sat in chairs with an end table and an unshaded lamp between them. Dooley holstered his forty-five-caliber pistol in the belt lying across his lap and snapped the cover closed over the butt of the pistol. Zeta finished wiping her fingers with a damp towel but took a second to sniff her nails.

Dooley looked up as he unsnapped the cover of a magazine pouch on the belt. "You can't be a good Pinkerton if you're going to fuss about the smell of gun oil on your fingers."

Zeta placed the towel on the table and picked up her wine. "If I'm undercover, I can't smell like I just cleaned a pistol. Remember: females don't shoot guns."

"Sounds like you'll make one helluva Pinkerton," Dooley said as he pulled the magazine from its pouch, "as you're thinking about the little things."

She winked and took a sip of her wine. Dooley winked back as he used his thumb to empty the spring-loaded magazine of its six rounds onto a rag sitting on the end table next to his wine glass. Once empty, Dooley picked up another oiled rag in his lap and wiped the outside of the magazine, knocking it against the table. After brushing away nonexistent sand, he picked up the oiled rag and a bullet.

"Never load a magazine to its capacity. It stresses the spring, causing failures. Just be in the habit of always loading the magazines to the same number of rounds. I always load with six rounds. Plus, if the man you're shooting at is counting, it'll throw him off his game."

She nodded as she watched Dooley wipe down that bullet before pressing it into the magazine. So, like the reloading of the magazine, or taking the blade of his steel-edged weapons to a whetstone, the afternoon continued as so. They wiped, cleaned, sharpened, folded, and stowed their possessions. By three in the afternoon, the second wine bottle was empty, the cheese was gone, but wayward raindrops still splattered against the windowpane. The bed was made and their bags, along with Dooley's weapons, web gear, and musette bag waited on top of the bedspread. Now, sitting back in the chairs, they enjoyed the last of the wine while pondering their future and looking at their meager belongs.

"Something wrong?" Dooley asked as he saw Zeta staring at her carpet bag.

Zeta turned to face Dooley. "When are we going to tell the American authorities about what is going on here? And why are you hanging onto that shoe?"

Dooley paused while staring at their meager belongings and part of the heel of the Mary Jane poking out from under the utility bag's flap. "Well, we don't know where we're headed, but we'll have to tell somebody. When that happens, though, I don't know, but we'll have to be careful who we tell and when. The minute we tell anyone, or as soon as they find out we're on to them, we can count ourselves out of a job. On the other hand, once we inform the American government, they may want us to continue as double agents. As far as the shoe, I have no reason to explain why it's still in my musette bag."

"Looks like your wanderlust is rubbing off as I don't mind being a double agent," Zeta said as she sipped her wine. "But it's hard to predict how your government will react. All I have to look forward to is going back to Shanghai to earn scraps while giving piano lessons and living with my parents." She paused long enough to look over at Dooley. "Well, I don't need the shoe, and it's not your size."

He looked at his belongings. "I guess you're right, and I'm also looking at unemployment. However, Utkin's paid me full up including what I left behind in Shanghai: five hundred and sixty dollars rounded up. That's what was in the envelope he left on the table at breakfast. You're welcome to half of it. It'll give us enough money to get us somewhere."

"Then what?" Zeta asked with a heavy voice. "That money will only go so far."

"Well, there are plenty of ways to make money once you get there," Dooley said.

"I hope you are not saying what I think you're saying?" Zeta asked as she gave Dooley a mock look of disdain. "You're a man. You can fix wagons and know something about motors. You can handle horses and fight as a mercenary or work as a pilot. I, on the other hand, am a woman with few skills. What's that saying? 'No matter which cardinal nature forces a young lady to pursue on the rose, the lassie will always end up in Mack's world.'"

Dooley nodded in acceptance. "Well, that sounds made up, but if you stay in a man's world then it's your fault. Do you remember what I said about my attack against that Red Russian machine gun nest? How it wasn't possible without knowing how to work with that gunner backing up my squad, and my use of a Thompson. My point is, knowing how and when to control your assets is an asset. All you need is a starting point with some seed money. My dough can be that start. Now, let's get your new life started."

Zeta smiled as she finished her wine. Placing the glass on the table, she stood and stepped to the bed to collect her carpet bag. Dooley did the same on the other side of the bed. After clipping his pistol belt around his waist, he stuffed his shingle axe into his belt. He then looped the draw string of his duffel over his shoulder, letting the duffel rest against his hip. He went to do the same with his musette bag, and as he did, he pulled the Mary Jane from it. He hefted it once before dropping it on the bed. Just as he was about to let go an explosion destroyed the quiet.

"What was that!" Zeta yelled as the bedroom windowpane cracked.

Dooley groaned as he dropped the shoe back into his musette bag.

*　*　*

Dooley and Zeta ran toward the black-grey pall towering over the tree line and staining the low-hanging storm clouds. As they were about to enter the forest, Tin-tin's head shot above the slope in the road hurtling itself in their direction. Dooley started waving his arms at the pony as he saw that Tin-tin was clearly in a state of panic. However, it seemed that once the pony recognized Dooley, he slowed to an unsteady gait, breathing heavy and snorting as he did. Dooley approached the pony and grabbed its mane. Holding onto the mane, he rubbed the animal's neck while looking at the pony's rump.

"Is Tin-tin going to be alright?" Zeta asked.

Repeating the pony's name, he let go of the mane and replied, "I'll tend to him later."

Minutes later, Dooley and Zeta stood among the carnage at the wharf, including the carcass of the newly arrived pony. It was still harnessed to the remnants of the wagon, which was on its side. The pony suffered several slashes to its body, and its head was nearly decapitated. Blood, oil, and slow rain ran through the cracks between the wharf's planks.

"Poor thing," Zeta said as they surveyed the scene. Both also heard men barking orders.

Along with the dead pony and the wagon, there were jagged chunks of metal and shredded steel plating scattered about the pier. There were also human body parts, including a hand. Not wanting to see what might be Mashka's remains, Dooley looked at the buildings along the waterfront. The front windows were blown out on all of them. Looking back to the source of the carnage, Dooley saw the steamship tied to the wharf with its bow, or what remained of it, only feet away from the sand of the beach. Lying across the road between the beach and the storefronts he saw what looked like a pipe among other metal debris. After a second, he realized it was not a pipe, but the barrel of an artillery piece.

With his first look at the new ship, he saw that it looked just like any other tramp steamer he had seen in the Orient. But what was once a two-story forecastle perched on the front of the ship was blown out, and the overhead deck of the forecastle was peeled back like the lid of a sardine can. The crane bolted to it was nothing but a mangled wrap of steel beams dangling over the side by wire cable. Inside the hole, he saw men with firehoses extinguishing flames. The thick black-grey pall above the ship started to dissipate and mix with the scudding clouds.

"I'm sorry, Dooley," Utkin said as he pulled up next to the American.

Dooley, still ignoring the flesh strewn about the wooden planks, steadied his eyes on Utkin. The wet weather flattened Utkin's black hair against his forehead.

Utkin nodded in acceptance. "Not to be callous, but it looks like your departure may be delayed. Please go back to the Brooks House. We'll sort this out."

The ex-sergeant nodded while reaching for Zeta's hand. She took it in turn and, as they started to walk back, they saw two sets of billowing sails emerge through the distant rainy haze.

* * *

Just like the dawn, the sunset was hidden behind a smothering of low-hanging clouds. Once returning to the Brooks House, Zeta and Dooley changed into dry shirts and calmed themselves with cold cider before searching out Tin-tin. Each carried a basket, with Zeta's containing cut-up carrots. Dooley's basket contained a towel, his bar of ivory soap, and a stoneware jug. They found Tin-tin north of the house along the edge of the forest. While grazing, the pony was still skittish, but after enticing him with pieces of carrots, they were able to get it into Mashka's laboratory. Once there, Zeta continued to feed the pony one piece at a time while rubbing its neck. Dooley, using fresh water he pumped into a bucket from a pump outside the shack, along with the towel, a bar of ivory soap, and a pair of brass pliers and a bottle of solvent he found on the workbench, cleaned the gashes in the pony's rump.

"What are you pouring on Tin-tin's rump?" Zeta asked as the pony nuzzled her palm for another piece of carrot.

With a wet, bloodied towel thrown over his shoulder, Dooley pulled a thumb-sized piece of steel from one of the gashes with the pliers. He dropped both on the workbench next to a Mason jar full of nuts, bolts, and washers before pouring more brown liquid from the jar into the wound. "It smells like turpentine, which both my father and uncle used on cuts all the time." While Tin-tin's rump was in front of the workbench, the pony's front end was tethered to a post in the center of the structure holding up a ceiling beam. "He'll be fine once it scabs over."

Zeta sighed as the pony licked her open palm. "It's apparent that the ship will not be going to sea anytime soon, but what about those sailboats? The submarine?"

Dooley removed the towel from his shoulder and used it to pat the gashes while answering, "I don't know, but it's starting to get pretty crowded around here."

Dooley dropped the towel on the bench next to the Mason jar and shrapnel and reached into the basket. Removing the stoneware jug and its cork, he kicked over the bucket.

"Is wine good for horses?" Zeta asked.

"Wine's good for blood. Any blood," Dooley answered as he emptied the stoneware jug. "Pop gave Alice and Betsy each a bucket of beer every night, and they've been around forever.

"He gave your horses beer?"

"Ale, pilsner, or lager; they didn't care."

* * *

As Dooley and Zeta watched Tin-tin gulp down the strawberry wine, the four Russian leaders sat around the table in the ship's wardroom. Light from the overhead lamp reflected off a bottle of vodka centered on the table and off the crystal tumblers in front of each man.

"What is the damage?" Utkin asked as he looked at the several radio messages on the table in front of Captain Lagos.

"The entire bow is a shambles," Lagos replied, "but if it wasn't for our present weather condition, we could get underway and reach a port with proper repair facilities."

"But how do you explain the damage? It does not look like we suffered an innocent collision with another vessel or had our bow stove in by a wave," Borodin said, reaching for his tumbler of vodka. "Is it possible to use the marine railway to house the ship for repairs? And how long would it take?"

"The damage can be explained," Lagos answered. "I can radio Mersk-Alba Headquarters and say the barrels of nitrates we were bringing back from Micronesia exploded."

Vostok spoke up and answered Borodin's other concern with a long sigh. "A good portion of the machinery and equipment we would need to repair the ship to any degree was lost in that explosion while trying to upgrade and reassemble the remaining torpedoes."

"It's a shame that the ammunition for the twelve-pound naval gun just above the torpedo repair shop added to the damage," Utkin added.

"Yes, it is," Vostok continued. "Also, the marine railway was not meant for such repairs. Lastly, Captain Bogdanovich will need to use that railway and what remains of the equipment we brought to install his submarine doors once he returns from his mission."

The men at the table fell silent while they sipped their liquor. After a few seconds, Borodin spoke up. "Well, it seems that we have a damaged ship, a schedule being impeded, the possible visit by an armed American destroyer, and a storm front that is wreaking havoc from Japan to Formosa. All of which is affecting our evacuation and the dispersal of our assets."

"And don't forget," Vostok spoke up, "we still have two valuable assets out there with air subs on board." He paused long enough to look out the porthole and the rain streaming past it. "I see that you have radio reports in front of you, Issak."

Lagos looked down at the sheets of notepaper while holding his tumbler. "Quite a number of vessels are reporting the same circumstances. One Japanese vessel is reporting its position and the fact that it is about to flounder. Other vessels are radioing their company headquarters indicating changes in schedules, all to avoid the worst of the weather. More germane to our situation, though, the captain of the SS Mongolia is reporting that he's increasing his speed to make Keelung before the storm front does. The captain wants to disembark his passengers, refuel, then depart before the weather worsens in that area. We can assume the captain of that destroyer is adjusting his transit accordingly."

"That sounds reasonable," Utkin said. "What about our assets, Issak?"

Lagos sipped his liquor before answering. "The submarine officer is reporting slow progress. He can only surface long enough to put some charge into his batteries. Igor is also reporting that he's had one lifeboat damaged but is making good progress, though. However, both are reporting doubts about their abilities to launch any air subs for reconnaissance."

"Should we recall them?" Borodin asked. "If they are of no use at sea, perhaps it would be wiser to have them closer to this island. Also, perhaps the weather may force the captain of that destroyer to change his plans or perhaps even sink it for us."

"We should be fortunate for the later," Vostok chimed in, "but in the meantime, I suggest we have our assets continue. We can recall them once we have more information. I also suggest that we have the crew aboard the Grim Reaper start our evacuation by removing the Hog Pen's staff. Afterwards, they can make their way across the Pacific, to Ensenada, for their first stop."

The men nodded in agreement just as a bolt of lightning flashed somewhere in the distance. The men looked at the open porthole as they heard the low rumble of distant thunder.

CHAPTER 30

NOW, BACK ON the porch of the Brooks House, Dooley and Zeta ate salad and baked chicken and drank white wine. At the same time, they talked with Utkin.

"So, we have no idea when we're leaving?" Dooley asked, removing a cucumber seed from his lip with his finger. "What about those sailboats?"

Utkin answered as he finished his wine. "They came here for shelter. As far as our vessel, the captain reports that the hull is seaworthy, but not the forecastle." Putting his glass on the table Utkin continued. "We will be aboard ship. In the meantime, I hope you've found enough to keep you entertained. The cook will see you in the morning."

"We'll be fine," Dooley replied while saluting with his glass of wine.

Utkin smiled at the countess before stepping toward the porch's steps. He stopped to look at Dooley. "I checked Tin-tin. You know horses."

"Thanks," Dooley said as they watched Utkin take the last step.

After their meal, Dooley and Zeta decided to check on Tin-tin. Dooley carried a kerosene lantern in one hand and a stoneware jug in the other. Zeta carried a basket of radishes. They slid the door back and saw Tin-tin next to the center post patiently swishing his tail and shooing flies from his rump. Walking in, Dooley held the lantern over the pony's rump while Zeta fed Tin-tin one radish at a time.

"What kind of flies are those?" Zeta asked. "And are those maggots in the wounds?"

The pony snorted and pawed at the ground impatiently waiting for an-other radish.

"Horse flies. Annoying as hell, and with a heck of bite," Dooley answered as he poked at one of the gashes. It was brown along the outer edges and filled with maggots. "And yes, they're maggots, which are a great form of old-fashioned medicine. Just like leeches."

"So, Tin-tin will be fine?" Zeta asked as she watched the pony chew a radish.

Dooley lifted the stoneware jug as he unstopped it. "He'll be just fine."

After refilling the bucket with wine and leaving the remaining radishes next to it, they returned to the house to get cleaned up and to retire to Zeta's room. They also waited for darkness, and when it came, just like the previous night, Zeta lay naked under her covers while Dooley stood at the door. Her hair was again sprawled over the pillowcase and about her head.

"Maybe one of these nights, we will be able to sleep together proper."

"Yeah," Dooley said with a grin, "but only when we're done dealing with hydro-airplanes that look like they're designed by H.G. Wells and Jules Verne after they spent a weekend together bending their elbows at McSorely's."

An hour later, Dooley found himself inside the cavern. He saw that the two wingless machines were gone, leaving him to focus on the winged craft from last night. Like last night, little ambient light entered through the aperture in the cavern's roof, but there was enough, along with Dooley's night vision and knowledge from last night's visit, to imagine himself flying that machine out of the cave once the doors were open. The only thing was to figure out how to power it up and how to open that double door. Walking the length of the ledge, he reviewed the cabling and crank system until he felt confident. Satisfied, he turned back to the winged machine.

Dooley tied the punt to the side of the aircraft just behind the wing. Once secured, he climbed up the side and onto the wing and reached up to open the hatch above the cockpit. A minute later, he stood inside what looked like the cross between the cockpit of an airplane and the control room of a submarine while standing next to the periscope with the end of it resting on the floor.

He reached up to close the hatch behind him. As his eyes adjusted, he looked at the source of the greenish illuminances. It came from a bubbled lens of a compass horizontally inserted into the console in front of the pilot's seat. Also, everything was made from polished aluminum, which reflected both the ambient light and luminance from the compass. His eyes went back and forth between the two seats and the brain-spinning number of gauges, labels, and levers about him. Against the side walls, just below the windows, were forward-facing tubes. Stooping down to get a better look, he saw a round hatchway under the windshield and between the two consoles. He pushed the door open and stuck his head inside. He saw a few gauges and other items, including a pipe high on either side that went from the console bulkhead to the nose of the machine. At that end, under each tube he saw what looked like the brakeman's handle of the trolleys he rode in Brooklyn, complete with the spring-loaded release grips. However, these handles were upside down. He also saw a Lewis gun, stacked magazines, and a metal tool kit, all fastened in place along the walls and under two fore-and-aft running tubes.

Pulling his head out of the space, he returned his attention to the seats. The left seat was, indeed, an airplane cockpit, while the right seat was like a miniaturized version of a submarine's control room. Turning around, he saw another hatch. After unlatching it, he pushed the hatchway open and saw what could only be described as a miniaturized bunkroom inside a miniaturized submarine. And just like the other compartments, Dooley could see that what space was not taken up by two bunks was filled with locker doors, gauges, tubes, valves, all made from shiny polished aluminum. There was also another Lewis gun held in place by clips against the overhead next to the hatchway and a hinged ladder in its upright stowed position, all reminding him of his mother's childhood toy: a German-made, nineteenth century, cutaway dollhouse the size of a suitcase.

* * *

"How's Rodham?" Hillary asked as he adjusted the helm while looking at the compass.

"Tied to the handrail on the stern and puking his guts out," Fowler answered as he pulled a pack of smokes from his pocket.

"His belongings?" Hillary asked as he adjusted the helm again.

Fowler explained as he held a cigarette out for Hillary to pinch with his lips. "He has a Cook County motor vehicle license, which expires next year along with his Chicago Public Library card. His army portfolio makes him out to be Captain Hugh Rodham of the United States Army, Philippine Department. Stationed at Fort Santiago, Manila. He's packing a government issue forty-five, two extra magazines, and a box of cartridges, but no military uniforms in his bag. Only civilian clothing, and good ones at that."

"Laundry labels?"

"Just like Harrison," Fowler said as he held out a lit match. "The laundry markings line up with his identification, and he has monogrammed handkerchiefs and a book just like Harrison did, but this one's Huckleberry Finn. I didn't see any scraps of paper with numbers on them. But there was a radio-telegram message typed on stationary from the SS Mongolia. The message appeared to be sent from his superiors. It said: 'Transport departed Hong Kong before dawn. Expected to arrive Keelung Harbor ten P.M. A ship's boat to collect you from Raphael's Steakhouse. Ship's captain will be under your direction. Good luck.'"

Watching Hillary exhale out of the corner of his mouth, Fowler continued. "What do you think? Is he a Red? Or is he Army Intelligence working a case?"

"Well," Hillary said, looking past the end of the cigarette and at the lubber line of the ship's illuminated compass. "Nothing says that Rodham's anything but a *bona fide* American army officer, so we'll just have to wait and see."

Fowler nodded as he pulled a cigarette from the pack for himself. "Do you think he'll figure out we're not heading northwest?"

Hillary shook his head slowly while keeping his eyes on the compass. Speaking out of the corner of his mouth, he said, "It's black as hell out there, and its overcast. Besides, he's too busy puking. And it'll be just as shitty in the morning."

Fowler nodded in agreement. "What time you want me to relieve you? It's midnight."

Adjusting the helm, Hillary answered, "Be back at four. Busachek will here at eight."

* * *

"I am sorry you spent the night sleeping on the fantail, Captain Rodham," Hillary said as he poured coffee for the army officer, "but fresh air is a time-worn remedy for seasickness."

The army officer slouched in the chair opposite Hillary. His black, wavy hair was hurriedly combed back, but his white shirt and grey slacks were still pressed after just being pulled from his suitcase. The ship lurched as it was hit another wave, and Rodham brought his fist up to his mouth as he reached out to grab the edge of the table with the other hand. He also looked at the open portholes, and at the salt spray blowing past them. Behind the spray he saw an ominous, overcast sky. After a half-burp, he haltingly spoke while letting go of the table. "I appreciate it, Lieutenant Hillary. I didn't know being seasick would be so miserable."

"Give it time," Hillary answered as he filled his own coffee cup. Setting the pot on the table next to a plate of bread and saltines, he pointed at the plate. "It'll help settle the stomach."

Rodham reached out an unsteady hand for his coffee while speaking. "I assume you've reported picking me up in Keelung, and that we are in route to Qingdao. We need to get to the Chinese coast as soon as possible."

"I did indeed," Hillary said as he too looked out the portholes at overcast skies, "report picking you up."

"Excellent," Rodham said with sullen, baggy eyes as he brought his coffee cup to his lips.

"But we are not headed there just yet," Hillary replied. Watching Rodham's eyes over the rim of the cup, Hillary was pleased with what he saw.

* * *

The sky above the Brooks House was nothing but a weighty, gray blanket pressing down on the island five hundred feet below.

"Definitely not flying weather," Dooley said as he took his eyes from the threatening skies back to the open book in front of him on the table.

Zeta sat opposite Dooley, but her attention was on Tin-tin. The pony stood in front of the porch patiently waiting for a handout. "Looks like you've found a new friend?"

"He likes the wine," Dooley answered as he picked up a strawberry for the pony.

"Are you serious about flying that thing off the island?" Zeta asked as she picked up her coffee cup. "Do we really need to?"

Dooley retracted his arm after Tin-tin snatched up the strawberry and continued to look at the book, which was an historic work about the Opium Wars between Great Britain and China. "I guess I'm just curious as to how it works, but there's too much to absorb with only two visits and one real look inside that thing. I'll go out there tonight. It's nice to have a backup plan."

Zeta turned her attention to the map in the open book. "How big is this storm?"

Dooley studied the map before answering. "Utkin said there's a low front moving away from the Chinese coast and east toward us and stretching north to south between Japan to Formosa."

He paused to point to an area hallway between Japan and Formosa but hundreds of miles to the east, out in the Pacific Ocean. "There's a number of islands between here and there, but most of them are nothing but exposed rocks covered in seagull shit. This is the best map I've found so far. I can rip it out of this book and use it to hopscotch our way west or north until we run out of gas. At least we'll get closer to some sort of land and not drift around the Pacific Ocean. I didn't see a radio on that thing, so our options are limited."

"It does sound like you're planning an escape on that thing?" Zeta asked.

"Just thinking aloud," Dooley answered as he heard the roll of distant thunder.

The morning drifted into the afternoon and remained just as wet and overcast. That said, the young couple still enjoyed the quiet day and walks when it wasn't too wet. Tin-tin dutifully followed in their footsteps. Although the pony was almost killed by steel shrapnel yesterday, he had no problem with keeping up with Dooley and Zeta. Dooley also saw that the gashes were healing nicely. By three in the afternoon, Dooley and Zeta stood on the dock where they disembarked from the submarine over two days ago. Tin-tin drank water from a rain barrel at the front of one of the damaged stores. The islanders, after inspecting Tin-tin's rump, continued their work on cleaning up glass and nailing boards to the window frames while the Russians were busy cutting away ragged steel with air-powered tools.

"Looks like the progress is a bit slow," Dooley said as he pushed his damp black hair from his forehead. The dock was now cleared from yesterday's explosion. He thought of Mashka. "And I see one of those sailboats is gone."

Vostok, wearing a pair of dirty coveralls, was wiping his hands with a rag; however, his grey hair and beard remained neatly combed and oiled. He looked at Tin-tin, who seemed to be waiting for Dooley and Zeta. "I heard you did a fine job of treating the pony."

"He'll live," Dooley replied.

"I'm sure he will," Vostok said as he shifted his eyes to the lone two-masted sailboat, which tugged at its anchor line like an impatient puppy railing against its fixed tether. "The captain of the other vessel said he needed to get somewhere and decided to chance it. As far as our ship if we can cut away enough damage to allow us to board up the forecastle and if the weather lessens some, we can get underway, and arrive at a place for proper repairs and to put you two ashore. I am sure you're ready to move on."

"Yes, we are," Dooley answered. "Yes, we are."

* * *

"It's almost 8 p.m.," Utkin said as he reclined in his chair while looking at the bulkhead-mounted chronometer. "What is the latest from your submarine officer? And Igor?"

Vostok, rubbing his hands together after pushing a piece of buttered bread into his mouth, answered. "My submarine is about four hours out from here, running with the seas, which is allowing him to run on the surface and use his diesels."

"Good," Utkin said as he reached for his wine glass. "And Igor?"

Captain Lagos spoke this time as he bit into a piece of white cheese. "He's about five hours out. With our assets back, we will have more technicians and equipment available to facilitate repairs to this ship. I've already identified sections of this ship that can be cut out and refabricated to help rebuild the forecastle. Igor is doing the same. Since he is conducting the internal modifications for his secret compartments and the installation of those submarine doors, finding that metal should be easy. Looks like we are back on schedule."

Reaching out for his glass of wine, Lagos washed the food down before continuing. "The Grim Reaper has reported the staff from the Hog Pen disposed of at sea, and, barring any unforeseen difficulties, the vessel will reach Ensenada in about a month."

"Excellent," Utkin said as he reached out to the plate in front of him. "While we lost a friend, it is still fortunate for us that the American destroyer sent out their Mayday calls."

"Yes," Vostok said as he lifted his glass of wine. "And according to his frantic reports, his ship floundered hundreds of miles to the west of us. Any help that did respond to their SOS indicated their own plights or were too far away to be of immediate assistance. I even found the message sent by HMS Krakatoa to be typically British: 'Have all survivors wear life jackets and group together. Be there by daybreak. God bless.'"

Utkin commented. "Leave it to the British to state the obvious." He paused to raise his glass. The others followed suit.

Chapter 31

"LAST CHANCE, ERNST. Stay aboard. We can reconnoiter the island then make our presence known in the morning," Hillary said as he held onto Fowler's shotgun.

Fowler and Hillary, along with others on the deck, were smothered by drizzle and the dark, starless sky above. But the seas were calm enough for Fowler to paddle the six-foot punt, now hanging over the ship's side by two ropes, the few hundred yards to the unseen shore. Seamen Krivor and Petty Officer Busachek stood by those ropes.

Rodham stood behind Hillary, and behind both Hillary and Rodham, a foreboding rumble escaped the bowels of the ship through three of the ship's four exhaust stacks. Hillary looked at the Number Two stack. While he would've ordered the boiler shut down as the emission of embers would have given away their position to observers, the burners decided for him.

"No, I'm good," Fowler said as he adjusted the straps and belts over his shoulders and around his waist. Under the musette bag, bandoliers, and cartridge belts, he wore his dungarees. The rest of his ensemble consisted of a black seaman's watch cap, navy boots, and Harrison's wristwatch. "Again, it's just after midnight so let me reconnoiter, and I'll see you at the wharf on the western shore at dawn. But, if anything happens, I can be picked up here."

Fowler lifted his hand and pointed at the unseen shore just as a flash of lightening highlighted the silver clouds miles away. The flash also profiled the island's north hill a few hundred yards away and Harrison's wristwatch only inches in front of Hillary. The haunting roll of far-off thunder followed the flash.

"Once Harrison's family get his belongings, they'll be looking for his pistol and that watch, which means I'll be getting a bill at some point. By the way, how did you get the watch?"

"I stole it from your stateroom," Fowler answered, "and whatever his daddy says it worth, I'll only pay ten percent."

With that last note, Fowler lifted his leg over the handrail. A minute later, he sat in the paint punt and reached for his shotgun. "You two mugs," Fowler said as he looked at the two men holding the ropes, "keep an eye on the skipper."

"You got it, Chief," Busachek said as he gave the chief boatswain's mate a nod.

Two minutes later, they watched as his shadow disappeared into the drizzling rain.

"Alright," Hillary said to the faces around him. "Krivor, get back on the bridge and relieve Grover. Have him stay by his Lewis gun. Remember, no lights, not even a cigarette."

Just then, Krivor spoke up quietly. "Looks like we have company. Look north."

Everybody's eyes turned to a point of light off in the distance. After watching the tiny, bouncing pinpoint of light, Hillary spoke up. "That's a masthead light."

"What do we do, Skipper?" Busachek asked. "Just as planned?"

After remembering their run-in with the ship at Bagay Alto, and its three machine guns, Hillary answered, "Krivor, get up to the bridge and turn us north. Keep just enough rpm for steerage. We don't want to create a wake for everybody to see. Also, keep us as close to the shore as possible. It's probably the ship we had our little dance with earlier. Busachek, get back to the deck gun and your crew, and wait. I don't want any shooting until I've reconnoitered the entire island, but if they shoot first, return fire, concentrating on the engineering spaces. Remind the men on the six-pounders to concentrate on anybody shooting at you."

"Anything else, Skipper?" Krivor asked.

"Yeah. When you get to the bridge, tell Mack to send up any black gang he can spare. Have them grab Springfields and shoot at targets of opportunity."

"Yes, sir," the men answered in unison and disappeared.

"What about me?" Rodham asked from the darkness.

Hillary kept his eyes on the bouncing white pinpoint while answering. "I've got a good crew, so you would only get in the way. Just stick with me. And no offense."

"No offense taken," Rodham answered as he carefully followed in Hillary's footsteps. "But do you think it wise getting involved in a situation without radioing your superiors? I know you said your radio broke down again, so why don't you just wait until it can be fixed? I also need to radio my superiors. To let them know my status."

"Well," Hillary said as he found the ladder steps and handrail that led to the bridge. He kept watching the distant pinpoint of light as he climbed those steps. "I don't know when that radio will be fixed, and I don't have any guarantee that whatever's going on with that island will suddenly just dry up and blow away."

During breakfast, Hillary explained to Rodham what they experienced over the last couple of days and why they were not going directly to the Chinese coast. Hillary, however, left out the fact that he and Fowler discovered Harrison's code book and were able to decode the message in his wallet. He also failed to mention that Demby saw Harrison trying to kill Fowler. Lastly, he neglected to say what specific type of aircraft attacked his men on the sailboats. The army officer seemed to accept everything in stride, including when he was told that the radio had broken down and he could not contact his Army supervisors in Manila until it was repaired.

Hillary stopped as he reached the starboard bridge wing. He saw the shadow of a man leaning against the railing of the bridge wing. He was pressing the stock of the Lewis gun against his shoulder. "Got plenty of ammunition, Grover?"

"Yes, sir," the man answered from the darkness.

"Good," Hillary replied. "Wait for them to shoot first. Then, shoot at anything you need to. More than likely their mounted automatics."

"Yes, sir," the unseen face answered.

Acknowledging with a nod, Hillary stepped into the bridge, pulling up to Krivor. Both, with Rodham behind them, looked over the ship's illuminated binnacle, and through the bridge windows. Still far ahead, the masthead light was becoming brighter and bigger.

"Maintain this heading," Hillary said as he reached into a shelf under the binnacle. Pulling out a black canvas hood, he draped it over the brass instrument. "I know you don't have any landmarks to line up on but do your best and let them slide past us. Hopefully, the captain of that ship has intercepted, or was sent, our Mayday calls and thinks we're at the bottom of the East China Sea hundreds of miles west of here."

"Yes, sir," Krivor replied dryly.

The men on the bridge remained quiet as they watched the masthead light. The seconds turned into minutes, and the apparition under it developed into a solid creature. A tramp steamer, with deck lights suddenly switched on, glided past the darkened torpedo boat destroyer.

"What're those things on its deck?" Krivor asked while keeping his hands on the helm.

Everybody could see two strange looking airplanes on the deck. Around the machines, black figures busied themselves by removing straps and climbing onto the machines. On top of the ship's forecastle, forward of the first airplane, a figure climbed into what looked like an operator's seat at the base of a crane. The ship also seemed to be slowing.

"Looks like a flying one-eyed whale and a fire-breathing dragon to me, Seaman Krivor," Hillary said, without turning to look at the expression on Rodham's face.

* * *

Just like the previous two nights, Dooley, dressed in his uniform and armed with his shingle axe and hunting knife, made his way to the cavern under the north hill. But before going inside the machine, he took the time to inspect the outside while sitting in the little punt.

He saw recessed vents along the fuselage, which could be used to release air from the ballast tanks honeycombed within the fuselage. He also found two holes right at the front of the nose of the machine. Each hole was about eight inches in diameter. Thinking of Tin-tin's nostrils, he stuck his hand into one of the holes and felt an angled door. His thoughts then returned to his bunk in the torpedo room of the submarine that brought him to this island. Lastly, he thought about the tubes inside the forward compartment with the trolley man's brake handles.

By midnight, he secured the punt to the side of the machine just behind the starboard wing and climbed up to stand on the wing. One of the first things he finally noticed were what looked like automobile gas tank caps, close to the root of the wing or next to the fuselage. Unscrewing the cap, he stuck his finger in and felt liquid close to the top. He smelled his finger while looking at the engines under the wings. *Well, got enough gas to get somewhere*, he said to himself.

Dropping through the single hatchway above the control compartment, he sat in the left seat of the air sub, inspecting the controls. The compartment itself was almost five feet from side to side and about five feet from the bulkhead right behind his head to windshield. Spacious compared to the cockpits of the trainers he flew, but it was still crammed with items just like those on the submarine. However, despite the darkness and the cluster of items, he was able to identify the rudder pedals, the control stick, and particular gauges and switches mounted to the console. After a couple of minutes, he told himself he could fly this thing. Now, being somewhat satisfied, he started to look around and took a second to look at the tube-shaped item clamped to the bulkhead just under the side windshield. Feeling with his hands, he could see that the thing had a rounded front end like a blunt artillery round but had a caged propeller at the other end. The whole thing was about four feet long. While he felt the item, he thought about the tubes going through the forward compartment and the open apertures at the bow of this thing. Along with two Lewis guns, this thing could fire at least two miniature torpedoes. In front of the torpedo, mounted against the gauge console was a hinged metal cap for the torpedo tube running from the console to the machine's bow. While noticing the details of the loading end of the torpedo tube, he saw what looked like the percussion cap firing mechanism for a musket, with a short lanyard hanging from it on the side of the tube.

Continuing his inspection, he sat in the right seat and remembered watching the helmsman and the diving plans operator on the submarine. Reaching down, he lifted the periscope from the floor to eye level. That was when he saw it had one handle on the aisle side, and a flip-down eye piece that he could look through it with his left eye while sitting. Lowering it, he finished his inspection and realized the craft did, indeed, not have a radio. Wondering for a second, he noted that each craft was unique, so perhaps it was just a matter of weight or space while trying to find the right attributes or characteristics for each type of aircraft. Anyway, knowing what he did not have was just as important as knowing what he did have.

Satisfied for now, he slipped out of his seat and crawled into the forward compartment. Like the cockpit, it appeared to be comparatively spacious except for all the tubes and things built into the nose. Feeling around, he found a chair folded against the bulkhead in front of the submarine operator seat. With his hand on the folding seat, he peered at the Lewis machine gun and pan magazines mounted to the side bulkheads under the tubes running fore and aft. Reaching up, he felt the latches that secured another hatch flush with the skin of the nose.

Again satisfied, he crawled out backwards and went to inspect the compartment behind the cockpit. He found that he could stand in this compartment, but just barely. Hunched over, he looked at the bunks on either side and two tall lockers. One contained a commode, a wash basin, and medicine cabinet: all aluminum. The other locker looked like a pantry stocked with canned goods, life jackets, and pan magazines for a Lewis gun. Closing the door, he looked up at the closed hatch, the hinged ladder folded against the metal ceiling, and the Lewis gun clipped into place. Stooping down, he looked through the open hatchway leading aft. Being so far back in the recesses of the machine, he could not see what it contained, but he smelled fuel and grease. It must be the engine for the propeller. Standing up, he wondered if the batteries needed to power the sub-airplane while submerged were beneath the aluminum deck plates at his feet.

Five minutes later, he closed the wooden door to the submarine cavern and felt the drizzling rain on his face. Satisfied with what he was able to comprehend so far, he stepped out of the doorway. Somewhere off to his left he heard a noise, but it was not the sound of the drizzling rain nor a boat engine. He pulled himself up against a tree trunk and pulled his shingle axe from the rope loop around his waist and his hunting knife from its sheath. The drizzling rain dropped from the branches above him, yet the noise of the precipitation failed to cover the slow steady footsteps coming in from his left. He turned his ears and eyes toward the footsteps. It was then that he saw glints of lights through the trees and behind the slow, but steady, footfalls. Watching the lights, he started to hear what he thought were the sounds of metal striking metal.

Hardening his grips on his weapons he saw the shadow of a man carrying a long gun. He did not look like any of the Russians he spent the last week with, so not really knowing what else to do and thinking about the ship off the coast of this island, he decided to take a chance.

"Looking for a beer, friend?" Dooley said quietly.

The man stopped in his tracks and threw the barrel of his weapon at Dooley's voice. The barrel almost took Dooley's nose off. "Who the fuck are you?" he belted out.

"Who the fuck are you?" Dooley returned.

"I'm the one holding the shotgun, friend."

"Good, you're an American," Dooley said with his voice still low and steady.

With the muzzle of the barrel still inches from his nose, the man spoke again, but quieter this time. "Yeah, but again. Who the hell are you? And what are you doing on this island?"

"First, you can take the barrel of that shotgun out of my face," Dooley stated. "Second, I'm Thomas Dooley, late of Brooklyn, and the US Army's 339th Infantry Division. You?"

While Dooley looked at the caution in the man's eyes, the man answered. "Ernst Fowler, chief boatswain's mate, currently of the USS Decatur."

The men paused to look at each other for a few seconds while the misty rain drizzled down their faces. Seeing honesty in the man's face, Dooley reinserted his shingle axe and hunting knife into the rope loop and sheath.

Fowler looked at the weapons. "No firearms?"

"I got weapons," Dooley answered as he stepped from the tree trunk, "and they're right next to a dry towel and a bottle of wine."

Just then, both heard the activity increasing through the trees, along with a boat engine.

"Something to do with you?" Dooley asked.

"No," Fowler replied as he lowered the barrel of his weapon, "Let's see what's doing."

The men turned toward the activity and walked through the forest. As they did, the lights and the noise became brighter and louder. In a few minutes, they found themselves standing at the edge of a narrow strip of beach. In front of them was the ship that Dooley saw on the marine railway earlier. It was also the same one that Fowler saw when they were looking for Mister Kermit and his men. It had a white light at its masthead and the yellowish deck working lights below. Black figures were busy on the deck of the ship helping guide a winged machine dangling from the cable of a crane into the water. The cable split into three cables just above the airplane's fuselage and were attached to the sides of the machine at the wing roots, and at the bow. In this case though, it was the dragon-shaped air machine Dooley saw earlier, but now with wings and attached engines and propellers.

"Behold the flying fire-breathing dragon," Fowler said aloud.

"What'd you say?" Dooley asked as the machine was being lowered into the water.

"I'll explain later," Fowler said as they both saw a motorized lifeboat and coxswain waiting off to the side. The engine exhaust from the boat bubbled as the boat bobbed in the water.

"It's their transportation," Dooley answered, "for those crewmen once those things are put up for the night. It'll follow that ship to a marine railway south of here."

"They left those things unguarded?" Fowler asked.

Watching Fowler think, Dooley answered, "They did before. Why?"

"Oh, nothing," Fowler answered.

Watching the machine being placed onto the water, they saw a man climb out of one of the top hatches and slide over the side to start unshackling the cables. At the same time, they heard an engine start and the water at the stern of the air sub started boil. The machine turned its nose toward the island's northern hill: toward them. Meanwhile, men on the ship's deck gathered behind the second machine and rolled it forward.

"Hence, the flying one-eyed whale," Fowler said, and before Dooley could ask anything, he continued, "You said something about wine?"

CHAPTER 32

"I HOPE YOU don't mind meeting behind the outhouse?" Dooley asked in a low voice as he poured a glass of wine for Fowler.

"As long as it isn't a target," Fowler replied in an equally low voice.

"What do you mean by that?"

"Nothing," Fowler said as he pulled his watch cap from his head and wiped his eyes of rain drizzle. After a sip of wine, he looked at Tin-tin busy lapping wine from a bucket. "Your pony?"

"The island's pony," Dooley answered, "but it looks like it's getting hooked on my wine."

"I've learned to never feed strays," Fowler replied as he placed his watch cap on top of the shotgun in his lap.

"Model 1897 Remington pump-action shotgun," Dooley mentioned. "Thirty-inch barrel, five-round external tube magazine firing shells packed with thirty-three-caliber shot. Or slugs."

"You know your shotguns," Fowler responded quietly. "Did you use one in Russia?"

"No," Dooley responded. "I learned about them from sergeants at Camp Custer who returned from the Western Front, or from old-timers who used them in the Philippines."

"Watch the old-timer crack," Fowler said as he inspected his glass.

The two men sat in chairs next to the outhouse under a slacking rain. While their voices were low and cautious, their eyes and ears were sharp.

Fowler kept his eyes on the trees to the north. Dooley kept his eyes on the rear of the Brooks House, watching in case Zeta lit a candle in his room. Meanwhile, Tin-tin finished his wine and stood there swishing his tail.

"So, this island is the base for a Red spy ring and infiltration network of the States? Huh? Never would've guessed it."

"I wouldn't have either," Dooley answered as he sipped his wine as well. "Just over a week ago, I was sitting in a bar in Shanghai drinking shitty beer wondering how I was going to get back to Brooklyn and not show up at my mother's doorstep looking like a bum."

"So, you fought as a mercenary? Outside Shanghai? And in Russia? As a soldier?" Fowler reaffirmed as he took his eyes off the forest to look at the black sky. "What's in Brooklyn?"

"A wagon repair shop, two old horses, my brother and my father arguing all the time, and my mother pestering me about eating my greens and getting married," Dooley replied, "which is why I was taking my time getting back there. But now it's not looking so bad."

"Well, boy, we gotta get there first."

Dooley sipped his wine before answering, "Well, Chief Petty Officer Fowler, my name is either Sergeant, Thomas, or Dooley, or any combination thereof, not boy. And I, and the countess, were about to leave this island, to warn somebody, but the arrival of your ship just might muck that up. Does your skipper know what he's doing?"

"He won't, and he does, Sergeant," Fowler replied as he drew back in his chair. "So, what do you, and your shingle axe, propose to do? And speaking of the countess, I only saw her for a second, but I bet she's got some nice gams under those slacks of hers."

"We weren't speaking of the countess," Dooley said as he looked at Fowler sideways. "And, as you said before, your captain will make his presence known in three hours. That's after he's had a chance to measure his competition. The problem is, he can only see what's visible to him. Also, we can't tell him of the threats not visible to him, like that submarine, and the little flying machines. Do you think he saw that tramp steamer dropping off the airplanes?"

"He did," Fowler answered. "You said the ship will go to the marine railway again?"

Dooley answered. "When the ship first arrived, they dropped off those two airplanes but without wings and engines and got that ship on the railway. I think the only reason why they got themselves off was because of your ship. Now that your destroyer has floundered hundreds of miles from here, they're going to finish whatever they started."

Fowler paused for a second. "So, the back-alley owl bends over to earn her coin."

Dooley thought for a second before answering. "I see your point."

"Anyway, it's the same ship, with its three Maxims, that attacked us at Bagay Alto, and it's those two same airplanes that attacked our men on two sailing ships. The bottom line is that Lieutenant Hillary will have figured out a plan to deal with any threat he's seen in the last hour, and he knows that I've seen the same threats. By now he's on his way around the island to see what will be next, including the remaining sailing vessel and that ship moored at the western dock. He also knows what I'm capable of—"

"What we're capable of," interrupted Dooley as Tin-tin came over to him. He reached up to rub the pony's forehead.

Fowler nodded while continuing. "And that means a British sailing vessel probably still armed with a BAR and a six-pounder, and with plenty of ammunition. Anybody on that yacht?"

"I couldn't say, but I'm assuming not as it looks like everybody's got something to do. Also, the ship that's tied up at the dock had its forecastle mostly blown off, including whatever gun was bolted to it. It's possible to assume they still have other surprises, though," Dooley said. "But I wouldn't make any sabotage too obvious. Don't need any fingers pointed at myself or the countess while we're still under the eyes of the Russians."

"Agreed," Fowler said as he reached to scratch his leg. "I can still swim out there and monkey with something. Is there any sugar in that house?"

"Yes," Dooley answered as he swallowed the last of his wine and reached down for the bottle, "but the cook will notice missing sugar. There are aluminum filings in one of those buildings though. I can start with the trainer and do something with the little sub-airplanes. I saw one leave last night, but it looks like there are still two inside those hangars under canvas tarps. From what I've been able to notice with those June bug airplanes is that they're each armed with a thirty-seven-millimeter anti-tank gun. I saw the Frogs use them in Russia. They can fire high-explosive and armor-piercing rounds along with a type of shotgun shell. I can do something with their all-metal bomber as well. But what about that ship at the dock?"

"I wouldn't worry about it," Fowler asked as he held out his wine glass. "By the time they get to the scene of combat, Rance would've taken care of any threats on the eastern side of the island, and he'll be ready to take that ship on."

"Sounds like you hold your skipper in high regard," Dooley said as he placed the bottle back on the grass. "I just hope that little air sub I've been inspecting inside the cavern doesn't get caught up in the fray. You know, just in case we need a getaway car."

"Yeah," Fowler answered. "I don't know how it's going to avoid any fight as I know my skipper saw those things getting put up for the night."

"I agree," Dooley countered, "but they left it behind for a reason, so I guess we'll just have to wait and see. It just might be the ace we need."

"Understood, but that still leaves, from what you said earlier, a submarine presumably with a load of torpedoes and its crew, at least six parachute solders from that flying outfit along with their pilots and aircrewmen, a dozen submarine raiders, and a few odds and ends."

"You're right," Dooley said. "I've had the opportunity to work with a few of those odd and ends, including a man called Morda. Be careful if you run into a blond-haired gladiator type carrying an entrenching tool."

"Some pretty tough heavies?" Fowler asked.

"The heaviest," Dooley answered as he inspected Fowler's weapons again. "But I've been good at taking care of myself. I just hope you can use all that iron. Or do you just like walking around looking like Pancho Villa shooting up cantinas in Juarez?"

"I've been known to crack a few skulls," Fowler finished as he looked down at Harrison's Rolex. It's almost three in the morning, which means we've got to move."

Both wiped their faces with their watch caps and finished their wine. As they stood, Dooley looked at Fowler's watch. "I didn't know the navy paid their chiefs that well."

Fowler hefted the shotgun in his hand. "Let's get going."

A few minutes later, after Zeta was told where the two men were going, Dooley and Fowler were inside Mashka's shed where Dooley repaired Tintin's wounds. The pony stood guard outside as Fowler felt the backboard of the workbench selecting tools.

"I have a pair of pliers," Fowler said as he slipped them in his musette bag. "And I see a file, wire cutters, and an adjustable wrench. Find what you need?"

Dooley stepped out from a corner. "I have an open five-gallon can of powdered aluminum. There's a jar of nuts, bolts, and washers on the workbench and a lid next to it. Go ahead and dump it out and, by the way, keep your eyes off Zeta's gams."

*　*　*

"I don't see the Grim Reaper, Skipper," Busachek said as he stood next to Hillary. Both stood in the darkness on the bridge wing. They saw only the British yacht. While riding at anchor yards away from the tramp steamer tied up to the dock, the working lights from the ship highlighted the two masts of the sailing vessel and its deck profile.

Hillary answered his petty officer as he saw his six-pounder. "Which means that, if our BAR is still aboard that thing, the Chief will have a reason to earn his pay."

"No worries there," Busachek replied, "but what about that tramp steamer at the wharf? It looks like it had an explosion or something."

Both men's eyes fell upon the shadow of the ship, and the flashes of light, arcing of sparks, and the movement of black figures. They also saw a trail of exhaust wisp away from one of the two smokestacks aft of the bridge.

"Looks like they're ready to get underway at a moment's notice. And I don't think that damaged forecastle will prevent them from doing so," Hillary replied, "or prevent them from shooting at us with whatever they may have hidden in that shack over the bridge. However, by the time they arrive on scene, we'll just be getting warmed up."

* * *

As Hillary ordered Krivor to reverse the ship's engines and back it into the darkness and drizzling rain, Dooley, walking along the tree line behind the outhouse, looked up at the sky. It was black as any sky can be before dawn, but he saw the twinkling from the occasional star through the thinning blanket of clouds. He stopped and looked past the outline of the privy and at the back of the Brooks House. There were no lit lanterns. With a sigh, he wiped his hands one last time with a rag and turned to the house.

As a scared Zeta, and tired pony, greeted Dooley on the back porch, Fowler waded out of the water. Stooped over, he stepped across the narrow beach. Reaching the trees, he lifted the shoulder strap of his musette bag over his head and sat next to his weapons and other items. After pushing his hair back with his fingers, he pulled the canteen from its canvas web cover. Half a canteen later, Fowler caught his breath. Replacing the canteen back into its canvas cover, he gathered his equipment while looking at the yacht and hoped he had done enough.

After swimming out to the vessel with nothing but his dungarees and musette bag containing the Mason jar and hand tools, he found a rope ladder slung over the side away from the tramp steamer near the stern. This allowed Fowler to board the vessel unseen. After rolling onto the deck, he listened and watched for signs that somebody was aboard. While waiting, he saw the result of their gunfight from Bagay Alto, and the fact that the Russians were in the process of repairing that damage. Pausing briefly while looking at the richly colored mahogany, he pictured Kermit reclining against an undamaged upholstered seat with one hand on the brass helm wheel. In the other hand, he saw Kermit holding a bottle of fancy beer while the summer sun shined on his face as he piloted his own yacht across Chesapeake Bay.

Reminding himself of his mission, Fowler cautiously stepped forward to see if the six-pounder was still mounted to the deck in front of the foremast. Stepping around the foremast, he saw the weapon, and in front of the barrel, he saw a hatch, presumably leading into the main cabin, and a hatch forward of that one leading into the forward bosun locker. The same space where the cabin boy hid out when the Lassiter Brothers seized this vessel. Stepping up to the hatch leading into the main cabin, he opened it and stepped down the companionway ladder. Walking aft through the vessel's luxuriously paneled interior, he still did not hear or see anyone's presence. Once he entered the galley, he took notice of the chart table and radio setup before setting his eyes on the BAR, with its cartridge belt and four double-magazine pouches, propped against the steps leading to the cockpit above. He went through the ammunition pouches and removed five rounds from each of the eight box magazines. Pocketing those rounds he found the extra ammunition for both the six-pounder and BAR and secreted the wooden cases into the vessel's bilge. Seeing no other weapons onboard he retraced his steps and stepped back onto the deck. After placing those pocketed BAR rounds inside a life jacket locker, he stepped over to the six-pounder. Pulling back on the breech-loading mechanism, he locked it open and used the file to shave down the firing pin. After about two minutes, he inserted a rag wrapped around his index finger to clear away the shavings. Letting the breech-loading mechanism slide forward, he wiped away any visible filings off the deck under the gun. After placing at least two obstacles in front of the Russians, he started on two more.

Stooping over the raised engine room access behind the cockpit, he entered the engine room and he saw a six-cylinder marine diesel. Unscrewing an oil cap, Fowler pulled the Mason jar from the musette bag and emptied the contents into the engine's valve cover. After replacing the cap, he stepped around the engine to the vessel's steering gear and found a linkage joint, then used his pliers to unbend a cotter pin and pull it out halfway. Hoping all the halfway steps were enough to impede any Russian effort, Fowler slipped back into the water.

Now, back on land, he refilled his musette bag, and gathered the rest of his gear and weapons. As he did, he looked at the ship tied to the dock. Knowing he could not do anything about the ship, he hoped Dooley did his part as well.

*　*　*

The aroma of freshly brewed coffee and baking bread added to the comforting tranquility of the mahogany-trimmed wardroom and its soft lighting. Both Utkin and Borodin, with washed faces, combed hair, and ironed clothing, each reached for a cucumber slice the cook laid out the rest of their breakfast. As the cook filled their coffee cups, the door behind Utkin opened.

Captains Lagos and Vostok entered the wardroom.

"You two are up early," Captain Lagos said. "Couldn't sleep?"

Utkin reached for his cup as he answered. "Good morning, Issak. I slept alright; despite being serenaded by the clamor of pneumatic tools. I can't imagine what it's like on the other ship."

"Same here," Borodin said as he reached for his coffee. "How are repairs going?"

Captain Vostok, who appeared freshly washed and wearing a pressed uniform, sat at the table and reached for a cup of coffee and a slice of brown bread. The three of them enjoyed their coffee while waiting for Captain Lagos, who stopped in front of the wash basin on the counter to wash his hands.

After a minute, Captain Lagos picked up the towel next to the basin and wiped his hands as he stepped to the table. Sitting down while dabbing a cut on his hand, he answered. "The repairs are going nicely as we've been able to harvest enough sheet steel from within the ship. I must say though, when complete, it will not be all that pretty, what with the tools and materials available to me right now. I also received word from Igor, and he said, after commencing his modifications, has come up with several sheets of steel that I can use. He has men loading them onto a wagon and it will be brought here with the wagon pulled by the island's pony."

"Is the pony going to be able to pull a wagon with sheets of steel?" Borodin asked.

Captain Lagos simply replied, "It appears that Sergeant Dooley has a way with animals. Anyway, with that material, I think we can be underway as early as this evening."

"Good," Utkin answered as he used a knife to spread strawberry preserves on a slice of brown bread.

"As far as getting my submarine underway," Vostok spoke, "I'll coordinate with Igor to make sure we are ready for our next phase."

Lagos smiled and nodded as he placed the stained towel on the table and reached for a slice of cucumber. "Well, the home office of the Mersk-Alba Shipping Line has announced in several shipping outlets the story about the nitrate explosion, so that will excuse our appearance once we are sighted. What are your immediate plans for this morning?"

Utkin answered while looking out the porthole. Although the sky was still dark, he saw the sun was ready to clamber over the horizon at any minute and the rain was, indeed, slackening. "Looks like the weather is going to start cooperating, which should make it that much easier for us to destroy any evidence of our presence."

The table fell silent as they continued to enjoy their coffee and, as Captain Lagos reached for a slice of bread, they heard the soft crack of distant thunder. The four men looked up.

"Thunder?" Utkin asked as he reached for another slice of cucumber.

"Didn't sound like any thunder I've heard," Captain Vostok answered just as another boom sounded. "That's not thunder! That's gunfire!"

* * *

Captain Igor Bogdanovich yawned and stretched, then stepped out onto the bridge wing and watched two men push a motorized boat off the beach. Below the captain's feet, inside the ship, his men spent the night working on their modifications while cutting out sheets of steel for the other ship at the same time. That made sleep a bit difficult for the few not involved in the work, including the airplane crews and pilots who decided to return to the ship and take advantage of its creature comforts. Stretching his arms out to his side, Bogdanovich stepped back into the bridge and looked at the ship's diagram sprawled across the chart table. Just then a man stepped in through the wooden door at the rear of the bridge. He held a mug of coffee in his hands.

Captain Bogdanovich accepted the mug and as he was about to sip from it, a loud crack boomed out behind the ship. "What the hell was that?"

His question was followed by a muffled explosion that he felt though his shoed feet. Throwing the coffee mug aside, he jumped out to the bridge wing. He turned aft and looked at an apparition steal from the distant early morning mist. The sight was followed up with a second booming crack and a ball of flame. He felt a second explosion though his feet.

CHAPTER 33

AFTER FOWLER GATHERED his belongings and weapons, he turned in the direction he came from. He already had an idea of the island's layout because of his research, but Dooley's information made it that much easier. The rain dissipated again, and the light from the sun, which still hung behind the eastern horizon and bank of clouds, eased the darkness. Minutes later, and partially out of breath, he came out onto the meadow where a Catholic church once stood and was still the site of the Spanish graveyard. Running through the very reason that started this adventure in the first place, he exited the meadow on the other side, and within minutes, returned to the spot where he met Dooley three short hours ago. By five-thirty, Fowler found the net-covered entrance into the cavern. After taking a breath, he spied a tree-fall depression halfway up the hill and above the entrance. He scrambled up the slope and settled down behind the fallen tree trunk.

After finishing the other half of the canteen, Fowler stared back at the beach, situating his weapons and removing what he felt necessary. While doing so, he looked past the tree trunks and at the approaches to the doorway. At the same time, he reached into his musette bag feeling for a sardine can. Finding it, he peeled the lid back and ate with his fingers. While hearing waking birds, he listened for gunfire, and as he did, he heard a noise. Looking down, he saw a man step into view and walk to a tree trunk. He fished in his crotch.

"Damn it!" Fowler said quietly to himself.

* * *

Dooley sat in the chair on the back porch having a cup of hot tea with Zeta. Though the morning promised to be busy they agreed on a hot cup of tea before it all started. While fully clothed in his uniform and weapons, Zeta wore a light blue, short-sleeve blouse, grey slacks, and athletic shoes. Draped over the back of her chair was the oversized Russian army blouse with a wool watch cap sticking out of one of the pockets. Dooley's duffel, now filled with what undergarments Zeta possessed and several cans of food and bottles of wine wrapped in towels, rested on the floor planks between their feet.

"So. There's no going back?" Zeta asked.

"The arrival of the destroyer threw everything I was planning out the window. It's going to be a battle royale around here in less than an hour, and I have a feeling Utkin will cut his losses, and our throats, given the chance. I just hope our 'malfunctions' are enough to help that captain."

Zeta asked slowly, "Were we ever valuable to Utkin?"

Dooley answered with a voice filled with sympathy. "Major Utkin is an expert stage manager capable of placing his actors under the most brilliant of lights. He, and his cohorts, are also experimenters or prospectors. Look at the machines they've created. Look at their plans. Both audacious in nature and futuristic in construction, yet simple in initiation and practice. Their machines and plans are nothing more than a well-dealt hand of cards. If something doesn't work, then they just discard, ask the dealer for a new card, and move on. Albeit with Utkin having a strong grip on the dealer's shoulder. We can be such discards, but valuable at the same time if only to confuse the man on the other side of the green felt. You were important to help retrieve their diamonds and could've played a vital role in the future. I was picked up as a piece of gold to be fashioned into jewelry and worn for its wearer's purpose. Instead, I turned out to be iron pyrite: fool's gold. I think we were valuable in the sense that Utkin has learned a lesson."

Zeta thought for a second. "Well, I don't mind being a piece of fool's gold myself."

* * *

"Rather gracious of him," Hillary said as he stood next to his helmsman and adjusted the chin strap of his helmet. Both men felt the rumble of their steam turbines under their feet as they pushed the ship out of the early morning mist and in view of their first target, which was about four hundred yards ahead. "Like a back-alley owl, clutching a twenty-five-cent piece in her hand while bent over a porch railing earning her silver."

"You do have a way with words, sir," Seaman Krivor smiled as he adjusted the helm wheel.

"I agree," Rodham said, standing next to Hillary, as he too adjusted his chin strap of his helmet. "Also, I'm no lawyer or judge advocate, but you may want to save some of that verbiage for your Board of Inquiry. Do you think it wise to fire the opening shots?"

Hillary returned the comment with a smile. "All I know is that the ship in front of us is the same ship that attacked us at Bagay Alto, and those two airplanes under that hill were the same ones that attacked my executive officer and men on the two sailing vessels. So, yes."

He stopped long enough to approach the sill of the bridge window in front of him. He looked down at Petty Officer Busachek and the gun crew. One member of the gun crew was stowing his bedroll behind an open case of ammunition. The other men were at their stations around the gun. They all wore their steel helmets. Speaking out the open angled bridge window, Hillary voiced his next order. "I'd say our guest was rather accommodating, Petty Officer Busachek. How about returning that courtesy with well-placed shots at the waterline and into her engineering spaces?"

Busachek looked up at the bridge. "Right up her ass. Aye, aye, sir."

With a nod, he watched as the crew trained and elevated the barrel of the weapon with the hand cranks. The sun was just making its appearance behind them, which helped reveal the details in front of the gun barrel. He saw the first third of the hull angled on the railway while the last two thirds were angled in the calm morning sea. Remembering the amazing speed the ship demonstrated at Bagay Alto, Hillary imaged the fantastic propulsion system inside the ship.

As he thought about the ship's disguised potential, he heard the crack of the Decatur's deck gun, saw the flash of the muzzle blast in front of him, and felt the blast pressure against his face. At the same time the round punched through the red-painted hull at the waterline. He imaged the explosion inside the engineering spaces, but before he had the opportunity to offer a congratulations, the gun crew was able to reload and retrain the barrel of the weapon. The weapon fired again, and the round struck the hull in the same area as the first shot.

"Very good, Busachek," Hillary congratulated. "Now we can take out flying machines." Hillary remained at the window but barked an order to the helmsman. "Turn us north, Krivor."

Krivor obeyed his orders and turned the wheel, which swung the bow of the ship away from the marine railway and into the northerly morning haze. As he did, the crews manning the six-pounders on the port side and stern joined in to exercise their own guns. Each was able to land a shot into the ship's bridge. By now, everybody could see smoke billowing out of open portholes along the ship's stern. At the same time, everybody on the forward guns and the bridge saw a motorboat heading north as well.

"It looks like the same boat we saw picking up men from the cavern under that hill only a few hours ago. Why is that boat going north?" Krivor asked. "I thought it brought back the crews earlier this morning. Or is it just trying to get away from us?"

After quickly thinking, Hillary turned around and grabbed the brass levers of the ship's EOT. He pushed them all the way back, then forward, leaving them on the "flank" speed slot.

Rodham looked at Hillary questioningly, and Hillary saw the look. "We saw that boat bring back crews from those flying machines, but perhaps not everybody."

As the thick creamy froth began roiling away from both sides of the sharp bow, Hillary and Rodham stepped out onto the port bridge wing. Looking down they saw several engineers with rifles, and the men on the only port-side six-pounder. The gunner holding the lanyard for that mounted weapon looked back at Hillary who gave him a nod.

Nodding back the gunner knelt next to the man aiming the mounted gun. And, as Hillary and Rodham returned their eyes to the motorboat, they saw the coxswain jump over the side of the boat just as they heard the sharp crack of that gun. A second later the stern of that boat exploded into splinters. As the destroyer sped past the now empty boat, the men with the bolt-action Springfields also decided to chime in for target practice. They all saw the Russian sailor swimming toward shore with the greatest of speed.

Hillary stepped back into the bridge and grabbed the handset for the ship's loudspeaker system from its cradle against the forward bulkhead under the window. He saw the island to his left speed past the bridge. He also saw the foliage become a more vibrant green. The sun was rising, and the skies were clearing. They had less than a mile to go. "Men! As you see, we've disabled the main target, and we're on our way to take out two others. The same targets that took out Mister Kermit and your shipmates, and it appears that those targets are armed and crewed. So, no matter if you're holding a Springfield, the lanyard for a six-pounder, or an oil can in the engine room, be ready for anything! That is all!"

Hillary rehung the handset and watched as the north hill came into greater detail.

"Do you think there's enough men under that hill to fly those things out?" Krivor asked.

Hillary kept his eyes on the hill while answering, "Yes, there is."

After answering, Hillary stepped behind the EOT. Ringing the brass levers of the engine order telegraph, forward, then back, he left the levers on "all slow." The ship's captain and the others standing on the bridge lurched forward slightly as the ship's engineers reacted.

Hillary turned to the army officer. "Please help Grover with loading magazines."

Rodham nodded, and as he stepped toward the door to the bridge wing,

Krivor spoke up. "Fire in the paint locker!"

Everybody who could watched as the sloping end of the north hill started to lift itself open, just like the tornado doors at the base of a house being slowly pushed open by somebody inside.

* * *

The sun finally climbed over the horizon and the bank of dissipating clouds, making the rushed walk through the forest that much easier for Dooley and Zeta. Dooley wore his army uniform and had all his weapons and canvas web gear strapped to his torso. He held the Thompson with the barrel pointing out in front of him. Zeta wore her civilian clothing with the oversized Russian army blouse enveloping her upper body and Dooley's duffel bouncing against her hip. While Dooley kept his eyes peeled for any threat, so many things were going through his mind, including the fact that, among the various Russian assets on this island, there was the barracks for the air assault commando about a mile from this spot. He remembered watching them drop from airplanes the other morning and what Utkin said about their climbing drills. He also remembered their obstacle course. Recalling what he said to Fowler earlier about being dressed like a bandito, he spoke to himself. "I sure hope Fowler knows how to use all that iron."

"What was that?" Zeta asked.

"Nothing," Dooley replied as the slope of the hill came into view through the trees. He could see the rectangular entrance built into the slope of that rise through the camouflage netting. As he came within yards of the entrance, he wondered why Fowler did not challenge them or call out.

"Fowler?"

"Up here," the sailor answered with a voice low but strong. "And keep your voice down. There're men inside this hill."

Both Dooley and Zeta looked up at the voice and finally saw Fowler's head and shoulders surrounded by the slope's foliage. A minute later, Dooley and Zeta were nestled with Fowler in the little depression with the barrels of their weapons laying across the tree trunk.

"What do you mean you saw somebody taking a piss?" Dooley asked. "I thought they all left for the ship at the railway."

"We assumed they would all go back," Fowler said.

"Damn it!" Dooley said.

Suddenly, the booming report of a ship's gun destroyed the early morning quiet and silenced the chirping birds. It was followed by the muted cracks of the ship's six-pounders.

"Too late to worry about it now," Fowler answered as he reached out to pick up his shotgun. "If there's enough men inside the cavern to crew up at least one of those airplanes, then Rance is in for a fight. We've never trained to fight airplanes."

Fowler was interrupted by the booming crack of another shell being fired from the deck gun and, again, followed by the six-pounders.

"Now that he's put some rounds into that ship, he'll beat feet to get up here and plug a bunch of shells through the fake side of the hill and into the cavern. But he'd better do so before whoever is under us wises up. Did you see a telephone or radio in there?"

"I think at least one of those machines has a radio," Dooley replied as he grabbed his Thompson, "but I think I can even out the odds."

"How so?" Fowler asked as they started to hear voices from inside the cavern. After a minute, those voices were drowned out by the sputtering start of an airplane engine.

They looked up the slope of the hill.

"They bored a hole through the roof of the cavern for ventilation," Dooley replied, "and it sounds like they're about to fly the coop. Fowler, you stay here, and watch for anybody coming this way. I'll get to the top of this hill and see what I can do."

"Remember to lead your target," Fowler said as he turned to face their front.

Dooley stood and saw Zeta looking at him with imploring eyes. "It's fine, Zeta. I'll be right back. And I'm sure the chief would not mind being a gentleman and offer up that shiny Colt."

Fowler, without taking his eyes off the forest floor in front of them, reached down and unsnapped the flap to the holster on his right hip. Pulling the pistol out, he handed it over to Zeta while speaking to Dooley. "Show her how to work it, and make sure I get it back. It cost me three months' pay," Fowler said as he reached back to the cartridge belt for another magazine.

Dooley set his Thompson down and reminded Zeta how to work the slide to chamber a round, to take the safety off, and to change out magazines. With a firm grip on her shoulder, Dooley grabbed his weapon and turned to scramble up the slope. As he climbed the hill, he wondered why the initials carved into the ivory pistol grips didn't seem to match Fowler's name, but his thoughts were disrupted by another crack of a six-pounder. Reaching the crest of the hill and standing among the thinning trees, he saw the opening that vented the cavern. Stepping up to the edge of the hole, which was about two yards in diameter, he saw the dragon-shaped airplane and a man climbing around it. The machine and man were illuminated by the rising sun.

They must've opened the doors, he told himself as he looked down at the airplane under him. His finger pressed lightly against the Thompson's trigger. It would be so easy to empty a magazine straight into the cockpit. He also thought about the remaining hand grenade in his musette bag. But he realized that disabling the machine there would block the use of that third aircraft.

He also heard a second airplane engine being fired up and stuttering to a start. Turning toward the east, he ran to the edge of the forest and looked down. The large, double doors were, indeed, winched open. Dooley turned to look south and saw the white frothy seas slide past the American destroyer's bow. Behind the ship, he saw what looked like a motorboat bobbing in the still, morning sea with thin, wispy black smoke drifting from it.

Behind the motorboat, at the marine railway, he also saw at least one other column of wispy smoke as well. Shouldering the Thompson in his hands, he thought back Fowler's statement about leading his target. Knowing that the short-barreled Thompson was designed for clearing dugouts and trenches he listened at the building crescendo of the airplane's engines. He knew the pilots conducted engine run-ups to make sure all the cylinders were firing properly before taking their feet off the brake pedals, but these were seaplanes, and brakes shouldn't work in this case.

Perhaps it was the confines of the caverns which magnified the intensity of the engine's rpm. Either way, he was glad, as the situation was getting him to think about his own flying ability. Going through flight procedures in his brain, he thought he could almost feel the rpm worm through the ground and the soles of his shoes. It must be hell inside that cave, he said to himself.

Keeping an eye on the water in front of the cavern's entrance, he saw movement as the floating machine inside was starting its take off and pushed the clear, blue water in front of it. Immediately, the front of the airplane became visible under his feet, and Dooley saw a man in the open hatchway with a mounted Lewis gun. That was when he pulled his trigger finger. The Thompson bucked against his shoulder as the polished nose of the airplane, and the gunner, replaced the blue of seawater in his open sights. Not letting go, he emptied the entire twenty-five rounds into the length of the machine as it filed past his iron sights.

Dropping the weapon from his shoulder, he saw the silver-skinned machine climb into the morning sky, wavering a bit. He also thought he saw a thread of smoke trailing behind it.

Exchanging stick magazines, he heard one of the engines for the dragon-shaped machine still in the cavern fire up. He waited for the other flying machine to bolt from that cavern while looking at the destroyer. Dark-blue-clad figures moved about the deck of the ship and its gun positions. Dooley turned his eyes to see the machine he fired at disappear into the clouds to the east and leaving behind a hint of smoke as it did. Almost feeling the rpm through his feet, he knew when it was time to tighten the pressure on his trigger finger. He saw the sharp nose of the machine and as he pulled on the trigger, the weapon bucked against his shoulder while the bow of the machine filled his iron sites. At the same time, though, the ground in front of him exploded. Jumping aside he saw a rear gunner sitting behind a double-barreled machine gun. The man stopped firing the weapon to wave at Dooley.

The sergeant shouldered his weapon again but dropped it back to his side as he saw that the flying machine was out of range. While doing so, he wondered how the crew of the second machine knew about Dooley standing here. With a nod, he accepted that those two airplanes were equipped with radios, which means Utkin and Vostok already knew what just happened.

Dooley listened to the silence behind him while thinking about the unique fight that would soon develop between airplanes and the destroyer. He also thought about the remaining craft under his feet and the soldiers that would be soon coming their way. Was there something wrong with the third machine? Why did the Russians leave that machine behind on more than one occasion? The only thing he could do now was find out why.

CHAPTER 34

UTKIN, BORODIN, VOSTOK, and Lagos stood on the bridge wing of the steamer that brought two of those men to this island. The men stared at the early morning sun and at a thread of rising black smoke staining the bank of silver-gray clouds behind it. While waiting for the radio operator, they speculated.

"Anytime a ship is in a repair facility, industrial accidents are expected," Lagos stated as he sipped his coffee. "Arching sparks may have ignited gaseous fumes or oil-soaked rags."

"Let's hope that whatever damage has occurred is minimal," Borodin said as he sipped his coffee. "That ship is needed for our next phase in Mexico and to refuel Vostok's submarine during its transit across the Pacific Ocean."

Just then, the ship's radio operator stepped out onto the bridge wing with eyes full of concern. "The marine railway is under attack by an American torpedo boat destroyer!"

"Impossible!" Borodin exclaimed. "We intercepted a radio message that said they were floundering hundreds of miles away from here."

Vostok and Lagos noted the grim in Borodin's voice. At the same time though they all noticed a strange twinkling in Utkin's eyes as a smile stretched the scar on his cheek.

"Well played, sir; well played," Utkin said with an appreciative sigh. A second later the major panned his eyes across their curious faces. Straightening up a bit, he answered their eyes. "What I mean is that we could be faced with a second torpedo boat destroyer, but I doubt that option. Instead, we received a fake message, which means our captain suspects something."

As the men seemed to accept Utkin's statement, he turned to the radio operator. "Damage?"

The radio operator answered. "Shells punctured the hull and exploded in the engine room, which started a fire, and a couple of other shells struck the bridge and the gun shack above the bridge. Also, the American destroyer is turning north and headed toward the cavern."

"Blast!" Borodin exclaimed. "It seems that he has had time to reconnoiter. I'd say that's rather ungentlemanly of him."

"Well, we can ignore his lack of politesse for now," Utkin said as he turned to face Lagos. "I suggest you remain here on the bridge and have your radio operator stay in contact with Igor. Did any of the aircrew remain with their machines under the north hill?"

"Two pilots and two crewmen stayed with their machines," the radio operator replied.

"Those machines have better quarters than staterooms aboard the ship?" Borodin asked.

Utkin turned to Borodin. "While each machine in that cavern differs in its mission and equipage, they are fitted with brief living abilities."

Lagos turned to the radio operator. "Tell the pilots they're about to be attacked. The last thing we need is for those machines to be trapped in that cavern while the destroyer pours in gunfire. Also, Vostok, get your submarine underway, and sink that interloper with the greatest of dispatch. Where's Sergei and his machine? His other pilots?"

"Sergei's machine is still on the deck of the submarine," Vostok answered, "and he's at the submarine raider barracks."

"Good," Utkin said with relief. "I'll telephone the barracks and have him report to the submarine and tell the pilots to man their airplanes by the Brooks House."

Lagos nodded to the radio operator who turned to step back into the bridge. "I'll have men get the yacht underway as well."

"Good," Utkin said as he looked over at Borodin. "In the meantime, you and I will collect my submarine raiders. I hope you are up for a bit of sport?"

"I am," Borodin replied, "but I am curious if that captain does send out a message concerning this island, and our presence here, won't the authorities be a bit confused or even suspicious? After all, he sent out a radio message indicating he was sinking. And the only remains found was a damaged emergency life raft with the ship's name stenciled on it. And that was recovered by HMS Krakatoa who reported finding no survivors."

"Yes, we do have concerns on that point," Utkin replied, "however, our moles in American intelligence can help with that issue. Anyway, curious arrivals to this island should still be days away. Also, as far as we know, that captain has only snippets of what is going on around here. I'll alert the parachute solders. They can deploy to the air submarine cavern to assist the aircrews and to start preparations for our departure as things are getting a bit heated. I believe we have enough explosives in each of the caverns."

The men nodded to each other and were about to separate when the radio operator stepped out through the bridge door again. "The pilots at the north submarine cavern reports they've flown out the Whaleshark and the Dragonwasp."

"Very well," Utkin said. "Radio back and tell the pilots to focus on the destroyer as best they can. We can get our assets up there to help."

The radio operator looked back at the men. "The pilot flying the Whaleshark reports he was fired upon as he flew out of the cavern by somebody from the shore, above the cavern, and his crewman was killed, and his machine was damaged. The Dragonwasp flew out and the gunner fired back as they did. The rear gunner said he saw a man wearing an army uniform and holding a Thompson submachine gun."

"What about the jitterbug? Utkin asked. "Is it still in the cavern?"

"No one reports flying it out of the cavern," the radio operator said.

Borodin looked at the other men. "It appears that either the American destroyer captain has landed an armed force or Sergeant Dooley has found a bit of sport himself. Or both."

Utkin spoke up. "We left that machine in the cavern as we had no need to use it. Now, I fear that we may have allowed a stalwart opponent from across the green felt to find a stray stick of dynamite and a fuse. I also know he is well armed with a match."

* * *

"Are you alright?" Zeta asked as Dooley slid into their depression. "We heard the gunfire."

Dooley wiped his forehead with the back of his hand as he answered. "I'm fine, and I was able to plug the first one and good. Couldn't do anything about the second one, though. I also think they were equipped with radios."

"Which means we'll get busy real soon," Fowler said as he held out his second canteen.

The ex-sergeant accepted the canteen and took a long draught before answering. "Which means we can't stay here. I've seen what those parachute solders can do."

"What will we do?" Zeta asked as she accepted the canteen from Dooley.

Dooley looked at Zeta. Wearing the black watch cap with her blond hair sticking out from under it while being enveloped by that oversized Russian army blouse, she looked just as innocent and demure as she did the night back at Vladivostok. She did not belong here. "The way I see it, we can make it to the beach, signal your captain, and swim out to them."

"Shipmate," Fowler responded as he accepted his canteen from Zeta. "I didn't get to be forty years old by making it a habit of walking in front of firing squads. We're all better off with us running interference. Any other ideas?"

"We could just split up and hide out. Wait for the dust to settle. I'm sure your captain, if he hasn't by now, will send out a radio message of some sort asking for help. But if it doesn't work out for your ship, then we're stuck until help arrives, and who knows when that'll happen. And the island is only so big," Dooley answered. "The only real option is for me to get into the cavern to find out if I can fly that machine. If I can, then we'll be an asset and help your captain. We could also fly from here and hopefully get rescued if we can land anywhere near civilization. Even if it's just an island or near a ship with a friendly flag."

"All that sounds good," Fowler said as he continued to look at the approaches to the door under them, "but you don't know how long it will take for you to figure that machine out, if at all. Also, they left it behind for a reason, and if we can fly it out of here, we risk getting shot down by the other flying machines. In the meantime, somebody's gotta guard this entrance, which would make it difficult for that somebody to get down to that door and inside the cavern to get aboard that machine if somebody does show up."

Dooley thought before answering, "Zeta can come with me. It's a Russian machine, so I will need help reading labels and such. Also, there's two Lewis guns on that thing. I can show her how to use them and she can guard the entrance from the inside in case anybody gets past you. And she can guard the entrance to the cave in case somebody swims around."

"Sounds good," Fowler answered, "but how will I get back in? I'll expose myself dropping down to the door, and I know none of those men have goobers for brains."

Dooley turned to look up the slope. "You can reposition yourself higher up. You can keep both your field of fire and high-ground advantage. When the time's right, you can drop through the vent and into the water below. It's quite a drop, but the water should be deep enough."

Fowler turned to look up the slope himself. After a couple of seconds, he spoke. "Should be deep enough, huh? But how will I know when it's the right time?"

"Good," Dooley said. "If I can get it running, listen for when the engines are running at a high rpm. Just like you heard with the first two. That means I'm about ready to take off."

Fowler lifted the shotgun from the tree trunk and panned the barrel in front of him. "Just don't jump the gun and chop me up with propellers on the way out."

With a nod, Dooley stood, shouldered his Thompson, and grabbed Zeta's hand.

"Hey," Fowler said. "My pistol?"

Zeta handed over the pistol and extra magazine, and together, the sergeant and the countess stepped down the hill and to the cavern's entrance. Pushing the netting aside, Dooley opened the door to the entrance and stepped inside with Zeta following.

As they did, Dooley could now see what he had walked through the previous nights. Once past the wooden structure they entered the tunnel that the Russians excavated through the side of the hill. Roughhewn through rock, they followed the length and curve of the tunnel and as they did, Dooley wondered why the Russians didn't simply tunnel straight into the cavern.

Maybe it was designed to act as a sound baffle, Dooley thought as he came around the second turn. It was obvious that the Russians left the sloping doors open, so when the two entered the cavern, Dooley saw the items he'd seen the last two nights and something else that he did not see before. In the back of the cavern were two stacks of dark green wooden boxes with rope handles. The boxes were the size of peach crates, stenciled in Russian, and stacked six high, with one crate sitting astride the two stacks. The crates were covered with camouflage netting.

"What's in those boxes?" Dooley asked.

Zeta looked through the netting before answering. "Some sort of explosive, and there's also a box of fuses or rope matches. That's the box on top."

"Good," Dooley said. "Looks like they used dynamite to blast out this cavern and will use what's left to destroy it when they leave, which is why the explosives and fuses are still here. But we might be able to use it ourselves. Come on."

Dooley stepped next to the edge of the quay wall and bent to untie the bowline for the punt. He stopped for a second, though.

"What's wrong?" Zeta asked.

Dooley did not answer right away. Instead, he turned to look at the entrance to the cavern and at the explosives. "Remember seeing the parachute soldiers throwing hand grenades?"

"Yes."

"Well, if they get past Fowler, they'll being running down that tunnel straight into your Lewis gun. And, just like Fowler said, they don't have peanuts for brains. Once they realize that, they could simply stay at the turn of the tunnel and roll hand grenades into the cavern where the explosions and fragmentation effects would be magnified in these confines. The hand grenades could also set off the dynamite. At some point, they will probably want to destroy this cavern, and need to destroy us, so doing both at the same time is quite efficient, even if it means the destruction of that thing in front of us."

Zeta looked at the stacks of explosives.

* * *

Hillary, like everybody on the deck of the destroyer, saw the aircraft dart from the entrance, and they also saw the thin trail of smoke trailing behind it. Sparks stood next to Hillary on the port bridge wing. Hugh Rodham and Grover stood next to him. They all wore their grey helmets, and the two officers took the time to don cartridge belts with holstered pistols.

"Behold the flying one-eyed whale," Sparks said.

Hillary, still looking at the flying machine as it flew eastward and away from them for a mile before beginning a wide turn to the south, answered, "No response to your calls yet?"

"Not yet," Sparks replied truthfully. "I got my striker on the set, but it looks like we're too far from Manila for them to receive a clear message, if at all, and the same with the consulate in Hong Kong and Shanghai. Also, I'm not sure what going on with the weather west or south of us. The closest American station that could receive us is in Formosa or Japan. It also doesn't help that I'm using a used vacuum tube meant for a Marconi model with less wattage. Too bad the replacement tube for our current model was defective."

While the first part of the radio operator's statement was true, the second part was not. Hillary and Sparks lied to prevent Rodham from using the radio for his own purposes. Rodham claimed to know nothing about radios, so it was that much easier to complete the ruse.

"Are any of our own navy ships within radio reach?" Rodham asked.

"And what do we tell them? We're about to enter the gladiator's arena with an airplane that appeared to have come from the pages of romance science novel and a tramp steamer that can go faster than a Baldwin Hydrofoil across Lake Michigan."

"The closest American navy vessels are the river gunboats in China, and they're hundreds of miles from here. So, no," Hillary replied truthfully as he avoided looking at Rodham. "However, there has to be American or European-flagged merchants out and about searching for any vessels that may have been stricken by the storm or at least trying to get their cargoes to port."

"Very good, Skipper," Sparks said, "but the last time I checked, most merchant ships don't have anything bigger than revolvers or bolt-action Enfields, so I doubt they'd be in a big hurry to get here. It sure would be nice if there was a British or Japanese warship on patrol."

It was at that point Hillary remembered the Royal Navy ship they saw in Hong Kong. It was also the one that replied to their fake distress call and reported collecting their damaged life raft. Not wanting to admit the worst scenario to Sparks, although Hillary assumed that the radio operator was probably aware of the dangers ahead, the ship's captain spoke. "We have it under control, Sparks. All I want to do is to let somebody know what's going on with this island in case somebody gets away from us. Keep trying to raise somebody and get a response."

"Yes, sir," Sparks replied as they heard the engines of another airplane. They turned to look at a sharply defined flying machine escape the cavern. It looked like a ground hornet escaping a suddenly disturbed hive. "I'll get a response."

Sparks stepped back into the bridge, leaving the captain, Grover, and Rodham alone. While the machine gunner watched the second aircraft gain altitude, he pressed his shoulder harder against the weapon's stock and followed the machine with his barrel. Meanwhile, Hillary shifted his focus back to the first aircraft as it moved in and out of the clouds in the eastern sky making a wide circle around the destroyer and heading south. It left a hint of brownish smoke behind it. Realizing that it was not an immediate threat, he turned his attention back to the second aircraft, which seemed to have leveled out at about a thousand feet and made a sharp turn toward his ship.

"Grover, I know we've never trained for aircraft combat, but if it comes straight in, don't worry about counting the bullets. If it turns sideways, try to lead the target as best you can."

"Yes, sir," Grover replied as he tightened his grip on the weapon and lined up his open sights at the distant flying machine.

Hillary turned to face Rodham. "I would appreciate your help with the magazines."

Rodham nodded as he adjusted the chinstrap of his helmet. They both then looked at the open weapon's locker on the bridge wing. Empty of its weapon, it still contained a drawer under the gun stand full of spare parts, a box of extra rounds, and cleaning equipment, a spare barrel clipped into place, and a stack of pan magazines secured in cubbies alongside the gun stand.

Their observations were disrupted by a burst from the Lewis gun, which was also followed by the boom of at least one of the six-pounders on the starboard side of the ship and the crackling fire of several Springfield rifles. The two officers turned toward the aircraft and the sound of spent brass casings being ejected from the Lewis gun striking the steel deck at their feet. The flying machine was a little less than a half mile to the east and a little less than a thousand feet of altitude, with its nose angling downward, pointing straight at the ship. The six-pounders on that side of the ship, the Lewis gun, and several Springfields kept up their fire, but from what they could see, the rounds did not appear to be striking their mark.

"Like honeybees attacking a black bear," Rodham remarked.

"We've never trained in anti-aircraft combat, nor do we have sights that help judge altitude and speed," Hillary replied, but before he could say anything else the nose of the dragon-shaped flying machine exploded into a burst of fire. "Son of a bitch!"

Hillary, Grover, and Rodham dove behind the steel of the bridge wing as the thunderous burst from the nose of the flying machine slammed into the steel of the ship's bow, which shuddered under the onslaught. The steel maelstrom was chorused by the screams of men. Hillary, and the others on the bridge wing, stood as the dragon-shaped airplane veered sharply, exposing its underside, and flew to the south, parallel to the ship leveling out as it did. While the six-pounders and rifles kept up their fire, the officers and gunner looked over the bridge wing and down at the deck gun.

Hillary's heart sank as he saw the screaming carnage.

The men who stood by the deck gun were either dead or still alive but with missing limbs or ripped open guts. Among the torn steel at the base of the deck gun, Hillary saw holes punched through the deck at the base of the gun mount. The holes were the size of golf balls, and smoke spiraled out as blood drained into them. Among the living was Petty Officer Busachek who lay at the base of the torn-up deck gun but was missing his leg beneath the knee. A couple feet away the amputated limb rested on a crate of ammunition. While the deck gun was ripped to shreds, none of the ammunition crates behind the mount were touched. Busachek was tying a handkerchief around the leg above the knee and at the same time ordering men who abandoned the two forward six-pounders to assist their shipmates. Everybody was screaming or yelling, but the bedlam did not distract Hillary. He looked aft and saw the aft six-pounder crews and engineers, with their bolt-action rifles, firing at the departing aircraft.

"Engineers!" Hillary shouted. "Keep your rifles but get on the forward six-pounders!"

"We've never trained on them!" one of the engineers yelled as he lowered his rifle.

"Your training starts now!" Hillary shouted back as he turned to face the doorway to the bridge. "Krivor, call down to sickbay and tell him we've got wounded."

"He already on it, Skipper," Krivor replied as he used a free hand to point through the bridge window. Hillary looked over the bridge wing ledge and saw the hospital steward with his first aide musette bag.

Hillary turned to face Grover and Rodham. "Grover, good job so far, but it looks like we're in for a fight. Go over to the other bridge wing and get the spare magazines from that Lewis gun locker. I'll get another case of ammunition in the meantime."

"Yes, sir," Grover said as he stepped away from the weapon.

"You want me to go down and help hospital?" Rodham volunteered.

"No, you stay with Grover," Hillary said as he stood next to weapon while trying to take all that had happened so far this morning, especially in the last couple of minutes. The first airplane disappeared, and Hillary thanked God for it not attacking them. He looked at the dragon airplane as it was making its way south. Its engines were like that of a distant gnat.

"I don't know who they are," Rodham said, "but they seem to know their business."

"You're right," Hillary said as he checked the condition of the Lewis gun. "To be able to fire a single burst and take out a deck gun, and its crew, from a half mile away while flying at a thousand feet and not touch the ammunition cases only feet behind it. That's called knowing your business. And with what can only be described as a fully automatic six-pounder machine gun in its nose. It must've fired a dozen rounds in two seconds."

Hillary paused as he saw Grover return, straining to hold the five, ninety-seven round pan magazines stacked in his arms.

Hillary stepped toward the ladder leading to the main deck. "I'm going to see what I can do with the wounded and get that case of rounds."

* * *

Captain Bogdanovich and others stood on the deck of their ship, witnessing the brief battle between the American destroyer and their Dragon-wasp airplane. They also saw the first flying machine, the Whaleshark, land on the blue sea just to the south of the marine railway. The pilot, having turned off the engines as he lined the machine up for a landing, completed an expert, power-out touchdown. He pulled back on the control stick just as he was about to land on the water, and the bulbous bow barely caused a ripple as the machine's hull glided on the water and settled in for a short transit to the beach.

Everybody also heard the little internal combustion engine inside the machine start up as its exhaust escaped through a port in the aircraft's tail. A wake bubbled up from the machine's stern as the pilot now engaged the propeller. The pilot could be seen through the cockpit's windshield as he switched seats and sat in the right seat and steered the machine toward the beach.

In front of the cockpit, everybody could see the open hatch in its nose and the unmanned Lewis gun with its barrel pointed upward. On the beach, waiting for the pilot and the dead crewman inside that nose, were the rest of the pilots and crewmen who spent the night on the ship. All of them wore their flying coveralls and held their leather helmets and goggles in their hands. At their feet, lying in the sand, was a folded canvas stretcher. They watched as the bulbous bow of the flying machine pushed itself onto the sand. Two airmen clambered onto the bow with one of them dropping his legs into the open hatchway.

Captain Bogdanovich turned his attention to the second airplane, the Dragonwasp, as it too lined up for a power-out landing. The pilot radioed that his gunner had fired on somebody standing on the hill above the cave. He also reported emptying a magazine of thirty-seven-millimeter armor-piercing and explosive rounds into the destroyer's deck gun. Seeing that all was well in in hand, Bogdanovich turned his attention to the radioman who just pulled up next to him.

CHAPTER 35

DOOLEY HELPED ZETA as she lowered herself into the cockpit of the airplane. Now, squeezed together in the tight confines, she looked at both seats and at Dooley's Thompson propped up against the back of the right seat. Its stock rested on two crates, one with dynamite and the other one with the fuse material.

"The left seat is just like being in an airplane, and I think I can fly us out of here, but I can't fly it and fight at the same time. There's a Lewis gun in the nose compartment, and one in the aft compartment. Come on."

Dooley stooped into the compartment behind the cockpit and as he did, he looked through the side window at the entrance into the cavern. Draped across the tunnel was the camouflage netting that covered the explosives. After removing the netting from the stacked crates, they reserved two crates for themselves while dumping the rest of the crates into the water. Once their explosives and fuse material were in the punt, Dooley went to the work benches to find bolts and a hammer so he could hang up the camouflage netting.

"This machine gun can do quite a bit of damage in the right hands," Dooley said as he straightened up and reached to unclip the weapon.

"You've been a good teacher so far," Zeta said with a smile.

"Here," Dooley answered with a smile of his own. Unclipping the weapon, he handed it to Zeta by the barrel and reached to open the pantry door. He pulled out a pan magazine enclosed in a canvas satchel from its cubby. Holding the strap, he reached up to pull down the hinged, spring-loaded ladder and locked it in its down position. It had a foldout landing, which he unfolded and locked in position He stepped up onto it, unlatched the round hatchway, and pushed it up and back into a locking position.

She held the weapon up and Dooley grabbed it by the barrel, which allowed Zeta to use her hands to pull herself up and onto the landing, squeezing in front of Dooley. She felt Dooley's chest against her shoulders, his thighs against her buttocks, and the handle of his shingle axe against the small of her back. His breath caressed her neck. Thinking back to the previous nights she continued to enjoy the sensation as Dooley's arms enveloped her while he flipped up a pintle mount in front of the hatch. After inserting the Lewis gun onto the thumb-sized stub of aluminum stock, he showed her how to load the magazine onto the weapon, how to operate it, and how to aim it. The view was excellent, except for the upright hatchway against the back of Dooley's shoulders and head. Dooley could see that, at this elevated position, the gun's operator could shoot at anything in front and on either side, while being somewhat protected from behind. To their right, was the entrance from the tunnel. At their front, was the cavern's entrance, and in front and above them was the circular vent with the straggle of roots hanging into the cavern.

"I'm going to the cockpit to figure out how to fly this thing. Get two more magazines, hang them from the ladder by their satchel straps, and stay on the gun."

Zeta nodded as she slid down and stepped off the landing feeling Dooley's body as she did. She waited for Dooley to step down, and when he did, he reached to unsnap the flap covering his pistol. He removed it from the holster, along with one of his magazines. He held them out.

"Keep these in your uniform pockets. Every good soldier carries a secondary, and every good Pinkerton carries a backup."

"Or a throwaway?" Zeta asked.

"Now you're learning," Dooley replied.

"Where's your secondary?" Zeta asked as she accepted the weapon and magazine with a proud smile.

He patted his shingle axe and sheathed hunting knife.

She nodded in understanding. "Dooley?"

"Yes," he said as he reached out to push some her hair behind her ear.

"When you went to the top of the hill, that American became a bit forward with me. Can you tell him we're involved?"

Dooley chuckled slightly as he dropped his hand and let it slide off her shoulder. "Bastard."

* * *

Captain Lagos felt the ship's propellers push his vessel closer to the eastern side of the island, and the American destroyer. Above his head, he could hear his gun crew move about as they used the hand cranks to unlimber and exercise the twelve-pounder deck gun. He glanced at the patched-up forecastle where the other twelve-pounder was once secreted inside. All that remained of the weapon was a bent piece of scrap lying on a beach behind them. Having just passed the closing doors of the of the submarine cavern, he took a minute to look east at Vostok's submarine, which was a mile ahead. Its bow cleaved through the smooth, early morning seas while leaving behind a broad wake.

"The pilot of the Dragonwasp reports he's taken out the deck gun of the American destroyer," stated the ship's senior radio operator who stood on the bridge behind Lagos. "Also, he's landed and picked up the rest of his crew."

"What about the Whaleshark?" Lagos asked.

"The pilot of the Whaleshark said he was fired upon by a single man with a machine gun as he left the cavern, and his gunner was killed. He's landed, and they've removed the body. They're also repairing electrical damage."

"Good," Lagos replied. "Is the American destroyer still making distress calls?"

"Yes, sir," the man replied. "But he's stopped radioing Manila or Hong Kong. Now he's sending out open distress calls indicating he's in combat with unidentified flying machines and has fired upon an armed merchant ship. He's also given his location, but no one has replied yet."

"Good," he again replied. "Remain with the radio and keep me updated."

"Yes, sir," the man said as he turned to the wooden door at the back of the bridge. As he reached for the brass knob, he heard a loud, echoing bang. He, and everybody else on the bridge, turned to see the airplane being shot from the foredeck of the submarine. A rising ball of black smoke from the powder-charged catapult rose from the submarine's deck. While the ball of black fell behind the submarine the single engine airplane pulled itself to about three hundred feet before Popov started to circle around the moving submarine.

With a smile Lagos thought about the upcoming engagement. It will not be much of a battle especially once Vostok's submarine arrives and launches his updated torpedoes. His thoughts though were interrupted by movement off to his left. Above the trees of the island, Lagos saw the large air bomber take to the sky with the two one-man air subs following it. As he saw the machines fly into the eastern morning sky, the junior radio operator opened the door bumping the hand of the senior radio rating. He looked at his senior before looking at Lagos.

"Sir," the man said, "the British yacht has a steering and an engine issue."

"Seems like we caused more damage than thought when we attacked the vessel," Lagos accepted. "Have them return to their anchorage for repairs and to finish preparations for their transit. And stay on the radio."

The man answered by stepping back into the radio room and closing the door behind him.

* * *

Borodin and Utkin met with the submarine raider commando. A dozen men stood outside their single-story wooden barracks near the submarine cavern and carried Fedorov automatic rifles, canvas web gear, and sheathed knuckle-duster fighting knives over loose-fitting field uniforms. They all could hear airplane engines from the airfield being fired up.

Utkin spoke to his men. "Men, we are to have a bit of sport this morning. It appears that Sergeant Dooley has turned on us. It also appears that there is an American destroyer off the eastern shore of this island and may have landed some sort of fighting force."

The men smiled. Morda's hand caressed the entrenching in his belt.

Utkin continued, "We will go to the railway to see if we can be any assistance. The parachute commando is headed to the airplane cavern. In both cases, though, when this matter is settled, we will return to collapse our caverns and depart this island as early as this evening. Understand?"

The men grouped in front of Utkin, and Borodin nodded.

Utkin nodded in response and turned to face the east. His men followed. They ran down the path that would take them to the island's central road. Holding their rifles in their right hands, their gait was strong and purposeful. Twenty minutes later, the force broke out into the meadow in time to see three aircraft lined up on the road. The large bomber was the first one in line with two little one-man air subs behind it, side by side. The small air subs were mounted on tracked catapult tractor-like machines with their engines screaming. Tracked just like the flying machines mounted on top of them, the catapult's explosive cylinder provided the power for the aircraft to be shot into the air. Behind each catapult and steering wheel, a man sat and held a lanyard to fire the powder charge by the almost centuries-old British percussion cap firing mechanisms. The two-seat trainer Dooley flew the other day was off to the side, and a man was doing something to the engine. The submarine raiders continued down the road past the flying machines. When they were in between the large bomber and the trainer, Utkin waved to his men and shouted, "You men keep going to the marine railway and we'll meet you there."

Utkin and Borodin peeled off and stopped to walk toward the pilot working on the trainer. His gunner stood behind him, holding a tool tray and two leather helmets. Like all the aircrews, they wore patch-covered coveralls. "What's wrong?"

The man who had his head stuck under the raised tin cowling replied as he turned a wrench. "I fired up the engine, but it looks like two spark plugs are misfiring. I don't understand it. I saw Sergei and the American fly it the other day and it flew fine, but no worries. I can fix it."

"Good," Utkin said. Not aware of the issue with the British yacht, Utkin left the man to his work, and turned to face the man sitting in the open cockpit of the bomber. Fully manned, the pilot appeared to be giving his gauges a check before taking off. Utkin offered a thumbs up. The pilot of the bomber replied with a thumbs up of his own as he took his feet off the brakes. The plane bolted forward and raced down the dirt road. As it almost jumped free of the dirt road, the two one-man air subs were shot off the catapults and followed in suit. The booms of the powder-charged catapults echoed across the meadow, and a dense billow of black smoke stained the clear air above each catapult. As the air sub closest to the two Russian leaders flew past them barely four feet off the ground, Utkin heard the airplane's single engine. Having heard the engines before, he knew how they were supposed to sound. Watching the planes fly into the morning sky, Utkin looked over his shoulder and at the pilot still bent over the engine of the two-seat trainer.

Utkin then looked at Borodin and jerked his head toward the east. The two men fell into a slow jog to follow their men and the airplanes. After a couple of minutes, though, Utkin's thoughts were confirmed as he saw the air sub with the rough-sounding engine start a wide turn to the south. Both men saw the trail of blue-white smoke develop behind the machine. The other aircraft turned to the north.

Catching up with the submarine raiders, Utkin mentioned his thoughts to Borodin. The man replied succinctly, "Looks like we will all be in for a bit of sport this morning."

While the submarine raiders made their way to the marine railway, the parachute solders slowed as they approached the slope of the northern hill. After having been warned about a man with a Thompson, they took no chances.

* * *

Fowler sat in his new position, which was another depression caused by another tree-fall closer to the top of the hill. Hidden behind the root ball of a rotten palm tree with the barrel of his shotgun inserted through the roots he watched the forest floor. While doing so, he thought of his commanding officer fighting for the life of his ship and his men. He had taken his eyes off his immediate front earlier and watched as the front of the dragon-looking airplane spit out a burst of fire. After that plane flew south, there was a lull, but Fowler knew it wouldn't last. According to Dooley, there were several other aircraft, and even though Dooley said he could disable them to a degree, he still feared for the lives of his shipmates and commanding officer. "Come on, Dooley, get those engines started!" Fowler said aloud as he returned his attention to the forest beneath him.

Just as he finished stating those words to himself, he saw movement. Lowering his head, he pressed his shoulder against the stock of his shotgun. At first, he didn't know what he had seen. It was just a blur among the trees. But after a minute, he started to see a form. It was a man, wearing camouflaged coveralls, a padded leather helmet, and high-top leather boots, cautiously stepping around a tree trunk. The man held a submachine gun and used the barrel to sniff the air in front of him. Realizing earlier that he might first sight his targets at the shotgun's furthest effective range, Fowler loaded it with shells firing slugs instead of buckshot.

Behind that man, Fowler started to see other forms. He looked down the length of his shotgun's barrel and took aim on the man's chest. Slowly, he pressed down on the trigger until it roared, and the stock jerked his shoulder back. At the same time, Fowler swore he could hear the digit-sized slug punch through the man's chest as it knocked him off his feet. Landing on his back, the man's submachine fell next to him with a thud. The forms behind him disappeared behind trees. As Fowler re-racked his shotgun, he was amazed not to hear men yelling out orders or the sound of confusion. But then he nodded in understanding as he hoped the people in the cavern heard the gunfire.

Inside the cavern, Zeta heard Fowler's shotgun as she stood at her post. She also heard Dooley talking to himself.

"Are you ok?" Zeta asked as she pressed her shoulder against the butt of the Lewis gun and pointed the barrel at the camouflage netting draped over the tunnel's opening.

"I'm fine, but everything's labeled in Russian," Dooley replied.

"Need me to read for you?"

"Stay on that gun," Dooley replied. "I got it."

For the most part, he wasn't lying. The rudder pedals and control stick were easy to figure out, and he was satisfied after testing them. The first gauges he recognized were the large, bubbled attitude indicator and compass centered on the polished aluminum console. Fixed on either side of them were other gauges including the air-pressure, engine rpm, and air-speed gauges. There were also several brass plaques printed with numeric scales, but most important were what looked like the ignition and battery and magneto switches. Since the wings were relatively high on the fuselage and the engines were under the wings, there was no need for fuel primer controls as the engines were gravity fed.

Looking for the fuel-tank indicators Dooley reached for what appeared to be the battery and magneto switches and turned them to what he thought were the on positions. After that, he turned the ignition switch for the starboard engine. The engine turned over and coughed a couple of times before catching. Blueish smoke shot from the exhaust manifold as well as the sound. Even from that one engine running a minimum of rpm, the noise was deafening inside the cavern. Letting it run for a few seconds, he saw the blue smoke dissipate as the engine warmed up.

He repeated the same process with the port engine. Once it caught, he took his eyes away from the engines and looked over his shoulder at Zeta's lower body. Dressed in slacks and with her athletic shoes standing on the ladder landing Dooley knew he had a good person on that Lewis gun. But he then thought about the dynamite on the starboard-side seat.

Letting go of his controls he leaned around the lowered periscope and moved the dynamite and fuse material into the nose compartment. Once back in his seat, he pushed in the throttle for each engine while keeping his hand on the airplane's anchor release lever at his side and under the short torpedo clamped to the side of the machine's frame.

That was when he finally had time to notice two other items, including a long stick marked with numbers and notches. He looked out the side windshield and at the gas tank cap. He now knew how to judge his fuel usage. The second item was a flare pistol clipped to the cockpit's frame in a canvas holster, along with a canvas holder with five shells. They were like shotgun shells, but longer.

He looked at his wristwatch before refocusing on how to release the anchors. The airplane was anchored with a forward and aft anchor under the nose and tail compartments and could be drawn up, by hand, if needed. But it looked like this lever was a quick disconnect feature which both anchor lines were connected to. Looking forward through the windshield, and at the roots dangling from the vent in the cavern's roof, he waited to see Fowler drop to the water beneath. While waiting, he felt the sound of the engines bounce off the walls of the cavern and seemingly through his body.

"Come on," Dooley said aloud even though he couldn't hear himself. It was then when he felt something hit his right shoulder. He turned in time for another spent cartridge to strike him, this time, on the side of his head. At the same time, while looking at the netting covering the tunnel's entrance, something out of the corner of his eye caught his attention. Turning quickly back to his front he saw Fowler, with his arms over his head holding his shotgun and both pistol holsters and musette bag folding away from his hips, falling as if in slow motion. In a second, though, Fowler hit the water and went under. While lined with stone rubble, the water was clear, and about eight feet deep. As Dooley watched Fowler pop to the surface with his shotgun in his hand, he thought about the cases of dynamite now lying at the bottom of that water under them. behind the tail of the flying machine. Looking past Fowler, who was now swim kicking his way toward them, Dooley appreciated the morning sun shining int the cavern entrance. He hoped, indeed, that he had done enough.

CHAPTER 36

AFTER FOWLER SHOT that first man, the other camouflaged forms disappeared behind the trees at the base of the hill. They remained silent, but Fowler knew they were already making their next move. He assumed at least one pair of men would stay in front of him in order to keep him engaged while the other pair would be intent on the cavern's entrance. The others would come at him from the sides or get up the hill and attack him from behind. As the barrel of his shotgun searched for targets, he heard an engine start. The rpm erupted from the cavern's vent up the slope and over his left shoulder. He also heard what sounded like distant cannon and automatic gunfire. He prayed for the lives of his shipmates and Rance Hillary.

While praying for the men, gunfire from the base of the hill brought him back to the threats in front of him. He hunkered down as bullets tore at the dirt and tree trunks above his position and at the root ball in front of him. Fowler peeked through the roots despite the gunfire and saw two men leave their protection and dart toward the entrance under him. He pulled the trigger, and the heavy lead slug knocked one man backward and, by the time Fowler re-racked the shotgun, the second man threw himself behind another tree trunk.

At that time, Fowler saw movement off to his left. He pulled the barrel from the tangle of roots and swung the weapon toward a pair of men trying to scramble up the slope through the trees. Fowler took aim at the man in front and pulled the trigger. The man bowled forward and screamed as he let go of his weapon and grabbed his thigh. The second man stopped long enough to let loose a burst toward Fowler's position, but he never had a chance to finish the magazine. Fowler put a lead slug into his head, knocking him over.

Then, without wasting a second, Fowler swung the barrel of the shotgun across his front and shot at another man running for the entrance before moving on to his right to fire at one of two men scrambling up the side of the hill. It was then that he heard the two engines inside the cavern increase to a crescendo.

While holding the shotgun in his left hand, he unholstered Harrison's pistol as he made it to the top of the hill. Running through the trees toward the hole, he fired the pistol at two men shooting at him from behind tree trunks halfway up the hill. He reached the hole and squatted to finish firing the magazine. When the hammer fell silent, he holstered the pistol and secured the leather flap. As bullets flew over his head, Fowler took a deep breath and rolled into the hole.

A second later, he slammed into the cavern's water feet first. As he went under, his feet landed on the rocks. Though weighed down with his weapons, canvas web gear, clothing, and musette bag, he used his legs to push himself to the surface. He opened his eyes and took a deep breath. In front of him, forty feet away, was the machine with its spinning propellers, screaming engines, and Dooley looking at him through the windshield. The pilot pointed his finger to the left side of the machine. Fowler also saw the countess, with her head and shoulders sticking out of a hatchway behind the cockpit, firing into camouflage netting hanging against the cavern wall. Though he couldn't hear the weapon firing over the howling engines, Fowler saw spent brass shells bouncing off the side of the airplane and splashing into the water around its hull.

Slinging his shotgun over his head and across his back, Fowler started kicking his way to the side of the machine. Keeping an eye on the airplane and the two people in it, Fowler made it around the port wing tip. Finding the footsteps and handholds, he pulled himself from the water and climbed up the side, stepping onto the wing while looking into the side windshield. Dooley, only inches away, pointed straight up. Fowler nodded while unslinging his shotgun and dropping it into the hatch stock first. At the same time, he saw Zeta fire another burst into the netting. He also saw a body on the other side. Grabbing the edge of the hatchway he pulled himself into it headfirst. Just as Fowler landed inside the cockpit, Dooley pulled the anchor release lever.

* * *

Hillary kept watching the skies to the south and could see several aircraft taking off. He turned to look at Grover and the stack of pan magazines next to his legs. Hillary also noticed Grover's shaking fingers.

"Just make sure you lead your targets, Grover," Hillary said as he patted him on the shoulder.

"Yes, sir," the young sailor said with a nervous sigh.

"Good," Hillary replied as he turned to Rodham who stood next to the captain's chair. "Wishin' you were back at Fort McKinley? On the post golf course?"

Rodham pulled a bullet from a metal ammunition box on the seat of the chair. As he pushed it into the pan magazine next to the box, he answered, "Too late to worry about it now, and sorry about your gun crew. Will your petty officer, the one called Busachek, make it?"

"He died before he got to sickbay," Hillary reported as he turned his eyes toward the grey-painted steel deck. "Loss of blood."

Just then, they heard the six-pounder on the ship's fantail bark, and the three of them turned to look past the four exhaust stacks and at the approaching aircraft. As they did, Hillary saw smoke and embers pouring out of the Number Three stack. Hillary envisioned his engineers trying to keep the dying boiler alive while it was eating its own guts, just as the Number Two boiler did after the relentless transit from Formosa. The other two boilers provided the required pressure, but the volume of steam needed to push the turbine blades for the two main engines was not there. Now, at reduced speed, all Hillary could do was fight off armed aircraft as he tried to escape this island. Taking a second to look at the island, he prayed for his chief petty officer.

Returning his thoughts to the fight, he saw the nose of the dragon-shaped aircraft tilt is as it came straight at the ship's stern. The two men at the mounted gun kept up a steady rate of fire as best they could with firing one shell at a time. No one could see where the shells were going, but at a half mile out, the nose of the aircraft exploded into a burst of flame. Just like before. At the same time, the ship's fantail and the steering room under it erupted into a cloud of steel slivers and paint and rust chips as a dozen rounds punched through the deck and exploded inside the steering gear room. After the explosive burst from the nose, the flying machine banked to starboard while continuing to fly toward the ship. As the airplane flew closer, the six-pounder gun crew got back on their weapon on the stern, and the gunner hand cranked the barrel to catch up with the forward movement of the aircraft and fired the round inside the breech.

"I lost steering, sir!" Krivor yelled out loudly as he turned the wheel to test the rudder while keeping an eye on the ship's binnacle. "The steering's gone!"

Still on the bridge wing, all Hillary could do was curse as he saw smoke pour from the holes in the fantail deck. "Damn it! First the deck gun and then the steering!" He jumped through the door and into bridge. "Krivor, work with Mack and use the EOT to steer with our engines. Keep the ship going straight ahead!" Turning his attention to the handset for the ship's loudspeaker system, he grabbed it and yelled, "You guys on the six-pounders: lead your targets!"

The stern gun crew and the crews manning the two six-pounders on the starboard side took aim at the dragon-airship as it was coming parallel to the ship three hundred yards away and at three hundred yards of altitude. Everybody saw a man's head and shoulders poke out of a hatch behind the cockpit and with what looked like a twin-barreled machine gun. The man started to fire at the destroyer. At the same time, the three six-pounders fired on the flying machine along with Grover on the bridge wing and the men armed with their bolt-action Springfields. The exchange of gunfire was furious, but with the machine gunner on the flying machine having the advantage of height and a larger, slow-moving target, the gunner easily found his targets as Hillary heard the machine gun's bullets smacking into the steel of his ship and flesh of his men. But just as suddenly as the duel began, it stopped. It stopped because of an explosion that blew off the flying machine's nose. Seeing that the air machine was made from metal, it still had to be thin-skinned and light enough to fly, so whatever set off the six-pounder round was a godsend.

The dragon-shaped aircraft wobbled as it veered away, leaving behind a trail of brown smoke. The Americans cheered, but that revelry was short-lived. Hillary, like everybody else, could hear the massive engines on a large bi-winged airplane coming in at its stern, and the storm of lead slugs spitting from its nose and chewing up the stern. Behind the bomber he saw another, smaller, airplane. Hillary looked over as Rodham handed Grover a full pan magazine.

Krivor, who had abandoned the helm and now had his hands on the EOT, yelled out, "Damn it, Skipper. Another one's leaving the cave!"

Hillary looked forward just in time to see an airplane bolt from under the hill. "Shit! They're already on us like a pack of dogs on a three-legged cat!"

Turning back to the large airplane off his stern, he saw it was continuing its stream of machine gun fire while closing the distance between the two. Hillary also saw that the six-pounder on the stern stopped firing. The one forward six-pounder on the starboard side was the only weapon available, and the crew did its best to keep up some sort of fire, firing down the length of the ship's deck. And joining in against the murderous machine gun fire, Grover turned the barrel of his Lewis gun aft and pointed it at the large airplane only a few hundred yards by now. Hillary started to dread the worst, but as he did, one thing happened that gave him hope at the same time. The large airplane's port engine suddenly emitted a huge puff of black smoke. A second later the engine exploded into a ball of flame.

Hillary, as well as everybody else still alive on the ship, watched the large plane, now on one engine, veer away just as the dragon airplane did only moments ago. Now slower, and with a profile to target, the men on the forward six-pounder, along with Grover on the Lewis gun, took advantage of the opportunity. The Americans watched in wonder as the flying machine detonated into a thousand pieces. Falling with the burning debris they saw a man clawing at the air as he fell. The destroyer men cheered as they just fought off a second flying machine; however, the cheer was short lived again. Hillary turned to look aft at a new attacker. Coming in from the stern, just like the previous airplanes, the new attacker was short and fat and appeared more like a carnival ride than a threat. However, he saw a muzzle flash with a cloud of black smoke rolling from its front and behind the aircraft. An explosion of water just off the side of the ship followed.

"Damned thing's firing artillery shells," Hillary cursed. At the same time, though, he thought he saw a glimpse of another aircraft off to his left. Taking a second look, he saw another stubby flying machine in the sky approaching from the east, coming in at their starboard side.

All went silent, except the sound of distant airplane engines. Hillary turned to see Grover accept a full magazine from Rodham and saw the heat rising from the hot barrel of the Lewis gun. On the main deck, he could hear men groaning and less-wounded men issuing orders to help whoever was still left alive. The ship had also just passed the cavern under the north hill and Hillary took a second to investigate the empty cavern. He took another second to think about the one last flying machine that bolted from the cavern.

Turning his attention back to the air assault coming in from the stern, he saw the machine in greater detail now, including what appeared to be tractor tracks under its fuselage.

"What kind of machine is that?" Hillary asked aloud to himself as the gun on that thing spit out another round. This time the round struck the ship. Still a few hundred yards out, the shell hit the deck in front of the six-pounder on the stern. He looked at Grover and his Lewis gun. "Got enough ammunition?"

"Got plenty of bullets," Grover replied, "but I could use a replacement barrel."

"Don't have time. Just keep firing!"

Grover answered by pulling his trigger, but as he tried to send those bullets into the stubby machine, the aircraft altered its course by swerving to the left and starting a wide circle.

"He's making a half circle and looks like he'll come straight in from our port side, just like the one that'll come in from our starboard side," Hillary stated. "Grover! Get that Lewis gun on the port bridge! Rodham! Help with ammunition!"

Before anybody moved though, they all heard the short burst of machine gun fire coming from somewhere in front of them. They all turned to the sound of that gunfire and saw the airplane from the cavern. It was a little less than one thousand feet of altitude and coming in from the northeast obliquely at the ship. However, instead of that gunfire being directed at the ship, it was shooting at the stubby little aircraft coming in from the port side.

Amazed at the possible turn of events Hillary, and his surviving crew, watched the new fight develop. The stubby little airplane changed course again and flew across the ship's stern toward its new opponent. Perhaps a half mile separated the two machines. At the same time, Hillary took a minute to look to the south. He saw one more, silvery-looking aircraft flying in with two seaborne threats further south. His heart sank.

"Grover, stay here and on the gun! Rodham let's see what we can do for my men! And get on a six-pounder if we can!"

Hillary, with Rodham following, ran for the ladder leading down to the main deck. As he waited for the dogfight to begin, his feet hit the main deck and next to a wounded man. The man, with a bolt-action rifle lying next to him, was tying a rag to his shattered knee cap.

"Start with Fireman Busch," Hillary said to Rodham as he looked off to the east and at a new threat. "You'll be okay, Joe. I'll be back."

"Yes, sir," the man grunted in pain.

Rodham knelt next to the man while pulling a monogrammed silk handkerchief from his back pocket. "Where are you going?"

Hillary looked down along the deck at dead and wounded men and at the new threats far off to the southeast. With a heavy heart, he turned to look down at Rodham. "I'm going to release the straps holding down the lifeboats while somebody still can."

On that note, Hillary stepped aft toward the starboard-side motorboat in its davit, and the six-pounder just aft of it. He stepped around wounded men helping other wounded men. As he offered words of encouragement, he thought about his suspicions concerning Rodham.

Maybe I misjudged him, Hillary said to himself as he reached up to the buckle for the boat's bow strap.

CHAPTER 37

THE SUDDEN EJECTION from the cavern was terrifying for all concerned aboard the airplane. While the noise of the engines reverberating off the curved walls of the cavern contributed to the anxiety, the idea of a novice pilot at the controls, the wing tips only feet away from the rocky walls, and over a hundred feet of tunnel to fly out of, took it over the edge. But as the airplane jetted from the cavern, Dooley, Zeta, and Fowler breathed a sigh of relief. With his feet on the pedals and his hands on the control stick, Dooley made minor adjustments to see how the airplane would react. It reacted as he thought it would. Now, with a bit more confidence, Dooley flew east while gaining altitude. He looked to his starboard, and his heart sank.

While the sight of the large bomber's port engine trailing black smoke was a cause of relief, Dooley saw other threats further south coming around the corner of the island. Trying to plan the next step in their salvation, he saw the engine of that bomber explode into a ball of flame. "At least that bomber's out of action," Dooley said aloud as he continued to fly the airplane east and gain altitude. While doing that he continued to sneak glimpses at the two seaborne threats and the remaining air threats. Fowler, holding his shotgun in his hands, looked out the windshield at those same threats. He turned to look at Dooley with imploring eyes.

Speaking loud enough to overcome the noise of the engines, Dooley yelled to Fowler, "Don't worry, Fowler! We'll help!"

Just then, Zeta poked her head into the cockpit. Blown about by the rushing air outside the flying machine, her blonde hair was a tangled mass. "I have two magazines left!"

Dooley turned to look at Fowler while adjusting the control stick between his legs. "Fowler! Get another magazine from the nose compartment and give it to her, then set up that forward Lewis gun! And remember, short, controlled bursts! And Fowler, I hope carrying all that iron around is worth it!"

Fowler leaned forward and looked at Dooley. "It is!"

* * *

Vostok stood on the deck of the conning tower of his submarine as it plowed forward. The sea behind it boiled as the vessel's two propellers drove the submarine toward their target. Far behind that V-shaped wake was the tramp steamer with Lagos aboard. Over Vostok's right shoulder, the morning sun broke free from a rebellious cloud. Off to his left, was their green-covered island. Two miles ahead, and just passing the northeast corner of the island heading into the open sea, was the American destroyer. He saw several whispers of black smoke stretching for the blue morning sky above it.

"That must be one hell of a captain," Vostok said to himself.

Even though the ship had been attacked by formidable machines, he had seen those same formidable flying machines knocked out of the fight. The remaining aircraft, starting with two tracked flying machines armed with thirty-seven-millimeter cannons and the Whaleshark armed with a single cockpit gunner, flew off the submarine's port side. As the Whaleshark flew past Vostok's submarine, he saw that its belly was empty. Designed by Utkin and himself, it was meant to be a flying submersible capable of flying long distance while carrying a container holding five hundred gallons of illicit alcohol under its belly.

At the same time, the June bugs were designed to fly the short distance from Cuba and the Bahamas to the Florida coastline and traverse its swamps to bring illicit alcohol to thirsty customers through the backdoor. They were not meant to be air fighters by any means, and the thirty-seven-millimeters cannons were more for keeping federal vessels at a distance. Assuming Sergeant Dooley was flying the last aircraft, the jitterbug, from the cavern. Vostok thought of the interesting fight that would soon occur. The jitterbug, which was designed to be a fast, torpedo-firing interceptor, was being flown by a novice pilot. But apparently not too novice.

Pondering the outcome, Vostok felt something touch his leg. He looked down and saw his officer clinging to the ladder and holding a piece of folded paper in his hand. Reaching into the hatchway, he grabbed the note and nodded at the officer, who held onto the ladder waiting for his next order. Vostok unfolded it and read the brief message. It was from Lagos. "Proceed with torpedo attack. Machine gun survivors but secure Friend if possible. We will return to dock and prepare to leave island. Return when mission complete. Two-seat trainer crashed upon takeoff. Wing collapsed. One June bug consumed its engine on takeoff. Sail yacht has mechanical difficulties. Seems Sergeant Dooley has been busy."

Vostok refolded the paper and placed it in his trouser pocket. He looked down into the hatchway. "Looks like the destroyer is dead in the water. Stay on this course and have the torpedo crew standby. Get a gunner up here with a Lewis gun and plenty of ammunition."

"Yes, sir," the officer replied as he slid down the ladder, letting Vostok return his attention to the fight in front of him. The jitterbug, presumably with Sergeant Dooley at the controls, flew straight in to engage the slower June bug hundreds of feet above the destroyer. At the same time, the Whaleshark was flying straight in at the stern of the destroyer.

* * *

"What's in those crates?" Fowler asked as he reached into the nose compartment for an extra magazine.

Dooley answered as his confidence at flying increased. "Dynamite and fuses."

"Dynamite? What the hell are Russians doing with dynamite aboard this thing!" Fowler yelled as he turned to hand Zeta a magazine. "We need to dump it over the side!"

Zeta accepted the magazine while looking at Dooley.

"I brought them on board. Figured they'd come in handy," Dooley answered assertively.

"Yeah, at blowing us to smithereens!" Fowler replied. "What? You got ammonia on the brain? All it would take is one stray bullet and we're done for!"

Dooley, flying the airplane and starting a wide turn back toward the ship, answered Fowler's complaint defiantly. "Well, then, Pancho Villa, you'd better keep them off our asses! Get on that forward gun! And, if you got time, see if you can arm some of those sticks of dynamite with fuses. Hope you still got your cigarette lighter!"

"Don't worry about me!" Fowler retorted as he turned back into the nose compartment. "I know what I'm doing."

Dooley's only response was thinking about his next step. Knowing that the only deck weapons the submarine could mount was at least one Lewis gun, his original plan was to attack the submarine with his machine-gun fired by Zeta to keep their heads down while Fowler could drop sticks of dynamite at the same time. However, the arrival of that fat airplane from the cavern and the small, stubby, tracked airplane interfered with those plans. It was then he saw something flash behind a cloud. It was another one of those stubby, tracked airplanes.

"Three separate flying machines and a submarine!" Dooley cursed aloud. After taking a deep breath, he made up his mind by pushing the control stick a little more to his right. At the same time, he grabbed the four-foot-long stick under the torpedo tube and used it to reach behind him and poke Zeta in the leg. Turning around, he stuck it into the forward compartment and poked Fowler in the back. Fowler and Zeta both turned to look at Dooley.

"We're going to take out the stubby, tracked machines first!" Dooley yelled over the engines. "They're no match for this thing! Also, they're armed with a fixed, single-barreled artillery piece that can fire big shotgun shells! Since they have to aim with the airplane, I'll come in at them from their sides!

Remember: short bursts! The destroyer can take care of the larger airplanes!"

Zeta and Fowler nodded and returned to their guns. Replacing the stick, Dooley saw the hinged two half doors in the machine's nose pop open, followed by Fowler's head and shoulders, and the Lewis gun. As he did, a strong draft now blew through the nose gun access and out of Zeta's position, which added to the noise of the engines. Also, because the hinged two half doors fell to the sides of the hatch, and the fact that the engines, propellers, and wings were directly behind him on either side, Fowler's field of fire was limited to an arc in front of him. Seeing that Fowler was doing well with his Lewis gun, Dooley looked beyond him and at the stubby, tracked airplane coming in at the destroyer from its port side. Its silver skin stood out against the green backdrop of the island. Dooley continued to go in at his opponent but, knowing height was a pilot's friend, planned on two, last-minute moves. After a glance, Dooley looked out the window at the fat airplane and saw that the pilot was still intent on attacking the destroyer.

Looking past Fowler's head and shoulders, he watched as their two machines drew closer to each other. As they did, the details became clearer, especially with the single-barreled artillery piece sticking out in front of the machine. Knowing that the pilot needed to get close enough to fire either an explosive shell or a shotgun-type of round to any degree of effect, the pilot was coming straight in at Dooley's airplane. Dooley gave him that courtesy, at least until the last minute. A quarter mile out from each other, Dooley pushed the right rudder with his foot and tilted the control stick, banking the machine slightly to the right. At the same time, he pushed in the throttle to increase the engine rpm to offset the loss of lift from the banking. Watching his opponent while in his turn, he also pulled back on the stick to increase his altitude at the same time. Closing within two hundred yards, and with some height above his opponent, Dooley pushed his stick forward, dropping the nose of the airplane to place the profile of the flying machine directly in front of the Fowler's and Zeta's Lewis guns. Neither person wasted time as he saw spent casings fly from Fowler's weapon and felt spent casings fall on his shoulder from behind. He watched as smoke started to pour from the airplane and pieces flew from its fuselage.

Finishing his pass over the stricken airplane, Dooley continued his turn, knowing there was another stubby machine somewhere behind him. As he did, he saw the larger, fat airplane with its single cockpit gunner, suddenly lose its starboard wing. The last thing Dooley saw of the machine was the wing going one way while the remainder of the craft spiraled toward the destroyer it was attacking. The destroyer, now dead in the water, gave rise to escaping spirals of black smoke, which looked like wraiths, complete with their present task: seeking a new haunting.

Dooley came out of his turn, now facing east, and at the bank of clouds. Somewhere in those clouds was the last short, stubby airplane and its cannon. Under him, he saw the stricken navy ship. He also saw the submarine maneuvering to line up its bow at the ship's starboard side. Now, only a few hundred yards separated the two vessels. There was no hope for the American ship, but there was one hope for them. He nodded to himself in agreement, and, as he started his turn to the northeast, Dooley felt the machine shudder through his foot pedals and stick.

Dooley turned to see Zeta still at her station. He also saw what looked like flickers of flame behind her in the small engine room compartment. He tested his controls, and the machine responded accordingly. As he did, Dooley looked out the front windshield and saw his last opponent drop out of the clouds many yards above and in front of him. He also saw Fowler reach down and pull his massive six-shot revolver and the fancy forty-five-caliber pistol from their holsters. Firing both, like he was a moving picture star, the airplane continued its downward angled path now only a hundred yards in front of them. As the machine filled Dooley's windshield, he thought he recognized Sergei Popov's face under the leather helmet. He also saw the pilot use his free hand to reload the weapon next to his head. Dooley pushed the stick to his right and, while doing so, smelled the acrid taint of gunfire replaced with something else.

Chapter 38

VOSTOK WATCHED AS the bow lined up on the space between the destroyer's first and second stacks three hundred yards away. At the same time, he watched as the multi-airplane air combat came to an end. The engagement with the second to the last June bug was decisive, with Dooley getting the better of the duel. Just before that, he saw the Whaleshark's wing blow away from the flying machine. Both spiraled into the sea behind the destroyer.

"Ready Tubes Numbers One and Two!" Vostok ordered down at his feet.

Vostok returned his eyes to the machine flown by Sergei. While Dooley was busy, Sergei hid behind the clouds to gain altitude. He appreciated his fellow Russian's skills, and even more so when Sergei dropped from the sky and fired a thirty-seven-meter round at Dooley. A blast of smoke erupted from the gun's barrel and stained the sky behind the downward-pointed machine.

"Tubes One and Two ready, Sir," the voice at Vostok's feet stated.

Vostok nodded while he looked up at the last two aircraft. Both were withdrawing from the fight, and both appeared to have suffered damage. "Fire!"

A second later, he felt the submarine tremble through the soles of his shoes as two torpedoes exploded from their tubes just under the water's surface.

As he watched the wakes of the two torpedoes draw lines toward the ship, he also saw the craft supposedly flown by Dooley fly off to the northwest, leaving a faint trail of wispy smoke staining the very blue sky. Sergei's machine made its way south. It, too, left a trail of smoke.

Returning his attention to the ship, he watched the warheads explode in brilliant flashes followed by columns of water and debris shooting into the air. He immediately felt the detonations against his face. Vostok looked down into the hatchway. "Slow speed ahead."

Looking back up, he spoke to the gunner. "Remember, we have one friend aboard that ship."

The man responded by leaning his shoulder against the stock of the weapon and firmly planting his feet. He, his assailant, and Vostok, watched as the geysers collapsed back onto a ship now in flames and breaking into three pieces. Sooty air shooting from the smokestacks replaced the water geysers. At the same time, he saw men leap from the ship and into the water. Closing in for the kill, Vostok took a second to look at the airplane flown by Dooley. Now, off in the distance, still heading northwest, he saw that the thin trail of smoke from a minute ago billowed into a thick, smoldering length of oily stain against the blue sky. Listening to the opening bursts of the Lewis gun, and the screams of men, he watched in appreciation as the flying machine that just escaped the carnage of the battle flew further from the island. Then, as if to signal the end of the day's fighting, a brilliant explosion flashed red at the north end of that oily black line. Five seconds later, while watching the burning black dot fall to the sea, Vostok heard the explosion.

* * *

Hillary scrambled to load the starboard six-pounder. Behind him, he heard gravely wounded men groaning as less-wounded men tried to care for them. At the base of the weapon's mount was the body of a young sailor. Hillary sighed as he remembered promoting the young man from ordinary seaman to a signalman rating at the start of their patrol. Bringing his mind back to the present, he leaned over and hand-cranked the weapon's elevation so that the barrel lined up on the oncoming aircraft. With a lanyard in the other hand, he watched as the airplane flying toward the ship at a slight angle, spit out a line of machine gun bullets. As the bullets started to reach the stern, he pulled the lanyard, and the weapon roared. Reaching for another round he was amazed as he heard an explosion. He looked up just in time to see the entire port wing blow away from the flying machine. His amazement, though, was interrupted as Grover, leaving a useless bridge, yelled at him from the starboard bridge wing. "Skipper! Torpedoes!"

Hillary looked at the submarine while dropping the lanyard from his hand. He also saw the white lines racing toward his vessel. "Grover! Get the men out of the engine spaces!"

Hillary then turned to round the end of the ship's superstructure to the portside, hoping to release the straps holding the lifeboat in that davit. Looking up and forward as he unfastened the first buckle of the lifeboat's strap, he saw the last aircraft, the last one that left the cavern and fought the other aircraft, fly off to the northwest, leaving behind a dense trail of thick black smoke. "I don't know who you, are but thank you."

Just then the ship under his feet exploded, and it seemed like he was being launched to the moon. He knew not how high he flew, but it seemed like he was in a spaceship of silence. While flying, he saw, in slow motion, parts of his ship and parts of his men, lofting into the air about him. All the suspended parts were bathed in a reddish-orangish glow. Along with hearing no noise, he also felt no pain. Suddenly, everything went black. How long he remained in the abyss he did not know, but when he emerged from the darkness, he found himself coughing up saltwater and oil. He also heard the screams of surviving men. He opened his eyes to burning oil and ears to the interruptive bursts of a machine gun. Like swipes from the Grim Reaper's scythe, the bullets collected the day's quota for its voracious handler. He saw the main deck of his ship awash with air and soot erupting from the ship's Number Two smokestack towering over him. Realizing now that his ship was dead, along with most of his men, he knew he had to stay alive, so that he could tell somebody what occurred on this island. As he kicked his legs to get out from under the ever-increasing tilting smokestack, he also kicked through the thick layer of bunker oil and flotsam. After a minute, his head rammed into something hard. He turned to face the upside-down lifeboat. Grabbing the gunwale, he pushed himself under while taking one last look at his command. All he saw was the top of his bridge as it slipped under the oil and debris, and the submarine on the other side. Pushing himself underwater, he came out of the water on the inside, but he could still hear the muted screams of men and gunfire. All he could do now was to try and survive this slaughter.

* * *

Ten minutes after the torpedoes exploded, the machine gunner removed his finger from the weapon's trigger for the last time, letting the smoking barrel tilt downward. Floating around the stationary submarine, in the oil-layered water, were bodies, pieces of bodies, and other debris, including the upside-down lifeboat drifting toward the beach. Rising air and oil bubbles escaping the now-sunken ship disturbed the flotsam.

Now that the sky above them was vacant of fighting aircraft and the destroyer was resting on the seabed under them, Vostok gave one more order. "Stow your weapon," he said as he turned to look at the deck aft of the conning tower. His feet kicked the spent brass layering the deck of the conning tower while doing so. He saw two of his men using a line to haul one man from the water. That man wore black socks, civilian trousers and shirt, a military cartridge belt with an empty holster, and a coat of bunker oil.

The man looked up at the conning tower and saluted. Vostok returned the salute. "Captain Hugh Rodham, I presume!"

"The very same!"

"Good. Get below and scrape off some of that oil," Vostok stated. Turning his attention to the hatch at his feet and kicking a couple of spent casings into the submarine, he spoke to his officer. "Radio the others and tell them the destroyer is gone. Suggest sending up crews and boats to start collecting any evidence of an American presence. And our men as well."

Two hours later, Rodham, now showered and wearing a new set of civilian clothes, sat at the wardroom table of the tramp steamer captained by Lagos. Rodham held a whiskey in his hand. The men around him were equally armed.

"It has turned out to be quite a day," Utkin said as he looked at the plate-sized chronometer mounted on the white-painted bulkhead of the ship's wardroom. "But our cleanup this afternoon is going well, which bodes for a successful departure from this island."

"What about Dooley?" Rodham asked. "And the Countess?"

"Don't forget the other man," Popov spoke up while turning to look at Rodham. "The one you call Fowler. He stood in the nose of the machine firing a revolver and automatic pistol like he was Allan Quatermain taking down a charging bull elephant on the Serengeti."

"I only met him a couple of times while aboard that ship," Rodham replied after sipping his whiskey, "but he came off as somebody that could match your submarine raiders."

Utkin answered their concerns while inspecting his whiskey. "In a way it is too bad my men did not have the chance to tangle with that man. Anyway, I, like most here at this table, saw the midair explosion, which accounts for the missing dynamite and fuses. For what purposes Dooley and Fowler had for the dynamite we are thankful to not have found out." Utkin paused to look at the American. "So, you never ran into Dooley while in Russia?"

"Only at Regimental parade," Rodham answered, "when he received his medals. That said, despite his grandiose citations, he was still flesh and blood."

"You are correct," Utkin offered. "I doubt he, or any of those three, survived that explosion. And while I welcome their demise, I also appreciate his companionship leading up to this morning. I will relish the events of this morning during our transit."

"How so?" Bogdanovich asked.

Utkin appreciated his whiskey. "Whether Roman gladiators or Sioux warriors, there has always been this sentiment: the greater the opponent, the greater the victory."

The others paused to look at their glasses.

"What I mean," Utkin continued, "is that we were like a well-trained team made of vigorous players, but one that has faced only scrimmage teams. You mentioned earlier, Issak, that Dooley has bloodied our noses.

I argue he trounced us within an inch of our lives. Dooley was quite an efficient pilot, and, perhaps, a teacher. By all accounts, Countess Zeta Tolstoy was proficient with that Lewis gun aboard the airplane. And the fact that they were aided by a chief petty officer armed with a shotgun and two pistols. I lost more than half of my air assault commando, and we do not have one flying machine left unscathed. This morning's beating has provided me with a month's worth of reflection that I will put to ink and paper during our transit across the Pacific. When we arrive in Latin America, we will have an updated field manual with new direction. For that reason, I salute our adversaries. *Caveat Emptor*! Winner beware!"

"I thought the phrase meant buyer beware," Captain Lagos said.

Utkin reflected on what Dooley said days before when back on the submarine. "I'm just repeating a piece of sage advice I received from across the felt."

Utkin, and the others raised their whiskey glasses.

"What do you propose now, Major?" Bogdanovich asked as he lowered his glass.

Utkin answered. "I propose we do the following, but first, I would like to commend Captain Hugh Rodham on his commitment to our cause. You stood on the deck of that ship in the face of withering gunfire. Your courage will be known to other family members. By the way, when was the last time you shaved?"

Rodham smiled in return. "Yesterday morning. Why?"

"Good. What I propose is for Captain Vostok and his full crew to take onboard Sergei's aircraft now that the engine has been replaced, Captain Rodham, and that damaged lifeboat from that American destroyer, along with a life jacket from that same vessel. Lash the lifeboat to the deck like we did with the submarine raider boats. After that, I suggest you, Vostok, get underway as soon as possible and go to the area where the American announced his floundering. Once in the proximity, keep an eye out for a ship, and when you sight a ship on the horizon, fire a flare and put Rodham over the side while wearing his oil-soaked clothing, the lifeboat, and life jacket and submerge. Your rescue, a bedraggled survivor identified as an American army officer, wearing a US Navy life jacket and aboard a lifeboat from the USS Decatur over two hundred miles from here, will solidify the captain's initial Mayday call and the fact of his floundering in stormy seas. You will state the ship broke in half and only you survived.

"Once Rodham is rescued, Vostok will turn and continue to his first scheduled refueling stop and wait for Igor's ship. I, along with my submarine raider commando, what is left of my air assault commando, my other men, and what parts of airplanes we can still salvage, will board Igor's ship for that same transit. The British yacht, with three crewmen, will follow. We can switch out crews during our transit. In the meantime, we will continue to collect any evidence of the American presence on this island, along with the bodies of our men. The evidence, and our men, can be properly disposed of later."

"What about the islanders?" Rodham asked. "They've seen quite a bit, which will conflict with the floundering story and my presence on a lifeboat hundreds of miles from here."

Utkin sipped his whiskey before answering, "I believe that our long-winded ruse, which we started months ago, will continue to serve us well. Just like a well-composed concert. When the dust settles, the Americans will have two scenarios. You may do your best, Hugh, at convincing your superiors of one. But if there is an investigation here, then we can leave pointing to rogue White Russians having a falling out. A time-worn domestic issue that Mr. Borodin can facilitate through the rumor mill in Shanghai, and one I can facilitate to the islanders. Due to your efforts in Shanghai, there is a storm of rumors tearing through Shanghai concerning a group of White Russian traitors aboard a stolen submarine, who raided an estate and killed three dozen Bolsheviks and are now in the possession of a cache of diamonds, including the Romanov sapphire, and such a collection of scoundrels naturally fell victim to greed. But if any blame is attached to White Russians for the destruction of an American naval vessel and its crew, that is even better, as it will absorb from the Bolsheviks. A situation that will stand us in good stead."

Pausing to look at Borodin and Lagos he continued. "Since your forecastle has been repaired, I would ask that you both return to Shanghai to resume your previous positions and solidify our ruse. Meanwhile, myself and Captain Vostok and our men, will comingle with the millions returning from war and disappear into the turmoil of a post-war decade and make occasional and appropriate appearances to advertise our commitment to fighting Bolshevism. I would ask everybody to wait for postcards alerting you to family reunions."

The men nodded as Utkin continued. "Although we will destroy what is needed to disguise our technical infrastructure and capabilities, we will leave behind copies of Russian literature in the Brooks House: Literature outlawed by the Bolshevik government. We should also place Russian-made materials, such as life jackets and clothing along the eastern shore. While authorities across the globe are looking for rogue White Russians such as myself and Captain Vostok, our movement will have the latitude to meld with American society and its criminal underworld."

"Thank God for Prohibition," Lagos said.

"I agree," Utkin replied. "Also, since Dooley saw fit to throw our dynamite in the water inside the north cavern possibly compromising its effect, I would ask that you divide your supply with my parachute solders to collapse both caverns."

Vostok smiled as he brought his whiskey glass to his lips. He finished his liquor and stood pushing the chair back as he did. He was joined by Rodham and Popov, and as they turned to leave, Utkin spoke to Rodham.

"And I will make sure you get a replacement copy of Huckleberry Finn."

Rodham nodded as he and the others left the wardroom, Utkin turned to Captain Bogdanovich. "How are your repairs going?"

"Well," Bogdanovich replied as he leaned back in his chair with his whiskey, "my custom-made propellers are fine, but the damage to the engine room, however, is a bit more problematic. Yet, we will be able to complete those repairs along with completing our efforts at creating our secret compartments and submarine doors in a day or so."

"Very good," Utkin appreciated with a smile. "Very good."

Chapter 39

AS SOON AS FOWLER fired the first of the rounds from his buffalo-killing revolver, Dooley saw smoke pour from Popov's engine. Dooley was also able to see the destruction of the American destroyer under him as well. He looked through the windshield and saw Fowler slumped against the mounted Lewis gun. He could not see Fowler's face but understood and gave the man a minute. While there were no more aircraft to deal with, there were three ships, with their crews, and men from the commandos watching them fly away. Grabbing the measuring stick he poked Fowler in the leg. After a second, Fowler brought his hands to his face before ducking down and turning to look up at Dooley. The draft going through the machine tore at Fowler's short, black hair and reddened his eyes and cheeks.

"I know what you're thinking, but we got to get out of here first!" Dooley yelled as he looked down at Fowler's red eyes. "And without being followed!"

Fowler nodded as he holstered his pistols. "Keep flying this thing but act like we're having problems! Slow down a bit too!" Without waiting for an answer Fowler reached to his right and released the clips holding the toolbox in place. Unsnapping the lid, he dumped the contents on the deck and selected a hammer and a screwdriver. Fowler closed the lid and used the tools to punch holes in the lid. "Give me that flare gun and two flares."

Reaching for the items, Dooley handed them to Fowler who, still on his knees, crawled into the aft hatch with the toolbox and tools. Still sitting in his seat, piloting the aircraft, he looked over his shoulder at the chief and Zeta.

Standing up in the rear compartment, Fowler unsheathed his bayonet and used its blade to tear at the bunk's bedding, stuffing shreds of wool blanket and mattress wadding into the toolbox before sticking his head into the small engine compartment aft of that. It was then Dooley noticed the shotgun-like blast in the aircraft's tail. He also now realized how lucky they were that Popov's aim was off just a bit. Returning his attention to Fowler, they saw him pull an oilcan and a pair of leather gloves from the compartment. Unscrewing the cap of the oilcan, he laid the open can on top of the wool and wadding. Dooley saw Fowler's hair being blown about by the draft and realized what the navy chief was up to.

Fowler placed one of the flares into the toolbox and loaded the other one into the pistol. Sticking the barrel into the toolbox lengthwise, and at an angle, he closed the lid and placed his knee on it. Averting his eyes, he pulled the trigger and immediately it seemed like the entire aft section of the plane would have been enveloped in a cloud of choking smoke, but for the draft rushing through the airplane pushing the oily cloud out through Zeta's gun position and the perforations in the tail. Now wearing the leather gloves, Fowler crawled forward, stopping in between the seats. Handing the flare gun back to Dooley, he said, "Give me another flare."

Dooley nodded as he looked in the compartment behind them. He saw, indeed, a great volume of oily smoke escaping up through the rear of the aircraft. At the same time, Fowler used his bayonet to snap the bands crimping the case of dynamite and the fuses in the nose compartment. From there he went to assemble the bundle of dynamite and flares, wrapping them together from a spool of wire from the toolbox. As he finished, Dooley commented on the length of the fuse. "Don't you think that fuse is a bit short?"

Fowler replied as he hefted the bundle in his hand, "I'll make the bombs around here!" Without waiting for a response, Fowler crawled back into the aft compartment and the billowing cloud of noxious smoke. Unseen to Dooley and Zeta, he wired the toolbox shut with wire and tethered the bundle to its handle using that same length of wire. Now standing, he stepped up on the ladder Zeta just got done using and reached into his trousers pocket for his cigarette lighter.

* * *

An hour later, Dooley, Zeta, and Fowler sat on a piece of exposed basalt not much larger than a baseball diamond, and only about two feet above the sea. It was covered with seagull shit, fish bones, and scales. They also took advantage of the shade offered by the rotting wooden hull of a motorized fishing smack. The faded writing on the bow and transom was in Japanese. Being so low to the water's edge, it was no surprise that the island was able to snare the vessel. Tilted over on its side, the three people sat under the overhead superstructure. The airplane that brought them to this island was tied to its broken-off bowsprit and covered with a roll of camouflage netting they found onboard.

"That was a good landing, Dooley," Zeta said as she reached into the can of ship's biscuits. "You did it like you've been doing it for years."

"I guess it was just one of many firsts today," Dooley replied as he sipped from Fowler's canteen. "And I'm glad that mattress stuffing we plugged into those holes in the tail are holding."

"It's not the first time I've had to resort to such actions," Fowler said with exaggerated slowness as he turned to look at Zeta. Lowering his voice, he continued. "I remember one time, off Madagascar, I was a castaway, and—"

Dooley jumped in, interrupting the chief as he looked at Zeta as well, "The way I see it, we have three options."

"Just so you know I'm not one for running away from a fight," Fowler interjected as he reached into his musette bag and pulled out a can of sardines. "And no one's ever choked on my heel dust."

"I know, Chief, but we must face reality. First, look at our arms. I have my weapons and a musette bag with bullets, magazines for my Thompson, and a beat-up hand grenade."

"I've been meaning to ask," Fowler said, looking at Dooley with one eye narrowed. "What the hell are you doing with a Mary Jane in that musette bag anyhow?"

"Long story," Dooley answered, "but that's not the point. My point is, between you, I, and the airplane, we have enough weapons and bullets at least for one more stand-up fight. We could stay here, though. We have the lifeboat rations you arrived with, what we stole from the Brooks House, and the emergency rations aboard the flying machine including fishing tackle. Also, the fishing boat is great for trapping rainwater. Once the rations run out, we can catch and eat raw fish. However, any chances of a timely rescue are unlikely. I mean, most ship captains with any brains learned to avoid this area."

They paused to look at the hull towering over them before Dooley continued.

"We could also keep flying towards Japan, Formosa, or some islands in between, but the problem is those lands are still hundreds of miles away, and we used up half of our fuel just getting to this rock, which brings me to our last option: we can use the other half of that fuel to get back to that island and finish what we started."

Zeta replied with a smile, "So, what are we going to when we get there?"

"That's still up in the air as far as I'm concerned," Dooley replied. "We could go in with guns blazing or we could go in and hide out. You know, wait until they leave."

"Well, all I know is," Fowler said as he put the unopened sardine can back into his musette bag, "I've got know what happened to my men and my captain."

* * *

The late afternoon sun inched its way toward the western sky and, now clear of dogfighting flying machines and clouds, it proved to be an idyllic sunset for those on the fantail of the tramp steamer that brought Borodin to the island. He sat at the table watching men aboard the anchored British yacht work at preparing the vessel for a trans-Pacific voyage. He enjoyed strawberry wine at the same time. It was from that spot, and a bottle of wine earlier, when he watched Vostok's submarine, the airplane, and an upside-down lifeboat tied to its deck depart the island.

"I must say, gentlemen," Borodin said as he raised his glass of wine, "the wine and cider is most excellent, and the beef is beyond reproach; therefore, I will surely miss this little niche."

"So, will we," Utkin replied as he looked over at Borodin, "however, our plan must continue. Starting with some of the more notable diamonds from Vladivostok. They will stand us in good stead once you get back in Shanghai and disperse them strategically. Zeta's father should be able to recognize the ones that make their way to his shop through fences."

Pulling the wine glass from his lips, Igor reached for an open bottle on the table. "My modifications are going well, and you can have your men start boarding when you like."

"I'll have them finish with tidying things up," Utkin said, pulling his wine glass from his lips. "They can start boarding this evening."

* * *

"Last chance to change your minds," Dooley said as he sat in the pilot's seat with his fingers on an ignition switch. Zeta sitting in the other cockpit seat, and Fowler sitting in the nose compartment facing them while forcing lengths of fuses into sticks of dynamite, smiled.

"Like you said," Zeta replied, "if we time it right, we can use lights from the ship on the railway to guide us back to the island once we're close enough."

"All I know is that you'd better be just as good with landing this thing," Fowler added, "without its engines, and at night."

Dooley nodded as he turned the ignition and listened to the port engine cough and sputter to a start. Behind the exhaust flume, the sun was already disappearing beyond the dark blue line of the horizon. Ahead of them, their fate awaited.

Chapter 40

THE LANDING WENT flawlessly and before the people aboard the aircraft knew it, the bow of the machine ground into the gravel of the beach. The same beach where the Russian motorboat landed to pick up the crews from the machines in the now collapsed cavern. The only light available, other than the compass and cockpit's red light, came from the stars above, which was enough to profile the beach and the tumble of rocks at the cavern's entrance. Two miles to the south, they saw flashes of yellowish deck lights from the ship still on the railway. Without a word, the three of them, working from the machine's hatches, spread the roll of camouflage netting over the aircraft. After Fowler and Dooley gathered their weapons and a coil of rope, they climbed out of the nose compartment hatch, one at a time, and slid over the side and onto the beach. After an hour confined in the aircraft during their return, any sounds were difficult to hear over the ringing in their ears.

"Looks like they're still at work," Fowler almost yelled out as he adjusted his weapons and web gear about his torso. "Whatever they're doing must be important."

"By the way that was a good landing," Zeta said as she joined the men, her voice almost as loud as Fowler's. "You seem to be a natural."

"Thanks, but we need to watch our voices," Dooley replied as he leaned his Thompson against the netting and pulled his shingle axe from his belt. "Fowler, tie the plane to the nearest tree. Zeta, help me gather tree branches."

"Are you sure they won't come back here," Zeta asked, "and find this airplane?"

Dooley replied, "They imploded their caverns. Also, I think they've got more important things to deal with."

Zeta nodded, and without another word, the three went to work. A few minutes later, they found the path leading toward the marine railway. As they walked in silence, with Fowler in the lead pointing his shotgun in front of him, they all thought the same thing: Somewhere behind them, over their left shoulders, was the ship that brought Fowler to this island. No one talked about it, but they all wondered if any survivors made it to shore and were now in hiding.

The three of them continued to walk. The night was comfortable, and the stars were bright. It seemed so pleasant now, especially with Zeta walking next to Dooley. The army sergeant listened to the night as the ringing in his ears started to go away, letting him hear the chirp of an insect and the scurrying of a lizard. At the same time, though, Dooley started to hear something else. His grip tightened on the Thompson. He looked at Fowler's back. "Chief?"

"I heard it, Dooley," Fowler replied quietly as he stepped off to the right.

"What the hell are you doing back here, Ernst?" a form asked as he stepped away from a tree trunk. "I got the feeling you got away on that flying machine. You should've stayed away."

The two men, with their faces a foot apart, nodded and smiled at each other. After a second, the man spoke again. "Got a butt?"

Fowler reached into his shirt pocket. Dooley and Zeta failed to see the relief in Fowler's face.

While waiting, the man turned to face Dooley and Zeta. "And who are you two?"

Dooley and Zeta saw a handsome man wearing what was left of a torn khaki uniform, a pistol belt with an empty holster, and a coating of dried oil.

Answering for them, Fowler gave the man a Camel. "What we have here, Skipper, is Sergeant Thomas Dooley, late of the US Army and of Brooklyn. The young lady is Countess Zeta Tolstoy, late of Shanghai and imperial Russia, and we came back to see what we could do to stop whatever is going on here. Is there anybody else? Busachek? Krivor?"

"Sorry," Hillary said as he reached out for the cigarette. After taking a light from Fowler, Hillary inhaled deeply while looking at Dooley. "Lieutenant Rance Hillary, captain of that ship and crew you helped try to save. Thanks for risking your lives, but it seems a wasted effort."

"I, we, tried to do our best," Dooley said, "and I am sorry for your loss. Also, I don't mean to be rude sir, but do you think having a smoke right now is a good idea?"

"They've been preoccupied all afternoon," Hillary replied. "Besides, as loud as you three have been, they would've been here by now if they weren't."

"So, what's doing, Rance?" Fowler asked as he lit his own cigarette.

"I know of a place where I can explain and get something to drink at the right time."

An hour later, they found themselves sitting in the same spot where Fowler and Dooley sat in what seemed like a century ago: next to the privy behind the Brooks House, which was now lifeless. The only evidence of life nearby was the occasional glint of light and clang of noise coming in from the marine railway. When they first sat down, while sharing wine, cheese, and bread, they watched Tin-tin pull a wagon heaped with duffels and supplies down the road to the railway. While one man sat in the bench seat holding the reins, other men walked behind the wagon. Some wore camouflaged coveralls and others wore loose-fitting raider uniforms.

"They've been cleaning up any evidence of their presence all afternoon. Now they're moving their soldiers to that ship on the railway," Hillary explained as he lifted a bottle to his lips. "They've also been busy recovering the bodies of my crew and theirs, along with floating debris or from the shoreline. Lastly, they either loaded what aircraft or parts of aircraft we didn't turn into Swiss cheese on that ship. Or sunk the scraps offshore. The bottom line is that the ship seems to have a special mission ahead of it. The other tramp steamer and yacht are still at the western dock, but it looks like they're departing with minimal crews."

"So, you came here to find your men. The ones on the sailboats?" Dooley reiterated.

"And to figure out why a naval officer tried to kill me," Fowler replied. "But we didn't know we'd run into an island full of Bolsheviks and frogman solders."

"Well," Hillary continued, "they are fixing up that British yacht and the submarine left with one of those short, June bug-looking airplanes, along with one of my wrecked lifeboats strapped to its deck. I don't know how they're going to implement their plans, but I'll bet it has something to do with Prohibition."

"So, you had a chance to figure out why that railway was so important?" Dooley asked as he reached for a piece of cheese. Grabbing a large piece, he leaned back and held it out for Zeta.

Hillary answered, "They're cutting out sections of the underwater hull and making water-tight doors. I guess so that they can deploy your frogmen soldiers or receive those flying submarines carrying contraband alcohol. That's how I figured out the Prohibition aspect."

"So, between us, we can fill out an encyclopedia for Uncle Sam," Dooley continued as Zeta broke off a piece of cheese. "The question then is, do we just lay low and let them go?"

Hillary responded, "But the problem is we do not know how long it will take for another ship to just happen by this island. If the Navy did not receive my Mayday calls, we could be written off as another victim of that storm. If they did receive my calls, I sent out Maydays saying we're sinking hundreds of miles from here, so my commander will be confused as hell. In the meantime, whatever they got planned will be in place when we do reach civilization."

"There's still that British yacht, but whatever happens, the Reds will be buried in so deep in American society the government will never ferret them out," Fowler finished, coughing slightly. "Also, I've never been one to take an ass-kicking without returning one in kind."

"You say you have some gas left in your machine," Hillary asked as he lifted his wine bottle.

"Yes," Dooley said as he looked at his trench watch.

"And it is a flying boat and underwater machine? With miniature torpedoes onboard? Along with a case of dynamite? And two Lewis guns? And several full pan magazines?"

"Yes," Dooley replied.

"Well," Hillary continued. "I know something about flying airplanes and submarines, so I can help. And Fowler knows something about explosives. And all of us know something about Lewis guns. But what about the damage to that flying machine? You plugged the holes with mattress stuffing, but we need something more substantial. What about the engine?"

"I looked at the motor and fixed a couple of things," Dooley replied as he bit into the piece of cheese in his hand. "And it sounds like you're planning on using that thing to attack the ship on the railway. Am I correct?"

"Yes, you are," Hillary replied. "And before you ask, the four of us attacking the ship from shore would only kick over the wasp nest and waste assets. Remember what you said about all those men onboard. Also, having Ernst plant dynamite to blow up the railway would just piss them off. And we still have men from the steamer and the yacht to deal with."

"By now, I think we have a rough idea of how many men we would be facing from that ship on the railway. What about the other two?"

"After what I've seen today," Hillary replied, "I'm guessing about a dozen crew on the steamer and three men on the yacht. About fifteen in total."

"Three men on a seaworthy sailing vessel," Fowler surmised, "with a radio set?"

Dooley swallowed the cheese in his mouth and nodded before continuing. "I can see a plan coming together and have an idea of what to replace that mattress stuffing with. That's if the Bolsheviks left stray items behind. Let's finish our wine and cheese and I'll check. You guys get more supplies from the basement. I'll meet you back at the airplane. We can attack at first light."

"Sounds fine," Hillary replied, "but if you happen to run into a spare sidearm, I wouldn't complain. I feel foolish walking around with an empty holster."

Dooley looked over at Fowler's two sidearms.

"I've gotten used to having a two-gun rig," Fowler replied. "I'm sure you can come up with an extra pistol. And while you're at it, I need something for the dynamite. Unless it's packed under the ship's keel, its explosive power is weak. And it's not much of an anti-personnel weapon by itself either. I need something to wrap it in. You know like a hand grenade."

Dooley looked first at Hillary, then Fowler. "You also want me to find an egg for your beer while I'm at it."

Minutes later, Dooley approached the shelter where Mashka conducted his experiments. He entered through a side door, which he left open behind him. Just like the other night, there were a few stray items left behind, including the nuts, bolts, and washers Fowler dumped on the workbench. Thinking back to Fowler's request, Dooley also grabbed a pair of wire snips as well. He set his Thompson on the workbench so he could use his hands to scoop the nuts, bolts, and washers into the musette bag hanging off his shoulder. He then spent another minute looking around for other useful items.

As he was about to turn to pick up his Thompson, he stopped. Something blocked out the starlight coming through the door behind him. He turned to see a figure standing in the doorway. The person wore a loose-fitting uniform along with unbuckled web gear draped over his shoulders and hanging from around his waist. The unbuckled belt contained a holstered Nagant pistol and knuckle duster trench fighting knife. He was armed with three other items: a sharpened entrenching tool clutched in one hand, a Fedorov submachine gun slung over his right shoulder, and a broad smile on his face.

"Good evening, Sergeant Thomas Dooley."

"So, you do speak English," Dooley replied. "No need for a Lewis gun?"

"Not this evening," Morda answered as he stepped back from the doorway and under the stars above. He looked up at the luminaries as he stooped to lay his Fedorov on the grass. Straightening, he slid his web gear from his shoulders and around his waist and tossed it to his left with one hand while holding his sharpened entrenching tool with the other. Dooley noted Morda's stance while remembering some of his readings. Yards behind him, the trees of the forest stood like legionnaires from the Praetorian Guard. Above them, the overarching mountain continued to stare at them like Cesar Nero himself, and the stars were like Rome's wealthy class looking forward to spectacular combat. It seemed as if Morda were a gladiator enjoying the noiseless roar of an adoring audience.

"I also speak Latin, Turkish and Greek. However, my linguistic ability is not important right now. What is important is how the next few minutes will end as I have no need for a cheater's weapon. I am armed with edged steel and lethal reactions instead. Also, I know you are wondering if you have the time to get to your Thompson before I can loft this entrenching tool through the door and into your torso."

Dooley sighed. "I'm disappointed that you think I'd use an automatic gun while walking onto the sand. I am also dismayed that you would think so little of me that it would take me minutes to settle this issue. After all, I wouldn't want to cheat our audience."

Morda looked over both his shoulders setting his eyes on the ranks of trees behind him. *"Veritas Odit Moras."*

"What does that mean?" Dooley said, unbuckling his cartridge belt while grabbing his shingle axe. After letting the cartridge belt drop to the floor, he stooped down to withdraw his hunting knife from its sheath. With a weapon in both hands, he stepped into the door frame.

Morda took another step back before answering. "It means 'truth hates delay.' Like the gladiators facing off while standing in the sands of the arena, pleasing the wanton bloodlust of senators above and the pedestrians below, I must know the truth. I've had no tension with you, but you have proven your worth in our presence, and you have proven that Major Utkin continues to be a good judge of men. Like the most proficient *lanista*, he selected you from the hordes crowding Shanghai, just as he culled me from the rabble overtaking the streets of Moscow holding banners and shooting their rifles in the air. He has selected us for the world stage. Although our audience will not have the opportunity to gossip about our fight to others at public wine houses. You and I are like gems sequestered under the cuff of a highwayman's boot. Forever priceless in existence, but a presence unknown to those around the wearer."

"So, you're a poet too? A romantic?" Dooley asked as he looked over Morda's shoulder.

"Neither. I am a victim of misplaced time. A castaway," Morda continued while shifting the entrenching tool in his hand. "While we embraced the long walk and exited onto the sand from the tunnel, we were not showered by scented scarves dropped on our heads by the wives of merchants. Nor admired by decorated legionnaires or blessed by the prayers and touches of pedestrians as we stepped past them. Our only audience are the over-indulged stars above and the stalwart pines at eye level along with a lonely swayback, and the prominent stare of a time-worn stone master. But I am not here for their approving eyes."

"Ah, the lethal rapture that drew special men to the sand," Dooley said as he stepped from the door frame. He used the hand holding the shingle axe to lift the strap of the musette bag over his head. Throwing it to the ground in front of him, it spilled its contents. He looked at the Mary Jane lying on the grass as he continued. "Gladiators entered the arena for any number of driven purposes: fame, glory; emancipation, to pay off a debt, or to earn living. I entered this stadium two weeks ago for five hundred dollars." Dooley finished by rotating his wrists just as he heard the soft thud of hooves. He looked to his right and saw Tin-tin making his way across the meadow behind Morda. The pony snorted.

"I disagree, Sergeant Dooley," Morda continued as he raised the entrenching tool above him, stretching his shoulders. "You did not enter this stadium for five hundred dollars. You stepped onto the sand for the same reason I did."

Shifting the entrenching tool in his hand one more time, Morda invited Dooley onto the level ground by taking one more step backward and widening his stance. Dooley accepted the proposal. As he stepped forward, he thought back to the nightly training on the deck of the submarine. Both were right-handed, had extremely sharp weapons, were fit, young men, and watched each other during the week aboard the submarine. Lastly, Dooley remembered the walk with Zeta when they saw Morda conducting his own exercises on the north side of the island. Dooley noted no deficiencies with

Morda. Did Morda note any deficiencies in him?

Now they were separated by only two yards, and the two men settled into a quiet moment while continuing to size each other up. They slowly poised their weapons as they did.

"How did you know I was here?" Dooley asked as he looked over Morda's shoulder at Tin-tin. The pony was swishing its tail and quietly snorting. Dooley also noticed the pony's moving legs.

"I just wanted to have one more walk around," Morda answered, shifting the entrenching tool in his hand. "To enjoy the quiet evening before boarding that ship on the railway. I let the others go before me, and I saw a shadow move under the starlight. I thought it was the pony at first, which seems to have taken a liking to you, by the way. Anyway, I wish you had seen my face when I recognized it was you. We all thought you were destroyed in that explosion. Which leads to the question: if you survived the explosion, what of the others."

"I was the only one," Dooley lied as he took a step toward Morda. "The tail of the airplane blew off, and I was at the controls. Everybody else fell out of the back. I was able to turn the thing around and fly back part of the way."

"And you swam the rest of the way?" Morda finished as he took a step toward Dooley. "That's quite a swim."

"I had the wind at my back," Dooley said as he lifted his shingle axe. At the same time, Tin-tin snorted again, and Morda narrowed his eyes. Suddenly he opened them wide, just as Dooley lurched forward. Morda responded by side stepping and raising the entrenching tool at the same time. Bringing it down, and across, he tried to use the flat side to knock the shingle hammer axe out of Dooley's hand. He missed the axe but connected with the side of Dooley's head, dropping Dooley to his knees.

"Oh, come now," Morda said as he recovered from his swing and took a new stance. "You have proved to be worthwhile opponent throughout this day. Why stop—"

But before he could continue, a shadow stole up behind Morda and brought down a large stoneware jug on the back of his head. Just as the stoneware shattered, splattering everybody with strawberry wine, Dooley leapt to his feet and drove his knife through Morda's ribs. An explosion of breath blew against Dooley's face as he looked into Morda's wide eyes. "Sorry to cheat you. This foreplay should have been more enduring."

Morda opened his mouth to speak, but only thick blood came out. Then his eyes closed.

Dooley kept the blade in Morda's chest as he guided him to the ground. Once on the ground, Dooley removed his blade slowly and stood. After a few seconds, he spoke. "I appreciate the help, but somehow it felt like cheating."

Zeta, with her index finger still in the neck ring of the broken stone jug, looked down at the body. "The secret of victory lies in the organization of the non-obvious."

"You're going to make on hell of a Pinkerton," Dooley replied. "By the way why'd you come here?"

"Sorry for cheating him out of a virtuous combat, but we do not have much time," Zeta answered. "And I only followed Tin-tin. I guess he wanted another bucket of wine."

Dooley shifted eyes from Morda's body to Tin-tin, who stood next to Zeta. He was licking the wine-splattered grass. "But we have time to replace that wine with a fresh jug. It's the least we can do. Get another jug and tell the others. I'll hide Morda's body and join you at the privy."

"They've already left for the airplane," Zeta said as she obeyed, leaving Dooley and Tin-tin alone for the time.

Turning around, Dooley gathered his musette bag and reentered the shelter. Making sure he had everything he needed, he slung the Thompson across his back and went to hide Morda's body. Under Tin-tin's supervision, he dragged Morda's body and gear to the tree line and returned to the privy carrying Morda's web gear and weapons. Minutes later, Tin-tin was lapping up a bucket of well-deserved cider. Dooley was petting its neck as Zeta, carrying a full, and bumpy, flour sack over her shoulder, reached out to rub the pony's nose one last time.

CHAPTER 41

WHILE MORDA'S DEATH seems a bit anticlimactic, he's still going to be missed, if not now definitely at their next muster," Dooley offered as he sat on the sand next to their flying machine. He shared a canteen of water with Zeta. The four of them sat with their weapons to discuss the next phase of their plan.

"I agree, and thanks for the Russian's weapons," Hillary said as he poked through Dooley's musette bag for the nuts, bolts, and washers. Holding up the shoe by the toe, he asked, "But what are you doing with a Mary Jane?"

Dooley looked up at the shoe and the huge heel. Thinking back to a comment Fowler made about his heel dust, Dooley replied, "Just drop it in the sand."

Hillary sighed as he dropped it in the sand next to him. Continuing his digging, he pulled out other items, including a hand grenade and a box of cartridges and placed them next to the shoe. "I see what you mean about machines so fantastic that they defy reality but so simple in construction they can be repaired by any jughead with a wrench. At the same time, though, I'm surprised that they didn't have a complete damage control kit. They knew they could get shot at."

"Yes," Dooley replied, "but they probably never thought they'd be shot at by their own machine armed with a thirty-seven-millimeter cannon firing shells packed with shot the size of golf balls. The hardware in their bolt kit was meant to replace snapped aluminum bolts and plug bullet holes no bigger than standard thirty-caliber rounds. Anyway, did you have enough time to figure out how to help me fight it?"

"Well, from what I understand," Hillary answered as he started to fill his shirt pockets with the hardware, "you've been able to fight that thing on your own."

"I don't mind sharing the controls," Dooley responded as he took the canteen from Zeta's hand. "After all, you're a ship's captain. I was only an infantry sergeant." Taking a swallow, he handed the canteen to Fowler, who was busy wiping down Harrison's forty-five with an oily rag.

Fowler accepted the canteen and placed it next to a stick the length of an arm and wrapped with barbed wire. He went back to wiping down the weapon. It was as if he were making a show of it. "While you two are plugging the holes and getting the machine ready, the Countess and I will get the dynamite bombs ready. I see that you brought back British barbed wire. I sure wished you had found German barbed wire; better steel equals more shrapnel." Pausing for a second, Fowler continued. "You know this reminds me of a time down Borneo way. That was before you became the skipper, Rance. Anyway, I was about to—"

Zeta interrupted Fowler. "How's your head, Dooley? I heard the hit."

"Well," Dooley replied, "since I had to have had a thick skull to get into this mess, the flat side of that thing didn't bother me none."

"You were lucky he used the flat side and not the edge," Zeta added.

"He didn't want to end it too soon, and that was his mistake," Dooley replied while turning to smile at Zeta. "By the way, that was a pretty neat trick, hiding behind Tin-tin."

"I remember reading about American mountain men sneaking up on herds of elk hidden by their horses," Zeta smiled as she replied. "Since animals can't count, it was easy. I guess they were done with Tin-tin and let him go. He found us behind the privy, and I figured you could give him one more bucket of wine before we attacked the ship. That's where I found you two, and since Morda was busy enjoying the moment, I took advantage of his blunder."

Both paused to smile at each other.

Giving them a minute, Hillary, now with two pockets full of hardware along with more in his hands, spoke up. "Ernst, you can handle the dynamite bombs on your own. Countess, follow me. I'm going to give you a wrench to help. One of us needs to be in the water and the other person on the inside. Dooley, grab your gear and go down the path. You know what to do if somebody comes looking for Morda."

While Zeta and Dooley nodded, Fowler gave Hillary a sideways look as he holstered the forty-five. Reaching for the spool of barbed wire, Fowler saw Dooley reaching for his musette bag and the items next to it. "What about the Mary Jane? You hang onto it like it's a crown jewel."

Picking up the woman's shoe and hefting it, Dooley replied. "Don't know. Maybe it's my lucky shoe."

Minutes later, and a hundred yards away, Dooley found a fallen tree to sit behind. Looking down the moonlit path while holding his Thompson, he thought about the people behind him, worrying about one in particular. The minutes ticked by as he tried to think of every conceivable way to make sure she would get through this mess, but his thoughts were interrupted by Hillary.

"It'll be light soon."

Dooley looked up at the man. "Have a seat."

"Sure," Hillary said as he sat in the grass next to Dooley. Placing his Fedorov across the tree trunk, he continued. "It's about the countess, isn't it?"

"Is it that apparent?"

"It is. At least in her eyes. Don't worry. We won't let anything happen to her."

"She's young and deserves a chance," Dooley said.

"I know you're concerned about Zeta, but we also have a much bigger worry on our hands. A worry bigger than any of us," Hillary said as he picked at a blade of grass. "It's apparent you know what you're doing, and I hold myself in high regard. And I have a plan."

"What about Fowler? Would you trust him with our lives? Zeta's life?"

Hillary scoffed. "Ernst? Trust him with my life? Of course, yes. Now, would I trust him with my girlfriend, wife, or the key to my Bixby? No."

Dooley chuckled. "Well, I've heard about navy chiefs, but this one seems to take the cake, so him having keys to the liquor cabinet seems like a bad combination."

"Not such a bad combination with sticks of dynamite wrapped in barbed wire, though," Hillary replied. "Also, I've heard about army sergeants, but you don't seem as crusty as the picture I had in my mind."

"Give me time," Dooley answered. "But I know you didn't come here to compare navy chiefs and army sergeants. You have a plan?"

Minutes later, after having pushed the nose of the machine off the beach and into a growing dawn, Dooley watched as Fowler dropped his legs into the forward gun hatch. Reaching down, he saw Fowler straighten up with a Lewis gun in his hands. Seeing Fowler clip the loaded machine gun into its mount, Dooley reached for the starboard engine's ignition switch.

Although the easterly morning breeze was slight, Dooley still took advantage of it as he pushed the throttles forward. Taking off from a still sea while pointed toward a sun just now peeking over the horizon, everybody kept one eye on the facility to the south. Both Hillary and Dooley, strapped in their cockpit seats, saw Fowler standing in the nose gun position enjoying the takeoff like he was a kid sitting in the first car of a roller coaster at Coney Island.

Taking his eyes off Fowler and his gauges for a second, Dooley looked over his right shoulder at Zeta who lay in the small bunk. Her head and legs were braced against the bunk's enclosure wall. She smiled at Dooley. Smiling back, he thought about the bunk behind him, on the other side of the bulkhead. This one was filled with camouflage netting topped with tree branches. Turning his head, he saw Hillary reviewing the switches and valves around his seat. Morda's submachine gun was bound to the lowered periscope by a length of barbed wire.

Leveling out at five hundred feet, Dooley turned the machine in a wide circle, giving Zeta time to set up her gun. He looked down at Fowler's feet and saw a dozen two-stick bundles wrapped in barbed wire from top to bottom, standing against each other in the open wooden case. Each bomb had a length of fuse inserted into a stick, but the length varied from ten inches to two feet. Seeing there was no going back, Dooley set his eyes on their target.

"Are you ready?" Dooley asked over the sounds of the engines. After having flown the machine more than once now, he seemed to have gotten used to the noise of the rpm.

"Just remember, come in kissing the seas," Hillary replied, "so we can send the first two torpedoes right up her stern but give yourself time enough to climb out."

"You got it," Dooley said as he adjusted his controls and went into shallow decline centering the marine railway square in windshield. Fowler's back and head blocked out the ship itself. "Can you imagine just what they're thinking right about now?"

* * *

On the bridge, Captain Lagos was taking the ship to the railway to help pull Bogdanovich's ship off the structure if needed. Now, with the installation of the underwater doors complete, Bogdanovich pumped as much weight toward the stern of his vessel, including fuel, making it possible for the ship to start its next planned phase. What machinery they could salvage was neatly stowed as far aft in the main cargo hold as possible as well, along with any evidence of an American torpedo boat presence. Only the British yacht, with its three-man crew finishing repairs on the vessel's engine, remained at anchor at the western beach.

Enjoying coffee while standing next to his helmsman, Lagos saw the silvery glint climb into the early morning sky. Trying to comprehend what he was looking at the hairs on the back of his neck snapped to attention. At the same time, he smiled. "Damn you, Sergeant Dooley."

On the eastern side of the island, at the marine railway, those awake heard the airplane well before seeing it. Those same men gathered on the ship's bridge, main deck, or beach asking each other about the morning's disturbance. Captain Bogdanovich stood on the bridge wondering the same thing himself. At first, he, like everybody else was stupefied, but when he saw the airplane come out of its wide turn and line its nose up on the stern, the astonishment vanished, and lucidity took over. Yelling over the bridge wing, he shouted out orders. "Get on the Maxims!"

The men on the deck scrambled to remount their weapons, which were stowed in their lockers near the mounts. They raced against the speed of the flying machine, but they lost. At less than two hundred yards away and barely above the still cobalt waters, Bogdanovich watched as the two outer doors for the torpedo tubes in the aircraft's nose erupted with brief fiery flashes. Those flashes were followed by miniature torpedoes shooting from the tubes and two balls of black smoke falling behind the oncoming aircraft.

Standing on the bridge wing, impotent as a newborn baby, Bogdanovich watched the two, four-foot, battery-powered torpedoes drop to the sea and race to the stern of his ship. The torpedoes with their little electric motors and propellers were automatically activated by the small powder charges that launched the weapons from their tubes. Knowing he could do nothing about them, he looked at the man standing in the nose of that machine and at the countess standing out of the aft hatch. Her blond hair blew in the trailing wind. Both held the pistol grips of the Lewis guns in their hands and pointed their barrels straight at him. Nodding in understanding, he stated aloud, "Damn you, Sergeant Dooley!"

Finishing his curse, he stepped forward to check the progress of his machine gun crews and felt the five-pound warheads explode against the stern. Although the explosive force of the warheads was minimal and whatever damage just occurred could be repaired at a proper shipyard, Bogdanovich knew they were not at a proper shipyard. He also knew that the machine had two more torpedoes. Lastly, he thought about the petrol in his aft fuel tanks.

With no exchange of machine gun fire, Bogdanovich watched as the machine flew over the island's forest and toward the island's salient feature. Just then, the ship's radio operator appeared on the bridge. "Sir?"

"Radio Captain Lagos. Tell him to standby to pull us off this thing and to sink us at sea."

The man nodded as he turned back to the brown door at the rear bulkhead of the bridge.

Watching the airplane start a wide circle around the stone-faced mountain, the captain reached for the ship's announcing handset hanging from its cradle above the chart table. "Comrades, finish getting those Maxims mounted as they are not yet finished with us. You commandos, gather your weapons and deploy ashore. Be prepared to throw up a wall of lead. We will depart this island today one way or another."

Hanging up the handset, he watched the flying machine disappear behind the mountain.

* * *

"Do you think they both hit? And went off?" Fowler asked as he pushed the case of standing dynamite bundles further into the forward part of the nose with his feet.

Zeta, who just poked her head into the cockpit looked out the side window at the mountain's southern face. For some reason it did not look as dour from this altitude. Sensing the stone edifice was giving them some sort of approval, she answered, "From my vantage point, I would say yes."

"Good," Hillary said as he closed the hand-sized torpedo tube cap and secured its latch. "Pretty ingenious, these fellows. Battery-powered torpedoes fired and activated by powder charges no bigger than a deck of cards." He looked over at Dooley who just finished pushing the torpedo on his side into the tube and the two copper rings inside the tube that held it in place. Securing the cap, he saw the short rope lanyard hanging from the percussion cap firing mechanism mounted to the side of the tube's cap.

Dooley looked out the side window and at the tramp steamer from the western wharf. "Seems like somebody might need a tow."

"And that yacht is still at anchor," Zeta offered, "like you hoped Mister Hillary."

Everybody looked out the forward windshield at the beach ahead of them.

"Let's hope it still remains at anchor, at least through the next ten minutes," Hillary answered as he looked at the barbed wire holding his Fedorov against the periscope. "Ernst, be ready to pull those outer door handles at my order. Zeta, remember short bursts."

With the second phase of their plan in motion and everybody at their stations, Dooley leaned the control stick to fly the airplane around the north side of the mountain, while angling up to increase his altitude. Coming around the other side, he leveled out at a thousand feet while pointing the nose of machine toward the direction of the tin-covered railway.

"Aim at the section where they removed the ribs," Hillary ordered.

Dooley nodded as he adjusted the grip on the control stick. "Zeta, get on your gun, and be prepared for a helluva dive. Hope you're not prone to airsickness."

"I have never been on an airplane before yesterday," she replied. "So, we will find out."

"Good," Dooley answered as he looked down at Fowler's back through the hatchway in the console. He also saw the top of his head just behind the Lewis gun in the nose's hatchway. "Be ready to start flinging out your dynamite bombs."

He heard a muffled reply.

Flying level at one thousand feet he watched as the railway got closer. When he felt the time was right his grip on the control stick tightened. He reached for the torpedo tube lanyard at the same time. He saw Hillary reach for his lanyard as well. "Now!"

Just as Dooley screamed that word, he pushed the control stick forward, and the nose of the airplane suddenly fell away. The result was the tin-covered railway filling the windshield in front of them. At the same time, he started to hear the short bursts of the Lewis gun above and behind him, knowing that when he went into his dive from this height, the angle would not allow the Maxim gunners to elevate their guns from under their shelter. He also knew that the dive presented the smallest profile possible to the men beneath them.

"Open!" Dooley ordered as he saw empty shell casings fly into the cockpit from the compartment behind him.

"Door open!" Fowler replied almost immediately.

Lining the center of the windshield on the open space in the railway's crib several hundred feet beneath him, Dooley and Hillary started to see the dynamite bombs, with lit fuses, popping out of the hatch. Fowler, with a survival candle inserted into the wooden case, lit the fuses as fast as he could and tossed them out even faster. The plan was that between the angle of the dive, the Lewis gun, and the bombs, they could avoid taking any rounds in the attack, thus sparing the machine's hull integrity. The efforts by Fowler and Zeta seemed to work. At five hundred feet Dooley heard Hillary's order.

"Fire!"

Yanking his lanyard, Dooley heard and felt the powder charges catapulting both the torpedoes from their tubes. As he saw them drop straight toward the gap under the tin sheathing, Dooley pulled on the control stick. At first, it seemed as if the airplane refused to obey, but in a couple of seconds the machine succumbed to Dooley's command. With only about twenty feet to spare, the airplane flew over the tin sheathing just as Fowler tossed out his last dynamite bomb.

Pretending to hear that one last explosion, both Hillary and Dooley tried to look behind the machine while thinking ahead to the next, and final, part of their plan.

Chapter 42

AFTER ANOTHER SUNSET, followed by another sunrise, two people busied themselves by sitting on soft, green grass between two palm trees and eating peaches. A flare pistol lay on the grass next to a watch cap full of more peaches. Behind them, their army blouses and other pieces of clothing and kit hung from tree branches, enjoying the late afternoon breeze as well. In front of them, a few hundred yards out to sea, uniformed seamen worked to lower a ship's boat filled with other uniformed seamen. The setting sun many miles behind the ship silhouetted its profile.

"Is it over with?" Zeta asked as while wiping juice from her chin with the back of her hand.

Dooley, doing the same, answered. "I'm not much of a sailor, but that looks like a British warship complete with a royal naval ensign flying at the masthead, and uniformed sailors."

Zeta chewed the peach in her mouth while watching the seamen in the boat detach the davit falls. She swallowed before answering. "That means peaches will never taste the same."

"No, they won't," Dooley stated as they watched the helmsman engage the boat's throttle. "But it's too late to un-signal them now."

They faced each other and toasted with their half-eaten peaches.

Ten minutes later, they watched as one of the crewmen holding a coil of rope, jumped from the gunwale and landed on the grass in front of them. In the bow, a man wearing civilian clothes and combed black hair stood at the bow as if he were George Washington crossing the Delaware River. Standing there, with a broad smile on his face, the man looked at Dooley and Zeta.

"You look familiar," Dooley stated as he stood while throwing a pit over his shoulder.

The man answered, "It's not often I run into island castaways, but somehow you look familiar too, friend. Let's get some food and brandy into you and some soap and water on those faces; then we can figure out why. We'll talk in the morning."

Dooley reached down to grab Zeta's hand. She threw her peach pit over her shoulder.

"By the way, I'm Captain Hugh Rodham."

*   *   *

"That's one helluva story, Thomas. Especially about the diamonds," Rodham said as he laid his fountain pen on the pad of paper and rotated his wrist. "Let's give my wrist a break and have some more tea."

"Thank you, sir," Dooley said as he straightened up in his chair and sniffed at the morning breeze coming in through the ship's porthole. Still somewhat groggy and very sore, he held out his teacup for a refill. "And thank the officer for the use of his stateroom and his clothes."

"No problem with the tea," Rodham paused as he filled his own cup before setting the teapot on the cloth-covered table. Taking a second to look at the chronometer on the paneled bulkhead, he took a long sip of his tea. He also looked out the open porthole at the dark blue sky and felt the slow, rhythmic turn of the ship's propellers, which propelled them toward Formosa. After that sip, he lowered the cup into both of his hands as he leaned back in the wooden chair. "And I already thanked him. He took in donations from his officers and crew. And I've already told you there is no need to call me sir. You aren't in the army anymore. Just call me Hugh. However, once you finish this debrief, I need to have your cooperation."

"Cooperation? In what?" Dooley asked as he continued to enjoy the hot, soothing tea. Looking past Rodman's shoulder he inspected his US Army issue, including the musette bag. All of which hung from hooks next to the stateroom door.

"Please let me start from the beginning. Doing so will fill in the cracks and emphasize the need for your complete understanding and cooperation at the same time," Rodham explained. "After our regiment started preparations to be shipped back to the States, I opted for orders transferring me to the Philippine Department and continued with staff intelligence. That was earlier this spring, and as part of my duties in the Philippines, I kept up with monitoring Bolshevik intrigues. As I gathered intelligence, a picture started to come together. After explaining the vaguest developments to my supervisors, I was put in charge of completing my own investigations, which ended up finding about you and the countess."

"Well, Hugh," Dooley replied, "I didn't mean to get involved with Bolsheviks. I was just trying to earn some money from what I thought were White Russians. I'm not a Bolshevik."

"I know you didn't, and I know you're not," Rodham said as he sipped his tea. "And I know all about your involvement, along with the countess. Both of you, along with Hillary and Fowler, were swooped up into something much bigger than any of us. Something so big it is endangering democracy and the United States as a whole. Do you understand what I am saying?"

"I do," Dooley answered.

Rodham studied the ex-sergeant's face as he answered. "I know you do, Thomas, but I need you to finish telling me the rest of your adventure. I also need to know if Lieutenant Hillary or Chief Fowler ever brought my name up."

Dooley narrowed his eyebrows before answering. "No, they didn't, but why would your name come up? Did they know you?"

"I can see where you might be a bit confused, so let me explain. The problem is that we, I, do not know who is involved. We could be talking about a staff officer stationed abroad in an American territory, an officer in command of a ship or regiment, or somebody on the General staff in Washington DC. That is the reason why I require your complete cooperation. Again, I hope you understand what I mean by cooperation."

Dooley nodded over his teacup. "I do. But you seem to know something I don't."

Rodham leaned forward to place his teacup on the table. He looked at Dooley as he did. "I spent last night ashore, with the Brits, trying to figure out what the hell was going on with that island and taking notes. While we did not find any of the ships, airplanes, or submarine you just informed me of, we did find three bodies. One of them was the Russian you killed. And the other two were Hillary and Fowler. The Brits buried them and marked the graves for later recovery. From what you said, you only knew those men for a few hours, yet you seemed to be quite impressed with them. I'm sorry for your loss, but I must emphasize the complexity of this entire thing. It is hard to describe the scope of the threat at hand but let me just say the Bolsheviks have spun a quite a web and have any number of recruits ensnared in their operations."

Pausing to take a second to look out the porthole, Rodham continued.

"I am not suggesting that Captain Hillary and Chief Fowler were part of a Bolshevik operation. I am just trying to trace out the web spun by the Bolsheviks. I don't, I can't, even trust the captain of this British ship, which is why I am asking that you and the countess keep your involvement in this scheme to yourselves. In fact, I am going to have to require it. I hope you understand. There is quite a bit that nobody needs to know about."

"How did you end up here? On this ship?" Dooley asked over the rim of his cup.

"Fair enough question, Thomas," Rodham said as he reached for his teacup. "It turns out I was on special assignment in Shanghai at the same time you were. Part of my investigations led me to Formosa. From there, I secured a secret means of transportation, as both rumors and facts were coming together into a picture that did not bode well for America. I wanted to find out what was going on at that island for myself. But the ship I was on was caught in that storm and, just like others caught in that tempest, I was cast about at sea. The captain of this ship put to sea to fulfill his duties, which included inspecting the security and safety of British property. On the way, they happened to collect me. I identified myself to the captain of this ship as a yachtsman, but with attachments to the American government. He and his crew have no idea of my real mission, nor do they need to know. I know everything sounds so fantastic and even very disjointed. It's going to be difficult for me to wrap this entire operation up into a report that can be read, believed, or even understood. I can barely understand it myself, but again, I cannot state how important it is for you to keep your knowledge to yourself. This whole mess is much bigger than you or I. Do I have your word, Sergeant Thomas Dooley?"

"Yes, you do, Hugh."

"Good," Rodham said as he reached for his fountain pen. "Let me refill the pen and pick up after the part where you dropped the second pair of torpedoes into that ship on the railway."

Dooley leaned before continuing. "Well, I guess we could have done any number of things, but Hillary's plan made the most sense, at least at the time. After dropping the last dynamite bomb and firing those last two torpedoes, we flew away but saw a great column of smoke as we did. Our goal was to damage that thing as much as possible, then to find a way to call for help. The next thing we did was to fly over to that British yacht and have Zeta fire the Lewis gun in the nose to keep the heads down of whoever might be aboard. At the same time, I slowed down enough and came low enough for Hillary and Fowler to roll out the rear hatch, with their weapons, and swim to the vessel. I did a few circles to the south of the yacht, and Zeta continued to fire occasional bursts at the stern. While the Russians were hunkered down, Hillary and Fowler planned on climbing up the anchor line and stowing themselves in the bosun's locker."

"So that," Rodham jumped in, "when the time was right, they would emerge and take the vessel over and use the radio."

"Correct," Dooley continued. "But I guess it didn't work out so well since you said the Brits found their bodies ashore. Anyway, after we saw them climb over the bow, Zeta and I continued to the north shore. The idea was for us to go our separate ways so that there was some chance. Anyway, I landed the plane about where you found us, and we covered it with a roll of camouflage netting and secured it with pieces of wire, along with some tree branches. Hillary figured out how to operate the machine as a submarine and showed me how to sink it, which we did. We submerged to the bottom just offshore. At a depth of about thirty feet. Shallow enough for us to escape if we couldn't raise it but deep enough so that it might not be seen from the surface. The netting was meant to help hide it if the water was exceptionally clear. We also wanted to be close enough to swim to shore while wearing clothes and carrying my weapons. We resurfaced the submarine after sunset and scuttled it. We then swam ashore and remained hidden. We figured by then the Russians would have given up looking for us and left the island. Are you going to tell the navy about it? So, they can recover it?"

Rodham answered while laying down his pen. "Don't worry. I'll let the proper authorities know where it is. In the meantime, it is almost ten. Go ahead and see if the countess is awake. Bring her some tea and keep her company until we arrive in Formosa."

Leaning back in his chair he paused before continuing. "I say Thomas, I really do envy you."

"How so?"

"I mean that you are free of the army and travelled half the world, and you are now free of the mess behind us. I suggest you plant your heels, sharpen your oyster knife, and travel the other half."

Dooley focused on the musette bag while answering. "Sounds like good advice."

* * *

The following day, Zeta and Dooley found themselves sitting at a street-side café. They sat with their backs to the building's stone wall and faced a morning breeze coming off a busy Keelung Harbor on the other side of the wrought-iron fence and brick-paved road in front of them. They sipped their coffee as they watched the motorboat that dropped them off only minutes ago power itself back to HMS Krakatoa, which now rode at anchor on the other side of the wide bay. Dooley watched that motorboat until it passed a two-masted sailing vessel that only anchored itself some minutes ago. He looked at the vessel as it came to anchorage while he, Zeta, and Rodham were being taken ashore. For some reason, that sailing vessel was familiar.

Thinking about the fancy yacht, he also thought about the two men who were intent upon seizing that British yacht back at the island. Instead, they found themselves buried in shallow graves on that island. Sighing, he took his eyes from the yacht and looked at Zeta.

"So, I guess this is it." Zeta stated as she removed the coffee cup from her lips. Her blonde hair was neatly combed and held back in a ponytail with a piece of blue ribbon. She, like Dooley, still wore the clothing and shoes donated by the crew from HMS Krakatoa: Long sleeve, white, linen shirts, grey, pleated slacks, and saddle shoes with wool socks. Neither of them had belts.

On the brick pavement, and next to Zeta's feet, was a barely filled pillowcase stenciled with the ship's name. At Dooley's feet was a threadbare Royal Navy issue seabag. It was full and looked lumpy. The growing lunch crowd, mostly well-dressed European businessmen or tourists gave Zeta long-nosed looks as they were seated in the open space. Both noticed the looks.

"I don't believe so," he said, as he placed his coffee cup on the table and sat back.

"What do you mean?" she retorted. "We're sitting here with nothing but donated clothes on our backs, what undergarments I stuffed into a Royal Navy pillowcase, two hundred and fifty dollars in my pockets and are waiting for that man Rodham to return with tickets. I'm supposed to catch passage from here to Hong Kong and then onto Europe. You're supposed to catch passage from here to Hawaii and then to Panama. Will we ever see each other again? Even Rodham said we're not supposed to have any future contact until his investigation is over with and he contacts us. And who knows how long that will take and how will he know where we'll be in two weeks? In two months? Or in two years from now? How am I supposed to find you?"

"He's with the government," Dooley answered while noticing the dread in Zeta's voice. "So, he'll find us, but that is not important right now."

"How is that?"

"You've seen me with that book about Panama," Dooley responded. "The one Rodham borrowed from the ship's captain, and gave to me, right?"

"Yes, why?"

"Like you said earlier, I have skills that I can use. I can find myself a grub-stake in Panama."

"Fine, but how will I find you?"

Dooley answered. "And we've looked at the maps in the book. Together. Right?"

"Yes," Zeta said as she crooked her head slightly to the side.

"Well, once you use your female intuition and pick the right town, just take a left after passing the first shithole bar you see."

"Fine, but how am I supposed to do that on two hundred and fifty-five dollars?"

Dooley smiled as he leaned to his right and opened the donated seabag by pulling on the drawstring. Reaching in for a second, he withdrew his hand holding the Mary Jane. Closing the seabag by pulling on the drawstring with one hand, he placed the shoe on the table. Both heard someone gasp from the table next to them. They ignored the man's wife.

"What am I supposed to do with that?" Zeta asked with a twinkle in her eyes.

"If you want to be an international Pinkerton, you're going to have to start thinking like one, and that starts with being inquisitive and always asking yourself questions."

"Such as?"

"Such as why was Olga wearing shoes like this in the middle of the escape? With heels that big or tall?" Dooley paused before continuing. "Also, how did she take a machine-pistol blast to the back and survive that without a scratch?"

Dooley stopped and let her look at the shoe. They could hear the murmuring around them. She continued to examine the brown leather shoe with its one strap and huge heel. Finally, she looked up. A broad smile overtook her face. "When did you figure it out? Or have you always known? What about you?"

The twinkle in Dooley's eyes matched his smile. "The edge of my oyster blade is just fine, so it's time to use your own whetstone."

Shocked with so many emotions she almost missed Dooley kicking her foot. She looked up and saw Rodham walking down the sidewalk toward the café carrying envelopes in his hand.

Picking up the shoe, she unfolded the top of the pillowcase and placed the shoe inside. Turning her attention back to the man in front of her, she picked up her coffee cup and smiled. "I remember those maps in the book, and I remember what you said about having a penchant for idling away your afternoons in shitholes."

"The culture tends to be a bit less stuffy and a bit more colorful in shitholes," Dooley said as they watched Rodham step off the sidewalk and through the gate of the wrought iron fence. He wore the same donated civilian clothing as Zeta and Dooley.

As Dooley watched Rodham approach their table, he saw the sailing yacht obey the stiffening morning breeze and shift at anchor. Though many yards away, he was able to now see the white French doors on the transom and the two-word name above them. Dooley reacted by sitting up straighter in his chair.

Rodham waved a hand at a server while placing three envelopes on the table.

Dooley and Zeta looked at the envelopes, and Dooley saw Zeta holding back a tear.

Rodham pulled the chair back and hiked up the legs of his trousers before sitting. He also saw the look in Zeta's eyes and sighed as he saw what she was looking at. The top envelope had a stamp in the upper left corner. The stamp identified the envelope as stationery from the Central Pacific-Occidental Shipping Line. Centered on the envelope was a name written in blue ink.

He was about to speak, but the waiter arrived with a tray. On it was an empty coffee cup and shiny metal coffee pot. After setting the tray down and filling the cups, the waiter left.

Watching him walk away, Rodham spoke slowly. "I understand that you two have had quite an adventure the last couple of weeks and may have grown close to each other. It all became so apparent and astounding as I typed up the story you dictated to me. The intrigue, the skullduggery, and the subterfuge could not have been placed better in any novel. Also, the technology is beyond belief: Flying machines that double as submarines and tanks, advanced electrical designs for airplanes. Machines made of aluminum and with only one set of wings. Ones that can be disassembled and crated like a Sears and Roebuck made-to-order prairie house. Even a fully automatic or electrically powered artillery piece that can fire a dozen explosive rounds in a single burst. Then there's the special troops including the parachute soldiers, air assault pilots, frogman commandos, and submarine raiders. It's all beyond imagination. Are you sure you never mentioned any of this to anybody aboard the Krakatoa? Nobody?"

"No," Dooley said. "The only contact we had with anybody on that ship was you. Also, I can understand about keeping mum about the Russians, but the airplane technology? Why does that need to be kept a secret? Wouldn't it be better for everybody to know?"

Rodham sighed. "Good. I'm glad you've kept everything to yourselves. As far as the advanced air and marine technology, I wondered the same thing myself. However, once I radiotelegraphed the report to my superiors, my superiors required that any information about that technology be kept top secret. Pardon the pun, but they mean down to every single nut and bolt. In the end, we are in a new century with governments having a new world view. That adage about gentlemen should not read another gentleman's mail is out of fashion. We also have new technologies as a result of the war, along with the rise of corporations. I guess what I'm saying is that we now have knowledge that the average citizen does not need to know about. Agree?"

"I guess so. But it's a shame about Fowler and Hillary as they could have added quite a bit to your report." Dooley paused to enjoy another sip of coffee. "How'd they look? I mean they weren't too chewed up by machine gun fire or anything. Also, the island is populated by feral hogs."

Rodham answered slowly. "I was told they did receive quite a bit of gun-fire."

Looking out into the harbor, and at that sailing vessel at anchor Dooley asked, "Then if the Brits never saw them before, how did the Brits ID the bodies?"

"Their uniform stencils," Rodham answered. "Why?"

"Nothing," Dooley replied as he took another look at the stern of that yacht one more time before turning to Rodham. The name read: Mary Jane. "What about us?"

Rodham sipped his coffee before answering. He saw the fear on Zeta's face and sighed before answering. "These envelopes were given to me by our consulate. Each one contains tickets for our future travels along with ten twenty-dollar notes. I am aware of your destinations and am given complete authority to cable and deposit small funds into bank accounts once you arrive there. There is contact information in your envelopes. I will let you know when you are free to discuss what you've seen and to meet, but until that moment, you two cannot have any contact. Please bear in mind the agreements that you both have signed. And the subsequent ramifications if those stipulations are violated. Questions?"

He received no verbal response.

Nodding in acknowledgement, Rodham picked up the top two envelopes with one in each hand and held them out. "I've also been asked by the government to thank you for your service."

As Dooley and the countess reached for their envelopes, Dooley noticed two things: Zeta's shaking hand and a man now standing on the stern of the Mary Jane.

CHAPTER 43

SO," **MAJOR UTKIN** said to the man sitting opposite him, "we've enjoyed two whiskeys each and I haven't seen you light a cigarette yet."

Hugh Rodham, sitting opposite Utkin, smiled as he reached for his whiskey. "I see what nonsmokers mean about the habit. It is rather distracting."

"Very good," Utkin complimented. "It is also bad for teeth. Anyway, I believe your ability to stand up to the withering fire stood you in good stead as it earned you a chair at the table. Also, I've received your official report, the one that did not make it to the headquarters of the US Army's Philippine Department, the one summarizing the events from the last two weeks in detail. I must say that Dooley does have quite an eye for detail, so I'm glad the report the Army and Navy did receive will serve our purposes and has closed the book on that investigation, thus setting you free to pursue your interests. That said, do you think Sergeant Thomas Dooley will keep his word? Despite being, directly or indirectly, involved with the loss of assets destined for operation in Latin America, I would still like him available if needed. The countess as well."

Hugh Rodham was fingering the rim of his whiskey tumbler while observing the pedestrian traffic along McKinley Boulevard, the main street in downtown Manila. Among the passersby, two young Filipino women, wearing lightly colored summer dresses and carrying small clutch purses, walked by. They peered discreetly over their shoulders at the two men sitting at a table in front of an open-door café. Like the women, both men wore loose-fitting and lightly colored summer tropical attire of their own.

"Yes," Rodham answered. "Fortunately, for us, he will keep his word. I only knew him for two days, but he struck me as a man of character and integrity, especially since the wording of the 'agreement' he signed was quite direct. 'Under threat of federal internment for any length of time deemed necessary and at an undisclosed location, I agree to not divulge, orally or in writing, the events of my life that have occurred between the dates of June 15th to June 30th in the year 1919 unless directly contacted by a duly authorized agent of the United States Federal government carrying the proper identification.' But they can always suffer fatal falls or auto accidents with appropriate timing."

Major Utkin smiled at the news as he lifted his whiskey to his lips. "Well, we must thank those mysterious forces who helped forge such predictable qualities as character and integrity. It is always nice to have an ace up one's sleeve."

"You are right there," Hugh answered as he held up his hand at the young, black-haired man standing behind the bar just inside the stucco-covered building. "What are your specific orders?"

Major Utkin sighed contently as he lifted his glass and tossed back the last of the whiskey. Placing the empty tumbler on the table, he answered Hugh's question. "Like Sergeant Dooley, I am to book passage on the next cruise ship leaving Manila for the States via the Panama Canal. Once I arrive in the United States, I am to make my way to New York City and set up a business in Manhattan. The committee has determined that America's next financial crisis will take effect by 1928, or 1930 at the latest. In the meantime, I will solidify my financial holdings in preparation, as gold, silver, and gems, unlike government-printed currency and corporate stocks and municipal bonds, will always maintain their value. I have also been researching the social columns and have two or three young women of appropriate breeding and family stature that should suffice as the mother of my offspring."

Major Utkin fingered the long scar across his cheek while continuing. "Being a man of means along with a well-documented war record, I shall have no problem securing the right woman, along with the blessing of her father.

With the coming financial collapse, I will make sure that my future father-in-law, and the fathers of my paramours, will certainly be grateful for my financial grounding."

Just then, the Filipino bartender arrived with a wooden tray, a bottle of Old Forester bourbon whiskey, and two fresh glasses. He quickly and, quietly, replaced the empty glasses with full ones and left the men to continue their discussion.

"And you. Are you still keen on establishing yourself as a businessman in the textiles industry? In Chicago?"

"After long consideration, I, Captain Hugh Rodham, hereby officially resign my commission as an officer in the United States Army after having served honorably in the completion of my obligated time of service."

"Officially?" Utkin asked.

Rodham answered. "My commanding officer begged me to stay in. He said with my experience and qualifications, the Army or the government would be an excellent place for a young handsome man such as I. However, I also explained to him that after having spent time at a university followed by my time in service traveling through Russia and Asia and experiencing many different adventures and contacts with new ideas and cultures, it is time for me to settle down and start a family. He agreed and signed my resignation, albeit with reluctance. The paperwork is being processed while we speak, and I too shall follow you back to the States as well. I will return to my hometown of Chicago, Illinois, and start a business of my own."

Rodham paused to look at his glass before looking at Major Utkin.

"That said, Sergeant Dooley or Countess Zeta Tolstoy would have no knowledge of my resignation, so anytime in the future any correspondence or contact with them would still be official. At least as far as they know."

Major Utkin looked back at Hugh and smiled. "Textiles? Have you established connections?"

"I've been watching the social columns myself and reading between the lines. It seems that a family patriarch is preparing for a rather lucrative involvement in Prohibition. This patriarch, head of the Bronfman family, has migrated to Canada to set up the infrastructure, and is planning on a return to Chicago within in a year. Chicago will become a major actor in an illegal industry, an industry most likely to create quite a bit of confusion and distrust along with a good financial investment, which means it will survive America's next financial crisis."

Major Utkin repeated slowly, "What a way to enrage, and distract, the democratic and peace-loving Americans more than by having the federal government create an entirely unwelcomed and armed department of the government to enforce a law pushed onto the citizenry by a small clutch of high and mighty politicians led around by the wives in the Woman's Temperance league and the Ku Klux Klan."

"You are correct," Rodham agreed. "What a way to pit Americans against each other to create mayhem and distrust."

"Looks like it is all coming together," Utkin said while turning his attention back to the street traffic. "Do you have any love interests targeted yet?"

"Two or three young women shall prove to be useful assets and serve as dependable mistresses and mothers of my offspring." Rodham stopped to sip his whiskey before continuing. "I have even started to think about the names of my children. The captain of that destroyer had an intriguing name. The first name of my first daughter. I have also been watching another family, the Kennedys, which should prove useful as well when the time comes. What about Gorki? What are his plans?"

Utkin paused for a second before returning his attention to the table. "Lieutenant Petro Gorki is in the process of becoming Doctor Drake Moray, late of Montenegro, and receiving documented credentials, which will help him start a residency at a new medical setting in New York City, where he hopes to become a very influential member of the medical staff: one that is admired, well-respected, and listened to. As far as his love interests, he will have no problem producing an entire brood of children from a line of socially connected women waiting for his attention at the urgings of their fathers and husbands. As far as Morda, he will be sorely missed, but I have already groomed a replacement who should have no issue with fulfilling his mission with the women. He will work his way into collegiate athletics and is making inroads into being accepted as a senior member of the KKK. The rest of my team will also be successful in their future endeavors. After all, our effort is not a sprint: it is a one-hundred-year marathon."

"Excellent," Rodham said, "and what are our plans for the next gathering? And what of Borodin, Lagos, Bogdanovich, and Vostok? And that British yacht?"

"Since we had to use the ship captained by Lagos to pull our vessel off the rail and sink in deep water, Borodin and Lagos are using their vessel to resupply and refuel Vostok's transit across the Pacific. Both will have a nice reception in Ensenada. As far as the British yacht, we have no idea but can only assume that it, and the three men aboard, succumbed to the forces of nature. After all, it is still typhoon season. But despite our setbacks, I will have no issue setting the foundations for the financial future of our group. Since every sound business venture does require a regular review by board or senior family members, we will conduct what I would like to call our Five-year Plan. Starting in 1925, and every five years hence, you will receive a postcard in the mail from a person called Mothershed, signaling our group's meeting location, and the meeting will occur five days from the post stamped date on each card."

Rodham nodded and clasped his tumbler, lifting it in salute. Utkin did likewise and their glasses clinked together. After each took a long sip, they placed their glasses on the table and watched as the two Filipino women who had passed by earlier returned, pretending to talk to each other while keeping their eyes on the two men at the table.

The two men looked at each other and smiled. Both rehoisted their glasses.

Utkin broke the silence by saying, "Here's to our children, grandchildren, and the mayhem they will cause Mister Hugh Rodham."

Rodham returned the salute. "Here's to the next one hundred years and Operation Crossfire."

Printed in the USA
CPSIA information can be obtained
at www.ICGtesting.com
LVHW051214170923
758377LV00010B/109